"Dr. Perkins?" A kid was in the doorway, holding a bouquet of roses.

She got up. "I'm Laura Perkins."

"See how considerate Ian is?" Rita said. "See?"

"They're beautiful," Laura remarked, admiring the fragrance, the deep burgundy hue. She opened the card. The words blurred. She trembled, dropped the card, and stood with her hands flat against the desk, the incubus of the man tight inside her skull, pushing her head down, that dryness like hot, sticky straw filling her throat. DENISE LOVED ROSES & I KNOW YOU WILL TOO. xxx

Terrify, unnerve, attack, kill. The lurid passion of his intention was clear.

Her eyes flew from the card to the roses—such a deep, deep red, so exquisitely lovely, and so filled with thorns—and she slammed her arm against the beautiful white vase and shouted as the bouquet shot across the room, the roses leaping out every which way and finally landing like bloody footprints on the floor. . . .

IN SHADOW

Trish Janeshutz

BALLANTINE BOOKS • NEW YORK

For my parents
with love and thanks

Library of Congress Catalog Card Number: 85-90764

ISBN 0-345-32469-2

Manufactured in the United States of America

First Edition: December 1985

Special thanks to my agent, Diane Cleaver;
to the juggler for his humor; to Griffin;
and to Mary and Greg Anderson for the
mountains of paper.

PROLOGUE

University of Miami

HE WATCHED AS she made her way through the trees toward the parking lot, her lovely head jerking at the slightest noise. She clutched her purse to her right side and her briefcase to her left, as if to draw the air around her for protection. She knew she was being followed, he thought; and her terror thrilled him. He could imagine the adrenaline coursing wildly through her body, impelling her to look around. But she wouldn't. In the dark, dry leaves crackling underfoot, knowing would be worse than what might only be imagined.

The walkway turned to damp ground, muting her footsteps. Clouds sailed in front of the quarter moon; he heard her suck in her breath. It was a sound women make when they are afraid or aroused, and it grated on his nerves. He ran his damp hands along his slacks, clenching and unclenching his fingers.

The only clear sound now was a train in the distance, hurtling through the warm humid night. Denise, Denise, he thought, it could have been so different. If you'd been good. He dug his hand into his pocket and his fingers closed around the knife. It seemed warm, suddenly heavy, as if imbued with consciousness, with an awareness of what it would have to do.

When the last of the train sounds left the air, she heard him and spun around, a hand flying dramatically to her heart. Then she saw him and laughed nervously, her eyelids fluttering. "Christ, you scared the hell out of me." An admonishing tone, he thought, one he knew well.

"I called the house." He smiled. His tongue darted into the corner of his mouth. He wouldn't give her the satisfaction of an apology. "No one was home."

"Viki's staying with relatives for a while in Orlando. School's out, you know." She laughed again. It was an unnatural sound, and he wondered why he'd never noticed it before. "I've had the feeling ever since I left the lab that I was being followed. You really frightened me."

They stopped by the hedge. The trees rustled in a momentary breeze. She cocked her head ever so slightly, her dark eyes

1

coming together in a frown as if she'd practiced this expression in front of the mirror like an actress and was using it for the first time. She brushed a hand through her lustrous chestnut hair. "So, what was it you wanted?"

He wanted to trace her petulant mouth with the tip of his finger. Such a perfect mouth, eyes, such a perfectly lovely face, he thought. That was her sin; she was too pretty, too perfect for another man. Any man. Then he thought of how she'd betrayed him and looked away so she wouldn't read his intention on his face.

"I didn't want to interrupt you while you were working."

"That doesn't really answer my question."

His fingers tightened on the knife in his pocket. "I guess I just wanted to see you, to—" The expression on her face stopped him. There was a softness in her dark eyes, a childlike adoration in the way she touched the side of his face. He thought of the way he'd spied on her earlier that night, working with such absorption in her lab. He had watched as she held test tubes up to the light, mixing her magic, scribbling notes. His original plan was to confront her there, in the place she held in the highest sanctity. But there were other lights in the building, another teacher working late upstairs.

"Oh, Bucky," she was whispering, "it just won't work for us, you know? I'm sorry for— I mean, we've been over this a million times. I— Oh, God. I loved you so much. We loved each other, didn't we, Bucky? Didn't we?" Her hands moved to his shoulders. He slipped his arms around her, drawing her against him, remembering what they had done to each other, what she had done to him.

His cheek was against her hair, such soft hair, healthy. Everything about Denise was healthy and beautiful. But she was a whore, a thief, a liar. She had betrayed him.

Her perfume tickled the inside of his nose. He recognized the scent; it was one he'd given her when— No, he wouldn't think about the past. That part of his life was over. Denise dropped her head back, looked at him with those deep, soulful eyes. "You understand, don't you? You understand why I did what I did, don't you?"

He kissed the knuckles of her hand, then her mouth. Everything about her was familiar. For a moment, it startled him, this familiarity. She tasted so good.

"It was fine with us," she said, pulling back, "fine until the very end, you know?" There were so many things he wanted to say, to confess. How he'd followed her, spied on her, discovered the truth—the many truths. Her life was layered like an onion, and he wished he could peel back every separate layer to arrive at the core. *How many other truths are there, Denise?*

He brought the knife from his pocket. Clicked it open. The blade was long, thin, so very sharp. Her mouth pressed against his again. She tasted of honeysuckle, and as he touched the blade ever so lightly to her side, he thought she also tasted of death, as though her body sensed what was coming. Then he pushed the knife hard against the fabric of her dress, and as the blade penetrated her flesh, between the third and fourth ribs, he felt a chill along his spine. *You made me do it, Denise, you made me.* There was only a moment when she struggled, when that sucking noise started in the back of her throat, then died with her scream as the blade pierced her heart.

She fell limply against him. He removed the blade, guided her gently to the ground, wiped the knife clean on the grass and dead leaves. He touched the side of her face with the back of his hand. "You shouldn't have made me do it, Denny," he whispered. *You shouldn't have been so bad.*

A sense of urgency nibbled now at the edges of his mind as he thought of the lights that had been on in Denise's building. Suppose the other woman was already on her way to the parking lot? He slipped on a pair of gloves, glanced through Denise's purse, opened her briefcase, and went through papers and her gradebook. His anxiety proliferated by the moment. The notebook, where the hell was it? He had seen it many times before, three-ringed, black, the sort of thing in which a little girl might record her secret thoughts. He was so certain she would have it with her. She said she always carried it, and hadn't she been scribbling in it when she was in the lab?

He closed his eyes for a moment, remembering precisely when she'd told him she carried the notebook with her at all times. He could still see the way she ran her hands along the sides of her dress, too, straightening it. She'd been wearing a wine-colored dress that day, made of a soft, shiny fabric like satin. There wasn't much he would forget about her. Especially her lies, her betrayal.

He went through her purse again, then squeezed his eyes shut, wanting to cry, scream, rage. She'd taken her secret with her. She'd lied even about the notebook. He rocked back on his heels, struggling to contain his rage, then returned everything to the briefcase, shut it, set it on the grass beside her. His anger abated. He was, after all, a reasonable man. Perhaps there were never any notes; perhaps she was just scribbling away like a two-year-old, recording nothing.

He heard a noise behind him; his head jerked around. He squinted into the dark but saw nothing. He was jumpy, that was all, and nervous about the other woman who had been in Denise's building. Maybe she'd started down the path, had seen him, had seen what had happened, and had run off to call the cops. Maybe even as he sat here, smoothing Denise's shirt, touching her cheek again, the police were circling the campus, closing in on him.

No, no, there would've been sirens, flashing lights. Everything was fine, of course.

He kissed Denise on the mouth, fascinated by how lovely she was; by now she looked to be merely sleeping. Her skin was still warm. He peered into her eyes, so dark, so vapid, then closed the lids and glanced around for something with which to cover her. He didn't want her to get wet if it rained.

Kneeling, he scooped leaves in around her, patted them along the sides of her body, sprinkled them over her chest, legs, around her neck. His hand paused at the side of her face; a finger caressed the cool surface of one of her earrings. His heart lurched. Like the perfume, the earrings were a gift from him. Carefully, he removed them, slipped them into his pocket. He then set her briefcase flat on the ground, close to her right hand, tucked her purse in the curve of her left arm. Just as the pharaohs were buried with the artifacts of their lives, so would he send Denise into oblivion with her personal effects.

Then his sense of urgency tightened its hold on him. He leaped up, glanced once down the path where Denise had come, wondering about the lights in the building, about that other woman. *Had she seen anything?*

He hurried off through the dark, Denise's earrings clasped tightly in his hand.

4

PART ONE

Blind Man's Bluff

1

THE BODY WAS gone by the time Conway got there that morning. It was beginning to rain and some of the guys were roping off the area where Denise Markham had been found. He saw Tillis, decked out in uniform, standing in front of the last trailer with a man in blue work clothes who was tapping his temple with a grimy finger and rolled his Rs as he told Tillis off.

"Everryone here, crrazy. Locos. You no ask *me* questions, you go find man who does this terrible thing," said the man, flipping his cigarette from him and jamming his hands into the pockets of his baggy pants.

"Mr. Panzo," Tillis said impatiently, "you gotta try to answer my questions, all right? You understand?" Tillis had a wad of tobacco in his cheek, and his face was a vibrant pink, as if he'd just stepped out of the shower. As Conway approached, Tillis saw him and hurried over. "Man," he breathed, "I'm glad you're here. This dude here, José Panzo, he's the maintenance guy who found her. Doesn't speak very good English. I haven't been able to get very much outa him."

Conway stuck a finger lightly in Tillis's cheek. "Maybe because *that's* in the way and he can't understand you."

"Ha-ha, Conway."

"So what do you have on the lady chemist?"

"A perfect thirty-five/twenty-four/thirty-six, ole man, take my word for it." Tillis hooked a thumb in the waist of his pants, hoisted them up under his belly.

"What else?"

"Got inventory of her things there on the clipboard"—he motioned over to the steps where Panzo was now sitting—"including the keys to that real nice TR Seven out in the parking lot. Nothing unusual. Money's still in there.

"The woman who answered at the home number says she's the housekeeper and that the lady of the house, Mrs. Markham, left Saturday around six and that was the last she saw of her. Don Markham—the golf pro, if you follow the sport—is on a two-month tour and coming back early, as soon as he can catch a flight. A ten-year-old daughter, Viki, is with Markham's relatives in Orlando. I spoke with them and they're going to tell her what happened." He pushed the wad of tobacco into his other cheek and shifted his weight from his left foot to his right, as if his body had to be balanced according to where the tobacco was. "This woman, the aunt, said the husband will be in touch as soon as he returns. The Markhams were in the process of getting a divorce. Although it beats hell outa me why a man would divorce a woman who looks like she does."

"Any sign of a struggle?"

"Nope. Doesn't look like it. No external signs on the woman. Captain Truro spoke with the university prez, who wants to play this real low key. They aren't going to cancel evening classes. Shit, low key, this man says. This woman was knifed, and it sure looks like it might be connected with the deaths of those other two women, Conway. But the prez says he'll only cancel classes—get this—for an act of God. Like a hurricane."

"I wish you'd left the body here until I arrived."

Tillis threw up his hands. "Not my fault, Conway. Flaherty took photos, the ambulance got here, and off she went to the morgue."

"I'll take the briefcase and handbag with me when I go," Conway said, and walked over to where Panzo was sitting. "Señor Panzo, I'm Detective Conway. John Conway."

Panzo slid his hands down the sides of his pants and they shook. "These people, they are locos. Questions, questions—they do more on the street, looking for the man who did this terrible thing, señor."

"Can you tell me what happened? *Que pasó?*"

Panzo ran a hand over his slick black hair. He was a short, wiry man with pocked cheeks and a gold front tooth. "I come to work. I walk *por aquí*." He ran a finger through the air, indicating the walk in front of them. "I see"—he pointed at his eyes—"two legs. They stick out." He bent his arms as if he were running. "I call *policía*. Tell them what happened. I sit here." He shook his head, made the sign of the cross against his forehead. "*Madre de Dios,*" he whispered. "She was a good lady. *Buena mujer.*"

"You knew her?"

"*Sí, sí,* she work like me. All the time. I tell her sometimes—no walk here at night. Not safe. She laugh, she tell me not to worry. She big girl." He rolled his Rs again. "She not a big girl at all," he finished softly.

"What time did you find her?"

8

"Five, maybe thirty after five. She there long time. Her hands"—he rubbed his own together—"verry cold."

Conway offered Panzo a cigarette and they sat there a few minutes, smoking, silent. The university was built on an old military site west of downtown Miami. Conway had lived out here as a kid, when there was nothing but runways and swamp grass, buzzards and barracks and an isolated community or two. Over the years the city had metastasized around it and the campus was now an oasis in a desert of noise and concrete. From where he sat, Conway could see the control tower, a spavined vestige of the old days that now housed campus security. The runways had sprouted tufts of grass. The barracks now paralleled two neat rows of trailers—"portables," the university called them—and together they accommodated the science and language departments until the new complex was completed. The buzzards had moved on; the swamp grass had been paved over. So much for the past, Conway thought.

"Señor," said Panzo, wiping an arm across his forehead. It was warm and still, and sweat left streaks along the sides of Panzo's face. "They say America is best country in the world, no? I hear this, in Havana. I see turistas come with much money. I ask, where you from? And always they say America. I come here, on Mariel boatlift. I get good job with the university. I feed my family. Then Señora Markham is killed. This not happen in Cuba. Only the soldiers kill. We no kill each other. Maybe this not best country, eh?"

Conway didn't know what to say to that. It began to rain and he and the Cuban ducked under the tin awning at the end of the trailer. In minutes, the rain was coming down hard and fast, drumming the roof and pouring off in streams. He was wearing sneakers and felt the damp seeping through the soles.

He stood with one hand in his pocket and the other holding a cigarette. His shoulders stooped. He'd been self-consciously tall as a kid and now carried himself that way out of habit. His face was boyish, except around his smoky eyes, where two deep lines jutted out from the corners, the result of squinting against the glare of a tropical sun. The end of his nose was sunburned, so he looked as if he had a cold. He did not want to be here.

He'd been packing to leave for Colorado when Truro had called earlier this morning. "I've got six guys out with the flu, John, and I'd appreciate it if you'd just drive over to the campus and take a look. Tillis is already out there."

"I'm leaving for vacation tomorrow," Conway had argued,

9

"tomorrow morning. I haven't had a vacation in two-and-a-half years, remember?"

"I know, I know. I'm just asking you to take a look." When Truro said this, a screen in Conway's mind had filled with an image of Truro sitting heavily on the edge of his desk, a cup of coffee in one hand, a cigarette in the other, perspiration beaded across his upper lip like a perforated line—a prime candidate for a coronary.

Now here he was. Taking a look. And of course Colorado was out of the question, and of course Truro had known that. So had Jenny. The minute Conway had hung up with Truro, Jenny had come to the door of the living room, a hand on her hip, that look on her face, and said, "Don't tell me."

"I'm just going to drive over, Jen. Take a look. That's all he said."

"Good-bye, Colorado; good-bye, Hawaii." She rolled her eyes toward the ceiling, flicked her blond hair off her shoulder as if it were tickling her neck.

"Truro's in a bind. Six guys are out with the flu."

"He *is* a bind, John." She turned on her heel, stomped back into the kitchen. He followed with short, nervous steps.

"C'mon, try to understand."

"Oh, but I do, I do. You're married to your job. I don't think it could be much plainer than that."

"I'll meet you in Aspen next weekend."

"Ah, yes," she said, nodding, "I know this routine. First, it's 'I'm just going to take a look, Jen,' and now it's 'I'll meet you next weekend, Jen.' Well, forget it. I'll go by myself. I've got a month off between flights and I'm not going to spend it sitting around Miami on my ass, waiting for you to sandwich me in between murders."

"I'll be back in an hour. We'll talk about it then."

"I won't *be* here in an hour, so don't bother."

She had, in fact, probably left already. So much for the present and the future.

"Señor Conway," Panzo said, glancing over at him, "who do this? Who do this to such a good woman?"

"I don't know." He wondered why people always seemed to think he had all the answers.

He waited until the rain had let up and steam was rising from the sidewalks, then said good-bye to Panzo and darted over to where Tillis and some of the others stood. "I'm heading downtown, so let me have the briefcase and purse. Someone's going to have to drive her car over to her husband's place. Check it out, will you, Tillis?"

"Gladly." Tillis eyed the bright blue sports car, sitting mute as a monk in the drizzle. "Maybe Markham will sell it to me cheap."

Conway picked up Denise Markham's briefcase and purse and walked off toward his car, no longer caring if he got wet. For a moment, the grandeur of the Rockies loomed larger than life in his head, blotting out the gray skies, the rain, the almost unbearable heat and humidity. Then he got into his car and started across town, thinking that maybe Jen was right about him. Any normal man would have gone to Colorado.

It was still raining Monday morning. Conway stood in the doorway of one of the barracks, shaking his raincoat, wishing he'd traded in his sneakers for a pair of real shoes. There were puddles in the parking lot where the TR7 had been and water rushing out of the corroding drainpipes at the sides of the trailers. Only three other cars were outside, and he wondered if today was a holiday he'd forgotten about.

His sneakers squeaked as he started upstairs to the second floor. The exiguously lit hallways smelled closed and unused and hummed with air conditioners on the verge of collapse. He fought back the feeling of general malaise that had plagued him since he'd gotten up this morning. Jen had gone on to Colorado without him. Stella, his ex-wife, had called to inform him that she hadn't received her check yet this month. And he couldn't help but feel some resentment toward Captain Truro for having called in the first place and taking advantage of his good nature.

The first office he came to was open. He knocked, peeked in. "Hello. Excuse me."

The woman behind the desk stacked high with papers smiled pleasantly as she got up. Black curls framed her face and there was a hint of color in her cheeks. Her eyes were a quiet, summery green. "Morning," she said, running her hands along her arms as she passed in front of the air conditioner. "You're not one of my students, so you can't be here about a grade."

"Detective Conway. With homicide."

That word, "homicide," always brought shadows to people's faces, he thought, and she was no exception. "Right. Come on in and have a seat. I'm Laura Perkins." She flung her arms out. "Excuse the mess. We're at the end of the quarter, and I'm way behind, as usual."

"Where is everyone?" he asked. "The parking lot is practically deserted."

"Most of the faculty's at home, grading papers."

Wonderful. He should have known there wasn't going to be anything simple about this case when he'd arrived yesterday only to find the body gone. "Denise Markham *did* work in this building, didn't she?"

"Right down the hall." Laura lit a cigarette as she sat in the chair across from him. "I hardly knew her, so I don't know how much I can tell you. She kept pretty much to herself."

"Were you here the night she was killed?"

"I was working late. Grading finals. I guess I left close to midnight. I don't usually like to stay that late here, but I lost track of the time."

"Do you know if Mrs. Markham was still here when you left?"

"The lights in the lab were still on, so probably. I parked in the back lot, though, and she usually parked out front, so I can't say for sure whether she was here or not. She might've already left and had forgotten to turn out her lights." She paused, sat forward. A thin veil of smoke rose up around her. "What time was she killed, do you know?"

"We'll know once the autopsy's been done. . . . Did she work late frequently?"

"She was always the first person here in the morning and the last to leave at night. She was primarily a researcher, you know. Oh, she taught an occasional chemistry course, but her passion was research. I've heard she was brilliant, for whatever that's worth. It's one of those words you hear a lot around here."

"Did she have any close friends on the faculty? Anyone in particular she was seeing?"

She crossed her legs at the knees, moved her foot in a slow arc. "She was a loner, Detective Conway. I've been here nearly five years and I don't think I ever saw Denise with anyone. As for whether she was seeing anyone—I thought she was married."

"On the verge of divorce."

"See"—she laughed—"you know more about this than I do. There isn't much departmental mixing here. She was science and I'm language, not that it would have made a difference where Denise was concerned. She didn't socialize with anyone, like I said. Madame Curie might've gotten a rise out of her, but not just someone she worked around."

"How'd the students feel about her?"

"I don't think they cared much for her, because she was

tough. Rarely gave anything above a C, and she had a bad habit of intimidating people in class."

Delightful woman, Conway thought. A beautiful bitch. "And other members of the faculty?"

"She was the first in the science department to be hired primarily as a researcher, so there may have been some professional jealousy.

Laura leaned forward, and stabbed out her cigarette. "The newspapers are drawing a connection between Denise's murder and the deaths of those other two women. Is that true? Do you think there's a correlation?"

"We won't know for sure until the autopsy's doné. But from the looks of it, Denise died the same way, and that makes three women in a month."

"So this guy's a nut."

"You sure the murderer's male?" he asked. Amateur sleuths abounded, he thought with amusement.

"Sam Spade I'm not." She laughed. "Was it really José Panzo who found her?" Conway nodded. "That's too bad. I know he was fond of her. I'd given him some books so he could study English on his own, and Denise used to help him with pronunciation. Seems like she always had time for him."

A beautiful bitch with a shade of compassion? "He said she was a 'good woman,' whatever that means."

"Then he was probably one of the few who thought so."

The rain was coming down in sheets now, whipping leaves and twigs through the gray light, and he thought about the floorboards leaking in his car and about how his sneakers were already damp and about how the weather in Aspen was a cool sixty-five degrees.

"Have you spoken to anyone over in the law school yet?"

"No, you're my first."

"Poor you. I'm afraid I haven't been much help. But Rita Lincoln might be. She teaches criminal law. Murder's her hobby."

"Gruesome hobby." Conway laughed.

"She's got the involuted mind for this kind of thing. We kid her about it all the time. I'm sure by now she's come up with a theory and a list of suspects."

"Then she's doing a better job than I am." He removed a card from his wallet, scribbled his home number across the bottom. "If you think of anything or hear anything, please give me a call. If you can't get me at either of those numbers, just leave a message."

Laura nodded, walked with him to the door. "Good luck, Mr. Conway."

"Thanks." If luck had anything to do with this, he thought, he was doomed and would have been better off in Colorado.

2.

Laura stood at the window after Conway had left, gazing through the gloomy light to the walkway below. In her mind, she followed it until she reached the hibiscus where Denise had been found. A chill passed through her. *Someone walking on my grave*, she thought. The suddenness of death, its proximity, had left her with a bitter taste of her own mortality. She was thirty-two years old and coming up for tenure this fall. Until this morning, when she'd read about the murder, her future had seemed utterly limitless. She'd never given much thought to what regrets she might have had for things undone, undreamed, unfinished. The death of a woman she barely knew had swept into her life like a hot, dry wind, disrupting her illusions, and now, suddenly, it was all she could think about.

She'd last seen Denise on Friday, standing in the hall with Panzo, the two of them paging through one of the textbooks Laura had given him. Denise had been pronouncing the word "owl," her mouth stretched oddly, exaggerating the sound. "Ow, José, like if I pinch you," she'd said, and had done just that, pinching him on the arm.

"Ow," he'd said, laughing, "*sí, sí,* owl. Owl."

Denise had glanced up as Laura had passed them, smiled in that distracted way she had, and then she and Panzo had moved into her office. When Laura had left that evening, Denise's car was still in the parking lot and the lights were on in the downstairs lab.

The newspaper said the murder had happened late Saturday evening. *But how late?* While she was sitting here in her office grading papers? Or maybe a little later when she and Rita were having a nightcap in Coconut Grove? Hopefully the latter, she thought. The mere possibility that Denise might've been killed while she was still on campus left a peculiar hole in the pit of her stomach.

It's tragic and I'm sorry, but I'm glad it wasn't me. She shuddered. It's the rain, she decided, rubbing her hands along her arms, wishing this vague and disturbing feeling would go away.

"Dr. Perkins?"

She spun around, startled. Tom Duncan stood in the doorway, his hairy arms dangling free of his rain slicker from the elbows down. His bright blue eyes stared out at her from beneath a mop of thick blond hair, and she wondered what it was about him she didn't like. She knew why he was here, and she walked over to her desk, reached for her purse, swung it onto her shoulder.

"I was just leaving, Tom."

"It's about my grade."

"We've already discussed it."

"You've just got to change it to a C, Dr. Perkins. Otherwise the coach is going to suspend me from the team."

"You know the appeal process."

"But that could take months."

"Look," she said impatiently as she moved toward the door, "you made it to class three times, got a C on the midterm, and flunked the final. That's an F in my book."

He followed her into the hall, stood so closely behind her that she could smell his after-shave. "It isn't that I didn't like American lit," he went on as if she hadn't spoken. "It's just that I was having some problems this quarter and I—"

"No," she said firmly.

"I bet that's what Mrs. Markham used to say."

Her eyes snapped to his face. "I wouldn't know. You *are* familiar with the appeal process, aren't you?"

"Sure," he replied. "And I'll win, too."

It probably wouldn't even get *that* far, she thought. The coach would relent not out of compassion for Duncan, but because *he* was the basketball team. Without him, where would the university be in collegiate competition? "Fine. I hope you do."

Duncan dribbled an imaginary basketball, turned from side to side as they walked down the hall. He made small clucking noises with his tongue against his teeth. "You always such a bitch?" he asked in a perfectly pleasant and casual voice, as though he were inquiring about the weather. A dimple grew at the corner of his mouth as he smiled, then deepened like a crater.

"I'll pretend I didn't hear that."

"Yeah, you do that, lady," and he dribbled off down the hall, hopping and sidestepping and making the weird noise with his tongue. She suddenly remembered that he'd been Denise Markham's research assistant at one time. She made a mental note to call Conway and tell him about it.

3.

By early afternoon, Conway was ready to quit and catch the next plane to Colorado. He'd spoken to a handful of faculty, and the emerging impression of the Markham woman was that she'd had little use for other people. No one seemed to know much about her, but most everyone agreed that if she'd been able to figure out a way to keep going without food or sleep, she probably never would have left the lab.

He'd contacted Joe Simms, the head of the science department, and even he had admitted he didn't know Denise very well. "She did her job, Mr. Conway, had published some excellent papers on enzyme research, but I can't say I really knew the woman personally. You know how these egghead types are—reclusive."

"Could you tell me something about the research she was working on when she died?"

"Well, Mr. Conway, we assume our people are professionals," Simms had said, "so we don't breathe down their necks. I couldn't tell you anything about her work, because we were all waiting for her to publish. It didn't have anything to do with enzymes, though. I can tell you that much." Which didn't tell him a thing.

As he thought about his conversation with Simms, he was coming out of the lab and saw a woman walking slowly around the area that had been cordoned off. One of her hands was loose on the rope; the other held the strap of her purse, which was over her shoulder. It was still drizzling, but she didn't seem to notice. Her blond hair reached thickly to her shoulders, so pale at the front it almost blended with her white jacket. She had fantastic legs.

"Lose something?" he asked.

She smiled as if she knew him, a quick, lovely smile that warmed his insides. Her face lacked the brassy prettiness that Jen's had; it was softer somehow, friendlier, with pale blue eyes that could probably speak paragraphs in a single glance. "Oh, Detective Conway."

He laughed. "Is it written somewhere that shows?"

"The trench coat." Her eyes twinkled; he realized she was poking fun at him.

He hooked his thumbs in the lapels. "But it's plastic."

She laughed. "Someone told me who you were. I'm Rita Lincoln. I teach here."

"Right. The lady whose hobby is murder."

"Laura Perkins. You've been talking to Laura," she said after a moment.

They started down the walk between the trailers, the scent of her perfume between them. "No interrogations? Don't you want to ask me what I know about Denise?" she said.

"Were you checking out the scene of the crime or something?"

"Boy, what sarcasm." She laughed again and he liked the sound of it—clear, sincere.

"I didn't mean it like that."

"Sure you did, but it's okay. I'm used to it. How about some coffee? I'll tell you everything I know about the woman. Which isn't much."

"That seems to be the general trend."

"Like Howard Hughes."

Rita got into her car and he followed her out of the lot and onto the old runway, which led to the main part of campus. She drove an old tan Volvo, with a long sleek back like a greyhound. It was badly in need of a paint job and didn't look like it could do much over fifty. So when it suddenly sped off through the oblique light, it took him a moment to react. Then he pressed the accelerator to the floor, grinning, saying, "I'll be damned," and the pavement flew toward him in a blur.

His speedometer needle climbed past eighty. Water tore off the windshield in opposing directions. The car hummed; it bumped and rattled across the tufts of grass, the holes, and the runway narrowed off forever into the gray, western sky.

Rita made an abrupt left turn. The car spun in a half circle; the tires screeched and steamed against the wet pavement. She made a surprisingly deft recovery, and by the time she approached the first stop sign, she was doing a respectable twenty in a fifteen-mile-an-hour zone.

"You must have secret aspirations," he remarked, pulling alongside Rita as she parked.

"That runway's just too tempting. You didn't do too badly yourself, you know. I was keeping an eye on you in the mirror."

"I," he said, "happen to have the same aspirations."

"Good. Then we should get along just fine."

They went through the cafeteria lunch line and sat at a table near the window. An hour later, when Laura came in, they were still there.

"So, Mr. Conway," said Laura, setting her tray on the table as she joined them, "did Rita fill you in on all her theories?"

Rita was eyeing the food on Laura's tray. "All sixty minutes' worth," she quipped.

"A meeting of the minds," Conway said. "And please call me John. 'Mister' makes me feel old."

"He thinks the guy who killed Denise was having sexual relations with her. That's just how he put it, Laura. 'Sexual relations,' " Rita said as if he were no longer present. "I disagree primarily with his semantics. 'Relationship' would be a

17

better word." She speared a leaf of spinach in Laura's salad and raised her eyes to Conway's face. "But that's a distinction which sometimes escapes men, isn't it?" There was no sarcasm in her voice; she was just poking fun again.

"I plead the Fifth." He glanced at his watch. "I've really got to run, ladies."

"Coward," Rita murmured.

Conway laughed. "Discretion."

As he was getting up, Laura mentioned he might want to speak to a student named Tom Duncan, who had once been Denise's research assistant. Conway jotted down the man's name.

"Oh, God," Rita groaned. "Duncan. Yuck. But while you're at it, you should probably talk to Frank Turnbalt, too. I think he knew Denise." She stabbed a carrot in Laura's bowl. "He's in the law building. Big shot from Harvard."

"Drive carefully, Rita."

"Chummy," Laura remarked when Conway had left. "Real chummy."

"What'd you tell him, anyway?"

"About your hobby."

Rita cut a corner from Laura's sandwich. "Attorneys don't have hobbies, Laura. They have law. Law and ulcers, law and diversions."

"My father used to say all lawyers are crooked."

"Okay, okay, some of us have law and swindles, how's that. Now, Hank's diversions are racquetball and magic. Mine are murder, fast cars, and, occasionally, sex. Just for the record."

"You make it sound like you're on the verge of divorce."

"We haven't been married long enough to get divorced, but we do have our moments, yes."

Laura watched Rita's fork swinging back and forth like a pendulum over her salad bowl. It dropped, impaling a radish. Rita's every movement, no matter how small, how trivial, was feminine, precise. It had been like that as long as Laura could remember. It was as if Rita had been born into a state of grace, blessed with alacrity, brains, and looks, the complete package. They'd been friends since they were kids, and Laura didn't think she'd ever met another human being as integrated as Rita, as complete.

Rita cut another corner from Laura's sandwich. "Did you eat, Rita?"

"Hmm. Sorry. Talking about murder makes me hungry. The other two women were raped, you know. Although they won't know about Denise until the autopsy, she didn't appear to have any contusions or abrasions. Neither did the other two." Rita picked up her spoon, dipped it into the heart of Laura's Jell-O.

"You know, it's a good thing I like you," Laura said, pushing her bowl of Jell-O toward Rita. "There. You finish it."

"Thanks."

"Maybe you're pregnant."

"Perish the thought." She nibbled at the salad, put her spoon down. "You know, it's too bad I'm a diehard from the old school of monogamy. Conway would be first on my list otherwise."

"He doesn't seem your type."

"I still haven't figured out what my type is. Hey, I almost forgot. If Ian's in town, why don't you two come over for dinner a week from Saturday?"

"Hank must be cooking."

"I sure wouldn't plan a menu two weeks in advance. When's Ian coming back, anyway?"

"Sometime this week."

"Boy, that sounds vague."

"It's always vague."

"Men." Rita sighed.

2

1.

THE HOUSE HAD always creaked when it rained, almost as if the cedar had some dim memory of itself as a tree, its branches weighted with the tricks of the seasons. It was an A-frame on a two-acre lot that backed up to a forest of pine. Some nights the scent of pine and the damp earth would follow Laura into sleep and she'd awaken believing she was somewhere in the New England woods. There was always a brief stab of disappointment when she looked out onto the roofs of other houses in the distance. In south Florida, the notion of country was an illusion.

She turned on her side and Emily strolled up from the foot of the bed, her striped tiger's face twitching. She stepped carefully over the hills and valleys in the sheets and stretched out beside Laura, purring. Laura glared at the phone, which had been mute for days, willing it to ring. It seemed she'd spent most of the last five months waiting for calls from Ian. When he wasn't on the road, he was preparing to hit the road, and when she didn't hear from him, she assumed the worst. And the worst was always a bright, lovely woman who knew all the right things to say over drinks and dinner and bed. Not that they'd ever discussed it. But she had met him on the road, in Key West, and look what had happened.

If she hadn't been in a hurry that morning; *if* she hadn't been annoyed that she would have to skip breakfast and sit through a polite luncheon with pompous educators dabbing at their mouths with linen napkins, glancing surreptitiously at the clock as they tugged at ties and panty hose, just itching to get away and drink themselves stinko; *if* she'd been paying attention to what she was doing, she wouldn't have plowed into the car behind her in the motel parking lot. She wouldn't have met him.

She'd no sooner heard the sickening crunch of taillights than a man jumped out of the car and marched to the back, his fists clenched as if he intended to damage the person responsible. He was muttering, "I can't believe this," as she approached.

"I'm really sorry," she said, "and I'll be glad to pay for whatever damages there are." The fenders were hooked. A deep gash ran through the paint near the license plate. "Should I go call a tow truck? Would that be easiest?"

He broke off a piece of taillight, dropped it in the dirt, brought the heel of his shoe down over it. The plastic splintered like bone. "The car's a rental," he said, leaning against it, folding his arms, and he looked at her as if daring her to say something.

"So I'll pay for it."

It was late January and the sky over his shoulders arched in a perfect, cloudless blue, brittle where the sun stood, deeper at the edges. She didn't want to argue. It was chilly standing out here, and she was hungry and already late. "Look," she continued, scribbling her name and work number on a scrap of paper and handing it to him, "you can get in touch with me here when you know how much. I'm late for this conference, Mr. . . ." Her brows shot up quizzically.

"Fletcher, Ian Fletcher."

"Well, Mr. Fletcher, I'm late for this conference just around the corner, and if—"

"Me, too."

"Me, too, what?" she asked, and they both laughed.

20

"The conference," he said, dropping his arms to his sides. "That's where I'm supposed to be, too."

"You're a teacher?"

He laughed. His eyes were the color of bitter chocolate, good enough to eat, and his thick chestnut hair was graying at the temples. When she'd first looked at him, when he was snarling and fussing over his car, she'd thought his mouth was mean. But the laugh transformed it. "Don't I look like one?"

"No. I don't know." Then she shook her head firmly. "No, you don't."

"I'm not. I sell word processors."

There didn't seem to be much to say beyond that, so she glanced back at the fenders. "How're we going to get them loose?"

"I hate conferences," he said, ignoring her question. "What about you?"

"I hate luncheons."

Laughing, scratching the side of his nose, he looked down at the ground where they stood, then deliberately brought his eyes slowly up her body to her face. "My," she remarked, "that was subtle."

"You're supposed to pretend you didn't notice."

"I'd have to be blind not to notice," she snapped, taking umbrage, not liking his game. "About the fenders," she went on, her tone clipped, impersonal. "Why don't we call a tow truck and you get estimates and so on. I've really got to get going. I'll be here through tomorrow."

She started to turn around, but he said, "Wait. Hold on. I apologize." He knocked his knuckles against the side of the car. "I apologize, Laura Perkins. Have you had breakfast? Let me buy you breakfast. Let me prove to you that I'm not really an obnoxious human being."

"That may take some doing."

"Come on. There's a place across the street." He was already touching the small of her back, urging her forward.

"What about the cars?"

"Forget it, sweet pea. This is Key West. Where anything goes."

They lingered a couple of hours over breakfast at a place on the water, then walked the labyrinthian streets that curled in on themselves like pretzels. He, born and bred in the town, knew the history of everything—docks, buildings, and cornerstones, who had slept where and when—and showed her the island as only a native could. It was no surprise they didn't make it to the conference and that she surrendered her room and moved into his, and no surprise they spent the next three days breaking all the rules here at the end of the line. She, the refugee of another affair, shed the skin of her famine and fell in love with the abandon of a tourist in a foreign country, traveling without a past. She was zipped into paradise and snuggled down inside it, loving how it fit.

And on the fourth day, it burst.

She'd asked one simple question: Have you ever been married? And before he'd even replied, she saw it in his eyes and her hands went numb, and the numbness worked down into her arms, across her shoulders, and then dug into her heart. She looked away from him, out over the deck of the restaurant where they were sitting. A winter moon was rising in the tropics. A couple strolled the beach below, just the way you saw it on postcards—arms around each other, heads bowed, bare feet leaving prints in the wet sand—and she thought, *A lie, all of it's a lie.*

"I didn't know how to tell you," Ian said finally.

There: that was the worst and the best of it. Affirmation was a blessed relief. She thought of a thousand things she wanted to say and would have except there didn't seem to be much point in it. She simply dropped her napkin next to her plate and picked up her purse. "Have a nice life, Ian," she said, and left.

She drove back to Miami that night and spent most of the next month forgetting. She discovered she could be a fairly rational human being, perhaps even a useful one, as long as she kept busy. So she set to work refurbishing the house. It was only when she closed her eyes at night and heard the wind through the pines that she felt the penetrating, obdurate vestige of her affections. Her arguments were the usual ones women use to talk themselves out of love: he was a liar and a bastard and of course unobtainable. She loved him because she couldn't have him, didn't she? Not that it would have made any difference to anyone but her. Yet it seemed important she understand the distinction.

The conundrum was resolved one Saturday afternoon when she was wallpapering her downstairs bathroom and the doorbell rang and it was Ian. Just like that. Without preface, perhaps afraid she would shut the door before he said his piece, he blurted, "It was a lie, Laura. I'm not married. I was involved with someone else and I was feeling pretty screwed up and it was just simpler to say I was married than to try to explain." He ran a finger under his mustache, looked down at the porch. "I'm sorry."

His shoulders sagged with the relief of his confession. She didn't know what to think, say, so she left him standing there and walked back across the room to her wallpaper. She finished brushing paste onto the back of a strip. She heard him come into the house and shut the door. The cat ran into the bathroom, poked her nose around the tray of paste, then plopped herself down on the carpet just outside and began to preen.

"Emily wanted in," Ian said, crouching down, stroking the animal's belly.

Laura fixed the strip of wallpaper in place. "How'd you know her name?"

"You told me. I remembered. When we saw Hemingway's house and all the seven-toed cats."

Laura ran the roller up and down the wallpaper longer than necessary so she wouldn't have to look at him. She couldn't think properly. It was too warm in the room. She remembered the day they'd gone through Hemingway's *finca;* he'd told her he loved her. She wondered if he remembered that, too.

"Is it over?" she asked finally. "Between you and this woman?"

"The week I got back from the Keys. I realized I just didn't care anymore."

"Does she live here?"

"Does it matter?"

"Yes."

"She lives in Gainesville."

"How long were you involved with her?"

"Off and on for about a year."

She kneeled on the floor again, cut another strip of paper while Ian held down the sides. She noticed his fingers were long, the nails a soft, salubrious pink. "Tell me if I'm violating the boundaries of propriety," she said.

"You aren't."

"I think what you did was cowardly, Ian."

"Guilty as charged."

That he agreed made it more difficult. How much simpler it would have been if he'd come here, apologized, and they'd argued. Then she could have said, There, I was right. He's a shit. I'm better off without him. But he wasn't the least bit pugnacious.

Laura picked up the brush, dipped it in the paste, drew it once down the length of the paper, then set it in the tray. She scratched her forehead with the back of her hand because the rest of her was sticky. "Look," she began, feeling a dull pounding at the back of her head, the parched thickness in her throat, "what do you want from me?"

"Nothing."

Don't tell me that.

"Then why're you here, Ian? What's the point?" She rolled back on her heels, saw the look that came over his face, and felt her insides turning to sand.

"I wanted to apologize. I wanted to tell you that something happened between you and me, Laura." He chose his words carefully, stepping back through their brief and colored past. "Something good. I guess what I want from you is another chance."

Give me a chance, he'd said that morning in Key West. Let me prove to you I'm not an obnoxious human being. She picked up the brush again, wanting to stall, think, to decide. She couldn't breathe properly around him. Then she dropped the brush, sighed. "God, I'm so easy."

Now it was June, and the doubt implanted by the first lie grew in direct proportion to the telephone's silence. She rolled onto her back, insomnia creeping through her by degrees, her obstreperous thoughts marching through the months, pushing into the dark corners of consciousness, rubbing up against old wounds. *This bed's too big for one, Laura.* Ian's townhouse in North Miami had only a double bed; hers was a king. How ironic that the size of a bed determined at whose place they spent most of their time together. And it wasn't fair, she thought. Since she was picking him apart, she might as well include that, too. This way, if anything happened, her house would be the place where all the memories were stored. Ian would be able to return to the clean slate of his rooms, none the worse for wear.

She closed her eyes, listening to the rain in the dark, the squeal of traffic in the distance, the immense silence drifting up from downstairs. It wasn't just her bed that was too large for one. It was the house, lot, the forest of pines in the back.

The sound of the rain receded. She turned on her side, waiting for sleep to come, lulled by the whisper of the wind in the eaves.

In the dream, the phone was ringing and Laura was running to answer it. She took the stairs two at a time, but they got higher and higher and the ringing got louder and closer and she called out for Ian to answer it.

The ringing continued.

She kept on running and began to gasp for breath, as if the air were thin, and when the stairs suddenly flattened out, like a rug pulled from beneath her, she fell forward and slid down almost to the bottom and had to start all over again.

She had to climb up through the dream as the ringing went on and on, so empty, so hollow, and when she was finally on the landing, she could see into the bedroom. Ian was there, the covers pulled over his head. On the nightstand the phone was ringing so loudly she had to press her hands over her ears. "Why didn't you answer it?" she shouted. And then a woman sat up in the bed.

"You were always so stupid," she said. Laura stepped closer. The air in the room was thick, gray. The woman, naked to the waist, hair falling over one shoulder, was Denise Markham.

"But you're dead!" Laura shouted at her. "You're dead. *Get out of here!*"

"Go away," Denise said. "We don't want you here."

Ian sat up, the covers falling away from him. "That's right. We don't want you here," he repeated in a monotone.

"But she's dead, Ian, and I'm alive," Laura said to him, poking herself in the chest.

Denise and Ian laughed, looked at each other as if she were no longer in the room. Their laughter was a low, intimate sound, and he moved slowly toward her, kissing her mouth and eyes and breasts, and the ringing went on and on.

Laura stumbled out of the dream, sucking at the air, covered with perspiration. The phone was pealing. Her feet were tangled in the sheets. Rain whipped the branches against the windows. She fumbled in the dark for the phone, knocked it off the cradle. "Hello?"

"Laura?"

The voice was low, strained, like a frog's. She thought it was a bad connection, because of the storm. "Ian, can you speak up?"

"Laura, I'm watching you," the voice whispered, "and when the lights go out, I'll be there watching you and waiting for you, ready to—"

She slammed down the phone, dived for the light. She turned the switch off and on, her fingers sliding around it, but nothing happened. She threw back the covers, sat up. He'd cut the wires. He was outside. Her head dropped to her chest and she clutched the sheet. *Don't panic.*

But everything went dead inside her and then a wind rose from the silence within her and fear slammed against her ribs like a tidal wave. She leaped out of bed. She needed a weapon.

Laura felt her way along the edge of the bed until she reached the nightstand. She jerked open the drawer, jammed her hands into the sea of papers and junk, feeling around for the scissors. The phone, she thought, spinning around, holding the scissors open, maybe he'd cut that, too. She grabbed for it, held it away from her ear, anticipating the ugly whisper of the man's voice. Outside, the wind blew furiously through the pines and the sky suddenly lit up like the Fourth of July. She held the phone to her ear and heard the dial tone. The storm, she thought, daring to laugh. It had knocked out the power.

She got up, pressed her face to the window, cupping her hands at the sides as she peered out into the wet, empty dark. The streetlights were out, the power everywhere was dead. Coincidence, of course. These things happened.

It thundered and she grimaced, pulling her shoulders in toward her body until the rumble passed, then she put the scissors on the nightstand and felt along the wall to the closet. Hurricane supplies. Center of the shelf. Her hands touched a shoebox; she brought it back over to the bed with her, hugging it like a teddy bear. Matches. Candles. Batteries and a flashlight. She pushed her thumb against the switch, holding her breath in that instant before she knew, then whispered, "God, great. All right," as the beam shooed the dark from the room.

The phone rang again. She moved to the top of the bed, pulling the shoebox along with her, and got in between the sheets. When the ringing stopped, there was only the voice of the wind and the rain shrieking in the endless night.

2.

The man held his hand to the phone awhile after Laura had hung up on him, as if to prolong the connection between them and the thrill snaking along his spine. His voice would now be a ripple in her consciousness. She wouldn't be able to answer the phone in the next few days without first thinking of him, of his voice.

She evidently hadn't seen him the night of Denise's murder; otherwise he would've been in jail by now. But she might have noted some detail which wouldn't fall into place until later. Yes, it would have been simpler just to kill her. Dead, she would no longer be a menace to him. But he wanted to play with her first, like he had with Denise. He enjoyed that surge of power he'd felt just before Denise had died. That instant when she'd fully understood what was happening, that *he*, her faithful Bucky, was about to end her life. He wanted to experience that with Laura.

He walked back into the bedroom, growing dizzy as Denise's face swam inside his head, the features separate—a mouth, nose, those dark, tantalizing eyes, that cascade of hair—then the features slid together and became Laura's face, then the faces of many women. He rubbed his eyes, fighting back confusion.

For a moment he wondered what he was doing. Who was this man who had zipped himself into *his* body, *his* bones? He ran his hands along his arms, watching as his fingers rubbed the skin, and tried to remember who he had been before Denise had betrayed him. The event had neatly divided his life: Before Betrayal and After.

Denise's fault, he thought. If she had trusted him, he wouldn't be in this predicament now. So in the end, Laura's death would be added to Denise's sins. He could see the tally in his mind, gold star deeds on the right, black star deeds on the left, like a Sunday-school lesson.

The bedroom had a musty smell to it, like a closed cellar. It was the scent of sex; it had permeated everything. It was a damp fungus, a subtle poison. He got into bed and the woman turned over with a sigh, seeking him in the dark trust of her sleep. His arms slid around her. Smooth porcelain shoulders, cool lips. She wiggled up against him like a bitch in heat, and her breath smelled faintly of wine, her hair of perfume. Perhaps she, too, would betray him. He had looked for the signs, waited for them, even expected them. Eventually, all women reenacted Eve's betrayal of Adam. His father used to say as much.

As a child, he had sometimes awakened in the middle of the night to his mother's soft sobs in the next room and his father's shouted accusations that she was unfaithful. The noise got so bad some nights that he had to drag his pillow and a blanket into the closet to get away, and even then the sounds had penetrated when his father was really mad. In the beginning, the ruckus had scared him, and once in the closet he would slap his hands over his ears and squeeze his eyes shut until it passed. But over the years, he'd almost gotten used to it. Expected it. And in the end, of course, he'd discovered that the beatings his father had administered to his mother were deserved. She'd run out on them both with another man. In the end, she'd betrayed him just as completely as Denise.

The woman beside him reached down, touching him as he grew hard against her. She urged him inside her, whispering something to him. He pressed his hand against her waist, holding her away from him, teasing her. She liked it slow. So had

Denise. But she wouldn't let him do to her the things he'd done to Denny.

"You." She giggled, fully awake now, struggling a little as he pinned her arms to the pillow and covered her mouth with his own.

Her legs opened and closed like scissors, then parted wide as the Red Sea as he moved inside her. Denise was burgundy, warm as blood. This woman was champagne, to be savored. Laura, he imagined, would be swift and cool, a northern river. The differences among women were sometimes subtle, he thought, often various, but they were all smooth and wet, and always there was this momentary, fragmented terror that he would lose himself inside them. Drunk one night, his father had confessed as much.

He felt the vacuum of the wasted months with Denise and moved hard and fast to dispel it. The woman squeezed her arms around him, squeezed his terror, the vacuum, from him; then, nibbling at his ear, she groaned, slowed, her pleasure now exquisite.

He watched it, this pleasure, sweep across her face in a storm. It excited him as deeply as Denise's terror had, as Laura's terror had tonight. Pleasure and pain were the same for a woman.

The woman's head moved from side to side and she made small, strange sounds deep in her throat. She was an animal beneath him. She scratched, moaned, lurched forward and wrapped her arms around his waist. They rocked back and forth. She nibbled at him like a little fish. The room grew diseased with the smell of their bodies and reminded him of those nights in his cramped closet.

He pulled out, urged her over on her stomach, and entered her from behind. "This . . . this is how dogs do it," the woman whimpered, trying to turn over, to free her arms. But he rode her hard and fast and she cried out as she came and fell stupidly against the bed, still and silent at last.

He decided she was ugly. Her hair was plastered to the sides of her face, and the back of her neck. He tried to remember where he'd met her, but it didn't really matter. She was just another woman. No one special like Denise. Like Laura.

"Let me up," she said. He moved away from her; she remained on her side for a while, her back to him, breathing so softly, motionless. Denise would always snuggle up to him after, no matter what he did to her. But this woman didn't. He reached out and dropped his arm in the small of her waist. His hand reached between her legs. She didn't move. "I'm not through yet," he said.

He took her roughly by the cuff of the neck, pulled her over against him. "You're hurting my neck," she whispered, a hand flat against his chest trying to keep him away. But he was stronger.

"You take," he said. "You always take, take, take." He pushed her head toward his groin and held it there until her mouth covered him.

3

1.

"THE AIRPORTS WERE jammed," Markham explained, handing Conway a glass of cranberry juice with a splash of vodka. "I wanted to fly to Orlando first, to be with Viki, and trying to change my reservations was nearly as bad as trying to get on the plane. Any plane." He sat down heavily. They were out by the screened-in pool, and although the rain had cooled things off a bit, a thin line of perspiration crossed Markham's upper lip. "I don't really know where to begin," he said, then smiled ruefully. "I suppose you hear that a lot."

"How long were you married?"

"Six years. With numerous separations in between. The marriage was a mess from the beginning, Mr. Conway. Denise was a rather complicated woman. Unique; an egghead. She was also compulsive and neurotic and way out of my league. She was a Ph.D.; I'm a jock with a high school education." He tapped a plastic swizzle stick on the rim of his glass and doubled it over his finger. "Part of the problem was that I have a son from my first marriage who lived with us off and on those first couple of years. Then there was Viki from Denny's first marriage, then there were Denny and me. We should have split for good a long time before we did, but when your first marriage fails, it's tough to admit your second has, too."

"Is Viki going to live with you?"

"She doesn't have anyone else. I adopted her when Denny and I were married. She's with my brother and his family until the funeral's over. She and Denise were going to stay here until my tour had ended, which was when the divorce would've been final.'' He paused, said, "She didn't want anything. Just her freedom, Viki, and that goddamned lab. Not even the house.''

Markham, Conway thought, was one of those men who aged gracefully and therefore gave the impression that he had things together. He reminded Conway of Jack Nicklaus—the same baby blue eyes and a boyish way of brushing his hair from his forehead as if it were an annoyance to have so much hair when you were forty-four. He wore madras pants and a lime-colored shirt, as if he were ready to go out and play eighteen holes, and was deeply tanned.

"Was her work what caused your final split?''

"Partly." He sipped from his drink as he gazed into the backyard. A wooden fence separated Markham's lot from the adjoining one. It was thick with vines and ivy and tongues of pale gold and scarlet hibiscus licking the air. A comfortable, private neighborhood, Conway thought. And Markham was a comfortable, private man. "When Denise and I met,'' he went on, "she was recently divorced from her first husband. I was on one of my self-improvement kicks at the time and had enrolled at the university for a chemistry course. She was the teacher. We had coffee one night after class and I guess that's how it started. Like I said, we were an odd pair, but in the beginning, it was good, very good.'' He glanced at Conway. "You ever been married?''

"Yup. For five years." Five long, long years, Conway thought.

"Curious institution, marriage. What are the statistics now? One out of two marriages ends in divorce? And I think the figures are worse for second marriages, if I'm not mistaken. And yet man, being the optimistic beast that he is, raised on fairy tales and forever-afters, keeps trying again and again, despite the odds. I'll probably get married again." He laughed. "Denny would've married again. We seem to need emotional involvement; it comes with the blood and the cells.''

Markham walked across the pool area to the screen, hands in his madras pockets. "I was married for ten years the first time,'' he continued. "First few years, the sex was fine, communication was fine. Then my son was born and sex became perfunctory and there was no time to communicate and before the ten years were over everything had skidded downhill. But with Denny . . .'' He shook his head, turned around. "She was insatiable.'' He walked back to the counter, picked up his drink, dropped more ice cubes into the glass. "It was her sexual temperament, though, which caused our final split and most of our problems, too." He paused. "Christ, I don't know what the point would be of going into all this." He twisted a new swizzle stick around his finger.

"Anything you can tell me would help," Conway assured him, understanding that Markham, for whatever reason, had a need to confess. He just needed a little prodding.

A minute passed in the dry whir of the electric clock mounted on the wall above the counter, in the cry of birds flitting through the garden beyond the screen, in the clinking of ice cubes in Markham's glass. "Denise wanted an open marriage. And I didn't. I figure if you're going to go through the legal hassles involved in getting married, why should the marriage be open? Just live together. Anyway, she began having affairs. Got into swinging. She wanted me to participate, said it would improve our communication." He laughed and it was a hard, torn sound. He stirred his drink again, held the swizzle stick back against the glass, and lifted it to his mouth. "This is embarrassing."

"Look, I can come back another day if—"

"No, no, maybe it'll do me good to talk about it," he said, and gave a small, nervous laugh. "Got to start somewhere, right?" He set the glass down. Tapped his fingers against the side. "I've been around enough to know what's going on in the world, Mr. Conway. But fundamentally, I'm a monogamist. Denise said I was a prig. Maybe I am. But there's something repulsive to me about exhibitionism. I haven't any desire to watch . . . to watch my wife with anyone else. I told Denny I wasn't interested. That was our first separation. It was an issue off and on. We'd split, get back together. Just about a year ago, though, she met some people in town and the whole thing started up again."

"People from the university?"

"Yes. And I guess some prominent people in the Grove and Miami. I don't know the names of most of them. But generally, they seem to think the rules don't apply to them because they have enough money to buy themselves out of anything." Conway noted the bitterness and contempt in Markham's voice. "Another drink?" Conway shook his head. "Anyway," Markham continued, "just before I left on this tour in April, we agreed to split." He hesitated. "Have you been over to the law school yet?"

"Yes."

"Then you've met Frank Turnbalt."

"Heard of him. Harvard big shot, right?"

Markham chortled. "Yeah, that's one way of putting it. He's

an adjunct professor, real estate law, I think, or some other damned thing. He also has a lucrative practice in the Grove, and his wife, Marie, is a prominent jewelry designer. It started with them. Like I said, about a year ago. I've only met the man once. Denny had them over for dinner one night, before I ever knew what was going on." He sank into the chair, the weight of his confession finally overcoming him. "He's witty, loud, and abrasive, especially when he gets into one of his I-know-how-to-make-money routines. He's obviously very bright and he makes sure you know it." He sipped, said, "Anyway, the Turnbalts are what led to our final split."

"Was Denise still, uh, involved with them when she was killed?"

"I don't know. She was in April, when I left on tour. I know that much because she came home loaded one night on cocaine and told me." He looked around, pointed. "She stood right there. In that doorway. She stood right there and told me she had just made it with Marie Turnbalt and what did I think of that? I told her what I thought of *that*." He snapped at the word, as if to bite it in half. "And it was the end of the marriage."

"Did she have any close women friends?"

"No. She was an only child and her folks are dead. She never had friendships like ordinary people."

"Then she and Marie Turnbalt weren't friends."

"Not like that, no. Funny, on the plane down here, I was trying to remember things about Denny. And I thought of something a little odd. About three weeks after I met her, we went to an astrologer. She was fascinated with stuff like that—the occult, astrology, just about anything associated with the paranormal. The astrologer told her she would die a violent death, that her sex drive was one of the strongest influences in her chart, and that she should guard against excess if she wanted to make it past forty. Makes you wonder."

He shook his head and Conway imagined him shaking his head for the rest of his life, puzzling over the conundrum of wife number two. "Mr. Conway, I know this is going to sound cold-blooded of me, but could you give me any idea of when the autopsy will be completed? I'd like to be able to plan something about the funeral. I've got to get on with my own life."

"I'll have to let you know." Conway didn't want to tell him that Denise's body was stored with fifteen others on the county's mobile morgue, a freezer disguised as a van. "Do you know what kind of research she was involved in?"

"What she did for a living was absolutely Greek to me, Mr.

Conway. I told you, I'm a jock,'' and he smiled at the term, poking fun at himself. ''She sometimes spent days in that lab, though, not even coming home to sleep. And I know she was there, because I used to drive over to see her. It was like visiting someone in prison or something.''

''You never discussed the research?''

''No. Not really. I knew it was something she'd been working on for years, though. She used to refer to it as her sixteen-year-old adolescent, suffering from acne and growing pains. You might ask her assistant, Tom Duncan.''

That name again, Conway thought. ''I haven't been able to locate him. I thought it was odd that even the head of the science department didn't know the nature of Denise's research.''

As Markham laughed, his eyes crinkled at the corners like crepe paper. ''Simms? He's been out to lunch since the day he was born. He doesn't give a damn what his people do, as long as they publish and don't miss classes.''

Conway told Markham he wanted to speak to Viki when she returned. At the mention of the girl's name, his face lit up for the first time since Conway had arrived. ''No problem. I'll call you. But go easy on her. She's as different from her mother as any two people can be.''

''Where's her father?''

''Last I heard, he was floating around Texas somewhere. He's a civil engineer with a drinking problem. No telling where he is.''

Conway wondered, suddenly, what the sum total of his life would look like to someone else. He could just hear Tillis saying: ''Conway? An officious prick.'' And Stella: ''That sonuvabitch was always late with the check and gave me high blood pressure.'' And Jen: ''No wonder his wife divorced him.''

He asked Markham to let him know if he ran across anything in Denise's personal effects related to her work, then the housekeeper came out on the porch and announced lunch was ready. She was Jamaican and spoke with that soft, melodious voice of the islanders. Conway had spoken with her earlier, but she'd been unable to provide anything more than she'd told Tillis on Sunday.

''Why don't you stay for lunch?'' Markham asked. He seemed eager for company and Conway felt a twinge of compassion for the man as he shook his head.

''I'd like to, but I've got to make tracks.''

A few moments later, Conway started down the front steps and along the walk that curved in between some higher hedges, past a rose garden with a statue, birdbath, a white picket fence, trees. There were a number of mango trees in the front yard and in one, near the gate, Conway noticed a little wooden house and guessed it belonged to Viki Markham. It had windows and a door and smacked of childhood secrets.

The neighborhood was an expensive one in Coral Gables, but lacked ostentation. The quality of life here was a state of mind. It was not the sort of place he would have imagined Denise to have spent six years. She belonged, he thought, in a high-rise where rooms were made of glass and looked out over the cerulean blue of the Atlantic. A place where she could kick up her feet on satin pillows after a day in the lab, a place where the name of the game was pleasure. He'd never laid eyes on the woman but felt this with a disturbing certainty, as if she were someone he might have known. She'd needed a kind of luxury Don Markham had been unable to provide.

The sun vanished behind a bank of clouds as Conway got in his car. He wiped an arm across his forehead, hating summer, hating the heat, wishing he, like Viki, had someplace to which he could retreat and shut out the world. He started the car, turned on the air conditioning, then rested his head against the steering wheel so the air blew directly into his face.

Motives, he thought about motives. Wasn't misspent passion its own reason? Didn't Markham have sufficient cause to have killed his wife? And what about Turnbalt?

Orgies and cocaine among the well to do; obsessions, the occult; and an egghead researcher living life in the fast lane. A turbid canvas, he thought.

He breathed deeply and thought there was something loose in the world. He had no name for the thing, but sometimes he felt it, as if somewhere in a remote spot, another Pandora's box were being opened and already the ills were taking form. He knew the contents of the box were going to tear into his life, knew it with the same certainty he'd felt about Denise and the high-rise. And he feared it.

2.

A perfectly lovely day, he thought as he turned from the main road onto the campus. Sunlight filtering through the trees like in those old films where God would suddenly speak to the faithful, the road shaded and peaceful, with just a sprinkling of students. A perfect day to return to the scene of the crime.

But he wouldn't stop. He wasn't that stupid. No, today he was in control of his life. His destiny. Daylight soothed his nerves, and smoothed out last night's wrinkled memories. Of the woman. The taker.

For a moment, Laura's voice drifted like smoke through his mind: *Hello? . . . Ian?*

Now his voice would be echoing along the back corridors of her mind.

The thought of her tickled his spine. He wondered if she would let him do to her the things he had done to Denise. The brass bed, the wonderful brass bed with the four gleaming posts. The silky, colorful scarfs with which he'd tied Denise's arms and legs. Laura would probably be squeamish at first, yeah, that's the type of woman she was. But he would teach her. Reward her if she was good. And punish her if she was bad.

He slowed as he passed the path that led to the hibiscus hedge, then pulled into an empty parking space. From here he could see the brightly painted flowers along the path, the low-hanging branches. He wondered where Denise's body was, then reached into his pocket and brought out one of the delicate gold earrings. He stared at it, then clasped it tightly in his hand as if it might connect him with Denny. Wherever she was. A lump swelled in his throat like a tumor and he quickly returned the earring to his pocket. *You made me do it, Denise. It's your fault.* And it would be her fault when Laura died.

Several students were coming down the path. He started the car, his hands slippery and damp now, his fingers fumbling at the keys. It had been a mistake to come here. It was too soon. His tongue slid across his lower lip as he glanced over his shoulder, pulled out of the spot. An image of Denise flared in his mind at that moment: Denise with the little vial at her nose, snorting the powder, then holding it up to him with a grin. *You next, Bucky.*

He hadn't liked doing it, not really, but he'd done it for her. She'd so obviously enjoyed it and he wanted to be part of her pleasure. Yes, he thought. Pleasure with Denise was a virtual smorgasbord. A pinch here, a dab there, snort this, drink that. Like Alice in Wonderland. Now the drug and Denise's betrayal were all that remained.

And the notebook, he thought, if indeed it even existed.

He sped off the campus, a man fleeing his own perdition, never suspecting that only weeks from now the drug and the notebook would be his undoing.

Putting men on the moon was the best thing that had ever happened to law enforcement, Conway mused, and patted the computer terminal. Without that giant step for mankind, his investigations would still be trapped in the Dark Ages, where a cop struggled from clue to clue in a clumsy breast stroke. He lit his twenty-ninth cigarette of the day, coughed, vowed to quit when this case was solved, and set it on the edge of the console.

He heard the night people next door and smelled fresh coffee. For nearly a decade these sounds and aromas had been almost like home. He typed in his code and the screen lit up.

HELLO CHARLIE. PDQ: ANNA GARCIA, BELLE GLADE. DOD: 5/9/85. DESCRIBE WOUND.

HELLO JOHN. PDQ/ANNA GARCIA. AUTOPSY RESULTS: DEATH BY KNIFE WOUND TO LEFT SIDE, BETWEEN THIRD AND FOURTH RIBS, PIERCING THE HEART. DIAMETER OF WOUND ⅛". NO DAMAGE TO BONES OR OTHER ORGANS.

*WHAT WERE RESULTS OF SPERM ANALYSIS?

TYPE A NEGATIVE BLOOD, JOHN.

PDQ: PENELOPE JOHNSON, FT. LAUDERDALE. DOD: 5/17/85. ARE SPERM ANALYSIS AND WOUND IDENTICAL TO THAT OF ANNA GARCIA?

YES.

*FORENSICS. PDQ: DENISE MARKHAM. DOD: 6/6/85. ANY INFO YET?

NEGATIVE.

*ANYTHING AT ALL ON DENISE MARKHAM?

CHECKING. . . .

The door opened and Pete Aikens lumbered into the room. "I thought I heard the baby clickin' away in here. What're you up to this late, Conway?"

He was a huge man. He filled the doorway, and when he smiled his teeth were so white against his chocolate face that they almost shone in the dark. He'd joined narcotics six years ago, and besides being an ace detective, he was the finest poker player Conway had ever been up against.

"I'm doing no good, black boy," Conway said, and Ake laughed.

The computer typed out: NO INFORMATION ON DENISE MARKHAM.

"The Markham murder," Ake said as Conway turned off the computer.

"What else." Conway sat down, lit another cigarette. The other had burned down and he tossed the dead butt in the basket.

"Got anything?"

"Yeah, a messy life."

"Tillis said you're waiting for the autopsy results."

"I really won't know anything until then. We might be dealing with another nut like Ted Bundy. Or the Boston Strangler."

"Or someone just trying to make her murder look like the other two. The newspapers covered all the details, remember."

"Yeah, I've thought of that."

"Hate to change the subject, my man, but weren't you supposed to be on vacation? You and Jenny?"

"She went."

"Aahh," Ake breathed, "women." Then he rubbed his hands together. "So let's play some poker Saturday night."

"Ain't they killin' crackers in youh neck o'dah woods, brothah?"

"All dah damn time, massa. Eight o'clock sharp."

Conway finished his cigarette, coughed, stabbed it out. "You ever thought about doing something else, Ake?"

"You mean when I grow up?"

Conway laughed. "Yeah."

"Nope." He scrutinized Conway. "You're dragging ass, Conway. Go home. Go to bed." In the doorway, he turned. "And remember, white boy. All work and no play makes a dull Johnny Conway."

The phone was ringing when Conway walked in the door of his apartment. He'd forgotten to hook up the tape machine. "Yeah," he said, grabbing it. "Conway."

"Sugar, that's no way to answer the phone." Jenny's soft southern voice sent delicious chills up his spine.

"Jen. Hi. I just came in the door."

"I know. I've been calling all night. When're you coming out here, sugar? It's been gorgeous."

"I don't know. There's nothing definite yet."

"John, you've got the time coming to you. Just take it. Truro won't do anything but assign someone else to the case. You're not indispensable, you know."

From "sugar" to "John," he thought. That meant he'd already fallen from grace. "I can't."

"Great. Terrific. We plan a month's vacation and you're stuck in south Florida and not making any effort to leave. That tells me a lot."

"Jen, please." He was tired. He didn't want to argue. He could almost see her on the other end, legs propped up on a chair in some cozy chalet, a glass of cognac in her hand. Jen's style, yes sir. Loose and free. "If I could, I'd be on the next flight. You know that, sweetheart."

"Right." She laughed. "I know that."

"Maybe you could fly back here so we could have some time together before your charter leaves."

"Nope, I don't think so, John. I wouldn't get to see you, so what's the dif?"

"I'll call you tomorrow night."

"Forget it." Then he thought he heard someone else in the background and suddenly understood Jenny had called to confirm he was *not* coming out. "Don't bother," she snapped, and hung up.

Same to you. Now she could screw her way to Hawaii, happy as a clam. In two months, she'd have someone else. Women like Jenny couldn't stand their own company too long.

He started into the shower, heard the phone ring again, took it in the bedroom.

"Joe's Grill."

"Ha-ha, Johnny-o."

"Stella. Little late for phone calls, don't you think?"

"If you answered my calls, I wouldn't be calling, would I. The air conditioning has broken down and I need the check to get it fixed."

"So go to work like everyone else, Stell."

"I can't. You know what the doctor says about my blood pressure."

"You know how much I make, Stella? You know how much I shell out between you and taxes, huh?"

"What's that got to do with anything?"

"How come I'm paying alimony if we never had kids, huh?"

Because sweet Stella had a hotshot lawyer, that's why.

"That would be child support, Johnny-o. And it's not that I didn't *want* kids, you know."

"Go back to teaching school and give me a break."

"Fat chance, sweetie. You made me like this. You put me *in* this state."

"Bye, Stella." He returned to the living room and connected the tape machine. Jen and Stella: stew and teacher: nymphomaniac and hypochondriac. So what did that make him? Old, he decided. Just old.

4

1.

DENISE MARKHAM'S OFFICE was tidy—not just neat and clean, but meticulously tidy. A wicker couch and chairs with matching tropical pillows dominated the area beneath the long window. The colorful cushions, the slant of the pale light through the blinds, reminded Conway of something out of the deep South, where mammies still moved through oppressive afternoon heat with trays of ice-cold mint juleps and faces set with infinite obsequiousness. The wall behind the desk was solid books, maybe a couple hundred of them. A quick perusal confirmed what he'd already suspected: heavy-duty stuff with titles he could barely pronounce. Her desk was bare, except for a small brass lamp with a wicker shade and a brass spittoon with colorful pens sticking up out of it. Two large cactuses in clay pots were beginning to wilt in the corner. Conway opened the blinds.

Puddles from last night's rain glistened in the sunlight. Through the rows of pines, he could see cars in the distance, making their way west on Calle Ocho. He turned his attention from the window and looked slowly around the room. He didn't know precisely what he was looking for, that was the problem. Some evidence of a secret life, but what?

He sat at the desk, ran his hands over the smooth, cool wood, wondering if Denise had been up here the night she was killed or if she'd remained in the lab. He jimmied the lock on the center drawer and began going through her things. Belongings always had a truth to tell and sometimes it didn't have anything to do with the truths you heard elsewhere.

He found a stack of correspondence, some of it still in envelopes, and spread it out on the desk. Most of it was old and concerned research—inquiries, replies, speaking invitations. There was a scribbled note from Viki, informing her they were having pork chops for supper, and something from Don Markham, written on a napkin, that read: "Sorry about last night. I love you. Don. P.S. Did you like the flowers?" But nothing much of interest.

Conway lit a cigarette and smoked in small, rapid puffs. He got up, moved over the edge of the wicker couch. The cushions sighed as he sat. It was still early morning, and for some time there'd been no sounds from the hall. Now he heard footsteps, coming this way. He stabbed out his cigarette, slipped across the room, and stood behind the door.

The strides were long, quick, and stopped at Denise's door. Conway's hand was on his gun. His gaze was fixed on the floor, where he saw the thin shadows of someone's shoes. Conway waited a moment, but the shadow didn't move. He suddenly threw the door open. A man stood there. At the sight of Conway, his arms shot into the air. "Hold on," he said. "Just hold on."

Raised on westerns, Conway thought. He hadn't even drawn his gun. "Who're you?" he asked, switching on the lamp because it seemed like the kind of thing the man expected.

"Duncan, Tom Duncan." He blinked.

"You can put your arms down, Duncan." Conway waved his hands and his brows shot up, throwing his forehead into a chaos of erratic lines. "See? No gun."

The kid passed a hand over his chin. Conway thought he needed a shave and that he had very long arms, like an orangutan. "You're the cop," he said blankly.

"Detective Conway."

"I thought I heard something in here. I figured maybe it had all been a mistake and she was still alive."

"No mistake."

"I was one of her research assistants. For a while."

"Yeah, I've heard."

Duncan evidently felt more courageous now, because he ventured over to the bookshelves. "Just look at this." He spread his arms out very wide, indicating the height and width of the shelves. "She musta been the best read lady between here and . . ." He hesitated. "Well, between here and somewhere, anyway."

"You a chemistry major?"

Duncan turned around. "Me? Hell, no. I'm here for basketball. Work-study program. School guarantees me at least twenty hours of work a week. I mean, I know a little chemistry, but I'm no whiz." He moved around the office now, passing a hand over the desk, shelves, the windowsill, then leaned down and checked the dirt in the potted plants. "God, these things are dry. Got any theories on the bastard who did this?"

"No, nothing firm."

Duncan straightened, leaned against the sill. His thick blond hair fell toward his eyes and he pushed it back impatiently. "Nothing firm. Yeah. As in life, so in death, isn't that what they say? Nothing firm: that was Denise's style all right. Nothing definite, nothing firm."

"You didn't like her?"

"Me?" He laughed. "Shit, every guy who was ever in her class was in love with her. Didn't matter how much crap she dished out. You ever see her?" Conway shook his head. "Well, too bad. No man shoulda ever missed laying eyes on Denise Markham, no siree. I mean, she was a looker to beat all lookers."

"That good, huh."

"But cold," Duncan said. "She was cold. Oh, Jesus, sometimes she could give you a look that would freeze piss in your kidneys."

"How long did you work for her?" Conway asked, sitting on the edge of the desk.

"Eight months." Duncan turned toward the window, shoved his hands deep in his pockets. "Until April." Conway noticed that his left hand came out of his pocket and pressed to his side as if he were trying to hold a rib in place.

"And what happened in April?"

Duncan dropped his hands, and as he turned Conway noted the red blotches of annoyance popping out along his neck. He ran a finger under his nose. "This is like *What's My Line*. You've sure got a lot of questions for a guy who hasn't got any answers."

And you've got a smart mouth, kid. "So what happened in April?"

"She got herself a new assistant because I had to raise my grades, so I couldn't work as many hours as I had been." He walked over to the air conditioner, turned it on, fiddled with the vents so they blew in his face.

"You know what kind of research she was involved in?"

"Nope, like I said, chemistry isn't my major. I was more her gofer than anything. You know, go for this, go for that."

"Was she dating anyone?"

"Oh, sure, man," he said, turning around. The air from the window unit ruffled the hair around the sides of his head. "She was always seeing someone. A woman who looked like she did never had to spend a night alone, that's for sure."

"You know their names? Ever see her with anyone?"

"Nope. She was pretty private. I mean, sometimes she worked in that lab for hours. I'd pop in and out with coffee or stuff from the library and she wouldn't so much as say, 'How're things, Duncan?' or, 'How've you been, Duncan?' Nothing personal. That was her style. Yup." He grimaced, pressed a hand hard against his side, stretched his body left, right, then let go. "Well, good luck, Detective Conway. I've gotta get going. Hope you catch the shit who did it."

"You going to be around all summer?"

"Me? Oh, sure. The coach has given me the summer to raise my grades. I was going to be suspended. Now I'm just on probation."

"Notify me before you leave town, Duncan. Just in case I have more questions."

"Sure thing, man," he said, and raised one of his long arms and was gone.

Two hours later, after Conway had checked her desk, filing cabinets, and behind the bookcase, he found what he was looking for. There was a clock on the wall just inside the door and when he unplugged it and removed the back, he found two envelopes. One contained a plastic bag rolled out like a worm that had about a gram of what he suspected was cocaine. He wet the tip of his finger with his tongue, dipped it inside, touched it to his lower lip. It numbed quickly.

The second envelope was thick. When he shook out the contents, he found two marriage certificates, a divorce decree from Denise's first marriage, a copy of her daughter's birth certificate, and two typed and dated letters, unsigned. It was a rather odd place to find official documents, he thought, but then, Denise Markham had not been a normal person.

The first letter read: "Denny, I think I'm going crazy with wanting you and loving you and I can't stand the situation the way it is anymore. So please, we've got to talk. 7/6/84

The second letter was dated only two months before her death and before she and Markham had decided to divorce. It was laced with wrinkles, as if she'd crumpled it in a rage, then changed her mind and flattened it out.

42

4/9/85

Denise,

You're trying to lay this heavy guilt trip on me about how I'm causing your marital problems and that's bull, my dear, and you know it.

Conway picked up the clock again, saw that it could also run on batteries, and on impulse popped out one of them. Very good, he congratulated himself, and untaped the key that the battery had covered. It looked like a safety deposit box key, but it was anyone's guess which bank and under what name.

The law school was identifiable by the statue of blind justice, balancing her scales, on the lawn in front of the building. It had once been white and untouched as an angel, but now it had rust stains around her base, bits of dried leaves and sediment in her scales, and a piece chipped out of her arm. Like the notion she symbolized, she was badly in need of an overhaul.

As he started up the wide sweep of stairs inside, hoping he might find Turnbalt in, Conway heard a voice behind him say, "Well, you're not supposed to be here."

Grinning, he turned. "Rita. Hi."

Her hair was different—drawn back from her face with two tortoiseshell combs, so that it moved as she moved, in a singular, graceful motion. "Don't tell me. You found the guy," she said.

"Sure. The butler did it."

She laughed and they continued up the stairs. "Isn't this a wonderful building when the students aren't around? It's the quietest place in Miami this week and the only place I can get anything done. That's why I'm here. What about you?"

"I'm looking for Turnbalt. You know if he's around?"

"I doubt it. You'd be better off calling him at home or at his office in the Grove. Not many of us are around this week. This is when the professors go off and have nervous breakdowns they've been postponing all year."

They stood at the mouth of the stairs for a moment and he wanted to say something clever to keep her talking, but nothing came to mind except Denise Markham's autopsy. "Feel like taking a ride over to the morgue?" he asked suddenly.

"The morgue?" She gave a small laugh, shifted her briefcase to her other hand. He smiled; it had apparently been the right thing to say.

"Morgue. M-o-r-g-u-e."

"Sure, why not? I've never been to a morgue. I'll pass on the bodies, though, Conway."

"Okay. No bodies," he promised.

It was bright and uncomfortably warm outside. Trees drooped with the weight of the sunlight and humidity. The leaves seemed pale, dry, browning at the edges. A week without rain here during the summer would mark the land for certain death, Conway thought.

Rita removed her jacket, carried it over her arm, slipped on sunglasses. He watched her peripherally, liking the way the light turned the white strands of her hair even whiter. She pushed her sunglasses back on her nose with a finger, looked over at him.

"You know," she said, "if Frank Turnbalt's on your list of suspects, I think you're wrong."

"Why?" He liked the way she said, "I think you're wrong," instead of, "You're wrong."

"Murder's not his game. Money is."

"How well do you know him?"

"We nod in the hall and are usually on opposing sides of any issue. Other than that, I really don't know him at all. Laura is the one to talk to. She and Marie Turnbalt used to be good friends. She knew her pre-Frank."

"She's the jewelry designer."

"Right. She's good, too, ever seen her stuff?"

"I probably wouldn't know it even if I had."

"I understand she's hit the big time. She's designing pieces for the Duponts, Kennedys, even Yoko Ono, before she stopped coming to their place in Palm Beach."

Conway unlocked the car. As Rita scooted in, she glanced in the backseat where his briefcase was. "Any goodies?" she asked.

He hesitated, hands on the wheel, the car filling with the warm air from the air conditioner. "You think we could consider ourselves to have a fiduciary relationship?" he asked, and she laughed. One of the combs had come loose in her hair. She lowered her head, held the comb between her teeth, caught the wayward strands, and pulled them into place again.

"Yes, I think we have a fiduciary, Conway. So what's the scoop?" she whispered in a commiserating tone.

Conway thought of Jen, who never bothered to ask about a case, and of Stella, who said cops were first in line in hell. And on his way across town, he told Rita about his conversation with Markham and Duncan and about his search of Denise's office. She burst out laughing.

"So the Turnbalts are kinks. Denise was a coke freak who may or may not have been screwing that beautiful but not terribly bright young man, Tom Duncan. My, my, you just never know, do you."

"What's Turnbalt doing at Miami if he's got a degree from Harvard?"

"Where should he be? Wall Street? Suffering from stress and high blood pressure? He's doing just fine here, Conway." And she added, "Especially with what Marie must be bringing in."

Conway parked at the back of the building, which lay between a long, squat row of bleached concrete warehouses. A forty-foot van was sitting in front of an open garage. "There's the county's portable morgue," he said, pointing. "For the overflow. That's where Denise is."

"How cheery."

They entered through a back hall and came out into a large room with five empty desks. It was quiet, the kind of quiet you expected in a morgue. "Everyone's gone to lunch," Conway said, looking around.

"Not everyone," corrected a voice behind them. They turned. "Oh. John. It's you."

Dr. Larry Pivot was a short, balding man with black frame glasses. He was terribly anemic looking, as if he'd spent his entire life underground. A white lab coat, too large in the shoulders, covered his jeans and a blue shirt. "Doc Pivot," said Conway, "this is Rita Lincoln."

"Hi, Rita," Pivot said with distraction, and looked back at Conway. "I know why you're here and I wish I could promise you something definite, John. But I can't. We're already backed up into next week."

"I just need to know a couple of real simple things, Larry. The diameter of the wound, if she was raped, and the blood type. That's it. Simple."

Pivot laughed. It was a funny sound, deep, like quick burps. "I'll try to squeeze her in before the end of the week, but that's the best I can do."

"It'll have to, I guess. I'd like to take a look at her."

"We just moved her downstairs last night. Out of the van." They followed Pivot to another hallway, then down several flights of stairs to a basement. Rita slipped her jacket back on; the air was cold and still. There were two connecting rooms, one that was floor-to-ceiling steel vaults and the other where autopsies were performed.

"Holds two hundred and fifty," Pivot announced proudly.

"Which isn't enough, of course. I keep waiting for the day death takes a vacation. Then I'm taking a slow boat to Egypt—or wherever the farthest port from Miami is."

He led them into the other room. A stainless-steel table stood as proud and large as the sun in the center of the room, reflecting fluorescent lights overhead. The odor of pHisoHex and alcohol and other disinfectants seemed frozen in the air. Instruments were laid out in aluminum basins and there was a refrigerator against the wall.

"This," Rita murmured, "would probably make me psychotic."

"You hit it, little lady." Pivot laughed. "Come on, I'll find Denise for you, Conway."

He said it like Denise Markham was a personal friend, a guest in his home. But then, Pivot was probably on a first-name basis with all of his 250 corpses. Conway could imagine the little man complaining to them in the morning, bidding them farewell in the evening. Pivot pulled out one of the lower vaults.

"Here she is. A beauty, isn't she," he said, flipping back the sheet. Rita moved away.

No matter how often he saw it, Conway was always startled by what death did to a person's face. All traces of compulsions, sorrows, joys, and aberrations had been wiped clean with a look of utter relief and peace. How did you read the history of a life in the face of the dead? he wondered.

Denise's skin was rubbery and wan, colorless, really, except for the lips, which were blue. Her dark hair was long and tangled, but the features, the bone structure, were very nearly perfect. Her face had symmetry. Her nose came gracefully away from her face, neither too large nor too small, and added an exotic touch to her prominent cheekbones. She had a long, swanlike neck and absolutely flawless skin. Pivot brought the sheet down a little past her shoulders and here, too, the skin was without imperfections. Not so much as a freckle. She was a looker all right. Duncan had been absolutely correct about that.

"Beautiful," Pivot breathed, sounding like an agent who had just discovered a potential star. He slipped the sheet back over her, pushed the vault into the wall again.

"Won't the tissues begin to deteriorate?" Rita asked.

"Not significantly."

"Her husband wanted to know about the autopsy, so he could plan a date for the funeral," Conway said.

"He'd be better off having a memorial service," Pivot replied. "I get so damned tired of people thinking they have to have a body present for the obsequies."

Conway smiled. "I'll pass that along."

Pivot brought his arm up, squinted as he looked at his watch. "My esteemed colleagues are due back any minute. I should be getting back upstairs. Can't have anyone thinking I've already caught that slow boat to Egypt." On their way back upstairs, Pivot asked if they'd seen the mobile unit. Before either of them could reply, he said, "With the murder rate like it is, we had to do something. Lots of drug-related murders since the boat lift, and then just the usual number of unsolved deaths. I'm telling you, the morgue is the most accurate barometer of a society's malaise. The world's a goddamned stinkin' mess."

"So that's a morgue," Rita remarked when they were outside.

"You couldn't wait to get out of there, could you." Conway chuckled.

"I go into a place like that and I think, Hey, Alfie, what's it all about?"

Conway chuckled. "Ask me something easy, like if there's a God."

"Glad to see Pivot enjoys his work," she continued with a grimace.

"People in this business develop thick skins."

Their eyes met over the roof of the car, hers cool as spring in the blur of sand and scrub brush diffused by the raw, white heat. Somewhere in the distance, crickets sang of their insatiable thirst. "Do you have a thick skin, Conway?" she asked.

"I don't know anymore," he replied, and got in the car.

On the way back to campus, they were caught in a traffic jam. The heat raised tempers. Horns blared. Cars pulled abruptly into other lanes, bumpers brushed. "Ever play blind man's bluff?" Conway asked.

Rita turned halfway in her seat, so she was nearly facing him. "Yeah, that's the game where ESP would help."

"It's how I'm beginning to feel about Denise's murder."

"Understandable. Like my husband would say, it's not that you're not looking hard enough, just that you're looking in the wrong places." She chuckled. "Hank used to be big on *Perry Mason, Petrocelli*, those attorney shows."

"What's he do?"

"What else? He's an attorney. We've got our own practice. No. That's not quite accurate. It's *his* practice run by a group of attorneys because he's not in town much. He's an amateur magician and does shows all over the state. He's very good," she added, as if to convince herself as well as him.

"How about a beer when we get out of this mess?"

"I'd love to, really. But I've got to get home." She lit a cigarette, cracked the window. "Laura and a friend of hers are coming for dinner a week from Saturday, so why don't you come, too?"

"Great. I'd love to. Thanks."

"Hank's cooking, which means we'll eat promptly at eight. He's very organized. Why don't you come by at seven? Bring a date, too."

Half an hour later, he pulled up behind her car. "Thanks again, Conway. It was interesting."

He waited until she was in her car, then headed across town to the lab with what he'd found in Denise's office. He decided he was probably not going to like Hank Lincoln just on principle.

5

1.

LAURA WAS ON her way out of her office when the phone rang. She grabbed it, said, "I know, I know. I'm on my way, Rita."

"Laura?"

"Ian?"

Her hand tightened on the phone as he laughed. A wonderful sound, full, perspicuous, and she imagined the way his eyes, browner than cocoa, crinkled at the corners and how he ran a finger under his mustache with its flecks of gray and how she felt her heart pushing insistently against her ribs, giving her away. How easy it was to forgive and forget the phones that didn't ring when they were supposed to, the small and petty annoyances that built up like sediment in the lines of communication. "We sound like a recording," he said. "How're you?"

"Okay. Fine. Where are you?"

"De Land. I'm not sure when I can make it back, babe. With luck, by this weekend."

"What happened?"

"I've got two new contracts and have a couple more irons in the fire."

The expression, his vagueness, that he was not coming back, it all irritated her. He chatted about his new contracts for a few minutes, and when she didn't say anything, he said, "Laura? Babe? You still there?"

48

"Yes."

"I read about Denise Markham's murder. I called you last night, but you must've been out." The second call, she thought, the one she hadn't answered. She told him what had happened. "Maybe you should change your number, that would probably solve the problem." Then he changed the subject and that irritated her, too. "Do they have any leads yet on who killed her?"

"No, I don't think so. Detective Conway, who's in charge of the investigation, has been talking with the faculty, but they haven't found anything."

"I hope you're not teaching any night courses this summer."

"I hadn't planned on it."

"Good. Until this thing's solved, I don't think it's safe to be on campus after dark."

She could see him saying this, too, standing in a phone booth, his eyes darting around the building as if he were looking for someone, his attention chopped up, a hand deep in his pocket, rattling for change. They hadn't been on the phone five minutes and already she'd slid from a high to a low, picked apart what she liked and disliked about him and thought: This isn't normal.

"Do you know where you're going to be staying?" she asked, leading him, waiting to see if he would leave a phone number with her. Then she remembered the dream she'd had about Denise and Ian and wondered if his interest in the woman's death was personal. She wanted to ask but couldn't.

"I don't know yet. I just got here. I'll call you in a couple of days, though, all right? Let you know something more definite."

"That's what you said last week. The last time we talked, Ian."

The silence was more of a hesitation, but she detected the impatience, knew he was rolling his eyes, glancing out the building again as if his salvation lay there, in the anonymous crowds. He was probably twitching in his suit—did he wear one? had he worn one in the Keys?—anxious to get off the phone.

"I'm sorry about last week, Laura. I was gone from morning to night."

There. She'd heard it. The edge in his voice, the aloofness. After a moment, she said, "I understand. Call me, okay? Now I've got to run. I was on my way over to meet Rita and by now, she's chafing at the bit."

"Love you, babe."

She wanted to say it, but again couldn't. It was as if a door had slammed shut in her chest. Afterward, she stood, her hand still on the phone, wishing she could take back the conversation, start it over again.

Coconut Grove, Laura thought, was sustained by illusion, just like Disney World. The crime was rampant, the streets at night were lit up like a carnival, and many of the old, spavined buildings had been carefully patched back together. But the air smelled forever with salt from the bay and students flew by on ten-speeds, hunched over into the wind, possessed of their singular goals, and there was something familiar, that sense of people not letting go. She'd lived here during graduate school, had sat in most of these shops and cafes at one time or another, probably looking as grave and insipid and self-contained as the students zipping by on their old bikes.

"I told you," Rita said, walking beside her with an armful of packages, "that shopping is the best cure for depression."

"I wasn't depressed."

"Oh. Right."

"Okay," Laura conceded after a moment, "I was depressed. Now I'm just poor."

"You're getting better, Laura, you know that? Two years ago, you wouldn't have admitted that."

"I was just admitting you were right," she said, and they both laughed.

What an obdurate friendship, Laura mused. They were equally stubborn and it had taken them many years to arrive at that point where neither took umbrage at hearing the truth from the other. They were in many ways closer than sisters, because there had never been a sibling rivalry between them. The friendship was unique for its honesty and implicit trust.

"Laura," someone called from the curb.

There stood Marie Turnbalt by her car, waving, one hand shielding her eyes from the sun. She looked like she'd just stepped off the shiny, slick pages of *Vogue*. Laura hurried over, set her packages against a post. The women touched cheeks; Marie's was cool. "It's good to see you," Laura said.

"It's been too damned long, Laura." Her arm rested along the open door of the white Mercedes and her other hand was at her throat, where her fingers were busy trying to untangle a pair of gold chains.

"What happened to the BMW?"

"*That* old thing died in the middle of the interstate one night. Frank bought me this a week ago." She ran her hand along the sleek, shiny sides, then patted it like a pet. A 450SL. The top was down and the interior was leather, the color of a palomino.

"It's a beauty."

"And drives like a dream," Marie said.

The first thing you noticed about the woman was her eyes. They were large, a watery green, like celery. Then, almost as an afterthought, as if it came from her eyes, you noticed she was beautiful. She vibrated. She looked to be a woman capable of enormous pleasure and reminded Laura of an impressionist painting, where no single form is precisely clear, but where the mood is the thing, a passionate, living color.

They'd first become friends eight years ago, when Laura was living in the Grove, going to school, and Marie was doing the local art circuit, trying to peddle her jewelry to tourists. It was a time in both their lives when each was striving for a goal and neither of them had known many people. Their friendship was as much a product of their compulsion as of their isolation, and they'd remained close until Frank had stepped into the picture.

Laura had never disliked the man, but she'd never trusted him. Ten years Marie's senior, he had money, was flashy, knew people. He had stepped right into Marie's life with his meretricious airs and took charge, as if by divine edict. He'd set her up in business. Bought her the right cars, clothes, introduced her to the right people. He'd dressed her up in the accoutrements of success, and in the most fundamental way, the Marie Laura knew now was her husband's creation.

"You've got us at the tail end of a shopping spree," Rita said as she joined them.

"How *are* you, Rita? Nice to see you again. I can't believe you two have been down here all afternoon, from the looks of it, and never stopped in at the shop. We have some *gorgeous* new stock. And not all of it's mine, either," she finished with a laugh. She lit a cigarette from a delicate, gold, monogrammed lighter. She had a certain impatience about her when she inhaled, but just the right degree of impatience, as if Frank had also prompted her on the correct way of smoking.

"I'm now poor and overextended," Laura groaned.

"Well, I've got the perfect solution to that. Frank and I were just talking about you last night, Laura. We haven't seen you in months. You've just got to join us in Juno Beach some weekend. We have a marvelous little place on the beach. We start off every morning with a Bloody Mary and a swim. It's glorious. You'd love it."

Laura noticed the invitation hadn't been extended to Rita. "I don't know about a weekend, but we should at least get together for dinner."

"Marvelous." Marie inhaled deeply once more from her cigarette, dropped it in the road. "I'll call you real soon. I've really got to run. Frank and I have an appointment with a detective tonight about Denise Markham's murder. It's tragic, isn't it. You're not safe anywhere anymore. I told Frank that the next time we move, it ought to be to Kansas or Iowa—someplace where cattle mutilations are the major concern." She waved, slipped behind the wheel of the car as if it had been made for her. "Nice seeing you again, Rita," she called, then honked, waved again, and was gone.

Rita gave a low whistle. "What's *she* on?"

"Oh, she's always been hyper like that. It's what keeps her thin, I think."

"You think that stuff is true? About her and Denise?"

"I don't know. If it is, you can bet it was Frank's idea and she went along with it to keep the peace."

"High price for peace, Laura. Unless you also happen to be into it."

That was the odd part, Laura thought. Even when she'd known Marie well, there had been a circumspection about her, as if she were afraid of letting anyone get too close. Truthfully, she didn't know the woman's sexual proclivities, because the only time they'd discussed it was in relation to Frank. She'd made sex with him sound almost mystical, like some endless acid trip whose goal was a perfection that passed mere orgiastic frenzy. Exactly what was to be perfect was never stated, however. Marie had assumed Laura had understood. Or perhaps it was one of those blind spots, where language fails you, and Marie had not really understood it herself.

"I'm not defending her," Laura said. "I'm just explaining." She pushed her sunglasses back into her hair, glanced across the street where her car was parked. "Christ, I got a ticket," she muttered, and walked quickly across the street, whipped it out from under the windshield wiper, and held it between her teeth while she unlocked the door and tossed her packages in the backseat. She looked down at the ticket. Her head snapped up, she unlocked Rita's door, said, "Get in, Rita. Hurry."

Her hand slammed down over the lock. Her eyes moved from the storefront, locked up for the night, to the buildings tipped with gold in the waning sunlight, to the lengthening shadows in the streets. She wadded the paper up, threw it to the floor. "It can't be *that* much," said Rita. "What's your big hurry?"

Laura spun out of the parking lot. *He could be anywhere*. She ran a red light. Horns blared in the hot evening light. She bit at her lower lip, saw Rita reading the note, looked at her anxiously, said, "What do you think? Am I jumping to conclusions?" She coasted into the Grove Marina, turned off the car, sat back.

Rita creased the note, running her finger back and forth along the edge of it, then tucked it in the seat between them. "Look, why don't you stay with Hank and me tonight? At least you'll get some sleep."

Laura picked up the note, read it again. Written in cutout letters, it looked like the work of a five-year-old child: LOVELy LaURa, I'M waTcHInG YOu & waITinG fOr ThE dAY i Can DriVE iT Up INtO YoU UNtiL yOu scReAm FoR mOrE aNd YoU WIlL wHeN tHe lIghTS gO OuT.

"Sleep," Laura said softly. "Sure. So I can sleep. The lady needs eight hours, doctor, and then she'll be just fine. Nothing to worry about." Her voice dropped to a terrified whisper. "Where *was* he, Rita? That's what I want to know. Where the hell was he? Watching all this time? And why *me*, huh?"

Rita took the note from Laura's hand, creased it again, dropped it in her purse. "I don't know what to say. But I think we should save this. Give it to Conway."

Laura let out a choked laugh, gazed out over the marina waters, rested her chin in the palm of her hand. "And what the hell's *he* going to do about it? Give me twenty-four-hour protection?"

"You're assuming this has something to do with Denise's murder, Laura. That's understandable. We're all edgy. But it might not be related at all. So you got a weird call and someone left you a note. Big deal. He hasn't harmed you."

That was her attorney voice, and Laura hated it. "Look, I'm not one of your whining clients," she snapped. "So stop patronizing me."

Rita didn't say anything, and Laura immediately felt ashamed. "I'm sorry, I didn't mean . . . ."

"Yeah, I know. Forget it. C'mon, we'll go get a bite to eat or something."

2.

The bar was noisy, smoky, and crowded. He ordered a Coke, and when he raised the glass to his mouth, his hand trembled. He wanted to laugh out loud as he thought of how Laura looked when she found the note. Her body's expression, he thought, smiling to himself. Her shoulders drawn up as if for protection, her head jerked around, eyes sweeping the twilight expectantly for another assault. *Those who betray must be punished*. It was the single axiom of his life he'd never violated.

The jukebox came on, tearing into the steady pounding at the back of his head and in his temples. He caught the bartender's eye, asked for a refill of Coke and a couple of aspirin.

"How about a hair of whatever bit you instead?"

"Aspirin's fine."

"Suit yourself," he said with a shrug.

The pain climbed down into his cheeks and was working its way into his shoulders, across his neck. The headaches had started months ago, when he and Denise were doing the drug pretty regularly. But there shouldn't be any correlation now, should there? He hadn't done the drug in . . . what? Days? Weeks? Funny, he could no longer remember.

"Here you go. Two aspirin."

"Thanks."

He stared at the tiny white tablets, remembering something. Denise popping two Percodan one night when she'd worked late in the lab and the pain in her head was so bad she could barely see. But the Percs had done the trick all right. Within an hour, she had brought the rope out of the closet and announced she wanted to play. So he had tied her wrists and ankles to the four posters of the bed and had started in on her. The feather, then pieces of silk, then his mouth and hands until he'd driven her into a frenzy and she was begging him to do it.

Laura would learn to beg like that.

He would break her down bit by bit, making her choke on her own filthy desire, and just when she'd cried herself into a false calm, he would drive himself into her and watch the pain becoming pleasure. The ecstatic misery of women, he thought. In lovemaking, they were naked right down to the soul.

He would teach Laura just like he'd taught Denise that *he* was in control. Like that night of the Percodan, when Denise had been free of her bonds, she'd grinned and poked him in the ribs, whispering, "Your turn now, Bucky," even though she'd known it wasn't part of the game. *He* made the rules, he had reminded her. Then she'd shouted he was spoiled and stomped off toward the shower in a bubble of cold, insouciant air as if she didn't give a damn. But she hadn't fooled him. If he'd followed her into the shower, they would have made love again and she'd have thought she had the upper hand. But really, women craved being controlled; Denise had understood that. She'd understood it even as he was slipping the knife between her ribs, even as she'd struggled and that sucking sound had risen and died in her throat.

He would make sure Laura understood, and today was only the first lesson.

He popped the aspirin in his mouth, washed them down with a sip of Coke. He pressed his fingers to his temple, massaging it, trying to will the pain away. *My first husband never told me no, Bucky. I despised him. He was weak. Are you weak like that? Can you deny me anything?*

He laughed despite the pain in his head. He'd denied her life.

Lifting his head, he gazed out through the window, into the twilight filling the space where her car had been.

Whose car? Laura's or Denise's?

For a moment, everything got mixed up in his mind. The faces of the two women were transposed: Laura's mouth became Denise's; Denise's eyes became Laura's. He pressed the heels of his hand to his forehead, grimacing as the pain exploded along his spine. He sucked in his breath, held it, and after a moment the pain lessened.

Better, a little better now. The aspirin were already working their magic and the Coke seemed to be settling his stomach. His thoughts cleared again. He congratulated himself on his ingenuity. The cops would be looking for the man who killed the other women, the man who used the stiletto.

It paid to read the news.

"You feel all right?"

He jerked his head up. Glanced to his right. The woman next to him was frowning, eyeing him in a way that made him uneasy, like maybe she'd seen him before but couldn't quite place his face. "Yeah. Fine. Just a touch of indigestion." He wrapped his hand around his glass, wished she would go away. *Vanish in a puff of smoke.*

"Boy, I know how *that* can be," she continued.

She was drinking one of those terrible concoctions of sweet liqueurs, something that no doubt had a name like skip and go naked or pink Russian. She was a student at the university, she said; and everyone needed a break from studying, right? So this was her break. It was a story he'd heard a million times, in bars just like this one, and he only half listened. In a moment, when he felt a little steadier on his feet, he would get up and leave.

He ordered a third Coke, and the bartender, assuming he was now with this obnoxious woman, set a refill in front of her, too, and added it to his bill. Her major was . . . She was from . . . She wanted to be . . . "What do you do?" she asked finally.

He looked at her straight in her pale, frenzied eyes and said, "I kill women."

Her face went as pale as milk and he nearly laughed. But then she brushed a hand nervously through her hair, sipped at her drink, and said, "Cute. That's a real cute line all right. Seriously, what do you do?"

Oh, he could peer down into those eyes of hers and teach her things. But the pain in his head was going away now and he felt drained; drained and tired. "I told you," he said, then smiled, slapped several bills on the table, got up, and left.

3.

"I really wouldn't let it worry you," Hank Lincoln said, handing Laura a drink. "This is some joker's way of amusing himself. Maybe one of your students who's sore about a grade. Or maybe some guy who's got five kids, a fat wife, and sells insurance."

"Yeah," Rita agreed. "A harmless Walter Mitty."

"But suppose he isn't either of those things?" She looked obliquely from Hank to Rita and then down into her drink. She touched a nail to an ice cube and stirred it. "Optimism. Right. I forgot."

Hank settled on the couch next to Rita. "What'd this Conway fellow have to say?"

"Pretty much the same thing you did." It was useless to discuss it, she decided. In fact, by discussing it, she was simply giving the incident more power over her life. Besides, men didn't understand this sort of threat.

"Well, you couldn't be much safer than right here," Rita assured her.

That, at any rate, was true. The Lincoln home was virtually impregnable, the kind of place that would have been a perfect fortress in a Colombian cocaine cowboy war. Several years ago, after the house had been robbed, Hank had bought a personal computer, embellished it, updated it, and it now ran the house practically single-handedly. A flick of the wrist could activate lamps, stereo, TV, air conditioner, hair curlers, coffeepot, or the electrical fence that surrounded the place. When placed on security command, the house went on autopilot, randomly turning on lights and sound equipment, giving the house a "lived-in" look when Rita and Hank were away. It could be activated from anywhere in the country by using a touchtone phone, and on more than one occasion Rita had called to have the air conditioning turned lower before she got home. The security system was the most sophisticated on the market and did everything, Laura thought, but shoot bullets. Hank's excuse was that he wanted to sleep in peace at night. But in truth, Hank, a man for whom most things in life had come easily, lived in a fortress because he feared what he couldn't see.

"Laura still needs cheering up," Hank said as he stood.

"Now you're in for it," Rita warned. "He just finished doing a benefit at the children's hospital recently and he's got a few new routines up his sleeve."

He was rummaging under the couch for something. "Kids love magic. They're naturals. They live inside it. They have an instinctive appreciation for it." He lifted a black case from under the couch, set it upright. "Be back in a flash." Laura glanced at Rita, who shrugged and made a face as if assuring Laura it wouldn't be bad if she didn't get impatient.

"Witness," Rita said, "the metamorphosis of one Hank Lincoln."

"I heard that, Ree," Hank called from the bedroom. He came back wearing a black cape, holding a black wand.

"You look like Zorro." Rita laughed.

"Ah," Hank said, tapping the wand to Laura's glass. Then a voice from the glass said, "The lady needs another drink."

"A ventriloquist," Laura said, delighted.

"I've been practicing."

"Well, I'm impressed."

"It's a new trick a week in this house," Rita said. Hank's expression darkened. His mouth grew tight. His usually soft blue eyes smoked. He touched the tip of the wand to his head, pushed back several strands of blond hair.

"Rita gets fed up with magic." His voice was obdurate, cold.

"Honey, that's not true."

"Oh, c'mon." Laura laughed.

"Admit it, Rita. You hate magic."

"Stop taking everything so personally, Hank. Christ." She started into the kitchen. "Frozen daiquiris coming up. What's your pleasure, Laura?"

"Whatever." She felt awkward and uncomfortable.

Hank grabbed the black case, slammed the door as he vanished into the bedroom. Laura followed Rita into the kitchen. "What's going on?"

Rita dropped ice into the blender. "He auditioned for a magic show on TV a couple weeks ago and found out today he didn't get the part. Hank doesn't take well to rejection. He has to win at everything, Laura. He can't ever be second best.'' She turned on the blender and for a moment neither of them spoke. Laura got two glasses from the cupboard. When the blender was silent, Rita spoke again, but her voice was lower, more cautious. "God, he's like this kid who never grew up. I mean, even if he practiced fourteen hours a day for the next twenty years, Laura, a Houdini he isn't. And on top of it, the firm's not doing so hot.''

"Since when?''

"Who knows.'' She dipped a spoon into the blender, sampling the drink. "Sam, one of the partners, mentioned that Hank's hardly ever in the office. I guess he's out practicing his goddamned magic tricks or something. I don't know.'' Her voice cracked, she paused, poured the mix into the two glasses, retrieved a third from the cabinet for Hank. Then suddenly her face caved in and she covered it with her hands. A sharp, dry sob escaped her. "A couple months ago, I was going through the office books and found six or seven substantial withdrawals from the company's pension fund. I thought maybe he'd decided to reinvest the money or something, so I went through his stock portfolios. I couldn't find anything. I looked in the savings passbook. Checked the IRA. The CDs. Nothing. So finally I asked him about it and he blew up. We had a terrible argument. Then a couple days later he admitted he'd used the money to gamble.''

"*Gamble?* Hank?''

"He said the company wasn't doing very well and that he thought he'd be able to make up some of the money at jai alai or the dogs.''

"How much money, Rita?''

"Oh, about twenty-five grand, give or take a few thousand.'' Tears had turned her eyes a paler blue; her mouth quivered. "We haven't been getting along very well since.'' Which explained her enigmatic remarks the other day in the cafeteria, Laura thought.

They heard Hank whistling. Rita glanced at Laura and shook her head, indicating that she should say nothing. Laura opened the drawer for a spoon and as Hank came into the kitchen, she was vigorously stirring her drink, chatting about school. *See, Hank? Just the status quo*.

"Well, girls.'' He grinned as if nothing had happened and slipped an arm around Rita's shoulder. "I see you've got the drinks department under control. Good, good,'' and he reached for the remaining glass. "I really do love my wife," he said gaily.

Then a voice from Laura's glass suggested they go watch the tube, and the three of them laughed. But as they started into the living room, Rita looked over her shoulder, her eyebrows shot up, and she seemed to be saying, *See? See what I mean?*

4.

Duncan had looked everywhere. Bookshelves, Denise's desk, filing cabinets, storage closet. And he hadn't found the notebook. But it had to be here.

Unless Conway had found it.

Of course. That had to be it.

He sank into the big leather chair where Denise always sat, and a sharp pain dug into his side and he doubled over. He broke into a cold sweat. It trickled down the underside of his arm, drenching the sleeves of his shirt. It wasn't fair. None of it was fair. Denise had sucked him in. She was a master at that. She was the spider who lured you into her web and as soon as she was done with you, she stung you to death.

"Oh, God," he whispered over and over again as the pain in his side climbed into his chest, heading straight for his heart. It was almost as if he could see the pain, marching, darting, finally bearing down. Her fault. It was all her fault.

He buried his head in his arms and began to cry.

6

1.

FRANK TURNBALT WAS not at all what Conway had expected. He had envisioned someone who was Clark Gable handsome and smooth, very smooth, but staid and perhaps somewhat constipated by years of university life. Instead, Turnbalt was very nearly bald, with a broad, sweeping forehead that gave him the look of an intellectual. His eyes dominated his face. They were a bluish green, the color of shoals in the Bahamas, a liquid light that provided the illusion that the foundation was deeper than you thought. He was well built. Self-satisfied. His charisma,

Conway thought, was a result of an absolute belief in himself. There was something in his demeanor that said you were a fool unless you were on his side of the fence.

They were on the porch of the Turnbalt penthouse. The floor was Mexican tile, shiny as glass, and the air smelled sweetly of roses and jasmine and whatever else grew up here at the top of the world. From where he sat, he could see the arch of lights along Biscayne Bay and the solitary blinking masts of sailboats in the marina. Turnbalt patted his midriff as Marie handed him a glass of cognac and said, "Not a bad way to live, is it, Mr. Conway."

"I used to walk down here as a kid and look up here and wonder how the other half lived."

"I've been down there. Grew up on the streets of New York and I was always looking up. Never much cared for it. Too hard on the neck." He laughed, stood. "You've got to see the view."

The three of them walked over to the wall. The lights of Miami spread from one end of the dark to the other, so profuse the black seemed to be swelling with a subcutaneous tumor, and any minute the skin of the sky was going to pop and the light and the stars and moon would slip through.

"It's not such a bad city at night," Conway remarked.

"The dark always hides the battle scars," Turnbalt said. He ran his fingers from just under his arm to the waist of his pants. "I've got a scar from here to here and you know, in the dark, women used to think it was romantic. That's rather how I think of Miami," he finished, and glanced at Marie. "My wife, fortunately, is used to it."

Marie sipped at her cognac but said nothing. Conway thought it seemed like she was waiting for her husband's permission to speak.

"What's the scar from?" Conway asked. Turnbalt was the sort of man, he decided, who had made the comparison in hopes Conway would inquire.

"Vietnam. You ever serve?"

"Nope."

"Blood shit of a war. I was Special Forces and they were all crazy. Anyone who avoided Nam was lucky. I got three Purple Hearts and lost a kidney."

"War stories," Marie said, returning to them with some dried leaves in her hands. "The sun's burning up these plants, Frank." She threw the leaves in the wicker basket next to the bar and Turnbalt shrugged.

"Marie treats her plants like kids," he commented. "So what

did you want to know about Denise Markham?'' he asked suddenly, after deftly avoiding the subject through drinks and dinner.

"I understand you knew her."

"I think we ate over at the Markhams' one evening, but I would hardly call her a close friend."

Slick, Conway thought. Not so much as a twitch on his face.

"She came into the store occasionally," Marie said, "and never left empty-handed."

Conway gave her his full attention. Marie Turnbalt was so vulnerably lovely, and so misplaced in her life, that just the sight of her injured him somehow. He guessed she was Frank's junior by eight or ten years, although she might have been younger. Her skin was as smooth as a child's and her hair, a deep, rich cocoa hue, was drawn away from her face with two small combs and then up in back, exposing her long, pale neck and setting off her incredible eyes. She shone and she glittered, and beneath the sophistication and polish Conway sensed the woman she'd been before Frank Turnbalt had come into her life.

"Did she ever come into the store with anyone?"

"No. Always alone. Well, no, I take that back. She came in a few times with her daughter." She sniffled, ran a finger under her nose, reached into the pocket of her skirt for a piece of Kleenex. "This cold," she muttered, and blew.

"She never came in with a man?" Conway asked.

Marie shook her head, sipped at her cognac. "No, not that I recall."

Frank patted his midriff again. "My impression of Denise, Mr. Conway, was that she was an uptight woman who could've used a good piece of ass."

Exactly the sort of remark, Conway thought, that he'd expected from Turnbalt. Marie flinched. "My husband has a somewhat tasteless way of putting things sometimes."

"I call it as I see it. There's a syndrome among university women, Mr. Conway, at least that I've noticed. Those who have been on the faculty as long as Denise generally have emotional and personal lives like roller coasters. They're wound up tight as drums."

"You think she was using cocaine?"

Turnbalt laughed. "If she was, good for her. Ideal prescription for frigidity."

The man didn't miss a trick.

Marie sat back on the wall, one arm around a post, her legs crossed at the knees. "Well, I felt sorry for Denise. She always seemed so . . . I don't know, lonely, I guess. You could tell she wanted to make friends, but had never learned how."

"My wife has a soft spot for orphans, waifs, the lonely. At heart, she's an idealist," Turnbalt remarked.

Marie glared at him, but Turnbalt missed it. They walked back over to the table and sat down. "Was she involved with anyone that you know of?"

Turnbalt shrugged, reached for the bottle of cognac, refilled their glasses. "Mr. Conway, if I kept track of all the gossip on campus, I don't know where I'd fit the rest of my life. You've spoken to Don Markham, haven't you?"

"Yes."

"Well, then you must know their marriage was in trouble."

Conway didn't reply.

"He's a pretty laid-back character," Turnbalt continued. "Never could figure out what he and Denise had in common. But he's one hell of a golfer. I always admire a man who's a pro at what he does." He capped the bottle. "What about you, Mr. Conway? You good at what you do?"

Conway laughed. Marie leaned forward, touched his arm. The gold pendant around her neck swung forward and those green eyes fastened on his with a kind of camaraderie. "Ignore him, John. He's being obnoxious."

Turnbalt patted his midriff, brought out a long, thick cheroot from a cedar box on the table. "Care for one?"

"No, thanks."

"Right from Fidel's best stockpile." He lit it. Conway asked if he had been in town the weekend of the murder. "Nope. We have a place up the coast, in Juno Beach. I can only take so much city and find I've got to escape on weekends."

"Are there neighbors who can vouch for your whereabouts?"

Anger flickered in the man's eyes. "Sure. Say, if we're under suspicion or anything, just come out and say so."

"At the moment, no one's under suspicion. I just don't want anyone leaving town in case I have more questions."

There was an awkward silence which Marie finally broke. "How about something to drink besides cognac, John?" She pushed away from the table, prepared to serve and pamper and play the perfect hostess.

"No, thanks. I've really got to get going. Thanks again for dinner."

Turnbalt left his cigar in the ashtray as he stood. He slipped an arm around Marie's shoulders and they walked him through the house to the door. Maybe he imagined it, but Conway thought

Marie held his hand longer than necessary. "Do come in the store, John, whenever you're in the Grove."

"I sure will," he said. "Night."

When the door closed behind him, Conway took several steps down the luxurious hall, then tiptoed back toward the hall. What the hell, he thought, listening at doors had helped Sam Spade on more than one occasion. Someone was putting the chain on and locking the dead bolt. He heard Marie say, "He knows something, Frank."

And Frank: "Don't be so goddamned paranoid, Marie. He's just a two-bit cop playing cat-and-mouse games. I know how these guys work. He's fishing, just fishing."

Conway smiled.

The elevator door down the hall opened and he hurried away.

"Mickey," Conway said as the Siamese sprang at him when he walked into the lab. He picked up the cat and put him over his shoulder. The animal purred with contentment.

Karen Pauling pushed away from the microscope and rubbed her eyes. "John. My God. Don't tell me it's already midnight." She held her arm away from her, squinting, trying to read her watch. "My glasses, where'd I leave my bloody glasses? What time *is* it, anyway?"

"Nine." He plucked her glasses from the top of her head, handed them to her. Mickey leaped to the floor and rubbed up against Karen's leg. "I know I'm being a pain, sweetheart, but did you get a chance to test that stuff I brought in?"

She was a stout, gray-haired woman who had been with the department ten years. The lab was her domain. She ran it with an iron fist but never demanded more of her subordinates than she herself was willing to give. It was a rare night that Conway didn't find her in here after everyone else had gone home.

"Yes, I did." He didn't like the tone of her voice. She opened a drawer, brought out the plastic bag he'd found in Denise's office. It was in an aluminum container, numbered and labeled. "It's not cocaine."

"It numbs like coke, Karen. I dabbed some on my lip."

"You shouldn't go sticking your fingers into strange stuff, John. You're fortunate you didn't trip out to the ozone. This stuff has an alkaloid base. Alkaloid of ergot, which means it has some of the properties of LSD. It can be absorbed through the skin, it's that potent."

"What else can you tell me about it?"

"At the moment, nothing. I intend to keep some here and run more tests, and I'm sending the rest to Tallahassee for analysis."

"How long will that take?"

"A week or two. They're backed up like the rest of us."

"I don't have two weeks."

"Hon, I'll do what I can on this end."

Conway grinned and bussed her on the cheek. "You're a doll, you know that?"

"It may cost you dinner, sport." She laughed.

"You name the time and place."

"Did you find any of her notes?" Conway shook his head. "Too bad. It might help to know what she was working on."

Karen returned the aluminum container to the drawer, locked it. "Hold on and I'll walk out with you." She glanced around to make sure she'd turned everything off. "Maybe this stuff will turn out to be a piece of nirvana, John. Or a memory enzyme. Maybe Denise Markham really *was* brilliant."

"Brilliant or not, her life was a sorry mess."

Karen picked up Mickey. "Ever find out what was in the safety deposit box?"

"I haven't even been able to locate the box. I've got some men checking savings and loans in the area."

"Ah-ha." She laughed. "That explains Tillis's mood. He stopped by this afternoon bitching about the heat and how he was sick of driving all over East Jesus trying to chase down a box."

"The man hates me," Conway said with a smile. "I just know it."

Karen gave him a maternal look. "You should go home and go to bed, John. You look like hell."

But Conway didn't want to go home. These days, home was four walls on the third floor of an apartment building filled with elderly people who'd migrated south to die. He'd spent the two years since his divorce there and it was an okay place to live—quiet, clean, and all those other admirable attributes—unless he had to kill time alone. Then it got to him. Besides, he decided, Stella had probably bombarded his tape machine with obscene messages because he still hadn't mailed her a check. Actually, he could think of a hundred reasons not to go home, but they all amounted to the same thing: Rita.

Conway drove over to the campus, talking to himself, trying out various approaches. There was feigned surprise: *Rita, imagine running into you here* (at 9:30 on the night you just happen to have a seminar); *what a coincidence*. Or the cop approach: *Hi, I thought you might need an escort to the parking lot.* The blunt approach: *I hope Hank's outa town, Rita, because I intend to kidnap you and do wonderful things to your body.* He still hadn't decided what to say as he ran up the walk to the law building.

Classes were getting out as he came in the door. He stood for a while in the lobby, smoking, perusing the bulletin boards, wrestling with himself: she was married (married women were trouble); she'd done nothing to encourage him (except the trip to the morgue, and he didn't know if that counted); and—what else? There had to be something else about her that was no good, but at the moment he didn't know what it was.

"Hello, Conway," she said, coming down the stairs. "You're still talking to faculty?"

That was it, he thought, that was the other bad thing. She called him by his last name. "How about a beer?" he asked quickly, wondering what had happened to his approaches. She hesitated. "If you don't think it's too late," he added, knowing time had nothing to do with her hesitation.

"I know a place up the street. Want to go in one car?"

"Sure. I'll drive," he replied, astonished that she'd consented to come at all.

"*Where* did you get this car?" Rita exclaimed as she got in. She ran her hands lovingly over the seats. It was a '67 Porsche that Conway had bought from a junkyard and rebuilt and refurbished whenever he had the time and money. "How come you've never driven it around here before?"

"And have some student vandalize it? Not a chance." He laughed.

"May I drive it?"

He handed her the keys and walked around to the other side. She scooted into the driver's seat, Conway got in and shut the door. "I want you to know," he said, "that you're the first woman who's driven this car since I've owned it."

"Really." She snapped the seat belt across her, not looking at him, then placed her hands on the steering wheel. She scanned the lights and switches like a pilot going through a preflight check. "Oh, boy," she murmured, "fasten your seat belt, Conway." She rolled down the window. He braced himself for a wild, reckless departure. But she backed out and drove normally until the road opened out into the runway. Then she revved the engine, sat back fully in the seat, one hand on the steering wheel, the other on the shift, and they shot out into the dark and the warm wind held him back in the seat like gravity. The blur of lights that was the campus fell away from them absolutely and there was only the sound of the engine, the wind, and Rita's laughter. The car purred under her touch. It turned on a dime. It performed without so much as a sputter, cough, a hesitation, as if the two were made for each other.

"For this car," she said, coming to a full stop where they'd started, "I would mortgage my soul."

Conway's hands ached when he let go of the edge of the seat. "I need a beer," he said, feeling the aftermath of motion sickness, shock, and perhaps even admiration.

"That stuff I found in Denise's office wasn't coke." They were seated in a college bar. He had his beer and felt human again as he told Rita what Karen had discovered.

"You think Denise was making it in the lab?"

"It's possible."

"Figures she'd have an angle. No one's *that* dedicated. So enter the new Albert Hoffman, huh. Maybe you can bottle, market, and sell it, Conway, then retire."

"Who's Hoffman?"

"The LSD chemist. I'm a veritable reservoir of trivia, you know."

"Really," he said.

"Really," she said. "I also used to sit on drug advisory boards all over south Florida where names like Huxley, Hoffman, Leary, and Alpert were tossed around a lot."

"I didn't know he was associated with LSD."

"That's because he just invented it; Leary got all the credit."

"You don't sit on the boards anymore?"

"No," she replied with a shake of her head. "I enjoy getting high occasionally and I felt like a hypocrite."

"That's ridiculous."

"Probably. But I stopped practicing law because I found I was incapable of creating a good defense for someone I knew was guilty. So now I just teach it. And one of the first things I tell my students is that you defend someone you know in your heart is guilty because it's your job to do so. If you can't, then you don't belong in the profession." She sipped at her beer again. "So that's my life story, what's yours?"

"You seem pretty certain of everything."

"Only stuff I know about." She leaned forward and tapped her fingers against the table. "But I'll tell you something, Conway. If I have any say in it, the next time around I'd like to have an I.Q. about sixty points higher so the bullshit doesn't touch me." She finished her beer and glanced at her watch. "I really should get going soon."

He nodded and a few minutes later they walked to the car, alone with their thoughts. When he unlocked the door, she was standing so close to him he could feel the heat of her body and almost taste the thin scent of her perfume. The door swung open. Rita stepped back, he turned, touched her arm, and there was an instant when her brows lifted with an unspoken question. Then the deep blue of her eyes twinkled and he kissed her.

His hands went through her hair and he didn't think he'd ever felt anything so soft. She stood tall, lean, and firmly against him, her hands cool through his shirt, then against his neck, and suddenly she broke away and touched the sides of his face. "No." Her arms dropped to her sides. "It wouldn't be any good. Not now." She looked at him. "Hank and I have discussed separating, Conway. I want to be sure I come to a decision with a clear head. If you were in the picture, I would not have a clear head."

His hand slid from her shoulder. He wanted to ask her why they were talking of separation, but now was not the time. He knew she would tell him when she was ready. "Are you still in love with him, Rita?"

She glanced down. The tip of her shoe shuffled through a pile of dried leaves. "We've been married about two years," she replied, which didn't answer his question.

They didn't speak on the way back. He pulled up behind her Volvo. She came around to his side, crouched down. "Things have happened between us, Hank and me, which shouldn't happen in just two years of marital bliss, you know?" and she smiled a little. "Thank you for letting me drive this wonderful car." She touched a finger to his mouth. "Just be my friend, Conway." She kissed him quickly and was gone.

The tape machine had been busy in his absence. There were at least ten calls from Stella, telling him he was a sonuvabitch for making her sit through June in the tropics with no air conditioning. At 9:40, his mother had called to say she'd heard from Jen and why wasn't he in Colorado taking the vacation he so justly deserved?

Jen hadn't called.

Don Markham left directions to the church for Denise's memorial service tomorrow and said, again, that he had to get on with his life and advised him Viki would be home over the weekend sometime. The last call came in at 11:45. He didn't leave his name, only a number and an enigmatic message that it concerned Denise Markham. Conway called the number and the man answered on the first ring. His voice was a scratchy whisper.

"This is Conway. Who's this?"

"I'd like to speak to you about Denise Markham."

"You'll have to be more specific."

"Would you be able to meet me at the Lauderdale Airport tomorrow? At three? Would that be convenient for you? If not, name the time and place."

"That's fine. Where?"

"The newsstand in the Delta terminal."

"How will I know you?"

"I'll know you," the man said, and rang off.

7

1.

CONWAY DROVE INTO the old neighborhood where he and Stella had lived in discontent for the better part of five years. The streets were familiar, but only remotely so, as if someone had described them to him a long time ago. Several joggers sweated beneath a canopy of trees, past the fenced-in yards where tricycles and toys lay rusting in the humid morning air.

The house was a split-level ranch on a dead-end street. When they'd bought it, the windows were so clean you couldn't tell there was glass between you and the outdoors, the yard was manicured, there were colorful flowers along the sides of the house. Now the grass was choked with weeds, the windows were filthy, and the flowers were as dead as the marriage. The disrepair, he thought grimly, reflected the state of Stella's life.

He pulled into the driveway and noticed all the windows were open. The air conditioning still hadn't been fixed. He wondered if her father had been supporting her through her mysterious medical malaise, and if so, why he hadn't paid to have the unit fixed. Her old man had plenty of money, the bulk of it made in crooked real estate deals, and he'd certainly never withheld aid before from his one and only daughter.

Conway held his finger to the doorbell until he heard Stella call from inside. "Hold on, hold on, I'm coming." Then, curiously, she asked, "Who is it?"

"It's John, Stella."

"John?" she asked as though the name meant nothing to her.

"John. Your ex. Remember?"

The chain rattled as she removed it. She opened the door a crack and poked her head out. "How the hell could I forget?" She opened the door wider. "Christ, John. It's barely seven."

She wore a colorful kimono that came to midthigh and was drawn at the waist with a black sash. There was a coffee stain on the front and she wasn't wearing anything underneath. She'd put on weight since he'd last seen her. Her face was plump, and damp with perspiration. One side of her hair was flattened out, as if she'd slept on it and hadn't combed it out yet. Smudges of mascara under the etioliated blue of her tiny eyes looked like bruises. She yawned, padded back into the house in her bare feet. He came in and shut the door behind him.

It was warm and still inside. There wasn't any breeze coming in through the windows and she'd neglected to turn on the ceiling fan. Dirty glasses and a pair of Budweiser cans were on the coffee table in front of the TV, ashtrays were heaped with butts, shoes were abandoned at the sliding glass doors that led to the backyard, clothes were draped over the couch. Sections of a newspaper lay scattered across the floor and magazines were sliding out of a wicker basket. Face to face with Stella's laziness, the very thing that had irreparably damaged the marriage, Conway pulled up a stool to the counter and just shook his head.

"Pleasant in here, huh," Stella said from the kitchen as she dropped the tea kettle onto a burner. "You coulda mailed the check, you know."

"I kept forgetting. Christ, Stella, this place is a pigsty."

She shrugged, retied the sash on her kimono. "Some people dropped by last night and stayed late. I just went to bed. C'mon, kettle. God, I need some coffee."

"I thought caffeine was bad for high blood pressure, Stell. And that *is* what you have, right? High blood pressure?" He brought out his checkbook and wrote a check.

"It's Sanka, John."

Conway tore out the check, set it on the counter. He heard something behind him, looked around. A man stood there in a pair of boxer shorts, scratching his head, yawning. He had hair to his shoulders and so much dark hair on his arms and chest he looked slightly simian. *Like Duncan,* Conway thought dimly.

"Man, what time is it? I feel like someone hit me over the head," he mumbled, rubbing his stomach, yawning again.

"A few minutes past seven," Stella told him. "Todd, this is John."

"Right. The cop. Howdy."

"We're living together," Stella announced with a note of triumph in her voice.

The tea kettle whistled. Stella took a cup from the stack of dirty dishes in the sink, rinsed it out. She spooned some Sanka into it, filled the cup to the brim with hot water.

Todd shuffled into the room, wrinkling his nose at the stale, warm odor in the room. "God, it smells like dirty shoes in here. You passin' around tea, Stell, or you just keeping it for yourself?"

"Oh, sorry," she replied with distraction. "John, you want some tea?" She turned on the burner again. "Or Sanka?"

Conway looked down at the check he'd just written. He fingered it, glanced at Todd with his musculature like a foreman's and a belly like Archie Bunker's. Todd, who had plopped himself down on the couch and was drumming his fingers against the edge of the coffee table, humming to himself. "Stell, what'd you do with the grass?" Then, remembering Conway was a cop, he grinned. "You gonna arrest me if I roll a joint, brother?"

Conway ripped the check in two, smiling broadly as he did so, then ripped it again. "What are you *doing*?" Stella shouted.

"I'm not supporting you and your boyfriend," Conway announced, and got up and started for the door.

Todd leaped forward, showing more energy in that single movement than he had since he'd walked out of the bedroom. "Hey, you can't do that. We need that bread."

"So get off your fat ass and go to work like everyone else." Conway slammed the door on his way out.

Stella ran out into the yard after him. "John," she called, then looked from side to side, remembering it was early and that she had neighbors. "John Conway, *you can't do this!*"

When he drove away, Stella was still standing in her stained kimono, a hand on her wide hips, staring after him incredulously.

2.

He waited until Laura's car vanished around the corner, then drove slowly around the block just to make sure. She was up mighty early, he thought. Maybe she was troubled by dreams. Or a voice. His. Maybe she was afraid if she hung around the house too long, he'd call. He smiled, pulled onto a dirt road. The car rattled through the thicket of graceful pines and stopped behind Laura's house.

He left the car where it couldn't be seen from the main road and started through the gray light on foot. The accretion of pine needles and leaves on the ground muffled his footsteps, and overhead a pleasant breeze played the branches like an instrument.

Stopping at the edge of the pines, he listened. He stood in the center of a vast, sweet silence. Only at the outer rim did the world pick up speed again: a semi grinding into a lower gear, a train pulling out of the station, shaking free of the night's torpor. He was safe, untouched: all systems go.

His gait was quick and purposeful as he moved away from the protection of the trees and into the backyard, to the porch under the weeping willow. He reached up, patting the flat metal surface above the porch light, looking for the spare key. He lifted the mat, checked the potted plants, and finally found the key lying inside the water dish of a tall aralia. He inserted it into the lock, and as the door swung open he thought: *My friend, you are a man acting with impunity.*

The air inside was cool, the light muted. He breathed deeply, with immense satisfaction, stepped out of his shoes, and walked barefoot across the tiles and into the living room.

The curtains were still closed, the windows buttoned up. He snuggled down into the air as if into a new suit of clothes. He felt the rooms as if they were extensions of himself. Her perfume had left a trail like footprints and he followed it, his smile widening as he climbed the stairs. Up, up, up into Rapunzel's tower. His gaze moved slowly through the loft just in front of him. Other aromas assaulted his senses: cinnamon, spice, clove, the delicate traces of bath oils, powder. Women's rooms were always so distinctly scented.

He sat on the top step, closed his eyes, let his mind wander through the immeasurable dark, touching every corner of the house. The rooms were imbued with her fear and it had taken form. *Why me? Why me?*

"Because," he whispered softly, then stopped. *Because why?* demanded an inner voice. He pressed the heels of his hands against his eyes until stars and geometric shapes lit up the black. His stomach churned at the sound of this inner voice, and his mind was besieged with images: Denise there on the path in front of him that night; Denise bucking beneath him like something wild, her eyes glazed from the drug; Denise's face as the knife slid smoothly between her ribs. *Why Laura?* the voice demanded, and he shook his head and leaped up from the step so quickly that he had to grab the railing to steady himself.

The drug, he thought. Prolonged use of the drug, with Denise, all those nights with Denise, had done something to him, to his mind. *What has Laura done to you?* the voice asked.

"She saw," he replied out loud. "She saw."

There was something about this that didn't ring true, but he didn't want to pursue it. He was here now. He had something he had to do. He pressed his hands to his ears so the voice couldn't be heard and fled up the stairs. He stopped in the doorway of the bedroom. For an instant, everything blurred in front of him: the foot of the bed melted into the window, curtains flapped in the closet, the mirror on the dresser toppled forward like an old tree. And for that instant, he understood, however dimly, that he wasn't right in the head. That his mind, in fact, swung like a pendulum from moments of perfect lucidity and sanity to the tottering brink and then over a step. Into the abyss.

Then his vision cleared and he couldn't understand why he was shivering, why his hands were so damp. After all, this was the heart. The source. He grew a little breathless at the sight of the unmade bed and suddenly flopped back onto it, arms out at his sides. The softness, the scents, he thought. He rolled onto his side, gathered the pillows against him, filled his senses with the aromas. This was why he was here. To know her. To know his victim.

But why? the voice persisted, fainter now, but still annoying.

"Why, why, why," he murmured. An unbidden image rose from the murky depths of the past: his father tearing through his mother's belongings one afternoon when he'd thought no one was home. He'd stood in the doorway a few minutes, watching his father, a madman, opening and closing his mother's drawers, scooping up lingerie, pressing them to his face. Then, perhaps sensing another presence in the room, his father had turned, and for a long time they'd simply stared at each other, the air turning thick and heavy between them.

"You wouldn't understand," his father had snapped finally, then shouted, his cheeks swollen like a squirrel's and pink as bubble gum: "She betrayed me, don't you see? I have to know who it is. I have to know. Now go away."

He squeezed his eyes shut against the memory, rolled onto his back, arms flung above his head in the shape of a V. Light played havoc with the shadows on the ceiling. The penumbra of the past lifted a little and in his mind he heard Denny say, "But you have someone else, so why can't I? He saw her flicking her hair off her collar. You owe me, he told her. You owe me.

This happened . . . when? He couldn't remember. He suddenly couldn't remember and flew forward as the abyss in his memory threatened to drag him down. His feet fell soundlessly against the carpet. He glanced around the room. He was sweating now. His purpose was consuming him, just as it had his father.

He opened the chest of drawers, shook his head. Nothing inside was folded, there was no order whatsoever. This was what he'd expected. He scooped his arms into the top drawer, dropped an armful of the lingerie on the bed, then kneeled and moved his arms under all the softness. A nightgown slid through his fingers and against his cheek. Such beautiful colors. Magentas, pale golds, greens, blues. He arranged the colors like a rainbow, from lights to darks, and folded everything carefully. Then he returned the clothes to the drawer in neat piles.

He moved to the closet. In his mind, he saw Laura standing where he was now, a hand at her mouth, trying to decide what to wear. Perhaps she even stood like this only a while ago, while he was waiting in the trees.

The closet, like the drawers, was a mess. Shirts were mixed in with pants, dresses with blouses. Her shoe rack was practically empty. The shoes weren't just thrown in the closet—she wasn't *that* bad—but were sitting in pairs wherever she'd happened to remove them. As he was replacing the shoes on the rack, he remembered his father had done the very same thing that afternoon with his mother's closet. Rearranged everything. Bestowed order. It was as if he'd hoped the order in her closet would move out into their lives as well. Well, he thought, he wished the same thing for Laura. Her life, like Denise's, was a mess.

He went to work on the closet with a loving diligence. When he was finished he stepped back, nodded his approval. A work of art. His father would've been proud. The solid colors formed a spectrum from the softest pearl to the deepest blue.

The top of the dresser was cluttered with bottles of perfume, tubes of lipstick, nail polish, jewelry. He arranged the bottles in a crescent and moved the lipstick and nail polish to a smaller half-moon inside. He then glanced around the room with satisfaction.

What else? He was forgetting something. He squeezed his temples with his fingers; the overture of a major headache was beginning. *Think, think.* Right. He snapped his fingers, his head jerked up. The envelope. He reached into his pocket, turned the envelope over in his hand, smiled. Wherever she went in the house now, she would find something of him, she would be reminded of him. He was courting her. It was important not to be forgotten.

Denise had forgotten him.

And now she was dead.

He turned the envelope upside down and bits of paper floated down to the sheets like confetti. He'd already inscribed messages on them. Denise had liked this game and he was sure Laura would like it, too.

But why? the voice whispered once more, but so faint now he barely heard it.

After he'd hidden the messages, he returned to the bedroom, picked up a tube of lipstick, uncapped it. It was a soft, moist color, like coral. He pressed the tip of it to the mirror and left a final message. She'd be sorry she missed him.

He started downstairs and peripherally saw a flash of color. He gripped the railing. There, crouched at a corner of the staircase, he saw the cat. "Here, kitty, kitty," he whispered.

The cat dashed into the kitchen. He followed, grinning, clicking his tongue against his teeth. "Here, kitty, kitty." He slipped his shoes back on, opened the door, and the cat flew out between his legs and vanished through the trees.

Outside, he returned the key to its hiding place, then hurried through the pines and into the center of the blissful silence once again.

8

TILLIS WAS AT the water cooler when Conway walked into the station. His head was tilted back and he was holding a triangular paper cup at his mouth. Water dribbled down his chin. It occurred to Conway that Stella and Tillis probably would make a fine pair, and he began to laugh.

"Glad to see you're in such tiptop shape," Tillis grumbled, wiping his arm across his mouth and wadding the paper cup in his hand. "Understand the university prez had a change of heart and is canceling classes in deference to the lady chemist. You going to the service?" Tillis aimed at the basket and let the cup fly. It hit the edge, bounced to the floor. "Shit," he muttered, and left it there.

"Yeah. Any luck with the banks?"

"Nothing. You know how many S and Ls there are in Dade and Broward counties, Conway?" Tillis followed him into the office. "If people from Venus landed here, they'd think we worshiped banks. There are more here in south Florida than there are in all of Switzerland."

"That a fact," Conway said absently, flipping through the mail and messages on his desk.

"I need more men, Conway."

"There aren't any more men."

Tillis's face was shiny and pink and there were deep circles under his eyes. He reached into his pocket for his pack of cigarettes, hit it against his finger, and three shot out. "I've got one shit of a hangover." He retrieved the cigarettes, and when he lit one his hand shook. He coughed. "I really should go to the Schick Clinic. Maybe the department would pick up the tab. I hear they make you smoke in a closet. That's how they kill the desire for nicotine." He coughed again, put the cigarette out, and got heavily to his feet. "Think of me when you're in that air-conditioned chapel and I'm trudging around in the heat that's ninety-one in the shade, Conway."

"Count on it. Get in touch as soon as you know anything about the bank."

"Sadist."

Conway popped a rubber band around his mail and called Doris Lummond, his contact at Ma Bell. "Hi, sweetheart," he said when she answered.

"Johnny boy. How've you been? What is it this time?"

"Am I such a thorn in your side?"

"Of course not. You break up the monotony. Do you know a person could die of monotony here?"

"I wish I could say the same. I need to know whose name five five two, two six four seven is listed under and where it's located."

"You want to hold or should I call you back?"

"I'll hold."

Conway sat down, swung around in his chair so he faced the window. Six stories below, traffic was stalled and snaked back farther than he could see. Waves of heat rose from the pavement, sunlight glinted off chrome. He was thinking of Colorado when the door opened and Larry Pivot said, "Morning, Conway."

"This is a surprise," Conway said, covering the mouthpiece with his hand. "I didn't think you ever left the catacombs."

"Private?"

"I'm on hold. Have a seat."

Pivot muttered, "Oh, hold. Ah, yes I know the feeling." He sat down, removed his black frame glasses, wiped them on the lapel of his lab coat. "I have some preliminary results for you on Denise Markham."

Doris came back on the line. "Johnny, it's a phone booth on the corner of Red Road and Federal in the Gables. Want the location?"

"No, thanks."

"Anything else?"

"Not right now. You're a peach, Doris. Thanks again." Conway hung up and gave Pivot his full attention. "Okay, what'd you find?"

"The wound was identical to the other two. Eighth of an inch in diameter, all the way to the heart. Swift and clean, in between the third and fourth ribs, left side."

"I'll be damned." Conway grinned.

"Hold on, friend. No evidence of sperm, no abrasions, not so much as a skinned knee. The lady wasn't raped. And without the sperm, we don't know if the blood type of Denise's killer matches that of the killer of the other two women."

Conway's mouth fell. He pushed away from the desk. "That leaves me back where I started. A killer with A negative blood and three women dead."

"Well, if you want my opinion," Pivot said, slipping his glasses on and pushing them back on his nose, "whoever did this must've known her well enough to get damned close to her, John. It would be difficult otherwise to get the stiletto in between the third and fourth ribs with such absolute precision."

"You could say the same for the other two women, then."

"Yeah. But there are some other important differences about Denise. For instance, her liver enzyme count far exceeded what it should have been. There was also evidence of enlarged lymph glands and the incipience of what looked like pneumonia." He said all this as if it should have been perfectly obvious to Conway what it implied.

"So?"

"A couple of things. The raised enzyme count could mean hepatitis, an enlarged or diseased liver, gallstones, a diseased gall bladder, maybe kidney trouble. Enlarged lymph glands are often found in drug addicts. As for the pneumonia . . . I checked a couple of possibilities, but couldn't find a thing. I'm sending blood samples and slides over to the medical center, John. I know it'll eat up time, but I'd like an internist to look at the results." Pivot removed his glasses once more, breathed on them, slid them back on his nose.

"So that's it?" Conway asked.

"For the time being, yeah. Sorry it doesn't clear things up for you." He paused. "I understand the memorial service is today. If he'd waited another twenty-four hours, he could've had his funeral, closed casket and all."

"I think Markham just wants to get on with his life."

"Understandable. Got in another three bodies last night. Shoot-out in Little Havana. Latin hotheads," he muttered, then pressed his hands against his thighs and got up. "Tempus fugit. Gotta run. Have a fruitful day, Conway. Go out and have some fun. Go to Disney World, laugh a little. When you deal with the dead all the time, you forget about living. Take it from a man who knows—it isn't worth it."

Conway gazed after the funny little man as he walked out of the office. Poor Pivot; he already looked half-dead.

The irony was that so many people attended the memorial service of a woman who allegedly had no close friends. They filled the doorway, Conway saw, spilled out onto the steps of the church and stood against the walls, watching the minister attentively, hanging on his every word as if for absolution.

The minister lit some incense and the holder swayed back and forth in his hand. Smoke drifted off into the air, mixing with the scent of the flowers arching in a half-moon in front of the altar. The minister was a short, squat man with a loud, clear voice who spoke with orotundity about the virtues of Denise Markham, whom he'd probably never met. He saw Don Markham sitting off to the side, in one of the front pews reserved for families and relatives of the deceased. His expression was masked, his eyes were bone dry. He tugged once at his tie, as if he weren't used to wearing one, but his gaze otherwise never left the minister's face. He sat with the housekeeper, and the absence of anyone else in the pew struck Conway with a kind of pathos. Denise had been an only child. Her parents had supposedly died in an auto accident somewhere in Westchester County, where the family had lived when Denise was young, still in her teens. Don and Viki Markham were her only surviving family.

The Turnbalts, people from the science department he had spoken to, Laura and Rita, Tom Duncan and several other students, and poor little Panzo, sitting off by himself: perhaps it was only curiosity and a sense of guilt that had drawn them here.

The death of a woman they'd barely known had punctured their ordered, sequestered lives.

A sandy-haired man sat between Rita and Laura, his arm along the back of the pew, fingers touching Rita's shoulder. Conway knew it was Hank Lincoln. And it bothered him. What had happened to their discussion about separating? Had it been shelved? Or had it been just something Rita had said because she actually was not interested in him and hadn't wanted to hurt his feelings?

Conway stared at the back of Rita's head, willing her to look around. He thought of how she'd touched her finger to his mouth and kissed him quickly, as if to affirm something in her own mind. He glanced away.

After the service, Markham stood by himself in the doorway, shaking hands with people as they passed through, thanking them for coming. When Conway shook his hand, he noticed that the man's eyes were now moist and three fine lines had etched across his forehead. "Good of you to come, John. Thanks very much. I'll be in touch as soon as Viki's home."

Outside, Conway saw the Lincolns, the Turnbalts, and Laura standing with some other faculty members he didn't know. He walked over to say hello and Rita watched him over Laura's shoulder.

"Afternoon, all."

"Conway, you look a little down in the mouth."

"How do you expect a man to look at a memorial service?" Hank said good-naturedly and introduced himself.

It was Conway's contention that you could read fifty percent of a man through his eyes and the grip of his hand. Hank Lincoln's grip was firm and his skin cool and dry. His pale blue eyes were as cold and barren as the dark side of the moon, until he smiled, and then you wondered how you could have thought such a thing. His coat was thrown carelessly over his arm and the tie against his perfectly ironed shirt was pulled to the side.

"I think he's entitled to look however he wants," remarked Marie Turnbalt. "Nice to see you again, John."

Frank Turnbalt nodded hello, patted his midriff. "Denise can be grateful for one thing, anyway. She doesn't have to return to the grind on Monday."

"Really, Frank," Marie said sourly.

"Denise was probably the only one of us who never thought of it as a grind, " Laura said.

Conway saw Markham coming out of the church with an armful of bouquets, followed by the housekeeper. Duncan was nearby, talking with an attractive redhead, and Conway noticed that he pressed a hand to his ribs, as if bitten by a jogger's cramp, and remembered he'd done the same thing that day in Denise's office. A hunch told him the observation was significant, even if he didn't yet understand how.

The final obsequies, he thought. All that remained now of Denise Markham lay in the memories of the people who had known her.

Suddenly, beside him, Laura gave a startled cry and ran over to a man coming out of the church with the minister. His head was bowed, his hands in his pockets, but when he looked up and saw Laura, he grinned, caught her around the waist. Conway, who didn't consider himself a sentimental man, thought there was something lovely in the intimacy of their embrace.

"Well, well, well," drolled Rita.

"Who's that?" Conway asked.

"That is Ian," Hank replied.

"The word processor man," Turnbalt said, "sure. I never forget a face."

Yeah, Conway mused. Turnbalt only forgot those he'd known. He watched Laura and Ian and felt a crescive, piercing loneliness dividing like cancer cells, striking him to the bone. He felt like he was standing alone in the heat, alive only within this terrible and peculiar pain of realizing you are the only beast on the Ark trapped in singularity. He felt the nameless thing loose in the world again, rising from this field of dust, this bed of heat, and the ills were no longer in the process of becoming. They were now formed.

Pivot was right, he decided. He *had* been too long with the dead. He looked down at the ground, rubbed the tip of his loafer on the cuff of his trousers, then glanced at Rita. She was already watching him, her gaze steady and soft, ubiquitous, and again he had the impression she was turning over a thought in her mind, trying to decide something about him.

"Glad to see you could make it back, Ian," Rita quipped as he and Laura approached.

"Couldn't stay away." He grinned. "I went over to the campus and the secretary said everyone was here."

As Laura made the necessary introductions, Hank reached into his pocket and brought out a hand puppet. It was a funny-looking thing with a grotesque face and a mop of reddish hair and a patch over one eye. "And my name's Diogenes," said the puppet.

Turnbalt, who'd absconded from the conversation until now, exclaimed, "Hey, you're good. How long have you been a ventriloquist?"

Diogenes bowed from the waist. "A mighty long time, sonny, long before you were born, that's for sure."

Conway laughed; the man was good, very good.

Turnbalt, a man for whom spontaneous laughter didn't come easily, actually burst out laughing, and Marie offered her finger to the puppet and said, "Pleased to make your acquaintance."

"*Ooohhh, my,*" crooned Diogenes, "you're a beautiful lady. Are you as honest as you are lovely?" He took hold of Marie's finger and shook it vigorously.

Conway noted that Rita watched with distraction bordering on boredom. "Diogenes," Rita said, her voice dry, "was of course obsessed with the way, the truth, and the light. For those of you who don't know your mythology."

The puppet turned toward her, moved its hands. "Please, we are in educated company. There's no need to be patronizing."

"I don't know about anyone else, but I've got to get back to campus," Rita said, smiling thinly.

"Pooper in every crowd," Diogenes moaned. As Hank started to stuff the puppet back in his pocket, it wailed, "Oohhh, no, please, I don't want to go back in there. It's dark and hot and lonely."

Hank rolled his eyes. "Lately, Diogenes has developed some rather odd compulsions. Behave," he snapped, pushing the puppet out of sight. The whole scene, short as it was, didn't sit right with Conway. It had gone from funny to something else, something he couldn't name.

"Poor little guy," Marie sympathized.

"Christ, he's not real," Turnbalt remarked.

"Could have fooled me," said Rita, who now seemed embarrassed by the entire display.

The crowd drifted toward the cars. Conway dropped back and walked with Ian and Laura. "Any leads?" Ian asked.

"No." Conway was accustomed to the question by now but tired of it just the same. "Did you know Denise?"

"I met her briefly, when I sold the science department their new computer. It's supposed to go into the complex they're building."

"I didn't know you'd met her," Laura said, looking at Ian.

"Months ago. I think she had to sign the requisition form because the department chairman was out that day."

"What was your impression of her?"

Ian thought about it for a moment. "Just offhand, that she was cold, sort of distant. And pretty, very pretty."

Conway stopped at his car. "Nice meeting you, Ian."

"Same here, Mr. Conway."

As he got in his car, he heard Ian tell Laura that he would pick her up by six for dinner. Beyond them, the Lincolns and Turnbalts were splitting up. Everyone was returning to their work routines and at the magical ring of five, they would reunite, the gemination completed.

Rita waved as he drove past her car.

9

1.

LAURA FROWNED AS she stopped in the driveway and saw Emily preening herself in a slice of hot light on the front porch. She was almost certain the cat had been indoors when she'd left this morning.

"Em, how'd you get out, anyway?" She dug into her purse for the key as the cat arched her back gracefully in the sunlight, then rubbed against Laura's leg, purring. "I know, I know, you're not saying. To tell you the truth, I can't remember if I let you out or not."

Except for Ian's unexpected arrival and the memorial service for Denise, most of today was a blur. She'd hardly slept last night, what with dreams blooming like bougainvillea in her head, finally driving her out of bed at 4:30 this morning. Her eyes burned from lack of sleep. She wanted to take a long, hot bath and a nap before Ian arrived, but she was almost afraid to close her eyes, so certain was she that she would see Denise's face again, as it was in the dream, just a skeleton with loose flaps of skin where the cheeks should have been.

She could still hear the woman's voice saying, *Go away, Laura; Ian and I don't want you here, Laura*, and she could see the way her mouth yawned open and closed as she spoke and how her teeth scraped together tightly as a saw against wood. Sometimes in the dream the faces melted together, then slowly took shape and grew into the faces of other people she knew. Rita. Hank. Conway. The Turnbalts. But it always found its way back like some lost homing pigeon to Laura's bedroom, where Denise and Ian lay side by side in bed, their movements abrupt, hollow, puppetlike.

The door swung open and Emily raced into the house and slid around the corner and into the kitchen. A rush of cool air brushed her face and legs as she stepped inside and shut the door. The rooms were quiet. The curtains were still closed and the light inside was diffused, cozy. Her sanctuary, she thought, slipping off her shoes and leaving them by the couch. She turned on a lamp and remembered the storm and the call and the light not coming on a few nights ago. She felt a momentary chill along her spine. She could not, even now, answer the phone without apprehension.

Laura left her things on the couch, slipped off her panty hose, and left them bunched on the cushion beside her. The luxury of living alone, she decided, was being able to leave things where you took them off, if you were so inclined.

Emily poked her head out from around the wall, her ears and tail twitching impatiently. She meowed. Laura pulled her blouse out of her skirt as she walked into the kitchen. Given her druthers, she thought, she would probably wear jeans all the time; just a button and a zipper got you in and out.

She fed Emily, scanned the headlines in the news, then wiggled out of her blouse on the way upstairs and flung it over her shoulders. She stepped out of her skirt, caught her toe on the waist, hopped into the bedroom. She tossed it and the blouse toward the bed and raised her eyes.

Stifled, ugly sounds climbed up from her throat. She grabbed for the spread, covering herself as she backed toward the closet. "Oh, God, what—" she whispered.

The letters dripped crookedly down the dresser mirror, cutting her reflection in quarters. *I see you now, Laura, even as you're backing away, looking over your shoulder for me, and one day you'll see me, Laura, I promise.*

She turned. Her vision blurred in a carnival of color.

The spread twisted like a boa around her legs and a long, hot wind raged through her, drying up her mouth and eyes and shriveling up her insides. *The closet, too.* She grabbed violently at a blouse and skirt; they came loose in her hand. The hanger banged against the wall, clattered, fell soundlessly to the carpet. She fled into the hall, clutching the spread, the blouse shaking with a terrible chill, her heart ramming against her insides like a bull.

He can't hurt you. He's not in the house.

Laura stopped. The vertiginous opening of the stairwell spiraled down before her and she grabbed onto the railing to steady herself. Water sighed in the pipes, the air conditioning clicked on. She shrugged the spread from her shoulders, slipped on the blouse. A false calm clamped down over her. *It's still light out*. That made a difference, she thought, even as she felt the fear building up behind her, ready to mow her down at the slightest sign of trepidation. She walked back into the bedroom. Her eyes darted from the mirror to the surface of the dresser where bottles and tubes of lipstick swung from end to end in an arc. What she felt most of all was a sense of violation, as if she'd been raped. He had intruded into the most intimate corners of her life, touched her belongings, her clothes, her—

"Where else were you, you bastard!" she screamed suddenly, and yanked open a dresser drawer, then another and another until all six tottered uneasily on their tracks. Shorts, bras, pants, nightgowns: all had been arranged in small, neat piles, in colors, like the clothes in the closet. She could almost see him standing here, where she was, touching everything, slipping his hands into the drawers, spraying her perfumes, infecting the very air she breathed.

Laura tore the sheets off the bed, the cases off the pillows, and tossed them in a heap on the floor. She started emptying the drawers onto the mattress. Colors fluttered soundlessly through the air, bright as confetti. Dirty, she thought, everything was dirty. She went into the closet, knelt in front of the shoe rack, flipping one shoe and then another over her shoulder until they were scattered behind her in the room. She stood, slapped an arm against the clothes hanging in such sweet and perfect order, stuck her other arm in between, and lifted things off the bar, dropped them on the bed, and went back and forth, emptying the closet. Her arm swept across the top of the dresser. Bottles, tubes, jewelry crashed against each other to the floor.

Which tube? *Which one did he use?* She crouched, uncapped them until she found the one he'd used. The end was squashed down like an overly ripe tomato. She jabbed it against the mirror again and again until the writing there was indecipherable and the lipstick was falling apart and her hands were smeared and sticky, as if with blood.

Turning slowly in place, the tube still in her hand, she looked at it, then the mirror, the bed, the empty closets and drawers. A terrible weight pushed down against her. She could barely lift her arms, her legs. It was the black of excess gravity. She lay back in all the clothes and shut her eyes. The tube of lipstick dropped to the carpet. *There, he's gone.* And she fell into a deep and dreamless sleep.

"Laura?"

The voice nipped and bit at her. Her eyes were heavy. Go away, go away.

"Laura? Babe?"

She climbed up through an impenetrable blackness as if she had been drugged. Her eyes opened and Ian was standing over her, a frown pushing down between his eyes. His hand was on her arm. Warm, she thought. He had such warm hands. She wanted to float into the brown of his eyes, sink down inside it, sleep.

Then she remembered and flew forward.

"How'd you get in here?" she demanded.

"Laura, babe, what *happened*? The mirror, this—this mess. What—"

"How'd you get in, Ian?"

"The spare key." He said this patiently as he sat beside her, his hand growing warmer against her arm.

"No. That's not possible. I locked the door. This morning. I locked all the doors."

"The utility room door, Laura. The spare fits." His voice was patronizingly patient now. He picked up the tube of lipstick, and over the curve of his back she saw the empty closet. "Babe, please," he said, raising up, capping the tube, setting it on the dresser, "tell me what happened."

She felt the scission in her consciousness. Part of her was still alone in the room, alone with the violation and the singular terror. She said, "The key, Ian. Where's the key?" and extended her hand. "I want the key."

"I left it where I found it. Outside. I kept calling and knocking on the door and ringing the bell and your car was out in front and I kept imagining you inside here bleeding to death or worse. Christ, I was practically frantic." She barely noticed that he spoke in a feverish rush.

"I've got to have the key, Ian. That's how he got in. I should call the police. Conway. I'll call Conway." She swung her legs over the side of the bed, shaking her head, saying nothing for the moment. She looked up at Ian, who was sitting beside her, surrounded by silk and cotton, waiting. "I'm going to buy a gun. I'm not going to live like this," she said. "I'll shoot him if he steps inside this house again. I swear I will.'' She paused. ''Conway, I'm going to call him. His card's in my purse.''

She got up.

Her purse, where'd she leave her purse?

''Laura,'' Ian said, standing now, his arms loose at his sides, ''please tell me what happened. Who're you talking about? What man?''

Her purse was downstairs, right, now she remembered. She touched her hand to the back of her shirt, pushing at the collar so it was closer around her throat. She started out of the room, remembered Ian, looked over her shoulders.

''Downstairs,'' she said, ''let's go downstairs. I want to get out of here. That bastard,'' she spat, and left the room.

2.

Conway's shoes whispered across the grass and dead pine needles. The sound traveled with an underwater clarity and mixed with the relentless cries of crickets, scratching at the heat. It was so still, so humid, he could smell the brackish tide from the canals, fitting down over the neighborhood like a dome. The stars were muddled and indistinct in the immense dark, and the moon sat on its haunches in a haze, as if covered with gauze, just over the roof of Laura's house.

He felt renewed annoyance that she'd called him. He was homicide. This was a B&E, something for the local cops. But in all fairness to her, he thought, the day had been an utter waste, anyway—from his stop at Stella's to his two-hour wait at Lauderdale Airport for the mysterious caller who had never showed. So what was one more stop? So what if it was eight o'clock on a Friday night?

The door opened before he rang the bell and Rita grinned at him and said, ''Hello, Conway, welcome to the Mad Hatter's tea party.''

''Rita, hi.'' The weight lifted from his shoulders and he stepped back, pretending to check the address. ''Do I have the right house?''

''You do. I stopped by for a glass of wine and stepped into an asylum.'' She opened the door wide. ''Come on in.''

He followed her through the house, glancing at the high ceiling, the exposed beams, the loft. He heard the drone of the TV in the back room. ''Have you eaten?'' Rita asked. ''Or how about a beer?'' She touched her hair, pushed it behind her ears.

The gesture, he thought, was as much a part of her as the color of her eyes.

"Yes, thanks."

Laura came into the kitchen, looking thin and undernourished in jeans and her bare feet. "Thanks for coming, John. I hope this isn't an imposition."

"No trouble." He pulled out a stool, sat at the counter. "What happened?"

"The same loony tune who left her the note," Rita explained, setting a beer and an icy mug in front of him. She leaned against the counter, arms folded, listening as Laura related what had happened.

"The bedroom's upstairs?" Conway asked.

"Yes." She bit at her lower lip and turned a pack of cigarettes slowly around in her hands. She looked as if she were on the verge of tears. "I'm afraid it's a mess. I ripped everything out of the closet, dumped the drawers on the bed, and scribbled all over the mirror with the lipstick he used. His hands had been all over everything," she finished softly.

"We checked the windows and doors," Ian said as he came into the room with a can of beer in either hand. "No sign of forced entry." He paused. "Long time no see, Mr. Conway." He dropped the cans in the trash and helped himself to another beer in the refrigerator.

"I think he must've used the spare key," Laura said. "When I left this morning, I'm sure Emily was inside. But when I got home, she was out. The only way she'll go out is through the door because she's got vertigo and the windows are four feet from the ground."

"I'll check just the same," Conway said.

"Grab your beer, Conway," Rita said. "I'll take you upstairs."

The room was spacious, with a large window that ran from end to end. The bed, huge as a ship, was directly under it and covered with clothes and shoes. Bottles and jewelry were strewn along a strip of carpeting near the dresser. The drawers were open and the mirror looked like a child's rendition of an abstract painting. It was a moment before either Conway or Rita spoke.

"*Mess* was an understatement," he remarked.

"Ravaged," she said.

Conway looked out the window and straight down. Unless the man had come in over the roof, there wasn't any way he could've entered through here. And to come in over the roof, he'd have to be Spiderman. They went back downstairs and outside. Laura had turned on the floodlights in the backyard, and as he and Rita made their way around the side of the house, she said, "Ian thought she should have called the local yokels, but Laura was adamant about calling you." When Conway didn't say anything, Rita added, "That was supposed to be a compliment, Conway."

"I guess today isn't such a hot day for compliments."

"Besides that depressing memorial service, what else happened?"

He told her about the phone call and his wait at the airport. "Well, don't feel bad," she said philosophically, "at least you haven't been abandoned, Conway. Hank left for the weekend. Another magician's conference. I mean, how many people can claim to have been upstaged by Diogenes?"

He laughed and thought it sounded like an invitation. Then he wondered if by "abandoned," she meant she and Hank were now separated. "I *was* abandoned. She went on vacation without me," he said. "She said I was married to my job."

"Are you?"

"Probably."

They stopped at the edge of the lot, which was lit up by the floodlights. "Where does the lot come out?" he asked.

"A dirt road. The people on the other side own it." She gestured toward the slab of cement in front of them. There were several large potted plants on either end of it. "Laura kept her spare key outside here somewhere."

"That door goes into the kitchen?"

"Yes."

They returned indoors and found Ian and Laura in the den. "There isn't much I can do but report it," Conway told her, settling into a chair near the window.

"That's what I figured," Laura replied. "And tomorrow I'm going out and purchasing a gun."

"I told her that's a little drastic," Ian said, and motioned toward a tray of cheese and crackers. "Help yourself."

"Well, I think it's a great idea. We've got one at home," Rita said. "Right next to the bed."

Ian laughed. "I don't see how the hell anyone could get into your place, Rita. You ought to see it, John. It's got more alarms and electronic gadgets in it than Fort Knox, and it's all run by a computer."

"Hank has a lot of hobbies," Rita said, as if she felt obliged to explain.

"If someone broke in here," Ian went on, "Laura would have to wait until he was three-quarters of the way in before she shot him, and even then she'd have to drag him in the rest of the way so she wouldn't end up with an assault with a deadly weapon charge.''

"What would you suggest, then, Ian?" Laura glared at him. "A bodyguard?"

Ian slipped an arm around her shoulder, kissed her quickly on the side of the head. "Of course. Me."

"You're always out of town."

Ian ignored the remark, offered Conway another beer. Conway glanced surreptitiously at Rita, whose legs were drawn up under her. She was evidently in no hurry to leave. "Sure. Another beer. Why not."

At midnight, four beers later, Conway stood on the front porch, saying good night to Laura and Ian. Rita was coming through the living room, checking her purse for her keys. Insects buzzed lazily around the porchlight and behind him loomed the deep, eerie soundlessness of another time. The air was perfectly still and hot, and he felt that if he turned too quickly, he might see himself as a kid, sitting in a canoe on one of the canals on a night like this, waiting for a tug on his fishing line.

He and Rita started down the drive, their footsteps a syncopated rhythm. The brackish smell was stronger now. Like rotting fish. He asked where Hank's conference was.

"Gainesville. Then he's doing a magic show at the University of Florida. He's popular on the college circuit."

"Why didn't you go with him?" *How could he not take you along?*

"Because classes start Monday and I've got a lot of work to do. I used to go, in the beginning, when we were first married, but he said it made him nervous to have me in the audience." She shrugged. Her voice was lower when she spoke again. "We've decided to separate. I'm moving into my sister's place this weekend."

Conway's heart flipped in his chest. "Why don't you move in with Laura? She could probably use the company."

"Ian lives there most of the time. And I wouldn't want to intrude. Besides, my sister's rarely home. She's in the travel business and always seems to be in China or Taiwan or some other place."

"Hank's quite a ventriloquist," Conway said.

"Yes, he's good. But I don't think he believes it. He wants to be the best. He knows he'll never be a Houdini and it seems to make him angry." She stopped at her car. "Well," she said, and they stood there, the night thick between them. "I think your coming over here put Laura's mind at ease."

"I wish there were more I could do."

"Night." She turned, then spun around and they both spoke at once, then laughed.

"You first," he said.

"No, you," she said.

"I think you know what I was going to say."

"So say it."

"No," he replied stubbornly. "You asked me to be your friend, Rita. Remember?"

"Okay. Then I'll say it." She turned her key around in her hands. "I want you to know. I want you to know so there're never any misconceptions between us. I don't understand what's going on between us, Conway. But something is. I'm in a vulnerable state at the moment, since I'm not quite sure what I feel about Hank. I don't know if it's fair to—" She stopped, got in the car, rolled down the window. "It isn't fair, I just decided. Forget that I said anything, all right? Good night, Conway. Have a nice weekend."

She started to roll the window back up, but he opened the door. "Why don't you leave your car here? It's not blocking anyone."

The porch light went off. Rita gazed at him in the dark. "And what?"

Conway dug his hands in his pockets, not taking his eyes from her face. "You're talking orthodontia, Rita."

"What?" She laughed. "What're you talking about?"

"My younger sister goes to bed with a guy once, and by the next morning she's planning orthodontia for the kids. She's figured it all out, their lives from A to Z. That's what you're trying to do, Rita. You've looked down the road a few months and are so damn certain you've figured all the options. But you haven't left any room for surprise. I don't know what to say about you and Hank. I don't know what to expect about your marriage. I'm not in a position to. But I'm willing to take the chance. If you'll let me. I guess that's what I'm saying."

She looked away, closed the door, rested her elbow on the window. Conway couldn't tell if his words had penetrated. "Not bad," she said at last, nodding. "Not bad at all, Conway. I'll follow you."

"This is it?" she whispered, getting out of the car, coming over to him as she looked around. "I smell water."

"Over to the right. A canal. These were built as condos about ten years ago and never made it."

Her eyes swept from the driveway where they stood, up along the front of the building where all the windows were dark. "It's so *quiet*," she said as they walked to the door.

"I may be the only tenant under eighty."

Her hand brushed the leaves of a plant. Her voice was quavering when she spoke. "What kind of plant is this?"

"I don't know." He felt light-headed, a little dizzy.

She was smiling, but it was a curious smile, not quite complete, as though whatever it was about him that she'd been contemplating since they'd met had just fallen into place. The smile dimpled the corners of her mouth and just barely dimpled the center of her chin. The light from the hallway inside shone thinly on her hair, fell onto her forehead, vanished into her cheeks, and reappeared along her nose. He touched a hand to her face. She turned her head, kissing it, her eyes shutting briefly, her hand covering his. "You want to stand out here all night?" she whispered.

They ascended the three flights of stairs without speaking. At the top, as he was looking for the right key, she caught her breath and said, "I thought you hated exercise."

"We've requisitioned an elevator. Last year, Mr. Light in twenty-one A had a coronary on the stairs. He was ninety-two."

Rita poked him in the back, chuckled. As they stepped inside, Conway went around turning on lamps. She left her purse in a nearby chair, examined a *mola* hanging above the couch. It was a handwoven, colorful design made by the Cuna Indians in Panama, a gift from Jen that she'd picked up on one of her layovers.

Rita moved slowly around the room, sometimes touching, sometimes just looking. Conway felt Jenny's presence everywhere, felt it suddenly like a stab of conscience. So many things in these rooms were connected to her. Things she owned, things that had been transplanted in the move from her place to his, gifts she'd brought him.

Rita strolled into the kitchen, held back the blinds, gazed out. Conway knew she could see the moon on the water in the distance and a spattering of sailboats tied behind homes on the canal. "You hungry?" he asked, opening the refrigerator.

"This place has a woman's touch, Conway. She the one who went on vacation without you?" He found her curiosity flattering but was surprised by her apparent lack of jealousy, sarcasm, or the other things he usually associated with such a question.

"She's a flight attendant with Pan Am," he explained, not wanting to discuss Jen. "Out of Miami."

Rita peeked in the fridge. "It's full," she exclaimed.

Conway laughed. It broke the awkwardness. "It usually isn't."

She opened the bins, inspected the shelves, lifted pieces of aluminum from their containers. "I *am* hungry," she said.

"Omelets? That about covers my culinary repertoire."

"Perfect."

They spent an hour over breakfast, and when they were finally making their way toward the bedroom, Conway shutting off lights behind them, Rita turned, said, "You know, I have a definite weakness for chefs."

They embraced. She tasted vaguely of cinnamon, he thought as his hands moved over the slant of her shoulders to the curve of her back. He held her face in his hands, and when they dropped to her blouse she stepped back, into the bedroom, and undressed herself. She draped her clothes over the back of the chair. Pulled down the sheets, drew the curtains closed, performed small rituals she had learned in marriage. Her impudicity was as innocent as a child's.

Conway's pleasure in her was so extreme, he forgot that in this very bed he and Jenny had fought and made love and held each other, that some nights she'd turned away from him and popped a pill to put her to sleep and popped another in the morning to awaken her. He forgot, really, that she'd ever been a part of his life.

Rita was a new continent—bold, shy, and starved. It was not a need for sex, for the act itself, but something stronger, deeper, a need to be held and whispered to, fussed over and caressed. When they finally moved apart, the air was as warm as the June night outside. She kept a hand on his arm, reluctant to break the contact. Her other hand was flat against her stomach. After a time, she raised herself on an elbow, touched her finger to his mouth as she had that night he'd left her in the university parking lot. When he smiled, her finger traced it all the way to the corners.

"What," he said. She turned on her side. His hand moved along her spine, counting the vertebrae.

She kissed him, her leg slipped in between his, and for a moment she lay with her ear against his chest. "Your heart. It gives you away."

He asked her what she was like as a child, suddenly wanting to know everything, to fill in the lacuna of the years, to hear details so specifically that he could imagine her at three, at twelve, nineteen, twenty-five, thirty. She talked freely, except about the years she'd spent with Hank. He and Rita existed within this room, now, and beyond that, he thought, nothing was certain.

When the light beyond the curtains began turning gray, Rita slept. He watched her, his arm falling asleep under her shoulders. He thought her face in the aftermath of lovemaking was not unlike the mask of death, that utter peace he'd seen in Denise Markham's face.

10

1.

IN THE DREAM, he was with Denise by the hibiscus. The knife was slipping smoothly in between her ribs and he felt her go limp in his arms as she made that sound in the back of her throat. He awakened drenched in sweat, his cheeks damp with tears, arms whipping at the dark. *Denny, Denny, why did you make me do it?*

In the beginning, things between them were good—no, perfect. From that first moment he'd seen her that morning in the jewelry store, where he'd gone for some last minute Christmas shopping, he'd known he would love her. He could still recall the moment when she'd glanced over at him as she'd waited for the sales clerk to return from the back room and her eyes had fixed on him with an odd intensity and something intimate had shot between them. He remembered the smooth curve of her jaw, the way she'd flicked impatiently at the hair on her collar, and how later, as they'd walked out of the store together, she'd said, "Have we met before? I just had the craziest sense of déjà vu."

And he, tricked by her beauty, her eyes, seduced by her very presence, had muttered, "I know what you mean."

They'd walked down the block and stopped at one of the cafes. For the next couple of hours, they had talked like old friends. Some months later, she'd told him she believed their meeting was karmic, some vestige of another life that had to be resolved. "There's nothing coincidental about any of this, Bucky," she'd said in that same certain tone he'd eventually come to despise. "Years ago, a psychic warned me I'd meet a man and—" Then she'd waved her hand impatiently and smiled in her mysterious way. "Never mind. Sometimes these things sound stupid if you say them out loud."

Denny, he thought, pulling the pillows up against him and squeezing his eyes shut against the memories, the ache, the truths. In another time and place, she might have been a mystic, working herself into a primeval frenzy, speaking in tongues, healing the blind and the sick. Instead, she'd only been a thief, liar, a whore.

He kicked off the sheet and got out of bed. He walked over to the window and gazed out into the hot, still night. His reflection was broken up by the spinning blue light of an ambulance in the distance. He watched a moment longer, transfixed, wondering if a time would come when he might cower at the sound of a siren because it was coming for him.

He shuffled back to the bed and lay down. The window, he thought, like his life, his future, was hermetically sealed. One could see out, but not in. As he closed his eyes, Denise's face pressed against the inner dark. He saw the months of their knowing strung out like a bridge of flesh, the two of them joined at the hip, the mouths gobbling up the drug as if it contained the secret of youth or eternal life. He hadn't touched it in weeks, but the memory of it left him with a sort of hunger. That was its danger and its seduction; Denise knew it.

The ache in his side kicked up again and bit down hard. His head hurt, his nose ran, he hadn't felt up to par in months. The drug, he thought, not stress. He knew.

As he drifted down into sleep once more, the thought of Denise rolled around inside him like a koan, impenetrable, oblique, and now forever untouchable.

2.

At nine, the phone rang. Conway's arm fell off the bed to reach for it, and beside him Rita stirred, opened her eyes, watched him.

"Hey, man, it's Ake. I'm over at Palmetto General and I think you should join me."

"I just went to bed."

Under the cover, Rita's foot rubbed against his and she turned her head to the side, so that one cheek lay flat against the pillow, smiled, moved closer to him. His arm went around her shoulders. He held the receiver away from his ear enough so she could listen.

"It's important. I have a hunch it may have something to do with the Markham case."

"Okay. I'll be there as soon as I can." He hung up, ran a finger along Rita's arm. "Breakfast?"

"I'm going to stay right here," she said, her voice quiet and sleepy. "If that's okay with you."

He kissed her shoulder through the sheet. "I'll be back in a couple of hours."

"I'll be right here," she promised, then closed her eyes and pulled the sheet around her as he got out of bed.

Forty-five minutes later, Conway was getting off the elevator on the eighth floor of the hospital and saw Ake standing at the nurse's station. He looked out of place in the bright, antiseptic hallway, his huge shoulders sagging with exhaustion, his skin that deep carbon you saw more of, usually, in the islands. He spotted Conway and came toward him with great, loping strides like some magnificent stallion. "What we've got, my friend, is one Jerome Blanchard, stockbroker, retired, and his much younger wife, Olivia, who was brought in earlier this morning, DOA." Ake paused. "He says she went into convulsions from a drug overdose."

"What kind of drug?"

"The man says coke."

"C'mon, Ake."

"I'm just telling you what the man said." He cocked his head sideways. "That's Blanchard at the end of the hall, with the doc."

Conway saw a disconsolate, overweight man sitting on the edge of the couch with his head in his hands. The physician was speaking earnestly to him and Blanchard just kept shaking his shiny, bald head. "Got the drug right here in my pocket," Ake said, patting his thigh. "I'll drop it by the lab when I split. Blanchard said it was in his wife's purse."

"And you think it's the same drug I found in Denise's office?"

"I do, I do. That's what my hunch says."

They walked down the hall to where Blanchard and the physician sat. Ake made introductions and Dr. Henry stood, nodding politely. "I'll have a report for you shortly on the ER treatment. We won't know anything definite until the autopsy, though." He motioned the two men aside. "If we'd known what the drug was, the medics might have been able to save her. I know Pivot is jammed up down at the lab, so if it would help, we could perform the autopsy here. With one of your physicians in attendance, of course."

"Thanks," Ake said. "That'd be a tremendous help."

Blanchard remained where he was, his pudgy fingers rubbing at his temples, the diamond on his little finger glistening in the light from the window behind him. His feet moved in and out of his bedroom slippers, as if he were shuffling across the floor in his sleep.

"Mr. Blanchard," said Ake, "I'd like you to tell Detective Conway here what you told me earlier."

Blanchard looked up through hooded, bloodshot eyes and dropped his arms to his legs, as if they were too heavy to hold to his face any longer. His nostrils flared as he sighed and rubbed a hand over his chin. He needed a shave. There were rings of perspiration under his arms. When he stood, he was unsteady on his feet, almost as if he'd been drinking. He gave Conway a limp, damp look, then his cheeks blotched with frustration, pain, perplexity.

"Sure. I'll tell him what I told you. I think you people are doing a goddamned lousy job protecting the taxpayers, that's what I think." He pointed vaguely down the hall, his finger wagging. "My wife, Conway, my *wife*—thirty-four years old with her whole goddamned life ahead of her—just died from a drug overdose, you get the picture? She died because you guys can't keep the streets clean, because smugglers are cutting drugs with all kinds of shit, and my wife's dead." His voice had risen to a fever pitch. The pink splotches on his cheeks had turned red; the end of his nose looked like a Christmas bulb. "Dead from a cocaine overdose, you got that?"

"Please, Mr. Blanchard. Sit down, get a grip on yourself," Dr. Henry said calmly. He spoke as if he were addressing a child. "Now. That's better. These gentlemen aren't to blame for what happened to Olivia." Blanchard, who'd fallen back against the couch, looked up helplessly at Henry, then his face sort of squashed up and he began to cry. Conway shuffled uncomfortably, sat next to him, and gave him a few minutes to compose himself.

"How do you know it was cocaine?"

"That's what she said." Blanchard sniffled, blew his nose in a soiled handkerchief. "I was upstairs. Asleep. Something woke me. Olivia wasn't there. I found her in the kitchen. Baking cookies. At five in the morning, she's baking cookies like it's the middle of the afternoon. She's laughing and carrying on like there's someone in the room with her. I asked her what she was doing and she looks at me in this kind of wild and crazy way and says, 'Mama, Jerry wants to know what I'm doing.' Then she giggles like it's the funniest thing she ever heard, giggling like a little girl with her hands at her mouth. I reminded her that her mother had been dead eight years. I went up to her, put my hands on her shoulders, and she . . . she shook them off like I was . . . Christ. Like I was going to hurt her or something. She was cold, God, she was so cold I could feel it through her nightgown. . . .'' He blew his nose again, wadded up the handkerchief, and started getting teary again. His face was waxen, the color of the dead, Conway thought.

''Go on, Mr. Blanchard,'' Conway coaxed.

''Well,'' he began, staring down the hall as if his past were unfolding there, in front of him, but at a distance, ''she shook my hands away and then started banging her fists on the counter. 'Mama's not dead!' she shouted. 'She's not, she's not. She's right here by the stove.' Then her head suddenly snapped back and she sort of sang, ''Toooo muuucchh cocaine,' and then she fell to the floor and went into convulsions. I . . . I got her tongue out, you know, and then the convulsions stopped; I called the ambulance and . . .'' He sat back, covered his face with his hands, and whispered, ''Oh, God, what am I going to do? Livvy, poor Livvy,'' and he rocked slowly back and forth in his seat, hugging his arms against him.

''She was hallucinating,'' Conway said.

Blanchard gulped at the air. ''She said . . . she said the walls were breathing and wanted to know why we didn't put up new wallpaper in the kitchen. But we don't *have* wallpaper in the kitchen. Then there was this stuff about her mother, talking to her mother. She . . . she was studying at the university, my Livvy, studying music. Oh, she had a marvelous voice, Conway. And she played the fiddle and the piano and she worked so hard.''

Except when she was doing drugs, Conway thought. ''Do you have any idea where she got the stuff?''

''No. I don't know. I don't want to know.''

''Had she ever used drugs before?''

''She wasn't addicted, if that's what you're asking.''

''*Used*, Mr. Blanchard. Had she ever *used* drugs before?''

Blanchard's hesitation was a dead giveaway. ''No.'' He worried his hands in his lap, ran a finger across his upper lip, said, ''Okay, okay. So she smoked and snorted occasionally, who doesn't? We get high to forget, right? No worse than booze. See this?'' And he patted his considerable stomach. ''Used to be twice this size. From booze. Olivia got me off the sauce. I was a mess. A forty-five-year-old mess. But I don't know where she got the stuff. I never asked. That was her thing, you know, and I went along with it because . . . well, because she enjoyed it and . . . I didn't want her to do it with anyone else.''

"You don't know who she might've gotten it from? Someone at school, maybe?'' Conway persisted.

Blanchard pressed his fists into his eyes, shook his head. "Oh, God, she was good, so very, very good,'' he whispered, and sitting back, he began to whimper again, his cheeks puffing out like a squirrel's.

"Mr. Blanchard, is there anyone I can call to drive you home?'' Dr. Henry asked.

"No, no. I can't leave. My Livvy might need me.''

Henry glanced at Conway and Ake. "If you don't need him anymore, I think I'm going to send him home. I'll be in touch as soon as we know anything.''

Conway motioned the doctor aside. "When the autopsy's performed, there're a couple things I wish you'd look for. A high liver enzyme count, enlarged lymph glands, and signs of respiratory infection.''

Henry nodded, made a note of it. A few minutes later, Conway and Ake were on their way down the hall toward the elevator. "When Blanchard is finished going to pieces,'' Ake said, "he's going to have to answer some questions.''

"You think the stuff has hit the streets?''

"It's possible, yeah.''

"No poker tonight,'' said Conway.

"No poker tonight,'' echoed Ake.

Outside, it had started clouding over again. The air was thick with heat, and in the distance thunderheads were climbing blackly into the sky. "Blanchard's treading eggshells, Ake. How about if I play good boy to your bad?''

"Great minds move in the same direction.'' He laughed. "You name the day and I'll be there.''

Conway looked up at the windows of the eighth floor, imagining Blanchard still perched on the edge of the couch, the pieces of his life scattered around him, his guilt pressing like a tumor against his heart. Conway knew the type; Don Markham was the same kind of man. Each harbored the ancient need to confess. It was one of those built-in defense mechanisms that ensured the survival of the species.

They went their separate ways in the parking lot and Conway paused a moment, watching Ake moving through the pale light.

It thundered. The sky to the south, where the dark clouds were building, grew jagged with lightning. Black and white, right and wrong, that was how Ake saw the world. Conway almost envied him that. He lived, instead, with the infinite gloom and confusion of gradations.

A while later, when Conway came into the apartment, he heard the shower. It drummed against the cool air, sent steam into the hall, was neither more nor less than he'd heard a thousand times before with Stella, with Jen, but it sent a chill up his spine; this was different.

The bathroom door was cracked and he peeked in, saw the blur of Rita's body as her arms lifted and her hands washed suds through her hair. A tide of emotion surged through him, larger than language, clipping that inchoate yearning he'd felt outside the church after Denise's funeral. The ceaseless skein of sounds, the murmur of the lover's lament: although now separated, she was still officially married.

He undressed there in the hall, left his clothes on the carpet, opened the door. It squeaked. "Conway," Rita called, "that better be you." He could see her foot, pink and warm like a flower, against the porcelain, and when he didn't answer, she yanked the curtain back. "Well." She laughed.

Drops of water stood at the ends of her lashes, and as she blinked they flew off and she pressed her fingers down over her eyes, blinked again, looked at him. The dimple started in her chin. He would memorize her like a blind man. He would be able to find his way from her throat to her knees, across wet skin or dry, and when she was away from him, in her other life, he would resurrect the memory and crush it against him like the real thing. He had, as Ake would have said, been bitten bad.

"You don't have to wait for an invitation, you know," she said.

"In that case . . ." And he stepped in with her.

After, when they were in the bedroom and she was drying her hair with a towel, watching him in the mirror, she said, "What is it?"

Conway pointed at the clean clothes in the chair. "You went home?"

"No. Since I'm in the process of moving, I've got some clothes in the trunk." She reached for a blouse, shook it, and her breasts vanished beneath the cotton. He watched as she zipped her magnificent legs into a pair of tight jeans. "I've also got spare fuses, hoses, a jug of water, battery, cash, matches, and so on. I'm well prepared for almost any catastrophe."

"Oh." He laughed. "Is that what this is?" The moment he'd said it, he knew it was the wrong thing to say. But it had been coiled at the tip of his tongue.

She tucked her hands in her pockets and her shoulders hunched up like a puppet's. "I'm not trying to think about it because I'm afraid if I do, I'll run like hell." Their eyes held. It was a tug-of-war, each of them pulling back, waiting to see who would give first.

Rita did.

She came over to him, rolled forward on the balls of her feet, kissed him quickly, and tugged on his sleeve. "Let's go take a drive to Nevada or something."

"The salt flats?"

"I thought the salt flats were in Utah." She followed him out of the room.

Conway heard a shake of keys on the other side of the door and thought, *Oh, Christ.*

"Sugar, I'm home!" shouted a jubilant Jen as she burst into the room. "Sugar . . ." Then she saw Rita, dropped her suitcase, and finished in a whisper, "Surprise."

"Oh, boy," Rita drolled, and rolled her eyes.

Jenny said, "My, my, isn't this cozy." She tossed the packages she was carrying onto the couch, whipped off the white straw hat she was wearing. Her blond hair tumbled out.

"Jennifer," said Conway, "this is Rita. Rita, this is Jennifer. And I'm John. John Conway. Now we all know each other."

"What's she doing here, John?" Jenny demanded. She swept a hand through her hair, put her other hand on her hip, then swung her purse off her shoulder and onto the couch with everything else. Like a cat, she was staking out her territory.

"Actually," Rita spoke up, looking quickly down at the floor, running a finger alongside her nose, finally lifting her eyes to Jenny, "I was just leaving."

"Really," said Jen, jutting out a hip, folding her arms, "don't leave on my account."

Rita smiled at Conway, winked. "Take care of yourself, Conway."

"His name is John," Jenny snapped as Rita started past her.

Rita patted her on the shoulder. "Relax, sweetheart, where's your sense of humor? Have a nice day, all," she said.

Jenny spun around, kicked the door shut with her foot. Conway dived past her, threw the door open, ran out onto the landing. "Rita!" he shouted. "Wait."

She looked up from the bottom of the first flight of stairs, hands still in her pockets, hair yet damp from the shower. "We'll drive to Nevada another day. Don't worry about it."

He watched until she reached the parking lot. He saw her run a hand over the roof of the Porsche, then she waggled her fingers at him, got in her old Volvo, and drove away.

3.

Duncan stood in the locker room in his shorts and T-shirt. He was dimly aware of the showers down the hall, the drumming of feet on the court overhead, and, of course, of the pain in his left side. It was an old friend, this pain. His reminder of Denise and of everything that had been.

His fingers twisted the combination lock three times to the right, then to the appropriate numbers. Right, left, right again. The lock clicked and the door swung open. He peered into the array of shorts and socks and shoes and remembered this was just how he was standing the day Denise had come here.

Duncan rifled through the clothes until he found his tennis shoes. He tried to push the memory of Denise away. But like the pain in his side, and the general malaise he'd felt for weeks, the memory was obdurate and stuck to the screen of his mind, sticky as gum.

"I understand you're going to be my research assistant," she'd said from the doorway. When he'd glanced around, there she'd stood in her magnificence, that beauty which was almost blinding, a hand on her hip as she'd looked slowly around the locker room. "I understand this is where you spend most of your time." When she'd finally gazed at him, her eyes had been cold. "Don't you speak?" she'd asked, her mouth stirring into a smile, her hand dropping from her hip, moving through her hair as she'd stepped into the room. "My *Gawd*, it smells terrible in here."

"Hullo," he'd said stupidly.

"You want the job or not? According to the terms of this work-study program, you have the right to refuse. You know any chemistry?"

"Some."

She'd rolled her eyes, sat down on the wooden bench, dug into her purse for a cigarette. She'd lit it, dropped her head back, languid as a cat, and blown smoke into the air. "What's 'some' mean?" she'd asked, and had begun firing questions at him. When he hadn't answered, she'd stopped, smiled again, stood. "I think you'll do just fine, Thomas Duncan. As long as you understand one thing.'' She'd smoothed down her dress, dropped the cigarette on the concrete floor, brought the heel of her shoe down over it. "I've spent the better part of my life as a chemist. My research is like my child. It involves something which could very well transform the way man perceives himself and the world. Do you understand the implications of such a transformation?''

"I think so,'' he'd replied, not having even the vaguest notion what she was talking about. He'd thought there was something frightening in the cold, dispassionate tone of her voice.

"Right." She'd looked down at the floor, the smile starting all over again. She'd raised her eyes. "If you're going to be my assistant, you're never to discuss my research. Not with anyone. If I found out that you have, I'll squash you. It's that simple. Do we understand each other?''

"You can't threaten me," he'd protested.

"I'm not. It's a promise. Not a threat."

"Maybe I don't want the job, after all."

"Fine." She'd turned and started toward the door.

He'd hesitated, but not for long. "Hey, look." He'd followed her to the door. "It's okay with me. Your terms."

That smile had grown on her face again. Her eyes had latched onto his and she'd reached out, laid her hand gently against his cheek. Her touch had been cool, soft. "Good. You won't regret it."

Two days later, he'd started to work.

A week later, they'd become lovers.

Duncan reached for his sneakers, sat on the bench, and slipped them on. The perfect woman, he thought grimly. Beautiful and brilliant and deadly. She'd used him just as she'd used everyone. And in the end, she'd squashed him, not because he'd ever discussed her work, but because she'd grown tired of him and he'd no longer served her purpose.

That was the story of Denise Markham, lady chemist, whore, his seductive Cleopatra for whom the end always justified the means. But he'd loved her; that, too, was part of the story. She was Eros, she'd mesmerized him, she'd permeated his soul like time.

The shower down the hall went off. He heard footsteps outside the locker room. The coach whistled and shouted, "All right, anyone left in there, get a move on. *Now*."

Duncan pressed a hand to his side, blew his nose once more. He touched the back of his hand to his forehead and wondered dimly if he had a fever. The pain in his side began to recede and there was only the perpetual but tolerable burning in the small of his back.

He was glad she was dead.

PART TWO

Pandora's Box

11

CONWAY WAS STANDING in the hall outside the office Monday morning, helping himself to coffee, when he saw Tillis rush in the door. His belly bounced against his belt, his arms moved at his sides like a tin soldier's, and he kept his gaze to the floor. There was a bulging wad of tobacco in his cheek and two neat rings of sweat under his arms, and it wasn't even eight o'clock yet.

"Hey, Tillis, whoa," Conway said when the man started past him.

Tillis stopped abruptly and for a moment seemed on the verge of losing his balance and falling forward. He wiped an arm across his forehead, muttered an expletive about the heat, said, "Conway, get your ass in gear. We're flying to Key West where a safety deposit box is just waiting for us to take a peek inside. That Markham dame was sure sneaky, ole man."

"*Key West?*"

Tillis smiled with satisfaction. "I'm not as dumb as I look. Had a couple men checking all the banks in the Keys and it paid off."

"I'll be goddamned." Conway laughed.

"Let's go, let's go. Williams is holding a plane for us. Twin-engine Beech."

Conway ducked into his office for his briefcase and on his way through the hall stirred cream and three sugars into his coffee. Tillis looked on sourly.

"You know what that shit does to your body, Conway?"

"No lectures. Please. I listened to a lecture most of Saturday and part of Sunday. One Jenny Garfield is a runner-up with the ex–Mrs. Conway for limited vocabulary in the area of verbal abuse."

Tillis laughed, pulled at his pants until they were up over his stomach. When he breathed, they slipped down again. "I'm on wife number four, man, and it don't get no easier. Take my word for it. Women are another species."

Outside, the sky drooped with black clouds. Thunder rumbled in the distance. "We're flying into *that*?"

"Above it, Conway."

"I hate to fly. I get airsick."

Tillis looked at him over the roof of the car, his pink face dark around the jaw, his wasplike eyes skewed up against the glare. "Just don't puke on me, buddy."

It took them forty minutes to reach Key West, and during most of the flight Conway lay in the backseat with an arm over his eyes, trying to forget that he was two miles high, that an elephant was squatting inside his stomach, that the only thing between him and the blue of the Gulf and the Atlantic was a few inches of paint and aluminum. He would think of something pleasant. Rita, for instance. But whenever he got as far as the Saturday morning part of his remembering, Jen would burst in with her wide-armed "Surprise!" and he would begin to feel sick all over again.

After Rita had left Saturday, he'd come back indoors to find Jen in the bedroom, madly throwing clothes into another suitcase, opening and slamming drawers. He'd stood there watching her as she'd marched into the hall, thrown open the linen closet door, said, "All these towels are mine. What's your lady friend going to use to dry herself the next time she takes a shower? Toilet paper?"

"All those towels *aren't* yours, Jen. The ones from Sears are mine."

She'd thrown her head back and laughed. "That's what I always liked about you, John. Class. You have so much class," she'd said, taking the towels out one after another until she'd had a small pile of them in her arms. As she'd started into the bedroom again, he'd blocked her way, reached for the pile, set them on the bed, and gone through them, checking the labels. He had already lost his towels and linens and all those other essentials to Stella. He didn't intend to have it happen twice. He'd separated his from hers, thinking how much this was like divorce. Jen had been yanking clothes off the hangers and they'd banged against the wall. Some of his things had fallen and she'd left them on the floor of the closet.

"You don't have to be sloppy about it," he'd said.

And then it had started. The accusations and recriminations, the shouting and the tears. And by Sunday morning, after a long and uncomfortable night on the couch, it was over. Just like that. She had only to pick up the rest of her things.

"You gonna survive back there?" Tillis called over his shoulder, a smirk in his voice.

Conway sat up, gripped the seat as the plane dipped three or four hundred feet, then put his face close to Tillis's ear. "I'll remember this one, friend," he said.

"Right." Tillis laughed and pushed the tobacco into his other cheek, and Conway was so close to him that the smell of it, stale, old, used up, forced him back into his seat.

"Been in the banking business nearly thirty years, gents," said Sam Pepper, VP in charge of bank operations, as he scratched his shiny head, bald as an egg's, "and here's where the truth about a man comes out. Throw a hundred-dollar bill on a table and the way a man reacts will tell you everything you need to know about him." He stopped as they reached the safety box area. It was quiet and cold, not unlike Pivot's morgue, Conway thought. Pepper looked at him over the rim of his glasses. "Not surprisin' that folks from your neck of the woods stick their money down here. Got customers as far north as Jacksonville and Tallahassee. Don't know what it is about islands, but people somehow think their money's safer surrounded by water." He chuckled, put out his hand for Conway's key, and held up its twin. "Let's match 'em, gents."

He walked down the long row of shiny boxes, his shoes squeaking as he muttered, "Nope, nope." Tillis looked at Conway, frowned, was about to say something when Pepper breathed, "Ah-ha." He inserted one key beneath the other, brought the box out, and set it on the table. "One of you gents care to do the honors?"

Pandora's box, thought Conway as he lifted the lid. The other two men crowded in around the table and Pepper let out a soft, low whistle. "Must be over a hundred grand in there."

"My Gawd," moaned Tillis, reaching in for a handful.

"Let me get a teller," offered Pepper. "Counting money's our business. We've got efficient ways of doing this." He walked off quickly toward the double doors.

"Start separating them into piles of five hundred, Tillis."

"How much do college professors make, man?" Tillis asked.

"Not much more than cops."

Tillis wet his thumb, began counting money. "Yeah, that's what I figured."

At the bottom of the box, they found an envelope addressed to Viki Markham. Conway held it up to the light, turned it sideways. A letter. And a thick one at that.

"Her kid, right?"

"Yes." He set the envelope on top of his briefcase.

"You're not gonna open it?"

"It's not addressed to me."

"What?" The tone of his voice implied that Conway had lost his marbles.

"If the girl knows anything, Tillis, anything at all, she might be more willing to confide in me if I respect her privacy."

He shook his head, wet his thumb again. "I hate mystery," he grumbled.

Pepper returned with a teller, who was carrying an adding machine. "This is Jane"—he glanced at the girl's name tag—"Jane Zolinski, and she's going to keep us accurate, gents." He pointed at the table. "Set her there, hon."

"Yes, sir; right, sir," said Jane Zolinski, obsequiously grateful to have been taken off the outside window.

Pepper's eyes swept across the table of money. "I remember the day they brought in the ten million from the *Margarita*," he said, planting himself next to Conway, reaching for a stack of bills. "Ever heard of her, gents? Spanish galleon which went down in the same storm as the *Atocha*. The divers came ahoopin' and ahollerin' into town that evening, never forget it as long as I live. Actually carried the stuff in right out there"—he pointed vaguely to the north—"down past Sloppy Joe's, right there to the steps of the bank. Ten million in gold and jewels, gents, never seen anythin' like it in my life. Drinks were on the house all over town that night."

He passed his stacks along to Jane Zolinski, now set up at the end of the table, efficiently counting the piles with a rubber tip on her thumb, playing that adding machine with a smile to beat Liberace's. The sounds of the machine rang out and echoed in the hollow, clean silence of the vaulted room, and behind it was the sound of a whispering Tillis. "Three hundred . . . four hundred . . . bingo. . . ."

"I'm a gambling man, myself," said Pepper. "You gents care to wager a fin apiece on how much is here?"

Conway laughed, slapped five dollars on the table. "Sure."

Jane glanced up from her machine, studied the men for a minute, said, "Count me in."

"Fine, fine," said Pepper. "Ante just went up to twenty smackers." He and Tillis brought out their five dollars. Jane Zolinski pulled her wallet out of her purse. Took a good look at the cash divided neatly into denominations. "I guess one eighty."

"One sixty-five," said Tillis.

"Even one fifty," bet Conway.

"Hmm," said Pepper. "Too low. Two hundred grand is my bet."

"Eeww," muttered Tillis, shaking his hand so his thumb snapped against his index finger. "Jesus."

It took them an hour to count and recount the money. The final tally was $175,000, making Jane the winner. "I'll be," said Pepper, glancing at her with new respect. "How long you been with us, hon?"

"Year and a half, Mr. Pepper. Sir."

"You play the dogs?"

She grinned. "Yes, sir. Jai alai, too."

"Maybe you're due for a promotion, yes sirree, anyone who's that accurate gotta have talents we can use. Isn't ten million, gents, but it'd sure buy me a ticket every year for the rest of my life to Pago Pago." He handed Conway some forms to sign and called in a notary public to witness the signatures. Jane Zolinski took her twenty dollars and returned to her cage.

Tillis emptied Conway's briefcase and began stacking money inside, whistling softly to himself, shuffling an occasional stack, straightening it, shaking his head. "I wish I wasn't so damned honest," he muttered. "Eeww, Jesus, what I could do with just ten grand." He looked over at Conway. "Even with ten grand, Conway, you can keep a woman happy. I'm telling you, with this I could hold on to wife number four."

Two hours later, after placing the money in safekeeping, Conway drove over to the Markhams with Viki's letter. The housekeeper let him in, and a moment later Markham came out of the back wearing madras shorts and a pale yellow shirt that matched the color of his hair.

"Conway. I just called your office a while ago to let you know Viki got in late last night. They didn't know when you'd be in. I've told her you'd like to speak to her."

They walked out onto the porch. The fragrance of roses floated in the heat. "How's she doing?"

"Surprisingly well. That *is* why you're here, isn't it? Can I get you something? A drink? Sandwich?"

"No, thanks." He sat down. Brought out the envelope. Markham frowned. Conway wanted to begin gently, but there didn't seem to be any way of doing that without lying, so he jumped in. "This envelope and a hundred and seventy-five thousand dollars in cash were found in a safety deposit box in Key West, Mr. Markham," and told him about the key he'd found in Denise's office.

"A hundred and—" he whispered, getting up with obvious effort, running a hand over his face, his blue eyes watering. The conundrum of wife number two was indeed, Conway thought, to be the scourge of Don Markham's life. "What else," he said quietly, settling his hands into his pockets, turning his back to Conway, "am I going to find out, Conway? Is there anything else I should know? Anything else you found in her office?"

He hesitated, then told him about the drug. "There was a drug-related death Saturday morning. A woman named Olivia Blanchard. If our sample of that drug matches what was in your wife's office, then it's safe to assume the stuff's hit the streets."

Markham turned around. The light was very bright against the side of his face, stripping it of symmetry, delineating the crow's-feet at the corners of his eyes. "Meaning that's where the money came from?"

"Possibly."

"Denise as a drug dealer?" He shook his head. "No, I think you're wrong, Conway. I can't see her doing that. Denise was a lot of things, but drug dealer wasn't among them."

"Drug supplier, Mr. Markham."

"Please. Just call me Don. My God, you know as much about me as my closest friends, so please. Don."

"Maybe the man who killed her was fronting the drug, maybe that's what her death was all about. Could be that she wanted out," he said.

Markham sat down, looking old and beaten. "No wonder she didn't want the house," he said. "Or anything else." He fingered the envelope. "You read it?"

"It's your daughter's. She should read it first."

"What should I read?" asked Viki Markham from the doorway.

"Hi," said Conway.

"You must be Detective Conway," she said, approaching without a trace of shyness, offering her hand. He stood. Her little hand got lost in his, then she sat in the empty chair between him and Markham. Her dark hair was pulled back into a pony-tail, setting off her disturbing dark eyes, high cheekbones, full, somewhat petulant mouth. She tucked a leg under her and the other hung loose and swung in a low arc, her toes almost touching the tiles. She glanced at Markham. "Is this for me, Daddy?" she said, tapping the envelope with a finger.

"Button," he said, leaning forward, "Mr. Conway found this with—well, he found this. It's addressed to you. It's from your mother. I want you to read it very carefully and then let Detective Conway read it, all right?"

She didn't take her finger away from the envelope, but neither did she pick it up. The ten-year-old eyes scrutinized him as her lower lip quivered. "My mom's not dead, you know. Nothing dies. It just becomes something else."

Markham's gaze met Conway's. "Like I told you, Denise had an interest in the occult and astrology and reincarnation, and I'm afraid some of it's rubbed off on Viki."

"Daddy, it's true. Mommy said energy doesn't die. She said Einstein proved that."

"Button, go ahead and read the letter and then let Mr. Conway have it. There might be something in there which will help him find whoever killed her."

She curled a finger around the end of her ponytail, looking at her name printed neatly on the envelope, then picked it up, opened it. No one spoke. Papers rustled and a breeze blew some dead leaves across the top of the screen over the pool. Viki read slowly, her mouth sometimes moving. Several times she rubbed her eyes, to keep back tears. When she finished, she dropped the pages on the table. "Mommy's not really dead," she insisted.

"May Mr. Conway read it now, button?" Markham asked.

Conway saw the conflict in the girl's face: the need to cling to the belief that her mother wasn't really dead, not six-foot-under, dust-to-dust-type dead, and the other need to retain something private if she were. She finally lowered her eyes to her hands, which were curled in her lap, and nodded.

Conway reached for the letter.

5/5/85

Dear Button,

If you are reading this, then it means something has happened to me and there are several things you should know.

First, I love you, honey. You have always been that one untarnished spot in my life, that part of me free, I believe, even from original sin. You are everything I am not and, God willing, will remain that way.

There is enough money with this letter so that you will never, as long as you live, have to depend on a man for survival, button. Daddy Markham will know how to invest it for you. You must take care of and love him with all your heart, honey. He's a very good man and loves you so much and has been a much better father to you than I have been a mother.

Even as I write this, the enormity of what you need to know almost overwhelms me. You so often asked me about your real daddy. I met him when I was 17. My own parents were dead, I was alone, terrified, very much in need of someone. I had no money, because my father was a gambler and had blown most of it in the stock market. Your daddy was older than I and very kind to me. He put me through undergraduate school and in his way, I think he loved me and I know he loved you. But we outgrew each other over the years. By the time I met Daddy Markham, your father and I had been separated for a long time and were in the process of getting a divorce.

About my research. I know you've often wondered exactly what I was doing all those nights I didn't come home, button. My work has represented 16 years of my life and I'm close now, Viki, so very close. I hope you never suffer from compulsions and obsessions, honey, because once one of them takes root, it becomes the only truth, the only thing which matters. I've had to be secretive about my work and I'm not too proud of some of the things I've done to finance this research. I may have hurt a number of people, but that couldn't be helped.

As for the nature of the research itself, think back. Remember the day you didn't want to go to school and I told you that if you could do what I was about to, you wouldn't have to go? Remember how I turned blue without holding my breath? Or how I could sometimes make my heartbeat sound like there were three hearts inside me instead of one? Or those experiments we used to do with one of us in the living room and the other in the bedroom? Well, that's what my research concerns. I've developed something which helps strengthen whatever natural psychic ability a person has. It's still in very rough form, there are yet serious side effects which must be eliminated, but think of it, button! Think how differently we would perceive our world and ourselves.

I haven't been well for some time and I know you've suspected it. Remember the story of Dr. Jekyll and Mr. Hyde? That's how I get. I don't change on the outside, I still look the same, but inside everything rattles loose and I go out of control, like Mr. Hyde did, only I don't kill people. Like a baker, I've sampled what I've cooked up in the lab all these years and it's damaged my health and I don't think I have much longer to live, which is why I'm writing this.

My research notebook is well hidden. This was necessary because there are certain people who would abuse my work—as I have admittedly done—and for the time being, it's best that it remain undiscovered. You'll find it in time, button, just as this letter found its way to you. You must think of it as a kind of treasure hunt, O.K.? When you find it, there will be other instructions with it. This, too, was necessary, since I obviously don't know under what conditions this letter has come to you.

Whatever else you hear of me, Viki, know that I love you, that nothing truly ever dies, that hobbits and aardvarks and daddies need kisses, that I want you to grow up tall and sweet and delicious.

Think of the rhyme you memorized, button, that's your clue.

Mommy

"What experiments was your mother talking about, Viki?" Conway asked.

She curled a strand of hair around her finger again. "We would sit in different rooms. I'd write down about ten things and then concentrate and see if Mommy could guess what they were. Then we would switch it around. It worked best, though, when I was the sender and she was the receiver."

"Did she guess right pretty often?"

"She never missed one, unless we'd been doing it for a while and then she'd get tired and couldn't get too many."

"Do you remember ever seeing your mother with a notebook? Her research notebook?" Viki shook her head. "Do you know what she meant by a treasure hunt and the rhyme you memorized?"

Markham looked up. He was folding the letter. There was a terrible, naked sadness in his face. "Easter," he said. "That's what we did one Easter. Instead of hiding Easter eggs in the yard, we hid clues. When Viki had figured out the clues, she found her rabbit, in a cage in the backyard."

"He sure was pretty," the girl said, sticking two fingers up behind her head, wiggling them. "These two big, white, furry ears, a funny pink nose, and red eyes, Mr. Conway. We named him Aardvark. Last Thanksgiving, we went away and my friend Mary Ellen kept him and he died. My mom said he died because he needed more hugs and kisses than he got from Mary Ellen."

"Denise had stories for everything," Markham explained. "She loved games. She wrote all the clues for the treasure hunt."

"The last one," said Viki, sitting forward, her dark eyes less sad now, "I remember the last one.

"First go to the garden where roses bloom,
Then nine strides in shadow to Hobbit's dune.
The prize you'll find in six steps to the sun,
Is yours for the keeping, since you have won."

"Hobbit?" Conway asked.

"Our dog," Viki said. "He has this grassy mound outside in the garden, under the old mango tree, which Mom called his dune. C'mon, I'll show you." Conway and Markham followed the girl into the utility room and looked out the window. The garden was a private world, Conway thought, with splashes of color that were roses and passion flowers, daisies and sunflowers. The mango tree with Hobbit's dune beneath made a perfect umbrella of shadow, its branches so tangled and thick that the sun barely penetrated. Just beyond it was a second mango tree with Viki's little house in it. Here, branches had been cut back so that the treehouse caught the full glare of the sun.

"Hobbit's not there now," Viki explained, "because he's at the vet. He's pretty old."

"What was your mom like when she was Mr. Hyde, Viki?" Conway asked.

"Real bitchy."

"Viki," Markham admonished in a paternal tone.

"Well, she was, Daddy, you used to say so, too. She yelled a lot. She was terrible. She and Perla—that's our housekeeper—had awful fights, Mr. Conway. Perla cried a few times." She looked down at her hands and softly added, "So did I."

Conway and Markham exchanged a glance over the girl's head. "May I take your letter with me, Viki? I'll have a copy made and return the original to you."

"You promise?"

Conway crossed his heart and raised two fingers. "Promise."

The girl giggled. "It's the other hand, Mr. Conway."

"Oh," he said quickly, and switched hands as he repeated the pledge. He brought out his card and gave it to her. "You be sure and call if you find or remember anything, all right?"

She nodded, then looked up at Markham. "I'm going outside. Mary Ellen's coming over, okay?" Then, as if remembering her

114

mother's words, she slipped her arms around his neck and kissed him on the cheek.

When Viki had left, the two men went back into the kitchen. Markham explained that Mr. Hyde used to do a lot more than yell. "Once after an argument, I left the house in a huff, and when I got back Denise had smashed all the mirrors in the bedroom and was sitting at the edge of the pool, her legs in the water. She was humming quietly to herself. I can tell you, it frightened me. But it terrified Viki. I found her hiding in her treehouse. I drove her over to my mother's for the night and it took weeks for her to come near Denise again."

"Did Denise explain?"

"When I got back from my mother's, she was still sitting by the pool. I told her as gently as I could that I thought she needed professional help and assured her I would support her in any way I could. She just sat there humming, twirling her foot around in the water." Markham's eyes clouded. The old pain returned to his face; it was obviously an effort for him to speak. "I—I grabbed her under the arms and pulled her to her feet and started shaking her. She was limp and unresponsive, and then she began clawing at her own face and she let out . . . the most horrible sound. God, Conway, it . . . it was an animal sound . . . almost primitive or something . . . a cry of such profound pain. . . ." He paused, rubbed his hands. "I picked her up and carried her into the bedroom. I gave her a couple of Valiums and she wouldn't let me leave. She kept muttering that she needed help. . . ." His voice dropped away in a whisper.

"But she didn't seek help."

"No. A couple hours later, when she woke up, she didn't even seem to remember what had happened."

"Was that the only time?"

"No. It happened five or six times between December and . . . and April, when I left on the tour. But it never happened again when Viki was around. But still, I was reluctant to leave her here during those two months. I don't think Denny would've laid a hand on her—she would've destroyed herself before she'd ever done anything like that. But just the same, I made Viki promise that if Denise ever went crazy like that while I was gone, she would go over to Mary Ellen's and call my mother from there."

They sat quietly for a few moments. "Did you ever see any manifestation of psychic ability in your wife?"

"I'm not even sure I believe in it. Oh, maybe little things, you know, like who's on the phone before you pick it up, hunches, but nothing at all like she described in that letter. Nothing like that."

Conway asked Markham about the astrologer he'd mentioned in an earlier conversation. "Was she here in Miami?"

"No, a place north of Orlando called Cassadaga. It's a weird little place. I'd never heard of it. But supposedly it was established nearly a century ago as a community for spiritualists—you know, psychics, mediums, astrologers, whatever. We were coming back from somewhere and Denny wanted to stop."

"You remember the astrologer's name?" Conway asked.

Markham thought about it. "That was six years ago."

"It could be important."

He rubbed his chin. "It was a woman. Her first name was odd, Figaro, something like that. No. Fedora, that was it. Fedora something." He shook his head. "This thing just keeps getting . . . Hell, I don't even feel like I knew the woman I was married to for six years."

He felt a wave of pity for Markham. More than anything else, the man impressed him as simply wanting to play a good game of golf, raise his daughter, and be happy. "I'd better get going. I'll be in touch, Don. Thanks again."

On his way out to the car, Conway thought about the little rhyme. Was it possible Denise had buried the notebook in the yard, near Hobbit's dune?

He saw Viki Markham and her friend sitting on the porch of the treehouse, having a tea party. Their laughter carried through the trees, into the scent of roses, out into the quiet street. It was innocent, he thought, that laughter. It was youth. It flattened out against his heart with urgent flutters.

Conway stopped at the lab on his way back to town. The first thing Karen Pauling said when he came in the door was, "You won't be surprised, John."

"Blanchard's stuff was the same."

"Sure was, whatever that means."

"Still no word from Tallahassee?"

"I called up there this morning," she replied, spinning around on her stool, pushing her glasses back into her hair, "and Harry Thompkins told me none too politely that he'd be in touch when there was any news. Don't call us, we'll call you, Karen, he says. This probably won't surprise you, either, but Dr. Henry told Pivot that the autopsy on the Blanchard woman showed a number of unusual things." She paused. Conway sucked in his breath. "She had a high liver enzyme count, enlarged lymph glands, and an acute respiratory infection. He wants to call in a pathologist—other than Pivot—because he found some things normally associated with AIDS.''

''What?'' exclaimed Conway.

''I'm not a physician or an epidemiologist, John, so I can't tell you much about it. Henry said he would mail you his written report.''

''I thought AIDS was associated primarily with gays and certain ethnic groups.''

''As far as we know, it's also transmitted sexually. I'm just saying this drug seems to cause similar symptoms, John, and we don't know why.'' She nudged back a strand of hair, then began counting off on her fingers. ''Enlarged lymph glands, a type of pneumonia called''—she opened a drawer and brought out a small notepad, which she flipped through—''pneumocystis carini. Dr. Henry intends to ask Blanchard if Olivia had suffered severe and sudden weight loss recently, as well as chills, fever, and night sweats.'' She paused, flipped through the notepad for several pages, pushed the glasses back on her nose once again. ''Henry says there's a wasting syndrome called lymphadenopathy, which includes all those symptoms and eventually breaks down the immune system. It's considered to be a possible early stage of AIDS.'' She shut the notepad and slipped it back in the drawer. Conway stood there saying nothing, feeling that he had stumbled into a nightmare.

''Now what?'' he said quietly.

''Well, in Tallahassee, they're feeding the drug to mice. Ake spoke to Captain Truro and he's going to exert pressure on Tallahassee to get this thing through.''

''And next we'll have bureaucrats down here demanding answers and just getting in the way.'' He ran a hand through his hair. ''Anything from the medical center about what the enzyme count means?''

''Nope,'' she replied, ''although Henry said it could be a symptom of viral liver disease, hepatitis B, which is transmitted by blood, semen, or saliva.'' She shook her head and smiled a little. ''Face it, John, not even the experts know exactly what they are dealing with here. Your lady Denise might as well have created a new species.''

''Yeah,'' muttered Conway, ''that's what worries me.''

12

1.

THERE WAS A reason he chose this particular florist, he thought, eyeing the sign over the shop door. But he couldn't remember what it was. Up ahead, the yellow school buses were chugging to a halt, their great hulking bodies sighing and fussing in the heat. Kids were flooding out of the buildings, and the road was choked with carpools and mothers in station wagons. The summer crowd, the flunkies, he thought, then remembered why he'd chosen this shop. This was where he'd find someone to do an errand for him.

A black kid, maybe eleven or twelve years old, was walking by himself, clutching his books in one arm, his legs periodically flicking out into break dance steps. "Son," he called out as the boy approached.

The kid looked up, squinted, switched his books to his other arm. "You talkin' to me, mister?"

"Yeah, c'mere a second."

The boy hesitated, looked around, picked up a large rock, and carried it over to the car. "What, mister?"

"What the hell's the rock for?"

"Ain't takin' no chances, mister, you know how it is."

Yeah, kid, I know how it is. "Want to earn forty bucks?"

"I ain't givin' no blow job, mister. Or doin' nuthin' illegal."

Idiot. He wiped an arm across his forehead, wishing the blasted heat and humidity would let up. "I'm going to give you forty bucks to walk into that florist shop across the street and order some flowers, roses. I'll give you ten now and thirty after. You interested?"

The kid winked an eye shut. "You also givin' me money to pay for the flowers?"

"Yeah. Now you can split with the flower money and what I'm paying you up front. But if you do it right, and don't rip me off, you'll walk away from here with forty bucks."

The kid lifted up on his toes, looked down toward the myriad buses at the end of the street, scratched his head, nodded.

"Okay." He dropped the rock, set his books on the hood of the car. The man handed him a piece of paper.

"Here's what the message should say, the person's name and address, your ten, and the money for the flowers. Buy however many you can get for a twenty."

"How do I know you're going to be here when I get back, mister, huh? Maybe you gonna split, maybe you gonna get the job done for less, huh?"

Smart-ass nigger. "Want to shake?"

The boy scrutinized him and shook his head. "No, I believe ya. Be back in a flash, Jack."

The man watched the boy strut off across the street, his legs moving in rhythm to some private tune in his head. He rested his head against the seat, closed his eyes, grateful for the momentary reprieve. He fanned himself with the newspaper, tried to imagine Laura receiving the roses. Had she found all the messages he'd left scattered around the house? Did she like the way he'd arranged her closets and drawers? He remembered the scent of those drawers, the touch of her negligees, bras, underwear, the silk and cotton, the colors, all the marvelous colors. *Laura, Laura, just wait. Before I kill you, we'll play games, such wonderful games.*

The inner voice rumbled at the back of his skull. He pressed his hands over his ears. "No, no, no," he muttered. "I don't want to hear anything you have to say."

But the voice ignored him. *Laura hasn't done anything to you. All you want is her terror, but it could be anyone's terror, couldn't it.*

He wouldn't listen. He flipped open the newspaper and began to read. But after a moment, the words blurred and he rubbed his eyes and looked up, waiting for the boy to reappear. He saw him still standing at the counter inside the shop and dropped his head against the seat once more.

Take a look at what you're doing, the voice whispered, and the man's head jerked up. He squinted against the glare of the sunlight on the hood of the car. His head began to throb as he fought the voice, tried to push it back down deep inside him. But now words began to form on the screen in his mind, words from something he'd read a few days ago: psychosis—mental derangement characterized by defective or lost contact with reality; a condition which—

He rubbed his fists into his eyes to efface the words. They blurred and re-formed again as shapes, images, bits of floating light. He heard Denise saying, "There seem to be some side effects of the drug," and distinctly recalled how her face was the color of marble when she said this. He even remembered the persistent cough she had and how her nose was always running and how when he touched her sometimes, her skin felt warm and dry, as if she had a low-grade fever.

Panicked, he groped for the glove compartment, grabbed the packet of Kleenex inside and a small bottle of Vitamin C. He blew his nose, popped four vitamins in his mouth, told himself the C would get rid of his cold and this fatigue that seemed to weigh him down from breakfast to dinner. But as if to convince him otherwise, the pain nipped him in the side and he winced.

A doctor, perhaps he should see a doctor, he thought. But he hated doctors, hated needles. He—

His eyes darted toward the flower shop. *C'mon, nigger, you ain't pickin' cotton. I don't have all day.*

He shook another vitamin out of the bottle, then returned it to the glove compartment. His head dropped back against the seat once more and he closed his eyes, waiting for the voice. Joan of Arc heard voices. Many great men and women have heard voices. He smiled.

"Mister."

His head snapped forward. Had he dozed? "Did you do it?"

"Yup."

"You got a receipt?"

"You didn't say nuthin' 'bout no receipt, mister."

"How do I know— Oh, forget it." He reached into his wallet.

"You think I stand in there all this time if I don't do what you ask? Shit, man, that lady was gettin' real suspicious, me bein' a black boy and all and waggin' twenty fat ones in her face."

"Okay, okay." He handed the kid the money.

The boy turned the bills over in his hand, then grinned. "Any time you want to buy more flowers, mister, I is at your service."

The man sat there a minute, staring after the kid, thinking of how Laura would look when she saw the roses, then read the note. He reached into his pocket for a handkerchief and his hand closed around one of Denise's earrings. Cool, smooth, and forever, he thought, removing it from his pocket. He held it in his palm, then turned it between his fingers. It was like a tiny golden sun. Suddenly, he felt like crying.

2.

Laura turned her purse upside down on her desk and picked the four notes out of the rubble of pens and lipstick and matches.

She lined them up, so they read almost like a letter, but with part of the body missing and no signature. Here in the daylight, at school, they almost made her laugh. They seemed so harmless. She could almost believe they had nothing to do with her life, that they were connected to some other woman and the concern she felt was like what she might feel for a friend.

Almost, she thought.

They were typewritten on what she guessed was a standard IBM Selectric:

HELLO LAURA,
  I'VE BEEN WHERE YOU ARE. I WATCH YOU NOW
   & FOREVER. BEAT YOU HERE, TOO.

Nothing obscene, she mused. It was as if he wanted to trick her with the cuteness. *See? I'm just playing a harmless game, silly. Nothing to be afraid of. Don't take me so seriously.* By hiding the notes in innocuous places that she didn't go to daily (the linen closet, under the kitchen sink, clothes hamper, the desk), he'd known she wouldn't be able to prepare herself whenever she reached in somewhere. Nor could she anticipate his next move, because he struck differently each time. The phone call, a note on the windshield, closet and drawers, and now these messages, she thought. It was a terror campaign and he was prolonging it, so that no matter where she was or what she was doing, every movement was accompanied by a ritual of circumspection.

Goddamned stinking coward, she thought angrily. He was coiled like a viper in the shadows of her life, but so far back in the dark that she couldn't see him. He was slowly narrowing the distance between them, but feinting first one way and then another, like a boxer, to throw her off the track. Then, when she least expected it, when he had the element of surprise in his favor, he would move in. *And then what?* Besides terrorizing her, what were his intentions? Was it just a sick little game, some perv getting his chuckles? Or were his designs on her larger?

Larger, she thought; she could feel it in her bones like a change in the weather. If his intention was control over her life, then he was winning. She still caught her breath whenever the phone rang, even though her number was now unlisted. The locks in the house had been changed and there was no longer a spare key outside. She couldn't approach her car without first looking at the windshield, and she couldn't walk into a room without thinking of rainbows. He had effected small but definite changes in her life and in her relationship with Ian.

Since the break-in, he'd been acting as if this were something *she* had caused, that she was somehow at fault. He hadn't said it, of course, but he didn't have to. The tone of his voice when he'd found her in the bedroom, the look on his face when she'd shown him the first two notes—these things were symptomatic. It was obvious he believed she'd made up the story about the intruder, that she'd destroyed her own room, written the notes, that she was, in fact, becoming unglued.

There was something else, too, something she'd avoided thinking about that now pressed urgently against her. Yesterday, she and Ian had driven over to his apartment so he could pick up more clothes. While there, he'd showered and she'd finished packing the clothes he'd laid out on the bed. She had picked up the slacks to fold them and his wallet, some loose change, and two credit card receipts had tumbled out. One was for a car rental at Fort Lauderdale Airport on June tenth, the day he'd supposedly called her from De Land. The other covered two nights (the tenth and eleventh) at a motel in Coconut Grove.

At first, she'd told herself there was probably some perfectly rational explanation that had nothing to do with another woman. Business, maybe something he couldn't discuss. She'd even considered the possibility that he'd had a last minute change in plans that had been so unimportant he'd forgotten to mention it. She'd told herself she was being unreasonably paranoid, that she was just on edge. But as the day had progressed, it had become easier to imagine Ian with another woman, the two of them sitting as close as Siamese twins on the flight from Tampa to Lauderdale; coupling with paroxysms of excessive emotion in their cozy motel room in the Grove; elegiac about parting and being parted. Of course he would have told this woman he was married. *She* had fallen for it, so why wouldn't some other unsuspecting woman?

Perhaps he was even trying to decide between her and this other woman, weighing them against each other like cuts of meat. This practice, after all, wasn't foreign to him. Hadn't she come into his life on the skids of another affair?

By this morning, she'd concluded he probably meant to tell her the news over dinner. Another Last Supper, like that night in the Keys. But because of the break-in, the notes, her "question-able" mental attitude, he'd decided to wait for a while. He would endure this out of some odd and distorted sense of respon-sibility to her. Ian's final act of martyrdom, she'd thought bitterly.

Now, this afternoon, she felt more detached from it all, found that she could observe it in an almost clinical manner. She'd decided Ian was simply one of those people who needed the eternal quixotry of new affairs to feel alive, virile. It was a pattern. Once he'd broken the news to Laura (if, indeed, the other woman had won and he'd decided to end things with her), then he would go to his new woman, confess that he'd lied about being married, and she, naturally, would forgive him. Six months or a year from now, Ian would dump her, too, and the pattern would repeat itself. Thirty years in the future, a wrinkled, gray-haired Ian would cut a ludicrous and pathetic figure, still trying to play the debonair ladies' man, suffering the pangs of separation from the beloved.

So she'd pieced it all together. How come it still stung?

Another curious thing was the literature she'd found. Last night while he was asleep, she'd shut herself in the den with his briefcase. She'd wanted to confirm her suspicions, to be done with the matter once and for all. So she'd gone through his papers, looking for an address book, letters, more receipts, anything. Instead, she'd discovered several scientific journals written in a language so technical it might as well have been foreign; three paperbacks on physics, one written for the layman and the others for scientists; a book that covered the research history on psychic phenomena; and a typewritten paper on something called Bell's theorem.

She'd removed the paper, copied it this morning at school, and would return the original to Ian's briefcase this afternoon when she got home. It had been a risk, but only a small one, since he hadn't taken the briefcase with him when he'd left the house and she would be home before he arrived. Tonight she intended to sit down with the paper and wade through it. She hadn't been aware that psychic phenomena interested him and suspected this other woman, whoever she was, might be the cause of it. She wondered if he was preparing for his expected leap into another life by paving a bridge of commonalities. She'd certainly never seen a surge of curiosity on his part about her particular interests. He read very little; in fact, she couldn't recall having ever seen him so much as pick up a novel.

What, exactly, did she and Ian have in common, anyway? What did they talk about? It panicked her for a moment that she couldn't remember.

"Earth to Laura," said Rita, coming into the office and plopping herself down in the nearest chair. "I'm ready to resign, aren't you? Let's resign together and make some sort of statement out of it, Laura. Like 'Down with the Duncans of the world' or 'Return the schools to the people.' I always feel like this during the summer quarter when the nitwits register.''

Despite her mood, Laura laughed. "Speaking of Duncan, he signed up for my American lit course. An elective. He's a phys ed major and already flunked my contemporary lit last quarter and here he is again. The kid gives me the creeps.''

"Duncan? The creeps? Oh, c'mon.'' Rita laughed. "I admit he's a pain in the ass, but you must be on edge or something if you really think he's creepy.'' She lit a cigarette, leaned forward to drop the match in the ashtray on Laura's desk. She saw the notes. "What're those?''

"My friend left some calling cards.'' She pushed them toward Rita. "Ian thinks I have some screws loose, you know, that I wrote these to myself, fabricated the story about the break-in and everything else.''

Rita gave her a Look. She'd been giving Laura Looks ever since they were kids. A Look usually consisted of the right corner of Rita's mouth jutting down while an eye shot quizzically upward. "That's unfair, Laura. If anything, he's solicitous. Or he was when I saw you two together on Friday.''

She told Rita about the receipts she'd found and the reading material. "The only reason he'd lie, Rita, is another woman. And don't tell me I'm jumping to conclusions.''

"I wasn't going to say anything.'' She sat there chipping the map of Spain into her nail polish. "Infidelity abounds.'' Bits of polish stuck to her skirt. Laura knew this Look, too. It was the "I've-got-something-to-tell-you" Look, the one that dated back to adolescent slumber parties when you confessed how far you'd gone with your boyfriend. The look was prepill, preliberated sexuality and dated back to the days of heavy petting and panting, but *no further*.

"Okay, let's have it,'' Laura said.

Rita raised her eyes. "I slept with Conway.''

"*Oh?*''

"*Oh?*'' Rita laughed. "That's all you've got to say?''

"Should I congratulate you or cry?'' She smiled; the question was like a password that got you into a private club.

"He's a very nice man,'' Rita went on, with perhaps a trace of both shyness and pride.

Which meant, naturally, that Conway was more than just a very nice man and that Rita knew this and Conway probably knew it, but that no one, particularly Rita, wanted to think about it much beyond that. Not right now.

"Hank and I both wanted this separation," Rita said when Laura didn't make any comment. "And I asked myself why I should be celibate when I know Hank isn't."

"How do you know he isn't?"

Rita made a face. "You always know."

"What about Hank?"

Rita shrugged. "He was out of town this weekend, but we'll still see each other, I imagine. Besides, most of my stuff is still at the house." She looked down at her hands, which were in her lap. "I don't know," she said softly. "A marriage begins with such high expectations, such wonderful hopes, and then somewhere along the way things begin to go wrong and . . ." Her voice trailed off and she stabbed out her cigarette.

Laura changed the subject. "You know anything about physics or psychic phenomena?"

"I'm a science flunky and my knowledge of psychic stuff goes no further than hunches and good ole intuition."

"Ever heard of Bell's theorem?"

"Sorry, kiddo." Rita shook her head.

"Maybe this other woman is a parapsychologist or something."

"*If* there's even another woman involved, Laura."

"Laura Perkins?" asked a pimply-faced kid from the doorway. He was holding a bouquet of roses.

"Yes, I'm Laura."

"Would you please sign for these, ma'am?"

"They're for *me*?"

"Yes, ma'am." He set the white vase on her desk and handed her the receipt.

"See? See how considerate Ian is?" Rita admonished her.

Laura signed the receipt and tipped the kid. Rita handed her the card. "They're beautiful," Laura remarked, admiring the fragrance, softening toward Ian a little. She felt the stirring of shame and was already wondering how she could make it up to him.

"It's romantic." Rita sighed, cupping her hand at the side of the bouquet as she leaned close to smell them.

Laura opened the card. The words blurred. She trembled, dropped the card, stood with her hands flat against the desk, the incubus of the man tight inside her skull, pushing her head down. The dryness inside her mouth was like hot, sticky straw filling her throat. Ugly sounds scraped and clawed at her tongue until it tasted metallic. It was a mistake, some terrible mistake. "Denny loved roses and I know you will, too. xxx"

Terrify, unnerve, attack, kill: the lurid passions of his intentions were clear and it had to be a mistake because she had never known Denise and she hated roses and he was a filthy, stinking coward.

Her eyes flew from the card to the roses—such a deep, wine red, so exquisitely lovely, and so filled with thorns. She slammed her arm against the beautiful white vase and shouted, "That bastard!" as the bouquet shot across the room. The vase shattered. The roses leaped out every which way and finally looked like bloody footprints in between the leaves, which had broken off and were now scattered across the floor.

Rita and Laura reached for the phone at the same time. The card lay on the desk between them. They looked at each other. Rita's eyes had turned to smoke. "The florist shop?" she asked.

"Yes."

"And then Conway."

"Yes, yes, then Conway."

Rita took her hand away.

The woman at the florist shop told her there was no way to check on who had purchased the bouquet. But Laura pressed the woman, gave her name, told her it was important, did everything but plead with her. The woman recognized her name and remembered that a black boy had paid for the flowers. Laura saw the Man, this faceless, nameless shit coward, paying the kid to do his dirty work. *Hey, little boy, wanna make a few bucks? Sure, little boy, it's real easy. . . .* Then she saw the flowers being transported from the refrigerator to the florist's hands to the vase to the truck to the delivery boy and, finally, to her office. Presto, bingo, change-o. Progressive and orderly, she thought. Terrify, unnerve: was he just beginning or was he nearing the end?

She was dimly aware of Rita's voice as she spoke to Conway and thought of the phone call the night of the storm. His voice had been disguised. Did that mean it was someone she knew? *But who?* Whom did she know that Denise had also known?

Turnbalt.

(Impossible.)

"He'll be here in half an hour," Rita said, hanging up.

Laura rubbed her eyes, hugged her arms at her waist. "Lancelot, Conway's turning into Lancelot, isn't he." Christ, she thought. Helplessness was the worst of it.

13

1.

FIVE MINUTES AFTER Rita's call, Conway was coming out of the building and saw Jen pulling up to the curb in her black Firebird with the tinted windows. The Jenmobile. Black like Darth Vader, he thought. She saw him, got out of her car, slammed the door behind her. Conway wasn't feeling much like Lancelot. He felt—and without due cause, he decided—like Judas.

She didn't walk. She marched, her arms swinging rhythmically at her sides, her legs lifting high, her mouth settled in a grim, determined line.

"You forgot to put money in the meter, Jen," he said, hoping the light approach would cool her mood.

"Fuck the meter," she snapped. "I'm here to return the keys." She held them up, rattled them. "All my stuff's out, John. I just wanted to deliver the keys in person, so I could tell you to have a terrific life, you shithead."

He extended his hand for the keys. "Grow up, Jenny Garfield. You've been sleeping with other guys as long as we've lived together."

"Grow up, Jenny Garfield," she mimicked.

He started away from her. No point in belaboring the issue. But then her temper broke loose like a foul wind. It was animal-like, vicious, wild. "You rotten sonuvabitch!" she shouted. "Fucking a married woman!"

The words echoed in the hot afternoon, and in his mind he saw them stopping traffic, the M, the A, the double Rs strung across the road like a chain link fence, then the I, the E, the D bringing faces to the windows. As he spun 'round, sunlight glinted off the chrome of a car, turning everything blurred and white, and she stood there in the harsh light, her face no longer young, just bitter and hateful. He took her roughly by the arm, led her around to the driver's side, and opened the door. "Get in, Jenny."

"Rita Lincoln," she spat. "Rita, who's married to Hank Lincoln of Barnett, Dolphin and Lincoln, isn't that it? The fancy law firm in the Grove. So now you've got yourself a little ta-ta

127

attorney and aren't you just on top of the world, sugar?'' Her gaze was an unrelenting dare. *Go ahead, John Conway. I dare you. Cross this line. Red Rover, Red Rover . . .* It wasn't the outburst that surprised him; Jenny wasn't raging because he'd slept with another woman, that was immaterial in her scheme of things. She was beside herself because the woman he'd slept with was an attorney. *That* surprised him. ''I wonder, Johnny boy,'' she went on, ''how hubby Hank would feel if he knew, huh?''

He saw red. She was flapping a cape in his face and he wanted to scrape his feet and snort and charge and hurl her bottom up into the air. Instead, he waited, said, ''I don't think your pill popping would go over well with your bosses, Jen, do you?''

''You wouldn't.'' She laughed, but her tone implied she knew that he would.

''Don't tempt me.'' He walked off, and a moment later the Firebird screeched away from the curb and shot down the street, horn blaring.

The floor squeaked in the barracks. Voices, coming from the basement where the lab was, struck the quiet. A girl laughed, said in a hushed, delighted voice, ''Tim, not *here*,'' and Conway smiled to himself, and when he looked up, Rita stood at the mouth of the stairs. She had a cigarette in one hand and the other was on her hip.

''That was fast, Conway. I'm glad you're here.''

She was lovely. She was the loveliest woman he'd ever seen, particularly since the last woman he'd laid eyes on was out of control. It must have shown on his face, too, like most things, he thought, annoyed that he'd never learned the art of disguise. Rita's cheeks flushed as if she'd read his mind. ''Stop that, Conway,'' she whispered, ''you're embarrassing me.'' Then she caught his hand, squeezed it, and they walked into Laura's office.

A vent was turned toward her desk and the air nipped at the sleeves of his shirt. Laura sat on the edge of the desk, one foot kicking out, back, the other planted firmly on the floor. He had the impression she wasn't sure whether to stay put or run. A small frown seemed permanently etched between her eyes.

He saw the flowers.

''I hope,'' said Laura, ''that you're going to tell me Denise didn't love roses.''

''The Markham yard is full of them.'' This neither confirmed nor denied anything, but it was the best he could do at the moment. She held out the florist's card and the notes, and he glanced through them as she explained what happened. The notes were pallid; it was the reference to Denise that said the guy meant business.

"Tell me if you think I'm wrong," Laura said, her voice strained, "but his strategy is evidently to terrify and unnerve, attack and kill. Right? Wrong? None of the above?"

Conway couldn't have said why, but he was suddenly sure this man had killed Denise, but not the other two women. "May I keep these notes?" Laura nodded. Conway pulled up a chair, sat down, explained about Olivia Blanchard and Key West, and his visit to the Markhams and the lab. "The drug not only seems to accrete in major organs, ultimately causing death, but apparently can trigger psychotic behavior and symptoms similar to AIDS, in that the immune system seems to become depressed. My feeling is that maybe with prolonged use, as more of the stuff accumulates in the body, the psychotic episodes worsen until the mind finally just snaps, like with Olivia."

"Surprise," Rita said softly. "Denise was even weirder than we thought. Next we'll find out the Russians are behind this because they're after Denise's formula or something, right?" She shook her head. "You still think this guy's responsible for the other two stabbings, Conway?"

"Tell me no," Laura murmured.

"We can't rule out the possibility," Conway said, "but personally, I doubt it. I don't think the guy is using the drug, either, although maybe he did in the past."

"It still doesn't explain why *me*," Laura said.

The victim's lament, he thought, and unfortunately, he didn't have an answer. Since he'd walked in here a week ago, it seemed his life had been speeded up, that the nameless thing was pursuing him, flapping its fetid wings, stirring up the smell of death, weaving illusions, garbling the message. For every answer he found, there was another question, floating in the muck and mystery that had been Denise Markham's life.

"How well do you know Turnbalt?" Conway asked Laura.

"I've known him for a long time, but not that well. I knew Marie first." She understood what Conway was getting at and shook her head. "No, you're wrong, John. Turnbalt's a lot of things, but he wouldn't kill anyone."

"Maybe not under normal conditions, but if he were under the influence of the drug . . ." He shrugged. "Well, the same might not be true, then. Would you mind if I came out to your place to look for more of these friendly notes?"

"Mind?" She laughed. "You must be kidding. I wish you'd move in. At least then I'd have police protection. Hey, would I qualify for protection?"

"I'll see what I can do," he promised, but didn't have much hope for it.

"What about the roses?" Rita asked.

A clap of thunder let loose outside, then the skies opened up. Rain was suddenly lashing the windows. "Let the roses rot. I just want to get outa here."

They walked downstairs and stood clustered in the doorway, peering into the gray, wet gloom. "You want to ride with me, Rita?" Conway asked. "I can bring you back later for your car."

Laura's eyes slid from Conway to Rita, then back outside, and Conway knew Rita had told her. It buoyed his spirits. The alliance somehow gave their relationship a validity beyond just the moment.

They ran out to the cars, and once he and Rita were inside the Porsche, the wipers making that lazy, persistent sound across the glass, he said, "I apologize for what happened Saturday, Rita."

She snapped on her seat belt. "Don't be. The lady lives there."

"Lived. She returned the keys this afternoon."

"Oh, boy, I'm really sorry if I fouled up—"

"It's been coming for a long time." He backed out and followed Laura onto the main road. At the light, he leaned over and brushed his mouth across Rita's cheek. "Did you get moved?" he asked.

"More or less. I was supposed to have a seminar tomorrow night, but it's been canceled. You free?"

"I'll make a point of it." Wind drove the rain across the road in violent gusts, and Conway finally pulled off to the side and cracked the window. The only sounds were the rain and the quiet ticking of the car's blinker. "I love you, Rita, is that crazy?" he said suddenly.

The watery blue of her eyes sought his. "I don't know," she said.

2.

The dream pressed against the flanks of Laura's sleep with an urgency like memory, opening slowly, as it always did: there, there was the quiet quarter moon lighting up the walk by the flaming hibiscus and the air growing sweeter with jasmine and the trees drooping with a melancholy heat. She heard whispered voices, like doves cooing in an eave, then a woman's laugh, soft and coy. The sound of it drifted through like summer, like smoke, and Laura wanted to push past it, into the deeper dark at the end of the walk, where her car was, push past all of it and out of the dream. But her feet took root in the cement. Her legs turned to putty. She was impotent with an irrational fear. If she moved, she would be seen. If she was seen, the night would split apart like an atom and she would be sucked away into the white and terrible truth.

She sank to her knees, pressed her hands to her eyes, doubling over, so her forehead brushed the ground. She waited for the moments to pass. She heard the woman who had laughed earlier sucking in her breath. Then the man whispered to her. Laura's own silence was a physical pain, beating her spine, whipping the inside of her skull, and she wanted to die, to sink into the ground and vanish.

The leaves rustled. She lifted her head and through the branches saw Denise sound asleep on her back and the man kneeling beside her, touching her cheek. Death swam in her eyes and she jolted out of the dream, gasping for air, thick with sweat.

Ian was on his side of the bed, sprawled on his stomach, sound asleep. Rain danced on the roof and windows. The TV was still on—snowy, buzzing like a swarm of bees.

Laura sat up. She tried to hold on to the dream long enough to see the man's face. But already it had moved away and she got out of bed, turned off the TV. She shuddered in the abrupt, absolute dark, feeling the Man's presence around her. Where else in this room, this house, had he been that she'd missed? They'd found three more notes—one in the pantry, taped to a box of GE light bulbs, a second taped to the vacuum cleaner bag, and a third curled inside a bottle of Tylenol. Seven in all. Were there more? Or was seven some magical number, perhaps a clue?

Oh, stop it.

She got back in bed. Ian turned in his sleep, reaching for her, his arm settling into the curve of her waist. The miasma of her terror and her solitude was compounded by what she believed was Ian's infidelity and that they hadn't made love since he'd left on his trip, over two weeks ago. The weekend had been riddled with tension; her desire for him, for sex, for any man, had slipped underground. When he moved against her, she thought of rainbows, saw the Man dipping his hands in her clothes, perhaps even rubbing them against his face or his groin, and after several overtures Ian had stopped coming near her. Then, Sunday, finding the receipts, she thought of this other woman when she looked at him, and once, when he had kissed her, the face of the Other Woman and the Man had melted perfectly together.

Her life was in an uproar, running amok. She stumbled into the morning pursued by dreams and fell into sleep only to find the dreams still waiting. Little by little, she knew she was coming apart at the seams.

"What time is it?" Ian murmured, moving up close to her.

"Around three," she whispered back, closing her eyes, ashamed that her desire should surface now, coming home to her like a puppy with its tail between its legs. He sensed it. His hand moved against her nightgown, sliding it up until his body was warm and familiar alongside hers. "I missed you, babe," he said softly, over and over, as he straddled her, as he drove into her with an urgency that frightened her just as the dream had. It hurt because she was dry and suddenly she didn't want him near her.

She stopped moving. She couldn't move. Her legs ached and the dream and the Man got all mixed up in her head and she began to cry. Ian held her in his arms, apologizing, thinking he'd hurt her. He kissed her head and she smelled the warm damp of his shoulder and the lingering scent of her perfume on the pillow.

She dabbed at her eyes with the sheet, angry at herself for crying. "Ian, how come you said you were calling me from De Land that day when you were really in Lauderdale?"

The emptiness whistled between them, dry and hot. "What're you talking about?"

She switched on the bedside light. It puddled along the edge of the bed, threw one side of his face into deep shadows. "I'm talking about credit card receipts. They fell out of your slacks. A receipt for a car rental and two nights at a motel in the Grove."

He propped his pillows against the headboard, sat back, had that incredulous expression on his face that she'd come to know so well. "You were snooping, Laura. God, I can't believe it." The chocolate eyes, once good enough to eat, turned darker, sour, accusatory.

"I wasn't," she insisted, holding the sheet up to her neck as if for protection. Her face looked ravaged. There were smudges of mascara under her red eyes and her hair was plastered to the sides of her head.

"It was business and I'm not supposed to discuss it," he

replied, no longer looking at her. She stared at his profile, stared until her eyes hurt. She wanted to believe him. But what, in the word processing business, could possibly be so secretive?

"Look, you don't have to lie. If there's someone else," she blurted, "then just have the guts to say so and—"

"*Someone else?* Laura, there hasn't been anyone else since I showed up here that day."

"Then what's so bloody difficult about the truth, Ian? You could have at least told me you couldn't discuss it."

"God," he said, throwing back the sheet, swinging his legs over the side of the bed. "Can't you trust me?" His voice was less quiet now, tinged with something like desperation. He got up, reached for his clothes. "It's almost four in the morning. I've got a meeting at eight. Maybe I should just go home and—"

She didn't hear the rest. Her terror of being alone in the creaking house, with her dreams and the dark and the Man only as far as the nearest shadow . . . No, it was worse than her desire to know the truth. "Ian, please, don't leave me alone," she whispered, hating the supplicating tone of her voice, the way she touched his shoulder with a cold, damp hand. She nearly choked on the words. She hated how she wanted to throw herself at his feet and beg him not to leave.

For an instant, she thought he was going to push her hand away. But then he slipped his arms around her. "I'm sorry, babe. I wasn't thinking. Of course I won't leave you alone."

Laura's cheek was pressed against his shoulder. She squeezed her eyes shut. *I won't ask any questions, I promise. Just don't leave me alone.*

They got back in bed. He turned off the light. They curled together like spoons, his arm at her waist, his warm breath against her back. She held on to his hand, ashamed of her fear, of the way she'd acted. After a while, she realized he'd fallen asleep and she was afraid to close her eyes and was, in the end, left alone anyway, with nothing but the infinite dark of the night and the uneven wheeze of Ian's snoring.

She finally went downstairs. She fixed herself a cup of tea, then sat down with the typewritten pages on Bell's theorem. The material was lengthy, complete with diagram and mathematical formulas. She read slowly, skipping the math, backtracking when she didn't understand something. At the end, Ian had made a page of handwritten notes, summarizing the material. As she went through them, she grew light-headed. Her stomach knotted. She felt as if she'd stumbled into a foreign country without the proper papers, uninformed about the language and the customs.

She realized she didn't know Ian at all and frantically read through his notes again and again, as if to glean a clue about who he was from between the lines:

> BELL'S THEOREM: The significance of the work, developed in 1964, seems to be that it demonstrates how some of our ideas about the world and reality are mistaken. If paired, subatomic particles that are identical in polarity fly apart and the polarity of one is altered by external stimuli, then the other particle changes direction immediately. In other words, there appears to be a faster-than-light communication between these particles, no matter how far apart they are or how long they've been separated.
>
> Physicists are divided on what this would indicate about our scientific structure of the world. But our people believe Bell's theorem could provide an explanation for certain types of psychic phenomena.
>
> Note: What sort of work are the Soviets doing related to Bell's theorem?
>
> Bell's experiments were duplicated by several universities during the 1970s, and the definitive test was conducted in 1982 by Alan Spect at the University of Paris.

Laura slipped the paper and Ian's notes into a magazine and hid them in a drawer in her den. Then she sat for a long time in the old leather chair, feet propped in the windowsill, as she stared into the rainy night. She would ask Rita, she decided finally. Rita would have answers. She had to. She always did.

14

1.

BLANCHARD'S CONDOMINIUM WAS as insipid, Conway thought, as every other high-rise in North Miami Beach, except it was newer. Tall and tacky, it formed an essential link in the concrete wall that blocked out the Atlantic. It was as if the buildings and the sea were engaged in some private, mortal battle of power and dominion.

The air where he stood tasted heavily of salt, but he couldn't see the water and noticed the sound of the waves had been reduced to some atavistic murmur of the unknown and the forgotten. It irritated him, pushed his youth farther back into the past, so that now he could barely remember when it had been any different. The coast had been pillaged for progress, and this morning he blamed Blanchard personally for the transgression.

He pried the lid off his coffee and sipped it tentatively. He and Ake had stopped at McDonald's on the way over, and the Egg McMuffin he'd wolfed down sat like a stone in the pit of his stomach. He felt hung over.

"Well, let's see what the big B has to say for himself," Ake said as he got into the car. "How's the coffee?"

"Rawtheh shiteh," Conway muttered as the first sip reached his stomach.

Blanchard's condo was on the tenth floor, and as they came out of the elevator, Ake whistled softly. Sunlight fell sharply across the deep, rich carpeting and stopped just inches from Blanchard's door. Cactuses in ceramic pots were thriving in the windows, dusty chandeliers hung from the ceilings, and at one end of the hall, furniture was arranged like a formal sitting room. Conway felt as if he'd stumbled into an expensive home that the inhabitants had suddenly evacuated. He envisioned Blanchard padding out here in the morning, wearing a robe and those stupid bedroom slippers he'd had on at the hospital, watering the plants, speaking softly to them, scolding them for one thing or another, then sitting on one of the chairs and pouring out his heart about dear, poor Livvy, victim of Denise Markham's misguided genius.

The man did, in fact, answer the door in a robe and slippers. His hair, what little of it there was, curled every which way and he squinted against the bright light. Over his shoulder, Conway saw drapes pulled across the terrace door and a spiral staircase twisting toward the high-beamed ceiling to an upstairs loft.

"Morning, Mr. Blanchard," Ake said, flashing his Pepsodent smile to show this was just a friendly visit. "Hope we didn't get you up."

Blanchard blinked, then rubbed his head and yawned and opened the door a little wider. "Haven't been sleeping well," he explained.

"May we come in?" Ake asked.

He hesitated. His soft, round eyes were like eight-balls, dull, black, reflecting nothing. He pulled the belt of his bathrobe tighter and let them in.

The room was tastefully and expensively furnished in chrome

and glass, cocoa and cream, and the pervasive mood was masculine. Blanchard opened the drapes and the thin bright blue of the Atlantic reached as far as the eye could see. A baby grand piano looked out over the sea from a corner.

"Got to have some coffee," Blanchard muttered. "You boys care for some?"

Both declined.

"Nice place," Ake remarked, sitting forward on the couch, eyeing the delicate watercolors hanging in frames on the walls. Conway got up and walked over to the piano. The keyboard gleamed proudly, like a mouth of polished teeth. He hit two notes, heard Blanchard explaining that Livvy had decorated the place and that she did, naturally, have impeccable taste. He hit two more notes, waiting for Ake to get things rolling.

"We'd like to know who sold your wife the dope, Mr. Blanchard," Ake said in exactly the same tone of voice he'd used to comment about the townhouse.

The coffee maker burped and dripped. Blanchard stared at it, as though the machine had spoken instead of Ake. "I told you before, I don't know." He sniffled. His nose turned pink, then deepened to a red like Rudolph's. Blanchard, apparently, had not yet finished going to pieces, Conway thought.

"We think you *do* know and just aren't saying," Ake continued, getting up now, going over to the counter and pulling out a stool. Conway followed. Blanchard poured himself a cup of coffee. The machine hadn't quite finished and some of the coffee dripped onto the burner. The smell quickly permeated the air. He sat down, resigned to the two men, resigned as a convict to his fate. "Please. I'm not well. The funeral's today."

"Mr. Blanchard," Conway said, "the drug you gave us is not cocaine."

"Dr. Henry told me." He reached toward a lower cabinet and brought out a bottle of Grand Marnier. He laced his coffee with it.

"Did he also tell you what the drug does?"

"Something about the liver," Blanchard replied, holding the mug with both hands as he lifted it to his mouth.

"Olivia's liver enzyme count was very high," Ake said. "Did you know the drug can trigger psychotic behavior with prolonged use? Did he tell you that, Mr. Blanchard? Or about the enlarged lymph glands? The possible breakdown of the immune system? Did he—"

"My Livvy was psychotic?" He looked miserable, Conway thought, his lip trembling, his eyes red-rimmed, puffy.

"Since you were also using it," Conway said, "I suggest you see your family doctor. You might have a time bomb inside you just as your wife did."

Splotches popped out on Blanchard's neck and cheeks. He drank deeply from the mug. "I don't know anything. I told you. I don't know where she got it from. I just know she's dead, that my Livvy is dead, and after today, she's going to be six feet under and that's all I know." His voice broke with a sob, his features squished together, and he hid his face with his hands. He put his head in his arms on the counter and made soft, pathetic sounds, half gasps, half sobs. After a while, he raised his head, pressed his stubby fists into his eyes, dabbed at his face with a corner of his bathrobe. He ripped a paper towel from the roll on the wall, blew his nose. The tip of it was now shiny, crimson. "I . . . I've been like this since . . . since Saturday. I j-just ca-can't seem to stop."

"Do you know Frank Turnbalt?" Conway asked.

Blanchard was peering into the mug. "Who doesn't?"

"Personally, I mean."

"He handled my first divorce and drafted my will. That's all."

That's enough, Conway decided.

"Know what I think, Mr. Blanchard?" Ake's voice had turned ugly, low and mean. "I think you're lying. I think you're a lousy shit. Your wife died of a drug overdose and you sit there expecting us to believe you don't know who sold her the stuff? C'mon, big B, even I could do better than that." His voice remained quiet; he was not a man who had ever had to shout to be heard. "You're just as guilty as the guy who sold the stuff, who're you trying to kid, my man?"

Blanchard's face turned pale as milk, curdled around the mouth. As he stood, he sank his hands into his bathrobe pockets. "Get out!" he shouted. "Get outa my house, I don't have to listen to this!" He grabbed onto the edge of the counter, gripping it until his knuckles were as white as his face.

"Calm down," Conway said. "Ake, why don't you wait downstairs, man."

Ake shot Blanchard one last contemptuous look, eyes pushed together in a tight, fierce frown, then rose. Blanchard let go of the counter, seemed to sway a moment, then turned in place, watching as Ake walked to the front door.

"That . . . that *nigger* isn't welcome in my house," Blanchard spat in a choked voice.

"He gets carried away sometimes. But he's just doing his job," Conway replied.

Blanchard sat loosely on the stool, like a punctured dirigible, shoulders sagging, his face falling with the weight of excess gravity, his hands moving again to the mug. "I'm going to leave you my card," Conway said. "I know you've got a lot on your mind right now, but if you think of anything, Mr. Blanchard, just give me a call, okay?" He removed a card from his wallet.

"Livvy's funeral's today," Blanchard repeated dully, then held the mug to his mouth, tipped his head back, and drank down his coffee and Grand Marnier like a child with a bottle of milk. Conway left his card on the counter, started toward the door. "Mr. Conway," said Blanchard, reaching for the cognac again, "you ever been afraid? Gut afraid? I mean, the kind of afraid where you don't want to close your eyes because you know you aren't going to like what you see when you do?"

"A few times."

"It's hell," Blanchard went on, pouring the cognac to the brim of the mug this time, not bothering with coffee. "It's hell, because you want to die, because you think that being six feet under is better than what's going on."

"Was it Frank Turnbalt who sold you the dope?" Conway asked.

Blanchard stuck his finger into the mug, licked off the cognac. "Get out," he said quietly. "Please. I just want to be alone."

"You're protecting the man responsible for Olivia's death, Blanchard."

The other man drank the cognac down, coughed, wipe his hand across his mouth. "Please. Go away. Just go away." He picked up the bottle by the neck, shuffled over to the couch with it. "Go or arrest me. But don't just stand there hassling me. Sure, give me the chair," he said in the same dull voice, gazing at Conway now from across the room. "What the hell's the difference." He drank straight from the bottle, then lay back against the cream-colored pillows and cradled the bottle in his arms.

Conway let himself out. Ake was waiting for him in the downstairs lobby. "How'd I do, mate?"

"Oscar performance. I think he'll come around. If he doesn't drink himself to death first."

"Dumb little shit protecting Turnbalt or whoever."

"Maybe he's just protecting himself," Conway replied.

2.

Upstairs, Jerome Blanchard was standing at the bedroom window, peering down ten stories to the parking lot. The ground blurred. The Atlantic blurred. His life was one big fat blur and he was scared, Jesus, he was so scared standing up here where everything should have been clear and where nothing was.

He was still holding the bottle. He rested his forehead against the glass, crying quietly, sniffling, taking an occasional nip from the bottle. His insides were burning up. He didn't want to die, he didn't want to go to jail, he just wanted his Livvy back.

He thought of her in the kitchen that morning, talking to her mother who was dead. His cries became deep, wrenching sobs. Oh, the terrible noises she had made, rolling about on the floor in convulsions, those horrible, primitive sounds gurgling in her throat as she'd begun to choke on her tongue.

Was that going to happen to him?

He had never done as much of the drug as she had, but how much was too much? What did anyone know? She was dead and the drug had made him feel oh, so damned good, good enough to forget he was fifty-five and balding and had a paunch, good enough to forget every ugly and terrible thing that had ever happened to him. And good God, once the stuff had taken hold, it had stroked and caressed the old libido until he'd known he could screw all night and into the next day and the next. It had made him feel as huge as John Wayne and as powerful as Don Juan, and even when he'd looked at himself in the mirror, he'd seen a man of twenty-five. The man he had once been, he thought, the man with a good build and a flat stomach and hair, lots of hair.

Livvy, sweet Jesus, Livvy. The drug had transformed her as well. Sometimes it seemed they'd been able to speak without words. They had only to look at each other in a certain way and suddenly he would find himself zipped up inside her bones and snuggling up inside her head and he would hear a tentative, *Jerry? Is that really you? Is this happening?* It happened, all right. And once it was over, there were no words to describe it.

Now Livvy was dead.

Blanchard stumbled away from the window and fell back onto the bed he'd shared with her for more than four years, back into the soft, plump pillows, back into the darkness of his own skull. He saw that filthy nigger's face all screwed up with contempt. *You're a lousy shit. . . .* Yes, he was. He was also a coward and he was scared and he was going to die, just like Livvy. He saw himself, his fat belly heaving into the air, falling down again, bucking like a bronco with convulsions, his tongue lolling back in his mouth until it gagged him. He saw himself turning blue as a bruise and suffocating to death.

He shouldn't have given the nigger the drug that night. But he hadn't been thinking straight then. Maybe he wasn't thinking straight now, either. Maybe he was on the verge of psychosis and in his next breath an organ would blow like a gasket. Which organ? *A major one.* Heart? Lungs? Liver? Where should he expect the pain to strike?

He tried to remember if Livvy had complained of pain. Only after she'd jogged, and then it was just a runner's cramp in the side. No big deal, yes, that was exactly what she used to say. "No big deal, Jerry, just a twist in the side."

And maybe psychosis was just a twist, too, a twist in the mind.

Blanchard turned over. The bottle tilted. Cognac dripped down the front of his robe and onto the sheets. The air smelled bitter and hot. He would sleep. When he awakened Livvy would be standing over him with her lovely, smiling face and she would place a cool hand on his head and sing in her soft, sweet voice which was youth and beauty, which was truth.

He had killed her: that, too, was truth.

"Oh, Christ," he sobbed, pressing his face into the pillow, wishing he could remember how to pray.

3.

Laura was safe here; she wasn't alone. Twenty-six pairs of eyes followed her as she moved back and forth in front of the class, lecturing on the dark nights of Fitzgerald's life that had produced *Tender Is the Night.* Like spectators at the Indy 500 or the Grand Prix who waited for the blood to spill and the guts to roll, her American lit students stuck around for the tales of love and ambition and incipient madness. It was the parts of the man's life they wanted, she thought, not its sum.

She knew this material well, could recite it by rote if necessary, but there were moments when she stumbled, paused, knew she was straining to hear something on the other side of the door. It was the maelstrom of her own fear she heard whispering along the crack under the door, pouring through the vents. *I am here, I am watching, I am waiting.* Chant, promise, it crouched in every corner of her life now and floated through her dreams with a lewd familiarity. The Man was out there somewhere. Perhaps he waited in the hall, the restroom, inside the car. He wore the face of someone she knew; she sensed it in some remote pocket of herself that could still view the events objectively. Laura, like Hank Lincoln, now feared what she couldn't see and longed for an impenetrable fortress with moats and video cameras, electric fences and a sophisticated computer.

A hand shot up in the back of the room. Duncan, poor Duncan. "Zelda and Fitzgerald," he said, uttering the names as if they were singular, "did he cause her madness?"

She wanted to shout at him, take him by the shoulders, shake him. *Madness? Who says it has anything to do with squashed ambitions and the loss of paradise? Who told you that, Duncan?* No, she thought, madness was to lie in an uncertain darkness, knowing that if you closed your eyes, the Man would get you from within and without, that he would chew his way through your life like a termite and then bloom in your head like bougainvillea. Madness was to gallop backward, mouthing your own name, listening for the echo in a mist where faces fell in on themselves and no one was who he was before. Madness just went on and on like a family curse.

Duncan stared at her with his wide blue eyes like those of a man in a trance, peering vapidly through her and beyond. *I know about madness*, the look said. *I know and I'm afraid of what I know*. The bell rang before she could reply to his question and she felt an immense relief at being free of his gaze.

"Dr. Perkins," he said, approaching her desk, "what's the answer about Fitzgerald and Zelda?"

Go away. Go away and leave me alone, Duncan. She couldn't lift her head to look at him. She was abruptly, irrationally, afraid of him. "Read the books on the list, Tom, and then decide for yourself."

He remained standing there. She dropped her notes in her briefcase, could see the blue of his jeans, the dark brown leather of his belt. She could hear the soft, uneven wheeze of his breathing and it brought goose bumps to her arms. Then he made a small sound, part sigh, part laughter, and shuffled out of the room.

Laura sank back in her chair, covered her face with her hands.

Stop! You're imagining things.

But she hadn't imagined the roses.

Or Ian's notes on Bell's theorem.

Or Ian's first tentative glance this morning across the emptiness of the bed, the glance that said, *Who is she? What have I gotten myself into?* And worse: *How do I get myself out of this?*

She could still taste the sting of sudden modesty as they'd turned their backs on each other like Adam and Eve after their fall from grace. And she hadn't imagined the separateness, as if everything were clearly labeled ''his'' and ''hers.'' She hadn't imagined that.

Tomorrow he was leaving for Orlando, he said, where two large firms were talking contracts. Just an overnight trip, he said, long enough for a presentation and signatures.

He said.

Had she imagined that?

''Laura?''

Her hands dropped from her face. Conway stood there, and she got quickly to her feet. ''Hi, John.''

''You all right?''

''Just a little tired.''

''I brought you a gun,'' he said, and handed her a leather pouch that fit into the palm of her hand. ''I can't get you police protection, Laura, because we don't have the extra men.''

She unzipped the pouch, removed the gun. It was cool and heavy against her hand, and completely foreign to her. ''Just show me how to use this, will you? Ian's going to be out of town tomorrow night.''

''It's a thirty-eight,'' he said, taking it from her, showing her how to load and unload it, clean and reassemble it. The whole thing seemed unreal to her, like something out of a movie. ''It's automatic, so once you pull the trigger, it just keeps firing. Don't ever pick it up and aim it unless you intend to use it.''

''Whose is it?''

''Mine.''

They drove to a gun store near campus that had an indoor firing range. The air smelled of metal, of gunpowder and men. There were bars and metal grills on the windows, across the cases of guns, and running the length of the door. The guy behind the counter was perched on a stool and wore heavy leather boots and a pair of six-shooters at his hips like Wyatt Earp. A Doberman was stretched at his feet, its nub of a tail twitching as it slept. They'd stumbled onto a movie set, she thought, and any minute now the director would rush out in a sweat, waving his arms and shouting, ''Cut, retake, retake!''

''Mornin','' said Wyatt. ''What'll it be?''

''We'd like a lane,'' Conway said.

Wyatt slid off his stool, brought two pairs of earmuffs out of a drawer. ''What kinda target?''

''Silhouette, four of them.''

"Type gun?"

"Thirty-eight."

"Need shells?"

"Yes."

"Ayup," he said, and laid everything out, including the bill.

Earmuffs in place, they stepped into the inner sanctum of the range. Empty shells littered the floor like peanuts. Shots coming from the other lanes were muffled as if underwater. Conway snapped a target between the jaws of a clothespin and cranked it out into the dusty abyss on a pulley. He removed the gun from the pouch with the respect of a priest for the host. He loaded it, moved the box of shells out of sight. Laura felt as if she should kneel and bless herself for communion.

Conway fired the first two shots. They hit on top of each other, right through the silhouette's neck. He passed her the gun. She held it in both hands, aimed for the heart, and fired and fired and continued to fire, thirsty for blood, anticipating the moment when the Man fell forward, riddled with holes. Conway touched her arm, pushing it gently down.

"It's empty, Laura."

He cranked in the silhouette. Two of her shots had missed the target completely. Two had hit in the leg. But one had gone dead center, right through the heart, and one was all she needed.

They went through five clips of shells, over half the box, and ravaged the four targets. When she walked out of the range, the gun was almost as familiar to her as her own skin. Wyatt, still on his stool, watching a customer at the end of the counter, looked up, asked, "So how'd the little lady do?" as if she weren't even there.

"The little lady," she said, "did just fine."

"Ayup," he said, and straddled the stool like a saddle.

Outside, Conway handed her a permit that entitled her to carry the gun with her. "Your diploma," he said.

"I appreciate this, John." She rubbed her thumb across the permit, wondering if in the end this would be the only diploma that mattered.

When Laura was back in her office, trying to plan her classes for the next week, her hand reached out now and then to feel the shape of the gun in her purse. It was reassuring, yes, but somehow tragic that she could feel safe only by possessing something so potentially deadly.

"Laura?"

His voice startled her. She hadn't heard him in the hall. "Hank, hi. What brings *you* over here?"

"I was looking for Rita and she wasn't in her office, so I thought she might be visiting you." He glanced around the room as he walked in, his hands lost in his pockets. "You've fixed it up nicely," he remarked. "Pretty view, too."

"Thanks. I can't wait until the new building's finished, though. I get tired of being in barracks. Makes me feel like I've enlisted or something."

He chuckled, sat down, got up, wandered over to the window, came back over, and sat down again. He seemed restless, troubled, as though the separation from Rita had affected him too deeply for words, Laura thought, and she felt sorry for him. "I think Rita's got a class now, Hank."

"Hmm, that's what the secretary said. She hasn't, uh, discussed any of this with you, has she?"

"You mean, about the two of you?" He nodded. She noticed the dark circles under his eyes, the deep lines that jutted from his nose to his mouth. "No, not really. You know how Rita keeps things pretty much to herself." It wasn't really a lie, she thought. Rita *had* discussed the situation, but not in great detail. Hank obviously didn't believe her. He smiled rather ruefully, ran a hand through his hair.

"I'm sorry. I wasn't trying to put you in a compromising position, Laura."

"Look, she just needs time to think things through, that's all."

"Yeah." He nodded. "Yeah, I guess we both do."

In the brief, awkward silence that followed, Laura wished she had a pot of coffee on, something she could offer him to lessen the strain between them. Hank smiled thinly again, pressed his hands against his thighs, and pushed himself to his feet. His fingers strayed to his tie, which he straightened absently, as though it were an annoyance. "Well, I'll let you get back to work. If you see Rita, tell her I stopped by, will you? That secretary over in the law building's a space cadet."

She walked him to the door, reached out and touched his arm. "I'll tell her, and take care of yourself, okay?"

"You, too," he said, and she watched as he made his way down the stairs, his shoulders hunched over as if against bad weather or pain.

15

1.

CONWAY WAS STRUCK by the silence of the village. Once a lively center of occult activity where flamboyant mediums spoke in tongues and spirits allegedly materialized and were photographed regularly, Cassadaga now slept among tall, ancient pines in the quiet pastoral hills an hour north of Disney World. The rambling wooden houses had fallen into disrepair; weeds and wildflowers had claimed many yards; and the savage June heat had practically dried up Spirit Lake. Only the hotel, a two-story Mediterranean-style structure built in the 1920s, seemed to have escaped the torpor that clung to the air like smoke.

They parked in front and went inside. The lobby had never escaped the decade in which it had been built. An old ceiling fan turned slowly overhead, rustling wilted plants in clay pots on either side of an old wicker couch. Several elderly people were sitting around, reading, talking quietly among themselves. Behind the bar was a young man on a stool, watching a small black-and-white TV. He saw them, grinned, hurried over to the desk.

"What can I do for you?"

"We're looking for an astrologer who lives here in the camp. Her name's Fedora," Conway explained.

"Did you check the plaque out front of the town center? That lists most of the mediums and such. If her name's not on the plaque, then she probably doesn't want to be bothered."

Rather than go back outside into the terrible heat and run the risk of not finding Fedora's name on the plaque, Conway showed the man his ID. "I'd appreciate any help you can give us."

He considered it a moment, then disappeared into a back room. He returned a few moments later. "She lives on Seneca Street. Her place is at the end, in a lot of trees so it's hard to see. Her name's Fedora Hopkins."

"Thanks a lot."

"Don't mention it."

They meandered past Spirit Lake, where tall old pines stood absolutely still, then down the hilly, quiet roads. The place had the feel of a ghost town, Conway thought. It was so quiet that he had the distinct impression that when the sun went down, coffins creaked open and the dead walked. Although most of the houses had signs out in front that read MEDIUM or PSYCHIC or REVEREND So and So, they saw no people.

"I think I read someplace that Cassadaga's dying," Rita said.

"Not hard to believe," Conway replied. "It's like *Night of the Living Dead* or something."

"I know. It was in the Sunday *Miami Herald*," she went on. "An article about how the old-timers here aren't letting new blood come in as psychics die off or move on because they only want spiritualists like themselves. People who talk to spirits, in other words."

"How cheery," he drolled.

The house was so far back off the main road in a cocoon of trees that at first Conway didn't see it. Grass was several inches high in the yard, a side of the front porch dipped ominously toward the ground, branches brushed the roof. Several cats roamed lazily through the brush and a cocker spaniel lay in a square of warm light on the walk. As they approached, it lifted its nose into the air, sniffed, barked halfheartedly several times, then made its way down the walk toward them, its old tail wagging as if they were old friends.

As the animal came up to Rita, she laughed, said, "Animals love me." The dog blinked its milky eyes at her, then jumped onto her knees as she crouched. Its long pink tongue slobbered up one side of her face and down the other.

The screen door opened and a plump woman with hair peppered with gray and eyes settling into a kind, wrinkled face waddled out onto the porch. She whistled for the spaniel. "What can Ah do for y'all?" she called out, shading her eyes with a hand. Over a faded blouse and slacks, she wore an apron with smiling sun faces on it. In between the faces was written Have a Nice Day. The apron was stained. Her sleeves were rolled up past her elbows, and bracelets took up several inches on either arm.

"We're looking for Fedora Hopkins," Conway said.

"That's me. You here for a reading?"

"Yes," Rita said quickly. "You were referred by a friend."

The cocker moved lazily up the stairs as Fedora snapped her fingers. "Where're y'folks from?" she asked.

"Miami," Conway said.

"Ooohh my, you've done come quite a ways, now, haven't

you. Come on in and get out of this dreadful heat. Come along, Spook," she said to the dog.

Spook, Conway mused. Wonderful.

The inside of the house wasn't much cooler than outside. They passed through a living room jammed with furniture, books, photos of children and grandchildren and family pets. The windows were open and the hot, still air was as thick as a furnace. She led them into the kitchen, chattering about how much cheaper a reading was during the summer. "Another week or so and Ah'd be gone. Fenny and Ah go north to the sister community during the summer. Cassadaga, New York, way upstate, near Rochester, where it's a whole lot cooler than it is here." She laughed and dabbed at her damp neck with a handkerchief.

Conway wondered if Fenny was another dog, maybe Spook's twin. He sat at the kitchen table, grateful he could finally breathe again. The kitchen and bedrooms, Fedora explained, were the only rooms in the house with air conditioning, and this was where she did most of her readings. "Ah don't know how civilized folks lived here before air and screens," she chattered, opening the refrigerator and bringing out a pitcher of something cold. She set three glasses on the table. "Help yourselves. Now, who'll be first?"

Conway and Rita looked at each other as Fedora took her seat at the head of the table. "I'll go," Rita said quickly. "What kind of readings do you do?"

"Gimmicks," the woman replied. "The *type* of reading is just a gimmick to focus the Power, you know?" She smiled broadly. "What matters is the result. What's your name again, hon?"

The Power? To focus the Power? This was beginning to sound more and more like stuff out of *Dune*, Conway decided. He heard Rita giving Fedora their names, then the old woman said, "Rita, yes, that's a mighty pretty name. You ever see Rita Moreno in *West Side Story*? My lord, how that woman can dance." Then she tapped her fingers against the edge of the table. " 'Bout the reading. My real love used to be the stars. But with these fancy computers that can spit out a chart in seconds where it used to take me a couple of hours, well, it just wasn't worth it anymore. So now Ah just set right back and close my eyes and let Spirit guide me." She sat back, hands folded on the tabletop, and closed her eyes. Conway wondered who Spirit was. Spook, Fenny, Spirit: a regular circus.

"Would you mind removing your earring, hon?" she asked Rita.

"Who's Spirit?" Rita said, unclasping her earring and handing it to Fedora.

"Spirit is the Power, although many folks here think of it as something outside themselves. Ah look at it as something we've all got to one degree or another." Her hand closed around Rita's earring and her eyes shut once more. "Let's see now. You're a teacher . . . somethin' to do with the law."

Surprised, Conway sat forward.

"Ah keep getting Libra," Fedora continued, opening her eyes now, looking at Rita. "You a Libra?" Rita nodded. "Great sign for the law, you know. Means you have an inbred sense of how to weigh both sides of an issue." She cocked her head to the side, as if listening to something. "Ah keep gettin' somethin' 'bout money, the loss of money, investments, loans. That ring any bells?"

Something changed in Rita's expression. "My, uh, husband was a gambler. We're separated now."

Conway's brows shot up. "Hank?" he exclaimed.

"It was a while ago," she replied evasively.

Fedora sat quietly for a few moments, eyes closed once more. The ticking of the clock on the wall seemed abnormally loud. Spook, lying in a corner, sighed deeply, rolled onto his back, and stuck his feet into the air as he stretched. "No children," Fedora said, "and chances are there won't be any. There'll be two marriages for you, hon, and . . ." She paused, looked at Conway. A chill snaked along his spine. She *knew*, he thought as she glanced back at Rita.

"You got your blind spots, hon, same as the rest of us, but if you can move past them, you'll . . ." Another pause, only this time she scrutinized Conway in a way that made him squirm. "You're a detective," she said flatly. She opened her hand, the earring dropped to the table. She got up, walked over to the sink, stood there with her back to them. "Ah'm right sorry, but you're going to have to leave."

"Please, Mrs. Hopkins," Conway began, getting up, "let me explain. My name's John Conway and I—"

"Ah don't 'preciate folks droppin' in here under false pretenses. You got questions, you shoulda mentioned 'em to begin with. Got enough trouble with local folks around here who think we're doin' the devil's work. Don't need no city folks messin' things up worse than they are."

Conway looked helplessly at Rita, who was already standing. "Did you know Denise Markham, Mrs. Hopkins?" Rita asked.

The quiet was tremulous, as if with excess weight. Fedora

turned slowly, as if it were an effort to move, and folded her
arms just under her breasts. Then her fingers ambled to her
throat and fiddled with a gold crucifix on a chain. Her bracelets
danced together. With her thumbnail, she made the sign of the
cross on her forehead.

"Is knowing the woman against the law?"

"You did a horoscope on her about six years ago."

"You didn't answer my question," she said to Conway.

"She's dead. I'm investigating her murder."

She whispered, "Murder," and her arms fell to her sides. Her
dark eyes turned moist, remote, inscrutable, and Conway had a
sudden hunch that Fedora Hopkins's knowledge of Denise went
far beyond a horoscope. She returned to the table, sat down,
sipped from her glass of lemonade, shook her head. "Oh, Lord,"
she said softly. "Sooner or later, Ah knew it would come to this.
Murdered. Ah wish Ah could say Ah'm sorry, but Ah'm not.
She was the devil's kind, son, take my word for it. Ever since
she was a tot, she was a strange girl who—"

"*Tot?* You knew her as a *child*?"

Fedora sighed, nodded. "She and her mama lived up the
street, where Jed lives now. Sara, that was her ma, was a
telepath, one of the best Ah've ever seen here or anywhere. She
had the Power and she had it good and some folks around here,
the ones who can still 'member, think it was the Power which
killed her. Truth is, she shot herself when Denny was sixteen,
maybe seventeen. She was never right in the head, poor Sara."

Rita glanced at Conway. "For a man playing a hunch, you're
not doing half-bad."

Fedora smiled ruefully. "Maybe you got somethin' of the
Power yourself, John. You know that to live here, you gotta take
tests? To prove you got it? Well, Sara took them tests and
popped the score better than anyone else had ever done. So they
let her move into what's now Jed's place, like Ah said. See, the
land in here belongs to the association, and it's leased to individuals for ninety-nine years. Ah own my house, but some of the
homes, like Jed's, are also owned by the association. Anyway,
Sara and Denny moved in."

"Where was her husband?" Conway asked.

"There wasn't one. Some thought Denise's pa was a professor
at Gainesville. Ah figure that was where the girl got her brains.
Now she had some of the Power herself, don't mistake me. But
she was smarter than her mama, smarter than most folks around
here. Used to read all the damn time. 'Course, there wasn't
much else to do back then. But no one read like Denny did. She

was readin' Einstein by the time she was thirteen. You 'magine that? Ah'm sixty-two years old and Ah can barely pronounce the man's name.''

"What did she do after her mother's death?'' Rita asked.

"Well, she found her ma, brains blown out in the bedroom, and you know, Ah never once saw the girl cry. Unnatural, that's what it was. She left town. Got herself married. Got herself a college degree, too. A couple of 'em. Never liked her first husband much. He drank too much. She brought him up here one day, to introduce him like, and he got drunk sitting right here in this kitchen. He had a lotta money and that was what Denny wanted most of all, I think, that and her stupid dream about some kinda drug which would tap the Power. That would strengthen whatever a person had.''

So that was it, Conway thought, the motive behind Denise Markham's obsession. "The drug became a reality,'' Conway said.

"Ah'm not surprised. She was one of those people who woulda done anything and used anyone to get what she wanted. Ah met Mr. Markham, you know, when she brought him up here one day. Ah'm pretty sure she told him like she told everyone— that her ma and pa died in a car crash in Beverly Hills or Scarsdale or some other fancy place. Even when she came here that day, she made it seem like she just happened to be driving by, you know, and wanted a reading. Ah played along with it; no harm done, really.

"Ah liked Mr. Markham. He seemed like a real nice man, but not her type. When they were leaving, she turned around and whispered she was going to marry him. He didn't know it yet, but that was when she decided, and she always got what she wanted.''

"Was that the last time you saw her?''

"Lawd, no.'' Fedora sat with her hands around the glass, looking tired and old. " 'Bout three years ago, she came up here by herself to ask a favor. She wanted me to find her some bona fide psychics who were needin' money bad enough to be in an experiment of hers where they'd take this drug that she claimed fed the Power. Told me she'd been workin' on it for thirteen years. Ah told her Ah didn't give a damn if she'd been workin' on it a *hundred* and thirteen years, Ah wasn't going to help her. 'If you need human guinea pigs,' Ah says to her, 'then use yourself. *You* got the Power, Denny,' Ah tells her, '*you* experiment on yourself.' '' She nodded. Conway had the feeling Fedora had replayed this conversation in her own mind so often through the years that in some part of her it was still occurring.

"See, John, Ah look at it like this. All of us got the Power—like you and your hunches—but some of us got more of it than others, and we've got an obligation to develop it, use it for good. Denny coulda been great, a leader. There was enough of her mother in her so that she coulda performed things the world would never have imagined. But she blew it. You can't get no drug that's going to feed the Power, not without damaging whatever is there to begin with. You follow?"

"I follow." But he wondered if Viki's experiments with her mother fell under the Power.

"Denny turned bad, her blood went sour. You don't tamper with what's God-given without reekin' His wrath, John. So no, Ah'm not surprised she was murdered." She paused. Rita lit two cigarettes, passed Conway one. " 'Bout a year ago, she showed up here again. Ah guessed she and Markham were having problems, because she was with another man. Bearded fellow, real nice-lookin'."

"Do you remember his name?"

"No, Ah'm not real good with names."

"Please try, Mrs. Hopkins. It could be very important."

"Why? If he killed 'er, if he's the one who done it, then he deserves a medal, John. See, this is all the worse 'cause she was one of us, 'cause her mama was one of us. She had it, Denny did, and she abused it."

"Can you tell me anything about him?" Conway persisted.

Fedora rubbed a hand over her eyes. "Just that he had a beard. Dark beard, full and thick. He was polite, too, real polite, like you don't see much in folks anymore. Ah doubt he even knew about Denny's research. She was like that, so secretive about everything, lyin' about her parents, about herself."

"Did you ever meet her daughter?"

"No, poor child. Ah hope she don't have none of her mother in her. Ah do have a photo, though. Yes sir, she sent me a picture last summer. Lemme get it for you." She got up, went into the other room. The door swung eerily in the quiet. Rita looked over at him.

"I'd like to go on record as saying this surpasses my seminar, Conway. In fact, this might be one of the strangest afternoons I've ever spent in my life."

He laughed.

Fedora returned with the picture and set it on the table. It was black and white, a Polaroid. Denise and Viki were sitting back on their heels in the grass. A dog was lying in front of them and Denise's fingers were lost in the animal's fur. Viki was holding a rabbit and the animals were watching each other. Both Denise and Viki were laughing.

He turned the picture over. On the back was scrawled: "Viki, Hobbit, Aardvark, and yours truly. 8/84." "Don't really know why she sent it, 'cept that she seemed to think of me as a relative or something. But that was probably because Ah knew her mother and the truth about her. You ever met the girl?"

"Yes. I like her."

"She got the Power?" Fedora asked warily, almost as if she were afraid to know the truth.

"She might. When you say Denise had it, exactly what do you mean? How much did she have? What could she do?"

"Couldn't say about when she was older, John, but as a girl, well, she could read minds like she was standing inside you. It was spookier than anything you can 'magine. Nothing, Ah mean *nothing* was private. She mighta had a little of that left after all those years of experimenting with her drug, but Ah doubt it. Myself, Ah don't drink or smoke, 'cause Ah'm afraid of losing things up in here," and she laughed and tapped the side of her head.

They exchanged numbers. Conway asked her to call him collect if she remembered the name of the man Denise had been with that day or if she recalled anything else that might help. "My opinion is still that whoever did this deserves a medal, but if Ah remember anything, Ah'll be sure to call you, John. My husband, Fenny, and Ah'll probably be up north then."

A husband? Conway thought. And what was *he* like? As they got up to leave, Fedora plucked the bill off the table that Rita had left there for her reading. "Can't accept no money for somethin' Ah didn't finish, honey. And if Ah wasn't so pooped now, Ah *would* finish it. This way, you'll just have to come back another time."

"Another time," Rita repeated, and glanced at Conway. "Yes, I think I will."

As they walked back down Seneca Street to the car, Fedora Hopkins, buttoned up in her apron with the smiling faces on it, stood on her drooping porch with Spook, gazing after them.

2.

At six o'clock that evening, while Conway and Rita were en route to Miami, Jenny Garfield was cruising at thirty-three thousand feet over the Pacific toward Bali, the final step in her flight.

She sat in the back of the tourist section, where the stews had six seats reserved for them.

It was only three in the afternoon California time, and there wasn't much to do between now and dinner. Her tray was down and she had a piece of stationery in front of her. She'd been composing the letter in her head for the better part of the day, and now the words came easily. She printed them in block letters, very neatly, so there could be no mistake about the message:

YOUR LOVELY WIFEY IS MAKING IT WITH DETECTIVE JOHN CONWAY. JUST IN CASE YOU'RE WONDERING HOW I KNOW, I FOUND THEM TOGETHER. AND IN CASE YOU DON'T UNDERSTAND THE PRECISE MEANING OF "MAKING IT," LET ME CLARIFY: SCREWING, NOOKY, COPULATING. THEY WERE DOING IT IN MY BED, MR. LINCOLN, AND CHANCES ARE THEY HAVE ALSO DONE IT IN YOUR BED.

Jenny reread it as she nibbled at the top of her pen. Should she sign it? Better not, she decided. There was probably some law against what she was doing, and the way her luck was running Hank Lincoln would probably know *which* law it was. If she didn't sign it, no one could ever prove beyond a shadow of a doubt that she'd written it.

Smiling, she folded the letter, slipped it in the envelope, addressed it. She would give it to one of the stews returning to California tomorrow. Hank Lincoln would get it at the end of the week or, at the latest, the beginning of next. It wasn't soon enough to suit her, but what really mattered was that he got it.

"Too bad, sugar," she whispered, running the flap along her tongue and creasing the envelope shut. "Too goddamned bad about you and your fancy lady lawyer." As for Conway's threat to tell her supervisor about the pills . . . well, he wouldn't do it. Who was he trying to kid? Messing up an illicit affair was *one* thing, but he wouldn't make her lose her job. That would be an amoral act.

Satisfied that she'd figured everything out, she put a stamp on the envelope, dropped it in her purse. *Now*, she thought, they would be even.

"It's crazy, Conway."

"Maybe, but it doesn't change my wanting to know, now does it."

They were standing in the kitchen of his apartment. The twilight was cut up by the venetian blinds and he could barely see Rita's face because there weren't any lights on. She had a hand on her hip, but the only reason he knew that was because the light shone through the triangle made by her arm.

"But this stuff kills," she protested.

"Not by using it once."

"You don't know for sure. Nothing is for sure about this drug."

He picked up the aluminum box from the middle of the table, ran his thumbs over the top of it. Pandora, he thought, here I come.

"Look, you've got labs and doctors and a medical center at your disposal. Let *them* tell you what the stuff does."

"Are the rats and guinea pigs going to tell me all about it, Rita? Are the little white mice going to say, 'Yes sir, Mr. Conway, we sure did communicate telepathically; yes sir, Denise was sure on the right track.' I've got doctors and a medical center and a lab who can't get their acts together enough to tell me anything for sure, and I'm supposed to sit around and wait for them to confirm, deny, or shrug their shoulders, right?" He shook his head and opened the lid. "No way."

She came over to him, put a hand on his shoulder. "Fine, I can understand your frustration, Conway," she said gently. "But it doesn't mean you have to put yourself on the line."

This close, he could see the liquid pale blue of her eyes, the way the light slid down to the edge of her nose, the graceful lines of her neck. "Why would people pay so much for this stuff that Denise would have a hundred and seventy-five thousand bucks? What's it do? I know that it numbs like coke, and Karen Pauling tells me it has some properties of LSD. But what else? Does it really tap what Fedora calls the Power? What's going on in the mind of the guy terrorizing Laura? Huh? Can you tell me that, Rita? Can little white mice tell me? Is it such absolutely fantastic stuff that people would risk their lives for it? This stuff's the key, Rita. And if I can figure out where it fits, maybe I can get to this guy before he gets to Laura."

Rita's hand dropped from his shoulder. For a full minute, neither of them spoke or moved. Then Rita walked across the kitchen to the refrigerator. She opened the door, brought out a carton of orange juice and two glasses. She filled them both to the top, set them on the table. "Okay, if you're going to be so pigheaded about it, put in a pinch apiece and let me get comfortable, call my sister, and tell her I won't be home tonight. You have enough food, Conway? I don't intend to get hungry." She walked into the living room, kicked off her shoes, picked up the phone.

"Let's forget it," he said, following her. "I don't think you should—"

She sat down, crossed her legs, pushed her hair behind her ears. "You think I shouldn't indulge? I've known Laura since I was three, Conway, I love her like a sister. Don't talk to me about not indulging."

There wasn't much he could say to that, so he returned to the kitchen, stirred a dash of the drug into the glasses, then put them in the refrigerator. He went into the den, stood there a minute thinking, looking around. Preparations, he thought, and reached for a blank microcassette and put it in the recorder. It was an Akai system, sensitive enough to pick up sounds anywhere in the room. He set another tape, notebook, and pen beside it. He brought in clean linen for the Hide-a-Bed, dropped it in a chair, activated his answering machine. He set the alarm. The room became a living, breathing thing, plugged in, turned on, ready to record and preserve.

"I'll be right back," Rita said, sticking her head in the room. "I'm going to get some clean clothes out of the car."

Conway nodded, returned to the kitchen. He checked out his food supply. On coke, food was something to be avoided, and on LSD, unless it was cut with speed, food was a new experience. So what could they expect from Markham Magic?

He opted for quick snacks: cheese, fruit, crackers, juice. He had no idea how long the effects of the drug would last, but this would probably be enough to tide them over for a day.

When Rita returned, he was sitting in the den in front of the TV, the glasses of orange juice on the table. She had changed into jeans and a cotton shirt. As she sat beside him, he said, "You sure?"

Rita laughed. "C'mon, let's get on with it."

He passed her a glass. "To the Power."

"Amen."

They clicked glasses and drank.

Jerome Blanchard was absolutely sober when he rang the Turnbalts' doorbell. There was a deep, hollow ache where his heart should have been, and he kept hearing the minister saying, "Olivia is with the Father now, the Father of us all. . . ."

The funeral was the most miserable thing he'd ever lived through. Worse than watching her lie in a pool of sweat after the convulsions, blood inching from the corner of her mouth because she'd almost bitten her tongue off before he could get hold of it; worse than her death. But he couldn't cry anymore. Everything inside him had dried up. In the end, he thought, only his bones and his black, execrable soul remained.

He rang the bell again and again, and Marie finally answered the door. She wore a robe. Her hair was in disarray. She was pale, sniffling, yet she still looked like Venus, he thought, like spring, like everything in the world that was good and true and forever, and he wanted to spit in her face as she said, "Jerry, honey, how nice to see you." He cringed as she brushed his cheek with her cool mouth and sniffled again. "Sorry I didn't answer the door. I've been feeling a little under the weather."

The words nipped at the edges of his mind, filling him with horror. *Marie, sick?*

She reached for his hand. "If there's anything Frank and I can do, Jerry, anything at all . . ."

"I want to see Frank," Blanchard snapped, finding his voice, remembering why he came here.

Marie stepped back, brought out a piece of Kleenex from her robe pocket, blew her nose. "Sure, Jerry, he's out on the porch, I think."

"I'll find my own way," he replied, moving away from her, grateful to have his hand back, to put distance between himself and her lies.

Turnbalt was sitting way at the end of the porch, his feet propped up on the wall, a glass of something in his hand. The lights of the city were a carnival of color, a deceptive parade that seemed to promise something, but Blanchard couldn't remember what.

"Frank."

Turnbalt turned around, got up, patted his midriff, and picked up his glass. "Jerry, old man. You look like you could use a drink. I'm glad you stopped by. We couldn't make the funeral because neither of us has been feeling up to par, but I just want you to know how sorry we are. What would you like to drink?"

"Nothing." He waited for Turnbalt to sit again, then pulled up a canvas chair. "It's got to stop, Frank. This stuff kills people. It killed Livvy."

"What're you talking about? They don't know *what* killed Livvy, Jerry."

"The drug killed her." Blanchard was surprised at how calm and rational he sounded, despite the seething rage that made him want to squash Turnbalt like an insect.

"Jerome, I'm terribly sorry about Livvy. You know that. I was very fond of her. But this stuff about the drug . . ." He shook his head. "It's just police hype to scare people. I heard the news tonight same as everyone else. It's just a ruse. The cops are trying to throw every coke dealer and user into a cold, white panic."

Such a way with words, Blanchard thought. "You're wrong. The stuff's not coke and you know it and I think I've known it all along. People don't pay for coke what they've paid for this stuff."

"Oh, Jerry, honey," Marie said, coming up behind him. "Frank's not wrong. Everyone knows that. You've said it yourself two dozen times." She sat on the arm of his chair. He wished she wouldn't do that, he couldn't think straight when Marie was so close to him. Things had happened in the past, things he didn't like to remember because he always felt so ashamed. He got up and walked over to the wall.

"So I was wrong about Frank being right," he said, looking out over the city, wishing he and Livvy had left. If they had, she would still be alive.

"All right, Jerry, let's look at the facts." Turnbalt spoke in his attorney voice that Blanchard knew so well. *Ladies and gentlemen of the jury, what we have here is one Jerome L. Blanchard* . . . "You've done damn terrific, admit it. Well over two hundred grand pure profit, right? Your initial investment was fifty-five thousand dollars. That's not a bad return on your money, now is it. Better than Treasury bills, the money market, safer than stocks. And you've still got money coming in, Jerome. You took Livvy to Europe and Hong Kong and . . ."

"And Australia," Marie added, "don't forget about Australia and New Zealand and all those pretty little islands in between."

"So if you blow the whistle, where's that going to leave you?"

Turnbalt was standing next to him now, the fetid smell of his cigar almost enough to make Blanchard puke. He was right, that was the hell of it. The deal *had* been profitable. Turnbalt somehow always made you think you'd come out smelling like a rose. The funny part was that *he* usually did, even if no one else did.

"In prison, that's where it would leave you," Turnbalt said. "You know what prison's like, Jerry?" Blanchard didn't bother to answer. Turnbalt didn't really want an answer. Besides, maybe there *were* no answers. "Just in case you don't know, let me tell you. You're never alone, Jerry. Never. Not when you eat or sleep, not when you shit or shower. It's you against them, and them is everyone else—the guards, other inmates, the system itself. How tall are you, Jerry?" Turnbalt glanced at him, looking him up, down, making Blanchard squirm. "Five six, maybe five seven? A guy who's short like you goes up for grabs. You find protection, friend, by becoming some nigger's sugar baby. It's real simple. All you do is screw the nigger and he protects you in return and maybe, just maybe, you make it through prison in one piece. And you know what you do with all that time, Jerry? All those days and months and years? You play it out or you hang yourself, those are your options.

"Think about it, Jerry," Turnbalt continued, pausing long enough to sip at his drink. "You wake up in the morning and you shuffle off to the bathroom to shave with your state-issued razor and then you shower with your state-issued soap and get into your state-issued blues. Then you eat your state-issued breakfast and go to your state-issued job and you sleep in a room with five or six other guys who've got just as much hate inside them as you do.

"Ever heard of the Understanding Room, Jerry? That's where they take you when they want some answers about what's happening on the compound. Doesn't matter if you don't know anything, as long as they *think* you do. The guards slap you around with their fists and their clubs and make you strip down so they can peer up your ass and maybe they even get it on with you, depends on the mood they're in. Then they leave you with mush and water, Jerry, just like in the movies, friend. You don't get visitors for two or three weeks, however long it takes for the cuts and bruises to heal. And you know what's worse, Jerry? No women. Night after night for months or years on end you don't touch a woman, and that's an ache worse than anything you've ever known. It gets so that it's the only thing you think about, Jerry, as you jerk off in the men's room and hope no one sees you. Got the picture? That's what prison's like, friend. Only worse, much worse, because it's happening to you, not on some screen in living color."

Blanchard looked over at him. Turnbalt stood there in his

designer shirt and slacks, sipping the best booze, smoking the best cigars, in the most expensive condominium in the Grove, and was married to a woman who could've walked off the cool, slick pages of *Harper's Bazaar*, and he was talking about prison as if he knew it from the inside out.

"How the hell would *you* know what prison's like, Frank? Get off my ass."

"I did time, that's how," Turnbalt said, his voice deadly quiet, the smooth, clever attorney tone gone. "I did time at Raiford, friend, the Rock. It's in Starke, Florida, ever been there? It should be on every tourist agenda, yes sir. Shit, they don't even speak *English* in Starke, I don't know what they speak. And at Raiford, you're doing time with the big boys, Jerry."

"Yeah, right. You did time." Blanchard laughed.

"Two years for manslaughter, when I was sixteen. My sentence was fifteen years, Jerry. It was the system's error, a case of mistaken identity, and I was eventually pardoned; went on to Harvard, and finally sued and won. But money doesn't begin to compensate for time you never get back."

"Now that you've heard the *whole* gruesome story," said Marie, coming over to the wall where they stood, "would you like a drink, Jerry?" She touched her hand to his shoulder and her perfume moved in around him like a web.

"No, I don't want anything to drink, and I don't want anything to eat. You can't keep selling this stuff to people, Frank. I don't care about profit margins and trips to Hong Kong. You're talking about people's lives, for Christ's sake. Doesn't that mean anything at all to you?"

Marie's hand dropped from his shoulder. "Oh, Jerry," she said impatiently. "You haven't heard a *thing* Frank has said. Of *course* lives matter to him, sweetheart, but where the hell would any of us be worrying about everyone else? We take care of our own, Jerry. And Frank's right about this police hype where the drug's concerned."

Blanchard's head was beginning to pound. "Conway knows something," he said dully. "He asked me point-blank if you'd sold Livvy the stuff." He saw Marie and Frank exchange a glance.

"Conway doesn't know shit," Turnbalt replied. "He's guessing, cops are always guessing. Look, Jerry, you're tired. Go home. Get a good night's rest. Go home and count your money. You put up your initial investment and that's all that was required. Let *me* worry about the fine points. As long as you keep your mouth shut, no one's going to jail and Conway can keep guessing until hell freezes over.''

Blanchard stood there a moment, gazing out into the dark. Then he turned and walked back inside. Marie followed him, took his hand. "Honey," she said quietly, her mouth very close to his ear, her hands at his face, her voice soft as summer, "you mustn't worry yourself so much. Has Frank ever steered you wrong before? Have I?" He wanted to fall into her eyes. She kissed him on the mouth. "Now if you want me to come over and look after you a few days, Jerry, you know I will. You remember, don't you, how it was before? Remember how it was the night the four of us—''

"Shut up, just shut up." He wrenched away from her, reached for the doorknob. "What do you know about anything, Marie? Christ. Livvy's just been buried and you . . .'' He was shouting now, his rage was pushing through the surface and he couldn't help himself. The words came in waves, slapping the air between them. "Hell, maybe Frank killed Denise, huh? Maybe that's why he's running scared and trying to make me run scared, too, huh? You know your precious husband so well you can say for sure he didn't kill Denise, Marie? You disgust me,'' he spat, and ran out into the hall, slamming the door behind him. Then he kept running on down the hall, the stairs, sobbing now, remembering, always remembering that night they'd done so much of the drug none of them could even walk and how they'd fallen into that bed and . . . Blanchard threw open his car door and took off into the night like a man fleeing his own perdition.

5.

In the penthouse, Marie Turnbalt remained by the door, frowning. For the first time in all the years she had known Frank, she was frightened. Little men like Jerome Blanchard could be dangerous when they went off the deep end. She glanced back onto the porch. Frank was still standing by the wall as if nothing had happened.

"You've got to do something," she said, walking out onto the porch. "He's . . . I don't know, Frank. Maybe I should go over there.''

"Don't be ridiculous. You think if you screw him he's going to be placated? Unless you enjoyed screwing him,'' he finished, his voice iced with sarcasm.

Marie looked down at the floor. "Suppose he goes to the

police?'' she whispered, biting her lip, afraid, terribly afraid now that everything had shot out of control.

Frank slipped his arms around her. Everything was fine when he held her, she thought. Nothing could touch her when he was near her like this. ''Blanchard,'' Frank said quietly, kissing her hair, ''isn't going to do anything.'' He held her back from him a little. ''Have I ever been wrong, Ree?''

''No. No, you haven't.''

She laid her head against his chest and closed her eyes. The beating of his heart was nice, so very nice. It made her drowsy, made her forget being afraid, made her forget almost everything. ''Frank, please don't take this the wrong way, all right? Because whatever your answer is, you know I'll be there.'' She paused, whispered, ''Did you kill Denise?''

She winced in anticipation of his shouting. But when he didn't shout, didn't even raise his voice, she lifted her head, looked up at him. ''Oh, Ree,'' he said, holding her face in his hands, kissing her. ''Of course I didn't.''

There, she thought. She had to ask and now she knew and now everything would be all right again. They stood there holding each other for a long time, and her mind drifted off into the warm, still dark. She was tired, so very tired.

16

1.

CONWAY HAD EXPERIMENTED a few times with hallucinogenics when he was in college, and usually the effects came on slowly, in steps, like an unfolding dream. But this didn't hold true for Markham Magic. This stuff hit him all at once with a wave of heat so intense that he leaped up from the couch, certain it was burning.

He was in the Sahara. He was the man in the beer commercial, stumbling from dune to dune in a hundred-and-ten degree heat, ripping off his shirt, slacks, shorts, until he was naked as a seal and buzzards were circling overhead waiting for the fall when he wouldn't rise again. The heat gripped him in the solar plexus, sprang into his mouth, and rode his shoulders like a monkey demon. His thirst was sudden and unbearable, but he couldn't move toward water because the demon was riding him to his knees, beating his spine.

His lungs burst into flame. The heat singed the inside of his nose, his brain. He smelled burning flesh. *Spontaneous human combustion*. That was what really happened to Denise Markham, and during the autopsy, when they'd found the charred remains of her insides, that bastard Pivot had made up the story about the liver enzymes because he'd been unable to explain what he'd found. It was perfectly clear now.

But just as quickly as the heat had swept through him, it vanished. He now sped through the white, gelid silence of the Arctic in a dog sled, and the cold had made his bones so brittle he knew if he sneezed, they would splinter like china. How come hell was fire? This was worse. His eyelids were freezing in their sockets. His fingers and toes were breaking off, neat as icicles. His heartbeat was negligible.

"Conway? Conway?"

Rita's voice was clear, but distant, someone calling in a dream, *Come back, come back, don't leave me,* as he swam for consciousness. When he looked at her, beauty as ripe and fresh as a child's, he realized he was neither hot nor cold now and that he'd never left the couch.

"The tape machine," he said, his words seeming thick as syrup against his tongue, "I forgot to turn it on." He rushed across the room, hit the button, grinned as the soft whirring broke the quiet. It was the purring of a giant cat, the soft, persistent beating of a mother's heart, heard in utero. It was his libido rolling over and over in a summer field like a dog with a terrible itch. By God, he was high, he felt good, better than good, he was a ubiquitous presence in a marvelous universe, and most of all, he wanted to fuck his ever-lovin' brains out.

It was as if he hadn't touched a woman in months, maybe years. The desire ballooned, fell in on itself, deeper than hunger. A collage of breasts and thighs and buttocks swam through his head in slow motion, congealed, marched backward and forward in time from his first girl when he was fifteen, in the sweet scent of hay, to Stella and Jen and Rita and others whose names he could no longer recall, but whose faces and bodies he couldn't forget. Libidinous kicks: I want, I need, I'm gonna go outa my miinndd— It inundated him like the heat and the cold had moments ago.

He turned. Everything slowed to a crawl: Rita's mouth opening, slow as a yawn, her words drawn out: "Meee, toooo, Conwaaayyy."

Did it hit her *like that?*

Rita's hand took a day to reach her mouth. She blinked, her lashes leaving elongated shadows on her cheeks. *Conway, your lips aren't moving.*

Neither are yours.

She smiled uncertainly, shyly. *Mess in here, I know. I should have cleaned house.* Then she began to laugh, her head thrown back, the tortoiseshell combs coming loose from her hair, which fell around her face like a veil. *If this is psychosis, it's not bad. Did you get the cold, the heat?*

Yeah, and this other. . . .

Really, Conway. And when she smiled, the dimple was there, huge as a crater. He followed it with his eyes as it grew even deeper, and when he touched his hand to her face, their skins formed a graft. Her mouth was cool, moist as a grape. They moved in a slow motion freedom, into the purr of the tape machine. He was lighter than air. The intensity of his emotions gripped him by the cuff of the neck, shook him. He wanted to cry, laugh, gobble her up in one greedy bite.

Their separateness vanished. He was stripped to the bone. They were buttoned up in the same ribs, breathed from the same lungs, were joined at the head, the heart. They were hermaphroditic mutants of Denise Markham's genius. In lovemaking, their very memories merged. It was glorious. He slipped through the years of Rita's past, read her cells like braille, and then he hit the brick wall of her marriage and nirvana caved in.

"That's hardly fair," she said, pulling away, sitting up, drawing her knees against her. Her cheeks were pink as if from sunburn. She held her hair with her hand, and he wondered what had happened to the tortoiseshell combs here in their bed of newfound knowledge.

"But I—"

There was no need for him to finish his sentence. She shook her head. "I don't want to know about the other women in your life, Conway. Not here. Not now. It's too . . . too close."

He wished, suddenly, for the small but necessary boundaries that separated people. They would suffocate in so much closeness. This, he thought, was the other side of the coin, the dark underside of Markham Magic.

The phone rang. The sound startled him. It was a rude reminder of the world that lay beyond the apartment. Rita laughed when Conway's recorded voice said, "I'm unavailable now, but if you'll leave your name and number at the sound of the tone, I'll return your call shortly."

"You're unavailable all right," Rita remarked. "Winged out. In the ozone."

The tone sounded. Stella's whine made Conway wince. "John, I know you're still angry and all, but the fact is, the court ordered you to pay the lousy two hundred, and like it or not, if I don't get it within the next few days, my attorney, Steve Jenkins, will be getting in touch with you. I don't intend to spend the rest of the summer without air conditioning."

"Thank you very much, Stella," he muttered, propping the pillows up, sitting back. He lit a cigarette, and as he passed it to Rita he felt her inside, leaving footprints across his cerebellum.

One giant step, Rita. Did you find Stella?

With pigtails and freckles.

We grew up together.

You see how it feels, Conway?

He smiled at her. Yes, he saw. The history of his marriage, however brief and impetuous it was, remained a thorn in his side. He handed it to Rita: Stella's pregnancy, the miscarriage, the marriage slowly coming apart at the seams until five years later, when they were finally divorced. Then, as if trading secrets like baseball cards, she waggled her fingers at him, inviting him in. It was like watching a movie, Rita and Hank meeting at a bar in the Grove, where he and his magic were the scheduled entertainment. Highlights of an eight-month courtship climaxed with an exchange of vows. Pandora's box, he thought.

He felt the external world pushing against the walls of the apartment. It was a wrestler weighing in at two twenty-five slamming tremendous shoulders against the front door. Paranoia swept through him like an insidious jungle rot. He put on his clothes, walked into the living room, listening carefully to every sound, checking the chain and the dead bolt on the front door. They were safe.

Conway peered through the kitchen window to the parking lot below. The Porsche was a beached whale in the moonlight and the windshield was its dead, dead eyes. The street beyond looked abandoned, as if an air raid had sounded and people were huddled underground somewhere, waiting for the bombs to fall, the sky to crumble in, waiting like Chicken Little.

In the canal, a sloop rocked back and forth in the breeze, restless to be loose from the dock and climbing the high seas. He had a wild, insane notion to steal the thing and saw himself and Rita on board, hoisting the sails and floating away from the dark in the beams of light like Winken, Blinken, and Nod. They would leave everything behind: the riddle of Denise Markham, homicide, all of it. He wanted to flee. It was more than a kittle in his side; it took root, sure as obsession. He saw them turning raisin gold during the forty days in the sun on their way to the Marquesas Islands. He wanted the boat. Now. Tonight.

He peered up and down the street. No cars, he thought, and no lights in the house. All he wanted was just a glimpse of what could be. Just the sight of Orion from the deck of a ship, that wasn't so much to ask, was it? *Riiitta. We're going to the South Pacific.*

They tiptoed into the hall, down the stairs, into the street. They dashed for the shadows, breathing the warm, spicy air, both of them barefoot and crazy and fleeing, the lady lawyer and the cop. He forgot about safety.

They skulked across the back lawn like commandos. He heard water lapping at the side of the sloop, filled up his lungs with the swelling rush of the brackish tide. They slipped from the grass to the dock, and the sloop moved away, coy as a flirt, rubbing up against the sides of the dock, drifting beyond them again. When his eyes followed the mast upward, it impaled the moon.

The wood was warm and damp beneath his feet. He ran his hands along the mast, rigging the rail which curved into a grin. It was his. It had always been his.

Rita tried the cabin door. It was open. Three steps and he was down. Moonlight filtered through the portholes, spilled across the tiny stove swinging back and forth on hinges, onto the mahogany table. They nosed toward the bow cupping out into a mouth of chocolate cushions. He looked into the head, noted the shower, the clean, colorful towels hanging next to the sink. He held one against his chin. It smelled of Tide, of childhood, warm from the dryer. He would probably find sheets on the bed and dishes in the cabinets and food in the fridge; Rita had thought of everything.

They went topside, laughing softly, delighted with their find. When he dropped his head back, he saw Orion facing Artemis in battle, the two of them lit up on the black screen of the sky. Navigation by the stars, my God, he could taste it. It was just a matter of untying the ropes and shoving off. With favorable winds he would be in Key West by morning.

He moved across the deck, his footsteps soundless, and began working at the ropes. They were wet, hardened together, sticky from the salt. Somewhere in the distance, the crickets started up again, and out on the canal, a boat putted by. Its wake reached the sloop in tiny waves like hiccups.

They would wait out the hurricane season in the islands,

maybe in Marsh Harbor or the Abacos, then head farther south in October, through the Panama Canal. Then forty days and nights of open sea, and by Christmas they would arrive eight thousand miles west of nowhere, down under, at the bottom of the world.

The rope at the stern gave way, fell into the water with a small, irritating splash. The sloop drifted out from the dock a ways and he kneeled down, watching the ripples spreading outward and the rope trailing beneath. Like a rat, he scurried to the bow, grappled with the ropes, anxious now, afraid that something would happen before they got away. Like a call, he thought, or someone dropping by. Hell, just look at the possibilities. Jen might drop in looking for something she'd left behind; Stella could arrive wanting her money; and then there were Tillis and Truro. He dug his fingers in between the ropes, pulled, grew red and hot in the face as he pushed a foot against the post that held the ropes.

A knife, he needed a knife. He got down on his hands, patted the deck for a knife, wondered why everything was out of place. Hadn't he brought a knife on board with the supplies?

Conway!

Rita, C'mere for a second, will you?

Conway, what the hell are you doing?

He jerked his head around. She stood on the stairs that led down into the cabin. He grinned at her. Moonlight burned the memory of her face into his brain. When had she gone back down into the cabin? Had she told him she was going to fix dinner? Sure, that must've been it. She'd told him and he, so engrossed in setting sail, had not heard. He should pay closer attention. What had Rita said they were going to have for dinner? Franks and beans? Tuna on rye?

The rope, I'm trying to get it unfastened.

Stop it! Look at us!

Conway rolled back on his heels, put his hands flat against his thighs.

He glanced at the dock, the stern, realized the sloop was now perpendicular, facing the house head on. The terrible truth of it hit him and he knew suddenly, irrevocably, that this was the key to Markham Magic: the myopia, the feeling that anything was yours for the taking, the arrogant certainty that you were invincible, above the law of either God or man. This, he knew, was the heart of the gradual psychosis.

"Jesus," he whispered, and grabbed the post with both arms like a dying man. He hugged. He held his legs tightly against the side for leverage. The sloop started slowly around. Rita was holding the stern rope, and when they were close enough to land she took hold of the post, stepped up onto the dock. She wound the rope several times, made Girl Scout knots. Conway let loose and stumbled back. His arms ached terribly. His shins throbbed. There would be bruises from where the edge of the sloop had bitten into the bone.

I think we'd better get out of here. She reached for his hand. Conway took hold, squeezed. But for one instant, the tug of his vision—the flight, the lure and promise of such a life on the sea—nearly kept him there. Once he stepped up, he knew he could not come back.

"Conway," she whispered urgently.

They ran; the air now smelled bitter and flat.

Much later, Conway woke with a start, sat forward, took inventory. Everything appeared to be in place, in order. His shins were tender, but he otherwise knew who he was and where he was and yes, his muscles all fit. His perceptions actually seemed sharper. He could hear the ticking of the clock in his bedroom and was certain he heard the beating of Rita's heart beside him.

It was raining—not hard, just enough to make the streets glisten. A comfortable sound, he thought, getting quietly out of bed. He went into the kitchen, gazed through the blinds, saw the sloop sleeping in the rain, and wondered if it had all really happened. Conway lifted his leg onto the chair, turned on the light. The bruises were there all right. He hadn't been hallucinating.

He called Ake. "Precinct twelve," said a sleepy voice.

"Ake? That you?"

"Conway. Where the hell've you been? I've left fourteen dozen messages on your goddamned machine. I hate that machine. Where are you?"

Bound for the Pacific, Ake. "What happened?"

"Oh, just the routine stuff, you know, like some of the mice screwed themselves to death."

"What?" Conway laughed.

"A Teletype came in from Thompkins around eight, straight from Tallahassee."

"Shoot."

"It says: 'Drug contains at least thirty-six different substances of indeterminate amounts. Maybe more, still testing. Massive doses were injected into a group of forty mice. Within thirty-six hours, eighteen of these were dead from exhaustion, dehydration, and cardiac failure. They refused to eat, guys, because they were too busy copulating. We lost them to lust. The remaining twenty-two were continued on the drug and were dead within four days of uremia, liver dysfunction, and a breakdown in the immune system. Drug evidently accretes in the liver.

" 'In the advanced stages, the drug causes extreme and inimical aggression. Ten of the twenty-two remaining mice would have eaten each other if they hadn't been separated. Drug has been recommended for code one list, although personally I feel it should be fed to the enemy so we'd win the war. Medical report and further test results to follow.' " Ake paused. "Are we at war, Conway?"

"Thompkins is still in Vietnam. Is that all he said? What's he mean by *massive*? What does that mean in terms of people?"

"That's all it said. The other thing is that I've got a tail on Turnbalt. Blanchard paid him a visit, and my man said he looked awful upset when he left. Tore outa the driveway like a bat outa hell and so on, that's how my man put it."

"And Turnbalt?"

"He left his place around seven-thirty, drove over to the campus for his class, and was home promptly at ten-fifteen. We've got a request in for a bug on his phone."

"Stay in touch."

"Hold on, man. A couple of other things. I'll have a psychological profile on our man ready for you in a couple of days."

"Who's doing it?"

"A friend of mine who works for the feds. It may give us some more leads. The last thing: Channel seven is going to run a spot on the drug for the next week and we've provided an eight hundred number for people to call, no questions asked. We're advising callers to see their family doctors and get rid of the stuff. It'll take people a couple days to realize there isn't any angle, but we expect to at least get the word out."

A bit of flotsam from the "trip" came loose in Conway's mind and floated to the surface. He didn't know *where* it had come from or why it had surfaced just then, but he said, "Hey, Ake. You ever heard of something called Bell's theorem?"

"What?"

"Never mind."

"Yeah, right. Talk to you soon, Conway."

After he'd hung up, Conway went into the den, got out an encyclopedia, thumbed through the Bs, looking for a reference to Bell's theorem. He thought about waking up Rita and asking her what it meant, since it was apparently something he'd picked from her head, but when he approached the couch, he saw that her hands were folded under her chin; she looked like a child who had fallen asleep while saying her prayers. He didn't have the heart to disturb her. He leaned over, brushed her hair from her forehead, kissed her lightly on the cheek. "I love you," he said quietly. She murmured something, turned on her side, her hands still folded. Then he found the letter Denise had written her daughter and closed the door behind him.

"You'll find it in time, button . . . like a treasure hunt." That phrase kept popping out at him whenever he read through the letter. Roses and aardvarks and Hobbit's dune: was the clue in there?

2.

Duncan came out into the dark silence of the court in his gym shorts, T-shirt, and jogging shoes. It was cool in here, it was wonderful in here, so deserted, so private, all his. He held the basketball in his arms, thought he felt it growing, pushing up under his chin, forcing his head back. He dropped it suddenly, heard it bounce, the noise echoing, the echoes growing smaller and smaller until it was quiet again. He breathed deeply. Lights, he needed lights.

He felt along the wall until his hand reached the switch. He played it safe, just in case someone saw the light in the window. He flipped on only one switch. A light glowed at the other end of the court, illuminating the basket, part of the bleachers. He started to dribble out onto the court, then sank onto the bleachers, too weary to move.

Lately, it seemed he needed more and more sleep. And he couldn't get rid of this persistent pain in his side or this cough and sniffles, and sometimes he was sure he was running a low-grade fever. But he was too frightened to check and know for sure. He held the ball between his knees, pressed his hands over his face.

"C'mon, Duncan, up, *up*," he whispered. He had to prove to the coach that he'd made the right decision in not suspending him from the team. He had to win this game against Florida State; yeah, he could do it, he *would* do it.

He got up, held tightly to the ball, dribbled across the court, fighting back weariness. He dribbled some more, loved the feel of the shiny wood under his feet. The ball was firm and hard under his hands, and when he let it go, he controlled it like a yo-yo. He dribbled down the court, jumped, poised the ball just above his head, held his breath, and shot. The

169

ball swished through the net, never touching the basket's rim and Duncan heard the crowd cheering, the feet stompin against the bleachers, the cheerleaders at the sidelines, and he caught the colorful blur of their uniforms, the fan of dark hair, blond hair. When he pivoted again, he glanced up and saw Denise sitting there at the top, watching him with a smile, watching only him, watching as if she would devour him with her eyes.

"Go away!" he shouted as the ball fell from his hands. He turned, slapped the ball with the flat of his hand, bouncing it higher and higher until he could dribble again. As long as he moved, her eyes couldn't touch him.

He flew from one end of the court to the other, sniffling, coughing, breathing so hard his chest ached. Perspiration dripped into his eyes, and the burning started in the small of his back and crept into his side. He grabbed hold of the ball in midair and doubled over it, whimpering. When he raised his head again, Denise was still there, grinning. He heard her say, *I'll squash you. It's that simple. Do we understand each other?*

17

1.

HE SAT ON the edge of the examining table in a paper robe, sorry he had come. The achiness he'd been feeling, the fatigue, were probably nothing more than his body rebelling against vitamins, certain foods, or insufficient sleep. It certainly didn't have anything to do with what they were saying on the news. Any moron could tell what the cops were up to. They'd even provided a façade of credibility with this 800 number, so the panicked would believe.

No questions asked. . . . Right. Sure. Instead, your voice would be taped and fed into a computer, and not long afterward the knock at the door would come, he thought. *Surprise, we know who you are.* . . .

Air from the vent overhead hit him in the back of the neck. He moved away from the table, noting the colorful containers filled with cotton balls and alcohol, assorted instruments, disposable syringes, and needles. He looked away. He hated needles. He was the kid who'd had to be restrained for boosters and vaccinations, the one who made dentists cringe when they saw him coming.

He remembered how one night two or three years ago, in a motel somewhere, he'd watched Denise inject herself with the drug. She had done it right there in front of him, and everything had swum in a vertiginous blur as he'd passed out. When he'd come to, she was standing over him, pressing a cold towel to his head. It was one of the few times she'd ever been tender with him.

"What's wrong with you, honey? You gave me an awful scare."

By then her eyes had had that strange, glazed look, and he'd known just by the way she was touching him, hands against his chest where the collar was open, that the drug had taken hold.

"How could you do that, Denny? How could you stick that thing into your arm?"

"You mean the needle? You're afraid of needles?"

And she'd laughed at him.

He leaned against the metal table. He didn't have to stay here. It had been a mistake to come. He'd been waiting—what? thirty minutes? forty-five?—too long. He was a busy man. He had things to do, responsibilities to attend to. He reached for his clothes, and just then the door opened.

"Bucky," said Doc Livesy, coming into the room with a stethoscope around his neck, that wonderful grin on his face, and his glasses pushed back onto his bald, shiny head. Like Marcus Welby, Livesy was part of a dying breed of family doctors. He'd known the man for a long time.

"Doc, I was just leaving."

Livesy chortled. "Now I know I'm as late as ever, Buck, but you got to have patience." He picked up the chart, dropped his glasses onto his nose. "How've you been, Bucky? It's been a while since we've seen you."

"I've been feeling tired and achy, like maybe I'm coming down with the flu."

Livesy set the chart aside, pressed the smooth, cool disk of the stethoscope against his back, moving it up and down and sideways like a marble in Chinese checkers. "Breathe deeply and slowly, Buck." The nickname came from his mother. Only Denise and the doc knew it; he hated it.

"Sometimes the aching starts in my lower back," he explained. That *was* right, wasn't it?

"Anything else?" Livesy asked, moving the stethoscope around to his chest, listening, frowning, instructing him to breathe, hold, expel.

He had a sudden urge to slap Livesy's hand away. He hated this, hated Livesy because he assumed, as all doctors seemed to assume, that the patient's body was *his* private domain. Now he moved the disk from his back to his chest so the paper robe slipped to his waist, so his ass showed.

"Still taking vitamins, Buck?"

"Yes. A through E."

"Uh-huh. Then for the time being, go off the Bs, okay? Some people have a reaction to them which begins in the lower back. In the kidneys." He pressed his cool, dry fingers to Bucky's side, moved them around to his back. "Could be arthritis, since it runs in your family. Have you been under any stress lately?"

This almost sent him into paroxysms of laughter. *Stress? No, not at all, doc.* "No more than usual. I'm too young for arthritis, doc," he said, laughing nervously, hating the sound of his own voice.

"No one's too young for arthritis, Buck," Livesy told him. "No one."

He picked up the chart, scribbled something. *What's he writing about me?*

"I'm going to send you over to X-ray, and when you're finished, step into my office, will you?"

Livesy opened the door, shut it behind him. He sat at the edge of the table, staring at the patterns in the wallpaper. Dark swirls ebbed and flowed across a lighter background. If he squinted his eyes, he could see faces there, in the designs. He could see faces and hair and mouths opening and closing like a fish's. He slid quickly off the table and a few minutes later was walking down the hall with a nurse, holding the back of his gown closed. Her name tag read Nancy Ewill, R.N. She didn't smile. He decided she probably didn't know *how* to smile. She didn't even speak to him. He felt small and terrible and alone. The gown was wet where he was holding it, and as he entered X-ray the paper ripped. He glanced over his shoulder and wanted to scream. The ignominious bare-assed patient: he was now one of those little old men you saw in hospitals, hunched over in his bones, shuffling in baby steps down a hall, clutching the back of his gown as he tried to cover himself. He clenched his fists, fought an urge to flee to the windowless room where his clothes were. Questions, there would be questions if he fled, he thought, unclenching his hands, forcing his face into a passive expression.

No one must ever know what he thought; that was the greatest danger.

Nancy Ewill took his robe, ripped as it was, and he had to stand completely naked with his stomach against the cold surface of the machine and then with his back to it, facing Nancy. She stood there watching him in her stiff uniform and starched cap, her unsmiling face as stark as a lunar surface, all that thick dark hair flowing out from under the cap in curls, loose curls, like Shirley Temple's. She *enjoyed* his helplessness.

He looked down at himself. His cock hung limply. Nancy Ewill, R.N., had probably seen dozens of limp cocks in her life. Bed baths for incontinents, postsurgical patients, sure, he thought, no reason to feel self-conscious. But when he looked up again, he could swear she was smiling—one of those smiles when you know the person was trying *not* to smile. Yeah, it was one of *those* smiles.

The overhead light came back on. She handed him a new paper robe, told him to follow her. "My clothes," he said, "are in the examining room."

"Lab first."

"Lab? For what?"

"Blood and urine." What an efficient voice she had, he thought, suddenly hating her.

"Dr. Livesy didn't say anything to me about blood tests." It was a mistake, naturally. Livesy was too old to be practicing medicine.

"It's right here on the chart," she replied, tapping a long, painted nail on the clipboard.

They stopped in the lab doorway. He held on to the jamb to keep from falling forward. Jars of shiny instruments gleamed at him. The aluminum pans were filled with sharp, ugly, hurtful things that swam in alcohol. No, he wouldn't step inside. He couldn't. Already, the smell in the room was making him feel nauseated.

A woman was sitting placidly on a stool with her arm straight out on the table, watching as another nurse swabbed her skin with cotton and uncapped the needle of a vacuum syringe. He looked away, fighting the black spots swelling behind his eyes.

"If you'll have a seat right here, please," Nancy said.

He stared at her name tag as if it were a riddle, as though it would cough up answers. He noticed how it sat on the curve of her breast, and lifted his eyes to her oddly soft and pretty face.

"Uh, Miss Ewill," he stammered, shaking his head, running a finger alongside his nose. He hesitated before he continued; it

173

was important that his voice be controlled. He tried not to look at the woman who'd just had her blood drawn. "I think I'd like to speak to Dr. Livesy first."

"He's with a patient. Have a seat, please." That last word was emphasized, strained. He could tell she was losing patience with him.

"I said I'd like to speak with the doctor first." His voice was harder now, more authoritative, in control. *Bitch, don't you hear me?* The women—the two nurses and the other who'd just had her blood drawn—were looking at him strangely. His gown was soaked under the arms, did it show? The paper stuck to him like a second skin. It irritated him. Everything irritated him. The lights were too bright, reflected off the aluminum containers, the metal at the bases of the syringes, the kidney-shaped dishes filled with cotton balls. The women irritated him most of all.

Nancy Ewill handed him a plastic cup. "Bathroom's down the hall. I'll go get the doctor, but in the meantime, you aren't afraid of peeing in a cup, are you?"

He laughed, even as he hated her. He knew her type. She would try to double-cross him. While he was in the bathroom, she would find an orderly to hold him down so they could take his blood. Vampires, he thought, a bunch of vampires. But he took the cup. He would fool her. "How much do you want?" He smiled pleasantly. "One cc? Two?"

"Whatever you've got," she replied sourly.

He sauntered off down the hall. *You'll get yours, Nancy Ewill, R.N., bitch.* He opened and closed the bathroom door, making sure it was loud enough for her to hear, then hurried into the connecting hall and into the examining room where his clothes were. He ripped off the robe, grabbed his slacks. There were voices in the hall and he gathered up his shirt and jacket and hid behind the door, which was partially open.

The voices passed. Just women talking about men, he thought. He could tell by the way they were laughing that they had just exchanged some small confidence. *Women kiss and tell.* This clinic was filled with neurotic women who enjoyed seeing men helpless and naked. He could easily imagine Nancy Ewill sitting over dinner with her boyfriend, discussing limp cocks. Oh, yeah, she'd get some chuckles on that one.

He was still buttoning his shirt when he stepped into the hall. He peered left, then right. By now, Nancy was probably knocking on the bathroom door, her knuckles tapping just so, naturally, because she was a woman who did everything "just so." Marriage to her would be hell; a man wouldn't be able to take a shit in private. But making love to her . . . well, that would be a different story. Her type always had this cool, detached exterior and an uncontrollable lust and passion inside, just like some heroine in a nineteenth-century romance.

The woman behind the desk smiled at him. He knew her; he had known her for two thousand years and couldn't remember her name. *Leah? Lucy? Laura?*

Laura.

No, no, no. Christ, what was wrong with him? He rubbed the back of his neck, felt the hot dampness there. *Louise. Right, her name was Louise.*

"Just bill me, will you, Louise?"

"Is the doctor going to see you again?" she asked, taking a pencil from behind her ear.

"No, not any time soon, I hope. Everything checked out fine, just fine." He wanted her to shut up so he could get away from here, breathe different air, blue sky, summer.

"Oh, wait a second. He wanted to see you again in a week, about those X-rays," she continued, flipping through the appointment calendar. "What day's good for you, hon?"

He looked uneasily over his shoulder. Any moment now he expected Nancy Ewill to come skidding around the corner, yelling, *Stop that man, don't let him leave!* "Any time. Whatever." A smile was impaled on his face and his feet were already moving toward the door. *Good-bye, Louise, good-bye, good-bye, thank you for the marvelous party.*

"Wait," she called after him. "Wait."

The door whispered shut behind him. He stood alone in the June heat. Birds on a telephone wire overhead twittered and fussed. He ran toward his car.

Five blocks away, he pulled into a shopping center. K-mart, Eckerd's, an A&P, he thought. Good, it was anonymous, and there was a phone booth, just what the doctor ordered. He laughed.

He dug into his pocket for his handkerchief. God, it was so bloody hot. He wiped his face, flipped open the directory, smiled when he found Ewill, N.T. Why was it women bothered with initials? Initials were a blatant giveaway that the woman lived alone, like Laura, he thought, living alone in that big, beautiful house. He jotted down Nancy Ewill's address and phone number, then glanced at his watch. Laura was probably at work.

Sure, where else would she be? She was conscientious, he

thought, like Denise, like Nancy. So many conscientious, castrating women in the world now, he decided. The women's movement had caused the world to backslide, to regress. But women weren't only inferior, they were a mistake in the evolutionary process. There were men everywhere who believed this; his father had believed it, and so had his father's father. It was a tenet, like religion, passed down through the family for generations.

He dropped a quarter into the phone, dialed the campus. The handkerchief was stretched over the mouthpiece. The sun bore down on his back. *Laura, sweet Laura, just wait and see.*

The secretary said she would connect him. The phone rang and rang. He turned his back as a couple passed and discreetly removed his handkerchief, then hung up. He realized he was grinding his teeth, that the sun was setting his back on fire. She was probably in the cafeteria, he thought, sipping coffee, taking a break, playing guessing games about who he was. But she'd never guess, she would never be able to paint a face on him, a name. He existed in the netherworld of imagination.

And by now, at the clinic, Nancy Ewill was probably discussing him with Louise or Livesy or someone. They thought they were closing in on him. He smiled.

He was a man not easily forgotten.

2.

The sun was as plump as a grapefruit in the white, barren sky, and it wasn't even noon yet. Waves of heat hovered over the road in front of Markham's house and insects whined in the absolute stillness. Except for Conway's sensitivity to the heat and the piercing clarity of certain sounds, he had come through his sojourn into Denise Markam's world unscathed.

He stuck his shovel into the ground and leaned on it as he lit a cigarette. The bandana around his head was sweaty and spots of salt had formed just under his temples. He was getting sunburned, and the sound of digging filled him with gloom. Markham's yard was cut up with holes from the fence to the roses to the treehouse, forming an erratic triangle. They'd been at it nearly three hours and hadn't found a thing.

Hobbit lay just beyond in the shade, panting from the heat, watching them with absorption. He was a beautiful old black collie who belonged in kinder weather and watched them only because they had torn into his dune and uncovered four of his bones. Every so often, the dog's eyes shifted out across the yard to the treehouse, as if he were remembering something, but he otherwise remained in the shade, unmoving, drooling, staring.

Tillis, working with a shirt on, his face already a soft pink, his pants rolled to the knees, looked at Conway and shook his head. His cheek, bulging unevenly with tobacco, caved in as he spit and let go of his shovel. "You sure you got that verse right?" he asked. He ran his bandana under the faucet at the side of the house, then slapped it, still sopping wet, against his forehead and retied it.

"Yeah, I'm sure."

"He's got it right," Markham assured them. "I just don't think the notebook is around here, that's all."

"It's got to be here," Conway insisted.

"Christ," Tillis muttered. "All we've got are four bones, two dead snakes, and a nest of ants. I'm telling you, man, this ain't no way to run an airline."

They retreated to the shade of a mango tree. A pitcher of iced tea and glasses were set up on the wicker table. Conway sank into a canvas chair. "Suppose Denise had died a natural death," he said to Markham, "so there wouldn't have been any reason to search her office. That means the key wouldn't have been found. Without the key, there wouldn't have been any money or a letter to Viki. Without either of those things, how could she be sure her notebook would be found? Or that Viki would get her money?"

"Meaning what?" Markham asked. "What're you getting at?"

"Meaning there must be a second key, which should've been found first. I think the key in her office was just a backup. A contingency."

"You think it's with the notebook?" Tillis asked.

"No, it wouldn't make any sense that way. The letter indicated a progression. The key, the safety deposit box, the letter, the notebook: her treasure hunt. This second key's separate."

"Even if you found it," Tillis began, "what difference would it make unless there was an explanation about where it fit? And how could she expect a ten-year-old girl to get all the way to Key West by herself, much less be allowed into the safety deposit box?"

Conway replied, "I think she confided in someone."

"Who? She didn't have any close friends," Markham reminded him.

"It doesn't necessarily have to be a friend. Maybe it was just someone who was blindly loyal."

Markham frowned. "I don't follow."

"I'm just speculating." Conway didn't want to go into it unless he was sure. He already felt as if he'd betrayed the man by not telling him about the trip to Cassadaga. But how did you go about telling a guy that the woman to whom he was married for half a dozen years never really existed? That her life was made up? That her parents were not, as Markham believed, from Westchester County, that her mother had the Power, that the woman was, in fact, illegitimate and had probably never set eyes on her father? You just didn't lay that stuff on a guy over iced tea, Conway thought.

"It still doesn't tell us where the notebook is," Markham said.

"The clue's in the poem, I'm sure of it," Conway murmured.

"I don't know." Markham gestured toward the garden. "So there's Hobbit's dune, and just beyond it where we put Aardvark that Easter morning. He was in a cage about six paces east of the dune, right under the treehouse. It was morning, the sun was in the east. We've dug east *and* west, though, John."

A car pulled into the driveway, stopped, and Ake got out. He came across the lawn with a grin on his face and a folder in his hand. After greeting everyone, he crouched down in the grass, flipped open the folder. "My buddy in the FBI? Well, here's the profile he came up with on Denise's murderer."

Markham's face paled. "I didn't realize the FBI's involved."

"They aren't," Ake assured him. "I sent him a copy of the autopsy report, photographs from the scene of the crime, and all the relevant facts I could think of. This is what he came up with. I made some copies." He gave Tillis and Markham copies and handed the original to Conway, then read aloud the note that accompanied the report:

Dear Ake,

The nature of Denise Markham's work and the apparent cumulative effects of the drug are important variables in determining the profile, so keep in mind this is only *a sketch. But I hope it helps.*

I outlined what I considered to be the pertinent facts and my conclusions, based on those facts. Let me know if I can be of further assistance. And good luck.

Best,
Jerry

Conway looked over at Markham, who was just sitting there, the report in his hand. "You don't have to read it, Don, if—"

Markham waved his hand impatiently. "Of course I'll read it," he replied, and walked away from the others with the report in hand. Conway sat back.

PSYCHOLOGICAL PROFILE
(re: Denise Markham)

FACTS:1) victim was stabbed; 2) stab wound between third and fourth ribs; 3) murder occurred late on a Saturday evening, during school break; 4) body was partially covered by leaves; 5) eyes were closed when victim was found; 6) victim wasn't raped; 7) no sign of a struggle; 8) although victim had pierced ears, she wore no jewelry except wedding ring; 9) purse and briefcase placed deliberately beside body.

CONCLUSIONS: The murderer had his own weapon, which points to a stalker, someone well organized and intelligent, who most likely lives in another part of town and drove to the campus. He knew the victim well enough to be familiar with her routine and schedule and also knew the area—i.e., that the campus would be deserted on a Saturday night during the break.

The precision of the wound and that there was no sign of a struggle indicate the murderer is someone the victim knew and probably trusted. He lingered afterward, covering the body with leaves, closing the victim's eyes, perhaps even removing a pair of earrings, then arranged her personal belongings in a ritualistic manner. These facts indicate:

a) that he feels some remorse;

b) that he might have been emotionally involved with the victim;

c) that the emotional involvement was probably reciprocal.

The theft of the victim's earrings, if it occurred, could be indicative of several things. Killers often carry away something that belonged to the victim so that the experience can be re-created in memory. While this may certainly be a component, the earrings could have an emotional connection—perhaps they were a gift from the murderer, or perhaps the victim had worn them on a special occasion.

The deliberate placement of the victim's purse and briefcase, the fact that no mutilation was involved, indicate the murderer is not an impulsive teenager or someone in his early twenties. Since nothing was stolen except, perhaps, a pair of earrings, robbery wasn't the motive.

The deliberate actions of the killer indicate a tightly controlled individual who must be the master of a given situation. He holds grudges, possesses cunning and above-average intelligence. He is probably college-educated, in his early twenties to late thirties, and is now under a great deal of stress and experiencing intense guilt about what he has done. Yet, he feels relatively certain he won't be caught.

Since there was no mutilation involved, he probably was raised by both parents during his formative years. His need for control indicates that he's probably had unsatisfactory relationships with women. The evidence doesn't point to a mass murderer. But *if* he used the drug over an extended period of time, he could be an extremely dangerous individual. He might, for instance, project his feelings about the victim onto other women—terrorizing them to feed his illusion of control.

My suggestion is to bombard the media, make him think the investigation is getting closer and closer to a resolution. Don't let him off the hook psychologically; he's feeling guilty and jumpy.

Conway glanced up when the radio squawked. "Shit," Tillis muttered, getting up. "That dispatcher loves tracking me down. I'm coming, I'm coming," he called out. "Just hold your horses."

Markham returned to the shade of the tree and handed Ake the report. "Well?" he said.

"It's a beginning," Ake replied. "And we've already started bombarding the media, like he suggested. Spots about the drug, news releases concerning the investigation, an eight hundred number to call for information."

"Hey," Tillis shouted, running back across the lawn, grabbing his shirt from a branch, "we gotta split. Blanchard is standing on a ledge ten stories up, getting ready to jump."

"*Jump?*" Conway leaped to his feet as Tillis wiggled into his shirt and ripped the bandana off his head.

"Is that the man whose wife . . ." Markham began, and Ake nodded. "Good God," he whispered, following the men to the end of the drive, "when is it going to end?"

"We'll get back just as soon as we can," Conway assured him, "and help patch your lawn back together."

Markham nodded. As the two cars peeled out of the driveway, Conway glanced back and saw Markham just standing there.

18

1.

JEROME BLANCHARD WAS drunk.

He was not standing on a ledge ten stories up, he was sitting, his legs dangling over the side, a bottle of bourbon between them.

He couldn't remember how he'd gotten out here or why he'd left the apartment. But he knew that as long as he didn't move and just kept on drinking, everything would be fine. The bourbon dulled the pain, even though it left him a little nauseated. Had he eaten anything? He couldn't remember. Twenty years ago, he could drink a fifth of bourbon a day, from morning to night, and feel just fine the next day. Twenty years ago, though, he was the big three five and in shape. Even his memory was in shape back then. His mind had been like a steel trap, ordered, indexed, cross-referenced. But twenty years ago anything was possible, and the future was utterly limitless. It had been going steadily downhill ever since.

He wiped one hand and then the other on his shirt, a T-shirt, it was, with a green alligator on it. Livvy had bought it for him in the Hong Kong airport, of all places. Now it smelled of hundred proof and was stained with orange juice, egg, bourbon, coffee. Funny, he thought, he must've eaten something today. Otherwise, how'd all the stains get on the shirt? Yesterday, right, he must've worn the shirt yesterday and pulled it on because it was the closest thing to the bed.

Blanchard poured some bourbon into his hand, splashed it on his face. The smell burned the inside of his nose, but it cooled him off. The heat out here was brutal; it was all this concrete. He'd been sitting here for a long time, since—when? But time was something he'd left under the bed with his slippers; it didn't count anymore.

He rubbed his fists into his eyes and could see all the dark in there. If he looked back far enough, he knew he would see Livvy's face, lit up like a saint's. A couple of times he thought he heard voices, but he couldn't turn his head because he was sure he would puke. If he puked, he would choke and would never have his answers. He wanted to tumble into the bone-white heat, where his life would flash before his eyes like it was supposed to do, flash with an absolute clarity that would burn away Turnbalt's voice saying, "Do it my way, Jerry," and the nigger's voice, "You're a shit, Blanchard," and Marie saying, "Remember when . . ." He wanted to know what his life had meant.

"Hey, Blanchard," someone shouted close to his head. He gripped the neck of the bottle. It was a pretty color, like the inside of an M&M. Cold crawled up his left side and the bottle blurred. This had happened before, sweet Jesus, he had seen himself sitting here like this, seen it in a dream or somewhere, maybe when they'd done the drug. Déjà vu, that's what Livvy would have called it.

"Blanchard," the voice called again.

Oh, it hurt. The noise pierced his skull. He looked slowly toward the balcony. He saw someone, a man, leaning forward, about to toss him a rope. The man's face was familiar, but he couldn't place the name. Twenty years ago, he thought, faces had been attached to names. "Go away," he muttered. "Please just go away."

"Listen to me, Blanchard," the voice demanded.

Turnbalt, he thought. Only Turnbalt spoke to him like that. *Do this, do that, Jerry. Do it my way.* Blanchard squinted, trying to focus on the man's face. He didn't look like Frank. "It's so hot," he said.

"Water? You want some water?" the voice asked.

He had bourbon, what'd he need water for?

But the bourbon was warm, too warm to quench his thirst. "Water, yes, that's what I want." He also wanted to get up and walk around, stretch his legs. His calves were cramping. But if he moved, he might move too much, and that was a little scary. He touched his tongue to the lip of the bottle and wished the voice would hurry up with the water. He would feel better once he'd had something cold to drink.

2.

Conway peered down ten stories. The fire department had just arrived and men were scurrying around in the parking lot like ants or Disney caricatures, clearing the area, waving their arms, bringing out the trampoline.

"Keep him talking," Ake said from the doorway, handing him a tall glass of cold water. He walked back inside with the walkie-talkie in his hand, said something to the men below that Conway couldn't hear.

The ledge was accessible. It was just a matter of climbing over the railing. But it was barely eighteen inches wide, Blanchard was about fifteen feet out and completely deranged. He wore a white shirt and his pajama bottoms and was so drunk he seemed unaware that his head was bleeding. Conway guessed he'd been out there nearly an hour before one of the neighbors had noticed and called in. Now the crowd below was growing as the curious wandered in from the beach, drawn by the fire trucks and sirens.

"Tell him Olivia's in here," Ake suggested.

"He's not *that* drunk."

"The man's lost it, Conway. You could tell him his grandmother was here and he'd believe you."

3.

The voice again.

Loud, terrible, that voice, telling him Livvy was inside, waiting for him. Then why didn't she come out onto the porch and talk to him? Turnbalt, sure, that was the reason. All along, Livvy had been fond of Turnbalt, she'd loved being with him that night when . . . when the four of them . . . He gulped from the bottle of bourbon, winced at the bitter taste, at the way it burned his throat as it went down.

"Here's your water, Blanchard," the voice said. "Now see if you can scoot over here."

If Livvy was inside, he thought, she would've brought him the water. The voice couldn't fool him. "She's with Frank," he whispered. His throat was so parched that it was hard to talk. He sipped from the bottle. "She's with Frank, I know she is," he said, louder now.

"She's in here, man!"

"You're lying!" Blanchard shouted, feeling the words clawing at his throat. "You're lying, whoever the hell you are, and just go away and leave me alone!"

He tipped the bottle to his mouth again, drank deeply. Some of the bourbon trickled from the corner of his mouth, down his chin. Livvy had gotten him into this, he thought, Livvy and Turnbalt. And Marie, too, he decided, lovely Marie with the angel's face and the devil's soul. He rested his head against the wall, curled his toes in the warm air, moved his ass little by little to the left. He heard Livvy singing; such a pretty voice, such a talented woman, his Livvy.

He drew his legs up against him, pressed his cheek to his knees, closed his eyes so he could hear Livvy's singing more clearly. *She could have made Carnegie Hall, she could have—*

He let his toes creep to the edge of the ledge, peek over. He felt a breeze, an emptiness, the abyss. He lifted his head. The voice was calling again, but he didn't care, couldn't even hear the words. Livvy was singing and playing the piano. It was a familiar tune, it dug into him, into his San Francisco heart. That was where they'd gone for their honeymoon: the city of lovers.

Blanchard began to weep. The bottle slipped out of his hands. He leaned forward to catch it and then he was falling in a slow motion freedom, into the warm blue where sky met sea. It was like being twenty-five again and the voice was gone and the air smelled so bitterly of bourbon. He felt a rush of heat, then the cold along his left side again. *It's your death, stalking you,* he thought. His eyes flew open and the pavement was rushing toward him like a black, yawning mouth, the mouth of a whale. A scream tore from his throat. *My answers, I still don't have my answers.*

Jerome Blanchard missed the trampoline by inches. He was doing fifty-two miles an hour when he hit the concrete. He bounced once before the horrified crowd, and ten stories above his splattered remains, Conway slapped his hands over his mouth. He made it as far as the kitchen before he got sick.

4.

Captain Truro blew into Conway's office like a foul wind, his bulldog's face sagging in the jowls, his eyes heavy as if with sleep. He was puffing on one of his putrid cigars and came in barking orders, demanding answers, his cheeks inflamed. Conway felt like punching him in the mouth.

"I've been getting calls since this morning. We've got people pressuring to tie this mess up. City Hall's on my back, Tallahassee's on my back, maybe even Christ himself is on my back and I just don't know it yet. The governor's gotten wind of this and he's sending one of his lackeys down here tomorrow morning to investigate."

Conway didn't bother looking up from Blanchard's bank statement. Tillis, on the other side of the room, continued going through Blanchard's canceled checks. It was Ake who popped to attention.

"What's the governor got to do with this?"

"His war on drugs," Truro replied, as if it should have been perfectly obvious. "Ridding south Florida of drug traffic." He poked the air with his cigar. "His assistant is going to want medical and lab reports, autopsy reports, answers. Most of all, he'll want answers."

"We're doing what we can," Ake assured him.

"Not good enough. Three people are dead and there might be more dead tomorrow. The eight hundred number has been swamped with calls. This man is going to want answers. Facts." Truro looked over at Conway, who had picked up his coffee mug and was walking over to the pot brewing on the counter. "What're the facts, John?"

Conway kept hearing Blanchard yelling, "She's with Frank," and Markham saying, "Who? She didn't have any close friends," and Laura muttering, "I hope Denise didn't love roses." He saw Blanchard squashed against the pavement like an insect and Turnbalt patting his goddamned midriff, puffing on his Cuban cigar, and the images stacked up in his head and toppled into a migraine. He suddenly hated Truro for the fat, incompetent bureaucrat he was, coasting along on the diligence of the people beneath him, not giving a damn about anything except how the department looked. Jen was right. The man was an asshole.

"Conway," Truro said, snapping his fingers.

"Get out of here," Conway said quietly.

"Excuse me?"

"Get out, Mike. We've got work to do."

Incredulity pulled Truro's sagging jowls even lower. His inflamed cheeks turned bright red. "You can't talk to me like that, John."

His voice was loud, abrasive, and Conway suddenly exploded. "Then don't come barging the fuck in here demanding answers to something you haven't bothered with since it started just because your ass is now on the line. Just get out and let us do our jobs."

Truro stepped forward, shook his cigar in Conway's face. "Now listen here." Conway slapped Truro's arm away. The cigar flew out of his hand, flipped once in the air, landed on the other side of the room. "I could have you fired for that," Truro said, his voice now low, mean, "and for some dozen infractions you've committed since you started on this case, including—"

"So fire me. It would be a blessing."

Tillis picked up the cigar, set it in an ashtray, sat down with the checks again. Ake said, "You fire him, you might as well fire me, too, Captain."

A lengthy silence followed. Conway was suddenly aware of all the tiny, persistent sounds in the room: the ticking of the clock on the wall, the sighing of the coffeepot, the occasional burp from the pint-sized refrigerator in the corner. Tillis finally cleared his throat. The flap of skin under Truro's chin shook like a frog's. "I want you both in my office tomorrow morning at eight," he said at last, then walked over to Tillis, extended his hand for his cigar. Tillis handed it to him. "Got that? Eight o'clock sharp tomorrow morning. And I want facts.'' He sauntered through the door and Ake slammed it shut behind him.

"My *ass*," he grumbled.

Tillis picked up his spittoon, spat. Now that the order of power was clear, still intact, he said, "In case anyone wants to know, there are still four boxes of canceled checks to go through.''

"I knew I should've gone to Colorado," Conway remarked.

"The man wants facts," Ake said, yanking out his chair, sitting down at the adding machine, "then fine. Let's give the turkey facts. Figures, Tillis, gimme some figures.''

"Hey, Ake, thanks," Conway said.

"Don't mention it, man.''

Three hours later, the facts were these: between April and December of 1983, Jerome Blanchard had liquidated $10,000 worth of stocks, another $17,000 in Treasury bills, and had sold a piece of property for $30,000. As far as they could determine, the money hadn't been reinvested—at least not in anything that had been recorded. According to his tax return, his income in 1984 was $40,000, and yet the man's ledger, maintained with a bookkeeper's neatness, showed some $155,000 of expenses over and above normal living costs. His tax returns for both 1983 and 1984 were signed by Frank Turnbalt.

"I don't understand why Turnbalt would sign his name to these," Tillis said.

"Arrogance," Conway replied with a certainty that surprised him. "He never figured anyone would get wise to him.''

"We could get a warrant tonight," Ake suggested. "No problem at all.''

"He'd get off, Ake. We need something a lot more solid.''

"So what do we tell this Peeping Tom from Tallahassee?''

"As little as possible. Tillis, I want you to tail Marie Turnbalt, starting tomorrow morning. My guess is this neat, exclusive drug ring is operating out of her store in the Grove, where south Florida's beautiful people buy their jewels and their highs. Just think of it, guys. Markham Magic is the newest thing, better than designer jeans.''

Ake leaned back in the chair, stretched his immense arms over his head. "There's got to be a middle man. I have trouble seeing Turnbalt peddling this shit himself.''

"I'm sure there's a middle man. But I think they're selling to close friends, the inner circle, you know, like stockbrokers, attorneys, Indian chiefs. A designer drug," Conway said, pushing away from the desk. "I say we take a ride over to Porky's. Got a job for him.''

Tillis rolled his eyes. "You mean bugging Marie's store."

"You got it."

"You know how Truro feels about using ex-cons," Tillis said, turning his hand over, examining his nails, buffing them on his shirt.

"I don't give a shit *what* Truro feels about anything," Conway snapped. "Porky's the best in the state, maybe in the whole Southeast."

Ake rubbed his chin. "Not only that, he owes me one."

Conway laughed. "You ain't all bad, boy, even for a blackie."

Ake wrung his hands and squealed, "Massa, massa, youse too good to me."

Tillis muttered, "Gawd."

5.

The closet door was open and Laura kept imagining the Man coming out of there like the creature from the Black Lagoon, hideous face part fish, part something else, and he would be whispering, "My rainbow, what'd you do with my rainbow?" He would slip a blade between her ribs before she could even scream. It had happened that quickly for Denise, she knew this just as she knew he was out there. Somewhere. She could feel it. She knew it in that inner place where you always knew such things.

She kicked off the sheet, pulled the phone closer to the bed, wishing she'd gone over to Rita's for the night or that she'd asked Conway to stay here. The gun was on the nightstand, with the box of shells, but seemed no more useful to her than sweet Emily, lying at the foot of the bed.

Laura picked up the receiver, thought of Ian's call earlier. He'd gotten one of the contracts. He would probably be home late tomorrow. He said.

She started to dial Rita's number but changed her mind. It was past midnight. She couldn't awaken Rita just because she was frightened. My God, she was too old for this nonsense. And besides, what was there to be afraid of? There was no one in the closet. No one in the house. She was sealed inside with her fear.

As she pulled the sheet around her shoulders, she felt Emily jump to the floor. A moment later, the cat passed into her field of vision, tail straight in the air, and leaped onto the windowsill. *Emily's heard something.*

Laura sat up, reached for the gun. The dull pounding started at the back of her head. She crept up to the window, staying low enough so she couldn't be seen passing in front of the venetian blind. She'd made it through last night alone and that hadn't been so bad, had it? Nothing had happened.

"Em," she whispered. "What's out there?" She touched the cat's tail, raised herself slowly, and peeked out.

Dark, horribly dark.

And the dark devoured everything except the tips of the pines, swaying in an occasional spasm of moonlight when the clouds cleared away. Then she saw it: movement, something.

You imagined it, Laura.

She crouched there as the pounding in her skull crested, moved away again. The floodlights, she thought, and tore into the hall. Her hand slapped the switches. She sucked in her breath. It should have been as bright as high noon outside, there should have been lights coming through the crack under the bedroom door.

There should have been and wasn't.

Laura flew into the bedroom, dived for the phone. The dull pounding became a roar in her head and of course the phone was dead and of course the bedroom lights didn't work and of course there was no storm to blame, not this time. He had cut the wires.

She scooped up the gun and as she started for the stairs heard him at the back of the house.

She cocked the gun, looked frantically around for someplace to hide. And then she remembered.

19

1.

THE WINDOW GAVE easily, almost soundlessly. He cut around the frame of the screen, pressed his hands flat against the sill, and pushed himself up and in. *You're a sick pup*, the voice whispered inside him. His sneakers sighed against the wooden floors.

A sick pup, yes, he thought it was probably true. Nancy Ewill, R.N., undoubtedly believed it. Denise had.

In the living room, two luminous balls were suspended in the air, moving as he moved. For a horrid instant, he was certain the balls were the eyes of a witch, that Laura had somehow conjured unspeakable perils from the primeval depths of her mind, that Denise had returned from the dead. Then he realized it was the cat, watching, waiting like a sphinx in the dust of forever, seeing it all. As he started up the stairs, the animal ran. He returned the knife to his pocket, barely aware that he'd even removed it. Another time, perhaps, he would teach the cat a thing or two.

He was perspiring heavily now. The ski mask, the dark clothes, kept his skin from breathing. And with the air conditioner off in the house, he would only get warmer in here. He gripped the railing, steadying himself.

At the top of the stairs he stopped, light-headed from remembering how his hands swam through the colorful silk of her underwear, gowns, how he transformed her closet into a rainbow. What magic he created, what beauty. Now his legs moved forward, propelled by that smoldering libidinous urge to conquer, to kill, to turn her into a pillar of salt for her sins.

At the doorway, he listened. He couldn't hear her breathing. He approached the bed, saw the sheets pulled back, the pillows heaped on top of each other, he saw she was gone. He spun around. The beam of his flashlight danced erratically across the closet and bathroom doors, which were open. *The game, this was a game, of course.* Like Denise's games, he thought. He kneeled at the bedside, smiling a little at this unexpected twist in events, pleased with Laura's ingenuity. He peered into the dark beneath the bed. Nothing.

He pulled at the sides of the ski mask, allowing his skin to breathe. When he let it go, it made a soft, sighing sound, and he fought the urge to rip it off, to show himself, to—

They were connected, he and Laura. He could feel it just as surely as if a copper wire running from her to him were glowing in the dark, *I am, you are* . . . The knife clicked open. He couldn't remember removing it from his pocket. This was what happened with Denise. It was as if the knife were a separate being, with a will of its own, desires and passions of its own. It lay sturdy and hard in his glove, an extension of his hand. She was here; oh, yes, he could *feel* her in the house, in the air. Suddenly everything inside him broke loose and he went after the room as if it were something living. He sank the knife into the pillows, ripping them up one side and down the other until the air was a shower of feathers and the pillows were limp as corpses. He stuck the blade into the mattress and drew it down the center, stabbing and stabbing through the sheets, into its very heart, then ran into the closet. For just an instant, he was a boy again, scrambling through clothes to hide from his father's voice and his mother's sobs. But instead of crouching, he lunged at the dresses and blouses, the pants and shirts, and he stabbed and stabbed.

He was breathing hard. Odors were released. Perfumes, powders, body smells. The scents flattened out against him until he began to gasp for air. He stumbled back, saw those luminous eyes like a witch's, rolled up on the balls of his feet, raised his arms, and hissed like a viper. The cat tore into the hall.

He jerked out the drawers in the bureau, impaled her clothes on the knife, knocked everything off the top—bottles, makeup, a ceramic frog bank, jewelry. *It was bad to hide, Laura. It was bad to hide and not come out. That isn't how we play this game.* He would punish her for doing this, he thought, punish her so she would learn, so she would remember. With his arm, he swept books from a shelf over the bed, then went after the blinds, clawing at them, swinging the knife at them until they were in a heap on the floor.

When there was nothing left to destroy in the bedroom, he flew downstairs, into the living room. He stood in the center, gripping his flashlight in one hand, brandishing the knife in the other, then fell on the chairs, the couch, the curtains. He dropped to his knees, dug his fingers under the edge of the carpet, pulled it away from the floor. *You see? You see what you make me do when you play your stupid hide and seek game, Laura? You see?* She was as bad as Denise, as stubborn. But he would teach her.

He toppled the bookcase, knowing how much she loved her books, ripped several magazines in two, knocked over plants, threw tufts of dirt into the air, then sliced the leaves of an ivy to shreds. *Punish, punish.*

A noise upstairs distracted him. The cat? He took the stairs two at a time, panting now, sure that the rooms were alive, bleeding, howling with pain. Jesus, it was a terrible sound. He slapped his hands over his ears, the flashlight tumbled to the floor, and the top of his body folded toward the bottom as a white heat burned into his side, forcing him to his knees.

He felt as though his flesh were being scraped along the surface of the sun. His blood would boil. He lifted the ski mask as far as the bridge of his nose, breathed deeply. After a moment, the pain and the heat passed. He pushed the mask back in place, opened his eyes, found the flashlight. Something near the wall caught his eyes. He moved toward it, laughed as he picked it up. Silly woman, he thought. In her haste to escape him, she'd lost her gun. He slipped the gun in the waistband of his pants, saw the box of shells when he returned to the bedroom, and swept them to the floor. It was possible she'd escaped out the front or back when he was jimmying the window, possible that she'd known he was coming. At this very instant, she could be hiding in the silence of the pines. Or it might be a trick.

Enraged that she might have outwitted him, he decided he

would check every closet, every nook and cranny in the house. He would check the garage, too, and the trunk of the car. But first he would leave his calling card, like the notes, only better. He unbuckled his belt, his jeans dropped around his ankles. He thought of Nancy Ewill, R.N., watching him as he stood at the X-ray machine, and he was so excited, it didn't take long. A few quick jerks and he came all over the torn sheets, the bed of feathers, the dead mattress.

Impatient to begin his hunt, he pulled his jeans up. If she wasn't in the house, he decided he would comb the entire woods out back from one end to the other. His car was parked out there. Perfect, yes sir, he would get her into the backseat, show her what happened to naughty girls. Then, if she was good, if she was nice to him, if she treated him right, he would teach her little tricks. He would teach her body maneuvers that he would eventually try with Nancy Ewill, R.N. He laughed out loud at the thought of Nancy's starched little white nurse's cap going floppy as a bunny's ears.

2.

Laura had climbed through the hole and was huddled tight as a question mark on a four-foot-square piece of paneling. It was above the closet in what was supposed to have been the attic, a project she had never completed. It would just be a matter of time before the Man realized the closet was open for a reason, that the gun was lying beyond it because she'd dropped it in her scramble up the shelves, when she was trying to slide the panel open.

Time: how much of it did she have? This was *his* time, she thought, which was no time, nowhere. She didn't know how long she'd been up here, but she could hear him on the rampage again, opening and slamming doors, systematically seeking her out.

Her lips were dry and cracking. She had to go to the bathroom. It was so hot, so dry and dusty up here, she couldn't breathe properly and was afraid she would sneeze. She was afraid her body, paralyzed with inertia, would betray her and he would hear. Pinpricks dug into her neck and shoulders. Every sound seemed closer than the last and brought terror one step further along her tongue. She clenched her teeth. Her buttocks were numb from sitting.

Laura finally lifted her head, rubbed her neck, froze as she thought for sure she heard him directly below her. Would he see the panel? Had she shut it tightly? Had the paint faded over the years so it would show? She looked down. Her hand was so near the crack that she felt air. She thought about moving farther back, away from the opening. But beyond the seams, beyond where she crouched, there was only insulation.

She waited. She could hear him lifting shelves, throwing things to the floor. She was suddenly grateful for the dark, realized he couldn't see the panel because he'd cut the wires, and she wanted to giggle at the ironic twist. She pressed her forehead against her knees, sliding against the sweat, growing sticky. Had he already found the gun? Probably. She thought of the silhouette at the firing range, remembered the one shot dead center. Had she not been so careless, in such a rush . . . *If only . . . Cut, retake, retake.* Senseless to count the ifs, she thought.

Her nightgown was filled with static electricity now and flickered in the dark when she lifted her head. Perspiration slid down the undersides of her arms, her neck and back were wet, and she heard him pulling boxes away from the wall, then suddenly kicking the door shut. Air, pushed up through the crack, brushed her hand, stirred the dust. She sat forward, back, imagining the layout of the house, wondering where he was. He'd been in the bedroom a long time. Would she descend into rainbows again? *Would she descend at all?*

Ian, where are you? Where the hell are you when I need you?

She grew dizzy peering into the dark, creating shapes from nothing. She lost touch with herself. She was floating in a tank of warm water, a sensory deprivation tank. She would emerge as the missing link of the species, either an evolutionary throwback or the next step forward, sure. It was perfectly clear now.

Laura drew her legs in closer to her body, locked her arms around them. Her bladder was going to explode. She would die of thirst up here, of dehydration, she would die in the attic of her own home. He would wait her out.

But he wouldn't stay in the house once it was light, would he? It would be too risky. Someone might arrive, someone— Was there a window up here? She'd been in the attic only once before, the day she'd installed the panel of wood, fitting it between the two beams, the day she'd decided not to complete the flooring because she didn't want to spend the money. If only she— *What? What the hell difference could it possibly have made if she'd spent the money?*

She closed her eyes, breathed shallowly, as if she were scuba diving and trying to preserve the air in her tank. The dark inside herself was a little easier to deal with than the dark outside. It seemed less permanent somehow, she could almost believe she was dreaming.

Get used to it, kid. She had no guarantee that dawn would

chase him away. After all, the day he'd come here, rearranged her room and her belongings, it had been daylight.

She would be missed at school, wouldn't she? Surely he knew this. Someone would come looking for her. *Rita.* Her secretary would call the house, and when no one answered she would get in touch with Rita. *But when?* Her first class wasn't until ten. When would her secretary think to call? By ten-thirty? Eleven? It was important to know the time. It had been shortly after midnight when she was going to call Rita. How long was it between then and when Emily had jumped into the window?

Why should he care if she'd be missed at school? If he found her, then she was dead and it wouldn't make any difference. If he didn't find her, if he thought she'd gotten out of the house, it still wouldn't make any difference, because the heat or her thirst would get her first.

She rubbed her forehead against her knee, felt the hot threat of tears. *Had he hurt Em? Would he hurt Em to get at her?* The thought of this, of finding Emily impaled or her stomach splayed open, made her catch her breath and clap her hands over her mouth as a sob escaped her. *Not Em, please not Em.*

She was doing time, she thought. But what was her crime? *Why me? Why me?* The profluent lament mocked her in the dark; it was a riddle, just another goddamned riddle. *Who? Who would do this to her? Whom had she angered or hurt so much?*

The weight of her insomnia this past week dropped away, bit by bit, as she waited. The heat made her drowsy. She floated off into the silence, into the warmth of her tank, and her head slipped away from the beam where it rested and into the insulation. It startled her, acted on her like an electric shock, pushed her forward. She gasped, waited for the door to fly open, the panel to shoot for the stars, waited for the Man's head to appear, for a Cheshire-cat grin to glow from the bottom of the closet as he shouted, *Gotcha, gotcha.* The attic filled with the pounding of her heart, became her heart, and the beams of wood were her veins, the blood pumping through, rushly hotly around and around. When she heard something below, her bladder let loose and tears finally came.

It would end. Sooner or later, he would have to leave. She could endure almost anything as long as she could see her way clear to the end. But how would she know when the end had come? *You'll know. You'll climb down out of here and put your ear to the closet door and take your chances. You'll know.*

Something brushed past the tips of her toes. "God," she whimpered, pulling her legs closer to her, as close as they would come. Was it fuzzy? She was curled into a ball, waiting for whatever it was to come back the other way. Rats? Roaches? Mice? Spiders? Her skin began to crawl with things. She scratched at her toes, ran her nails up her legs, her arms, scratching until she felt the warm dampness of blood.

Ants.

"OhGodohGodohGod, get away from me," she whispered, slapping and scratching now. Worse than the Man, worse than the dark, the waiting: her thoughts coiled into a tight, white ball of panic in her skull. She tightened her lips to keep from crying out, pushed herself up so that she was squatting, and hugged her knees tightly, her chin against the bone. She stood in her own urine, because the ants wouldn't come close to liquid unless it was sweet. She remembered this from childhood, remembered it because she and Rita had accidentally disturbed a nest of ants once. Oh, yes, she could see them still, huge red ants, the kind that grew in the tropics. Within minutes, the ground was swarming with them, and they'd finally escaped into the water and there they had stayed.

What river?

The Sewanee, in northern Florida, during junior high, yes, she remembered now. It seemed vitally important that she remember these small facts. The insects had swarmed along the banks for hours, waiting for her and Rita, stalking them as if propelled by some malign intelligence. She couldn't recall anymore what they were doing at the river, but it didn't matter. She began to cry, grew angry at herself for succumbing so easily. *Stop, take deep breaths, find a mantra, pray, do something.* But her arms and legs and hands itched, and once the urine dried up, once—

"Oh, please, just go away," she whimpered, squeezing her eyes shut.

3.

He had checked everywhere. She must have gotten out and had taken her keys, too, because all the doors leading outside were locked. Would a woman on the lam lock a door behind her? Would he?

He was suddenly afraid someone would pull off into the pines where his car was parked. Maybe some kids looking for a place to screw, maybe some drunks, he thought. He envisioned this so clearly, he was nearly convinced it had already happened, that his car had been reported and the police were on their way.

The rage of his destruction climbed up along the walls of dark in the house, evidence of his derangement. *Too far this time, he went too far.* He scrambled downstairs, remembering Denise and the light in Laura's window that night, Laura working diligently on her grades. *You should've stayed home that night, Laura, you should have stayed outa my way.*

At the back door he glanced over his shoulder, and the last thing he saw were the luminous eyes, following him. He ran off into the trees, into the dark safety of the pines.

4.

She was standing, feeling her way to the vertical beams. The ants were climbing all over her feet and even as she lifted one and then the other, slapping at them, brushing them away, she grabbed hold of the post and reached a foot out, feeling in space for the horizontal beam. Her foot touched it. She set it down carefully, then extended her right arm for the corresponding vertical beam. There was no wood paneling, just a long piece of scratchy pine about six inches wide.

Better than ants, stinging her, crawling all over her. Were they in her hair? The thought panicked her, her scalp began to itch terribly, she felt herself swaying as she straddled the beams. She reached out, hugged the vertical beam, held on, her nose squashed against it and filling with the scent of cedar. Slowly, she brought her other leg over. For a long time she didn't move. Didn't think. Barely breathed. Then the burning, the itching, started along her foot, then her ankles and arms and legs. She scratched, wet her fingers with saliva, rubbed them over wherever the burning was. The welts were swelling. Would the ants follow?

She could almost see this, an army of red ants moving along the underside of the panel, to the insulation, then across the great silver desert of aluminum and up along the underside of the beam on which she now stood. She would have to move again and again. She would have to keep moving until she was at the far end of the attic, where the dark was profound, an abyss, outer space. *And what lived there? Rats?*

She gripped the post until her shoulders ached, until her arms were scratched from the wood. She tried not to think about how her skin burned, tried to think of nothing but dawn, of the Man leaving. In her mind, she focused on the sun, blurred, white, rising in the June sky. She dozed, her forehead resting against the wood until it slipped. No sounds for hours, she thought, but it could be a trick. He could be sitting at the top of the stairs, waiting for her with *her* gun. What irony, if he shot her with her own gun.

But no, that wasn't his style.

She wasn't sure how she knew this, but it was a certainty like instinct. There were particulars she knew about him now, as if terror had created a new, sharper kind of awareness in her. Hatred, not sex, impelled him. It had seized his misogyny, inflated it, twisted it inside out.

Laura drifted in and out of consciousness, absorbed with the riddle of the Man, the terrible burning, certain she would die up here of thirst if he remained very long in the house after the sun had come up.

The dryness became a part of her, it had transmuted her body. It was foreign to her, no longer hers, this body. She came awake suddenly, her limbs tense. She'd heard something. Was he on the rampage again? She pressed her ear to the cedar, hoping the sound would travel through the wood as if through water. Was someone calling her? Was it *him*? Just a trick, that's all it was, just another trick.

She waited a few moments, then carefully stepped across to the other beam, where the panel was. She dug her nails in between the cracks, her senses alert for the first movement, the first sly touch of the ants, then lifted the panel back a little. Then a little more. And more. She gazed down, blinked. She was stiff from immobility. *Light, under the closet door. Or was it an hallucination? From focusing on the sun in her mind?*

Laura scooted closer to the hole, pushed the panel all the way back, and suddenly something behind her—*nails? Was there a pile of nails up here?*—slid clattering into the insulation. But she no longer cared. She sank her fingers between the mesh of the shelves and was so hurried, so careless, she fell the remaining distance to the floor.

Beyond the door, she heard, "Laura, what's happened? Are you here?"

Rita.

She grappled for the handle, crazy for light and for air and water, for the sight of Rita's face like a signal it was over, that she'd beaten the odds.

Still clutching the knob, she swung into the hall. The light hurt her eyes. Her mouth opened to shout Rita's name, but no sounds came out. They were lost inside her. They were buried in the dryness, which reached all the way down into the center of her heart. She released the knob, lying half in the hall now, and began to hit her heels against the door, harder and harder until she heard Rita on the stairs.

She lifted her head as Rita's face appeared at the top, as if over the dune of a desert, a mirage, an oasis, and then she passed out.

PART THREE

Hobbits and Aardvarks

20

1.

CONWAY AND AKE stepped through the debris. Now and then they glanced at each other and Ake shrugged his huge shoulders as if to rid himself of some terrible weight, but neither of them spoke. There wasn't much to say: the rooms said it all. Except that the walls were still standing and the kitchen was untouched, the house looked as if it had been gutted.

The curtains in the living room hung in strips and the rod had been pulled away from the wall on one side, giving the window a sadly lopsided look. The furniture had not been simply ripped apart, but the stuffing had been dug out and scattered around the room like confetti. In spots, the carpet had been torn from the floor, almost as though the man had dug his fingers beneath and pulled with a savage strength. There were books lying everywhere and the case in which they'd been was on its face, split down the back. Plants had been toppled, tufts of dirt flung as far as the kitchen. But the upstairs, particularly Laura's bedroom, had taken the brunt of the man's rage.

Conway had seen all the horrors of homicide: bodies shot up or stabbed beyond recognition, blood-splattered walls, clothing, hit-and-runs, faces squashed in like ripe fruit. But what he saw in Laura's bedroom was almost worse. It was as if the man's psyche had suddenly erupted, and rather than turn the knife on himself, he'd gone after the room. Bed, pillows, blinds, even the closet. There were nightgowns and underclothing scattered around, all of them torn, and little was left of the clothes in the closet. The two plants that had been by the window had been knocked off their stands onto the rug. Rage. And yet, the semen was deliberate. Perhaps that was the most frightening part of all: in the midst of his fury, the man had stopped, dropped his drawers, and jacked off.

"You'll be able to get a blood type from the semen, won't you?" Conway asked Pivot and Karen Pauling, who were kneeling over the bed, taking samples from the sticky feathers and material.

Pivot looked up, pushed his glasses back on his nose. "This

isn't my field, you know, John. I feel like puking, that's what I feel like doing. Corpses aren't nearly so messy."

Karen stood, placed her hand in the small of her back, and stretched. She pointed at Pivot and then circled her finger in the air at her temple and mouthed, "Crazy." "We'll try with the blood type, John. Shouldn't be any problem. If it's A negative, then you've got the same man who killed the other two women, huh?"

"Or I'm at least a little closer to finding him."

Ake was going through the closet when he suddenly said, "Hey, Conway, look what I found." He came out with Emily curled in his arms. "She was asleep on top of some clothes."

Karen Pauling came over and took the cat, cooing at her, scratching her under the neck. "I bet she's starved," she said, and went downstairs to feed her.

One of the exterminators stuck his head in the doorway. "Best keep the closet closed for a few hours, Mr. Conway. You don't want that stuff in the rest of the house."

"Was it a nest?" Ake asked.

"Yup, sure was. The attic was infested. Carpenter ants. Nasty critters. Not many houses in south Florida have attics, but the ones that do usually have the ants, too. They love the heat. Anyway, we got everything that moved. Must be a hundred and ten up there. How long did the lady . . . ?"

"About nine hours," Conway replied. Pivot made a face and shuddered. "Thanks again for coming over on such short notice."

"I hope they don't have insects in China," Pivot said, getting up. "Or wherever I'm going when I catch my slow boat. I hate bugs. I hate anything that crawls." He looked around the room. "I guess that about does it. Fingerprint people find anything?"

"Nope," Ake replied.

"Where's Truro?" Pivot whispered. "And his friend?"

Conway pointed down and snapped his fingers hard against his thumb. "Solving south Florida's drug problem."

Pivot rolled his eyes. "Bureaucrats. I'm telling you, Conway. It's a—"

"I know, Larry. It's a goddamned stinkin' world."

Pivot grinned. "You took the words right out of my mouth, John. I'll be in touch."

As he left, Conway heard Truro and Evan Sanborn, the governor's assistant, coming upstairs. "I hope I don't lose my temper," he whispered to Ake.

Ake shook his head, draped the ripped clothes he was holding over the back of a chair. "Don't bother. Let me do it for you," and he smoothed down his hair and tugged at the bottom of his shirt. "How do I look, Conway? Presentable enough to commit murder?"

When Rita's call had come through at nine, Conway and Ake had been in a meeting in Truro's office. Sanborn, who'd arrived only a few minutes before, had jumped up out of his chair and instructed the secretary to hold all calls.

"The lady says it's urgent," the secretary had insisted. "That Laura's half-dead."

"Who," Sanborn had asked, "is Laura?"

Conway had grabbed for the phone on Truro's desk. At first Rita's voice had been so soft, he could barely hear her. She'd said she was at a neighbor's house and an ambulance was on its way and that he'd better hurry.

"Has she been wounded?"

"I think . . . well, it looks like she's been bitten by something . . . and Conway, the house . . . everything's been ripped to shreds."

"I'll be there in ten minutes," he'd said, and hung up. Ake was already standing.

"Mr. Conway," Sanborn had begun in his crisp voice that still carried a hint of a Southern drawl, "we have a meeting to finish here and I—"

"You want facts?" Conway had said, knowing that any minute his voice was going to break and he would rush Sanborn and wring the man's neck. "Right? Facts? I'll show you facts, Mr. Sanborn. Come on, Ake. Our man struck again."

By the time they'd arrived, the ambulance had come and gone. Rita had waited long enough to tell them what she'd found, then gone on to the hospital. Sanborn's initial reaction was about what Conway had expected. He took one look around, said, "A drug caused a man to do *this*?" and immediately started barking orders to the police photographer, the fingerprint people, and whoever else was around.

Truro came into the bedroom. "I think we've done everything we can do here," he said.

And what exactly did you do? Conway felt like shouting.

"You boys about finished?" asked Sanborn, still looking cool as ice cream in his three-piece suit.

"No," said Ake, "we're not."

"I still need copies of the lab and autopsy reports, boys," Sanborn continued as though Ake hadn't spoken, "and I'd like you two to write up what you've done so far on the case, including any suspects you might have who—"

"Sanborn," said Ake, scratching his kinky head, looking down at the floor, then back up, "you want results? Then get us men."

Sanborn gave an amused smile. "And just how do you think I'm going to get you men, Mr. Aikens?" He snapped his fingers. "Just by doing that?"

Ake snapped his fingers and shuffled his feet. "Yeah, that'd do for starters. Then you might get on Thompkins's ass, up there in the lab? You dig? Tell him to get his act together a little more quickly from now on, so we can get some answers down on this end before the shit hits the fan. And while you're at it, Larry Pivot and his docs could stand another position allocation, so it doesn't take five days to get an autopsy done, and then, if you still don't have enough to do, you happen to know what cops make, Sanborn?"

Unruffled, Sanborn lit one of his skinny black cigarettes and said, "Salaries are not my jurisdiction; that's a local matter." He paused. "I understand this drug is able to tap psi power, gentlemen, is that true? If so, I'd like that included in the report."

Conway and Ake looked at each other. Ake just shook his head. "See ya around, Sanborn," he said, and walked out. Conway stood there, then went into the closet to finish bringing out the ripped clothes.

"The reports," said Sanborn, coming over to the door, "I'll expect to see them in the mail."

"Right," Conway muttered. *When hell freezes over.*

He heard Sanborn leave, came out of the closet with an armful of clothes, and draped them over the back of the chair. Truro, looking mean, disgruntled, whispered, "Don't fuck with Tallahassee, Conway," and left.

It was several hours before phone and power were restored and then only after lengthy hassles that exacerbated Conway's dislike of bureaucrats. Ma Bell wanted to charge for the cut wires; the power company said they needed a written report about the incident. Conway told them both what they could do with their demands. Everyone had someone to answer to. Everyone needed reports and verifications, statistics and facts. Didn't anyone give a damn that a woman had nearly lost her life and a maniac was still loose?

Ake came into the room and handed Conway the cartridge of shells they'd found on the bed. "You're going over to the hospital later?"

"Maybe tomorrow. I just called and Rita said Laura is allergic to ant bites, bee stings, and so on and is swollen up like a balloon. She'll probably sleep until tomorrow.''

"Ask her about the gun when you see her.''

"Yeah. I will. She may not want to talk about this, you know.''

"Hardly blame her. Ready to split?" Conway nodded. "Where's the cat?''

"Karen's going to keep him until Laura's out of the hospital.''

"I shoulda figured.''

As they passed through the living room, the sight of it still sickened Conway. He and Ake had restored the house to some semblance of order, but there wasn't anything they could do about the furniture, the carpet, the drapes. Rooms were extensions of personalities, of the people who inhabited them, but here, all traces of Laura had been effaced. The ghost of the madman howled out from the rubble, where strips of bright light fell unevenly almost to the kitchen.

Conway opened the front door. A car was coming in the drive. "Who's that?'' Ake asked.

"A man who should have been here,'' Conway replied harshly. "Ian Fletcher.''

The blinds in his office were halfway up as he spoke on the phone with Rita. He heard the hospital P.A. system in the background, imagined her standing at a phone in the hall, rummaging through her purse for a cigarette, the fine blond strands of her hair in front catching on her earrings.

According to Rita, the Turnbalts had left only a few minutes ago and somewhere out there in the long, hot twilight they were getting into their white Mercedes, unaware that Tillis had recorded every movement in and out of Marie's shop today, unaware that Conway knew about Blanchard's visit the night before he fell to his death, unaware of everything except their smooth, swift lives that offered the sweetest and the best that money could buy. They would return to their lovely, expensive penthouse to drink cognac on the long porch where the jasmine was thicker than the June heat, never knowing that he was going to pop holes in Turnbalt's arrogance so that it sank like a ship.

If Turnbalt were their man, would he be audacious enough to visit Laura in the hospital? Probably, Conway decided. At this point, *not* to visit her would arouse more suspicion. How much did Marie know? Given her long-standing, though no longer close, friendship with Laura, would she simply go along with it if she knew? Somehow, in spite of the control Frank exerted over his wife's life, Conway didn't think Marie would condone murder.

"Conway?" Rita asked. "You still there?"

"Still here."

"Want to pick me up tomorrow morning at ten?"

He swiveled back around, reached into his desk for a cigarette. "You know the answer to that."

"Maybe we'll make Nevada this time." She laughed.

"Are you staying overnight at the hospital?"

"Yeah, they wheeled in a cot. You coming by?"

"Sure. And I've got a man to stand guard outside her door, too." Something tugged at him, then he remembered. "Say, what's Bell's theorem?"

"Bell's theorem?"

"The night we indulged . . . I think it's something I pulled out of your head."

Rita laughed. "You make it sound dirty. You have a talent for that, Conway, you know?"

"You have any idea what it is?"

"Yeah, apparently a new hobby of Ian's," she replied, and explained what Laura had found in Ian's briefcase. "Some physicists think it might prove the existence of certain kinds of psychic phenomena, notably telepathy."

"Telepathy," he repeated, and wondered if Denise Markham had known about Bell's theorem. If so, it would have given her work a scientific foundation.

"Listen, Conway," Rita said, lowering her voice, "Hank's here. Visiting Laura."

"Oh." He hesitated. "Would you rather I stop by when visiting hours are over?"

"No reason to, I was just telling you so you wouldn't be surprised or anything."

"See you in a few minutes." He sat with his hand on the phone when they'd hung up, his thoughts drifting from Bell's theorem to Hank Lincoln, then back to Blanchard falling like a sparrow through the terrible heat.

Twenty minutes later, when he walked into Laura's room, the first thing he saw was Rita and Hank sitting on the vacant bed, and Ian in the chair next to Laura's bed. For a moment, it seemed that Hank's eyes met his, and Conway felt a brief but feral dislike for the man. Then the connection between them was broken by a chorus of hellos from the others, and he kissed Laura on top of the head and knew that his astonishment at her appearance showed. She was sitting up against some pillows, hair pulled into a loose ponytail. Her arms, face, and neck were covered with a clear ointment, but the large, ugly red welts still showed through. Her eyes and cheeks were badly swollen, as if she had been hit, but there weren't any bruises.

"You should see my legs and feet, if you think this is bad," Laura said. "I look worse than I feel, John, so don't try to hide your surprise." A corner of her mouth tried for a smile he knew was not going to make it.

"Was I doing that?" he asked, squeezing her hand.

"You were. My endotoxins ran amuck, the doctor said, whatever that means," she explained, and he laughed.

"She's being released Sunday," Ian said, as though he had something to do with the decision.

"How was your business trip?" Conway asked. *You shit.*

"Got two new contracts," Ian said. "And that means I won't have to travel as much from now on. I can hire one or two salesmen to do the legwork." He was sitting at the foot of Laura's bed and reached over and patted her thigh. "Not leaving my lady again."

Rita, still seated next to Hank, took Diogenes out of his pocket and slipped the puppet on her own hand, working its mouth. "What's *she* doing holding me?" Diogenes asked.

Conway smiled. Rita wasn't a ventriloquist, but she moved the thing more deftly than Hank. "Now I speak like a girl," the puppet said. "What's *happened* to me?"

"Hermaphrodite." Hank chuckled.

Diogenes popped its eye patch, clapped its little hand. "Hermaphro-what? What was that, Hank?"

Laura laughed. "Hank and Diogenes came to make me feel better."

"You bet," Diogenes said. "Hospitals are terrible places. Uh-oh," and its small, ugly face turned toward the doorway, where a nurse stood. "The big N is back."

"We *do* have rules, Miss Perkins," the nurse said, "about the number of visitors permitted at any one time." She tapped her watch. "Five minutes left until visiting hours are over, so I'll let you stay until then."

"She *needs* us," the puppet said, in Hank's voice this time. "We're making her laugh, helping her heal, don't you read the latest medical literature, ma'am?"

The nurse looked at Rita, who threw up her hands. "Wasn't me, honest."

Unimpressed, the nurse repeated, "Five more minutes," and left.

"Bitch," Diogenes muttered.

"No wonder I hate hospitals," Hank said, reaching for the puppet, stuffing it back in his pocket. He glanced at Conway. "How's your investigation going, Lieutenant? I hope you're close to catching this shit." He stood up, walked over to the window, and leaned against it, his arms folded across his chest. There in the light, Conway thought Hank Lincoln looked tired, his face sallow, as though he'd been shut up indoors for several years. The man was not, Conway guessed, taking well to the separation and he wondered if Hank knew about him and Rita. Probably, he decided.

"We're doing what we can," he replied, intentionally evasive.

"Any luck with that eight hundred number they've been flashing all over the tube?" Hank asked.

"Some."

"Is it true? What they say about the drug?"

"The drug can most certainly be deadly," he said, "with prolonged use. And evidently it can cause psychosis."

"Was the Markham woman mad or a genius?" Ian asked. "I mean, does the drug actually spark some sort of psychic connection between people?"

Conway did not look at Rita as he replied but relived that first nudge of her mind against his and remembered how their separateness had vanished. "Yes, it seems to," he said. Then, before he realized it, he continued, "There might be some scientific basis to Denise's work. Something called Bell's theorem."

Ian did not possess Frank Turnbalt's utter polish, and Conway caught the momentary change in his expression. "Which is?"

Conway reiterated what Rita had told him earlier. "Sounds fishy to me," Hank remarked. "How come there hasn't been anything about it in the papers? Something as big as this would be, should have been covered by the press, right?"

"It was first discovered in 1964, in Switzerland," Laura said, "and experiments were later run at Stanford. In 1975, physicist Henry Stapp called Bell's theorem 'the most profound discovery of science.'"

Ian stared at her. Conway smiled. Laura had apparently done some research on her own since her discovery of Ian's "new hobby." "How do you know *that*?" Ian asked.

She shrugged, glanced down at her hands. "I must have read it somewhere," she replied. "What's important, I think, is that Stapp made that statement in a work supported by the U.S. Energy Research and Development Administration, which shows

206

that even the feds recognize the potential value of such a discussion.''

''It's about time,'' Hank said. ''From what I understand, the Russians are way ahead of us in this field.''

''The Russians,'' Ian interjected, ''are most likely planning to use telepathy, psychokinesis, and other psychic phenomena in their spy operations.''

''Oh, c'mon,'' Rita said.

''In Russia,'' Ian continued, ''psychics are considered a national resource; in this country, they're thought of as charlatans.''

The nurse popped her head in the doorway again. ''Miss Perkins, visiting hours are over.''

Hank stuck his hand into his pocket and when he pulled it out Diogenes was fitted snugly over his fingers. ''We were just having a *fascinating* discussion about the Russians. What do *you* think about the Russkies, ma'am?''

Everyone, including the nurse, laughed. But as Ian and Hank rose to leave, Conway felt a vestige of tension in the air. He sensed that Hank wanted to speak to Rita privately; that Ian was curious about Laura's knowledge of Bell's theorem; and that he himself was suddenly viewing Ian in a different light. Was his interest in psychic phenomena coincidental? And if not, what did that imply?

Rita accompanied them into the hall, and for a moment he watched the three of them talking just beyond the door. Then Laura said, ''John, I thought it might save some time if I just wrote up what happened. Would that be okay with you?''

''Perfect.''

''About the gun . . . I think he took it. It slipped out of my hand when I was scrambling into the attic.''

Conway stuck his hand in his pocket and brought out a gun. ''I'm a veritable artillery. Keep this in your purse. It loads a bit differently, but it'll do the trick.'' He showed her how to load it and gave her a box of shells. ''Did Rita tell you we've got a man watching your room as long as you're in here?'' She nodded. ''So don't worry about a thing. Just rest and get well.'' He paused. There were so many things he wanted to ask her, but now was not the time. As if sensing his thoughts, she reached out, touched his arm.

''I intend to help you catch this bastard,'' she said.

Rita returned, rubbing her hands. ''Cocktails,'' she said, and brought a flask out of her purse. ''Scotch. Hope you two are agreeable.'' She found three paper cups in a drawer in the nightstand, filled them with ice, measured out the shots, and passed the cups around.

"Nursey would split a gut. Booze and a gun." Laura laughed.

"Nursey obviously has no sense of humor," Rita replied.

"Skoal," Conway said, holding his glass up. "To Laura's health." His eyes met Rita's, then he saw Ake behind her, filling up the doorway.

"Hey, you're just in time for cocktails," Conway said.

Ake smiled with distraction and as he came in the room Conway noticed the man's shoulders slumped with fatigue, that two deep lines formed a V between his eyes. Pandora's box had opened again; he could feel it. "What? What is it?"

"I just came up from downstairs," Ake replied. "The drug got two, OD by injection. Peg and Howard Marshall. Students. They were DOA, brought in from one of the local watering holes."

"Any stuff found?"

"Yeah. In the woman's purse." Then, as if noticing Rita and Laura for the first time, Ake nodded to them. "Sorry, didn't mean to barge in like this."

"No problem," Rita replied, and handed him a cup. "Here. Scotch on the rocks. For the road."

Ake flashed a smile. Raised his cup. "To Florence with the Scotch," he said.

In its heyday, the building had undoubtedly been a magnificent structure. Three stories with bay windows, white pillars in front like a Georgian mansion, and a wide porch where the Southern lord had probably sat in the evening with the family, perusing his kingdom. Even though the building had endured the years with a modicum of grace, there were scars. Water stains the color of brass, where the sprinklers and the rain had struck, marred the sides; the paint on the sway-back porch was peeling away in strips; the lawn was spavined, overgrown. But the ultimate indignity had taken place inside, where the once huge and beautiful rooms, the sparkling hallways with the grand chandeliers, had been divided into apartments, most of which were rented to students.

"So much for Southern gentility," Conway quipped as they came into the hall and scanned the mailboxes. The air smelled of spice and something bitter.

"Chitlins," Ake muttered, screwing up his face, pointing down the hall where the smell was coming from. "Stinko."

Somewhere in the building, a couple was arguing. Their voices carried into the stillness, reaching for a fever pitch. The two men glanced at each other and fled for the stairs. Domestic squabbles, Conway thought, were to be avoided at all costs.

Music pounded the walls of the third floor. Conway rang the bell, and from inside Duncan's apartment the needle scratched across the record and Duncan shouted that he was coming. A moment passed. There was whispering behind the door, the shuffling of feet and chairs, then the door opened a crack and Duncan peeked out.

"Oh, Mr. Conway," he said, his voice hoarse. He removed the chain, opened the door wide. He was dressed in a robe. He was barefoot. He looked as if he hadn't slept in a couple of days. His chin was covered with a light fuzz and his blue eyes were pale, bloodshot. Over his shoulder, Conway recognized the redhead he'd seen the day of Denise's funeral. She was seated at the dining room table, paging through a magazine. "I haven't been feeling too well," Duncan said.

"We'd like to ask you a few questions, Tom," Conway said. "This is Detective Aikens."

"Right now you want to ask me questions? Like I said, I'm not feeling too well."

"Right now," Ake replied gruffly.

"Yeah. Sure. Okay, man," and he stepped aside and they followed him into the room. Duncan sank onto the couch; the redhead eyed him worriedly. "This is Lucia," Duncan said, waving absently toward the woman.

"Hi," she said, raising her hand, attempting a smile, but obviously annoyed at the interruption. She passed a hand under her thick hair and flicked it off the collar of her blouse. "Want me to leave, Dunk?"

"Naw, I don't have nothing to hide from you."

"Depends," Ake remarked, sitting down.

Conway pulled out a chair at the dining room table. Lucia gave him a tentative smile. Her hand was playing at the collar of her blouse and a small frown had worked its way down in between her eyes.

The room wasn't bad, just old and sparsely furnished, a typical student's place. From where he sat, Conway could see into the kitchen. It reminded him of Stella's kitchen, dinner dishes still on the counter, the remains of what looked like spaghetti sauce drying and crusting on the plates, two yellow stains snaking down the oven door, and muck and dirt around the base of the fridge. He looked away. Lucia continued to turn the pages of her magazine.

"So what questions do you want to ask?" Duncan said, leaning forward, his arms resting on his legs. He ran a hand through his thick blond hair, smiled at Lucia.

"Point-blank," Conway began, "do you know Peg and Howard Marshall?"

"Yeah. He's in one of my classes. Why?"

"Because they're both dead."

Duncan's face turned pale as milk. "Dead?"

"Drug overdose. The same drug you and Denise were concocting in the lab for months," Ake replied.

Duncan didn't say anything at first. He stood, picked up Lucia's cigarettes off the table, hit the pack, took one out, tapped it against the table, lit it, coughed. Lucia seemed to be holding her breath, waiting. Conway realized she didn't have the faintest idea what was going on but was prepared to take her cues from Duncan, to provide an alibi if necessary.

"I didn't sell him or anyone a drug." He faced them. His expression said: *See? Read my face, I'm not lying*.

"Come off it," Ake told him. "You're lying. We know it and you know it, so why not just tell us the truth, son, or you're going to find yourself charged with murder."

"*Murder?*" whispered Lucia, closing the magazine, sitting forward. "*Whose* murder?"

"Of Denise Markham," Conway replied.

"That's bullshit, Mr. Conway," Duncan replied, his voice never changing, still cool, unaffected, as if they were not really in this room and Duncan were practicing lines for the school play in front of the mirror.

"I'll tell you what's not bullshit, son," said Ake in his best paternal cop voice, "and that's if you're charged with murder one, you can expect to face two more murder charges, an intent to commit murder charge, and a B and E charge. That's just for starters. The way I figure it, if you're convicted on all those *plus* the drug charge, you're not going to get out of prison before you're . . . oh, about a hundred and forty-five. You dig, son?"

Duncan just stared at him.

"What's he talking about, Tommy?" asked Lucia, getting up, smoothing down her blouse, reaching for a cigarette.

"And *that's* only if they don't give you the chair," Ake finished.

Duncan looked from Ake to Conway and laughed. "You guys aren't for real. You think you can just come barging in here at eleven o'clock at night, pointing the finger at me? For what? I haven't done a goddamned thing. All I ever did was become

Mrs. Markham's research assistant and shit, I can tell you, I wish I'd never laid eyes on the woman. There're plenty of people who could have killed her. People who had reasons, you know? People who thought she was a whore or a thief, or people who thought she had an ice cube for a heart, and people—like her husband, you know? Or Frank Turnbalt, huh? Or, well, any guy who ever slept with her.''

"Why Turnbalt?'' Conway asked.

Pink splotches were spreading across Duncan's neck and cheeks. He smoked rapidly, in short puffs, and began pacing around the room, running a hand through his hair, looking at Lucia, at Conway and Ake, then back at the floor. "Turnbalt, shit. He lah-de-dahs around the campus like he's some fucking hot piece of shit and the man's sick, that's what he is,'' and Duncan jabbed at his temple. "He's sick in the head, thinks no one knows about these parties he and his wife have. What a joke. *Every*one knows, it's the big rumor on campus. And—and Denise—Mrs. Markham . . . well, with the looks she had, it figured she'd be in swinging and screwing with the best of them. You think the administration would like knowing their star attorney from Harvard is into group sex? Whips and chains? You think that'll go over big with students? He had a motive for killing Denise, I didn't. I just worked for her, that's all.''

He sank into a chair, got up, grabbed for Lucia's cigarettes, lit another. "Honey,'' Lucia said, touching his arm. He yanked it away and walked back over to the couch, sat down.

"I think you've done enough of that drug,'' Conway said, "so that you've got a little time bomb ticking away inside you, friend. You know that it depresses the immune system? Like AIDS? I think you've had the piss scared out of you because you figure you're well on the road to ending up like the Marshalls and Olivia Blanchard.''

"Who's Olivia Blanchard?''

"Another of Denise's victims.''

"I didn't kill no one,'' Duncan said quietly, "and I don't know where you get off talking about B and Es and other murder charges and intent to commit murder and all the rest of it. I didn't kill no one.''

Lucia got up, came over to him, sat beside him. Again, she touched his arm. This time, Duncan didn't yank it away. "Of course you didn't, honey,'' she said softly.

"You *do* know about the drug, don't you,'' Ake said.

"Of course I know about the drug,'' Duncan replied. "I was

her assistant, of course I knew about it. Jesus. What're you guys, anyway, stupid or something?"

"Was she selling it?" Conway asked.

"I don't know."

"And you took the drug," said Ake.

Duncan raised his head. Lucia's hand was still on his arm, the bright red nails like flecks of blood against the tan of his robe. "I don't have to tell you guys anything," he said, "unless my attorney's present."

"Attorney?" said Conway, glancing at Ake.

"Attorney?" echoed Ake. "We're not arresting anyone, son. We're just trying to get some answers."

Lucia was worried. She searched Duncan's face with her pale blue eyes like ponds in all those freckles. "Dunk," she whispered, "tell them what you know."

"Just shut up, Lucia. You don't know what the hell you're talking about. Just shut up."

Lucia removed her hand from his arm.

"The lady makes good sense, son," said Ake.

"I don't know anything," Duncan repeated, his voice lifeless and dull now. "Just get out, will you? I don't know shit. I don't feel well." He sniffled, coughed. "I don't even know my name most of the time, so why don't you just get the hell out of here."

Ake and Conway stood. Duncan didn't bother looking up, but Lucia did and her eyes were frightened. "Let me suggest," Conway began, "that you go see a doctor, Duncan. Besides affecting the immune system, the drug also damages the liver, kidneys, and with prolonged use has been known to cause convulsions and psychosis. The catch, of course, is that so far, no one's been able to determine how long 'prolonged' is. It seems to differ with individuals. Oh, and don't be leaving town, Duncan."

"And don't get up," Ake added. "We'll show ourselves out."

When they were outside once more, Conway glanced up. Duncan stood at the window, gazing down at them. Lucia's shadow passed in front of the curtains. Somewhere distant, a siren sounded.

"So what do you think?" Ake asked.

"I think Duncan will come around. What bothers me is Ian," Conway replied, and explained about the papers Laura had found in the man's briefcase.

"Bell's theorem. You mentioned it before. You think Fletcher's involved?"

"I don't know. What bothers me is that Laura's going to be staying with him when she gets out of the hospital. So if he *is* involved, she could be in jeopardy."

Ake rubbed his jaw, jammed his hands in his pockets. "Maybe you should talk to her before she gets out of the hospital."

"And say what? I don't have any proof. I somehow have a real hard time seeing him as the killer, Ake. But if he *is*, I doubt he'd do anything to Laura while she's staying with him. This guy has been pretty cautious so far."

Ake stopped. "Maybe we should put a tail on him."

"Not yet. But let's just not dismiss him as being involved somehow."

"When this is over, white boy, what do you say we play some poker and get loaded, huh?"

"Sounds mighty fine to me."

21

1.

"MR. CONWAY?" A voice whispered.

"Hmm," he grunted into the phone, opening his eyes, gazing at the clock. Eight. And a Saturday not so long ago, Ake had called him at nine. He was working backward, he thought, and eventually he would work backward to the stroke of midnight and *presto*, he'd have his answers. "This is Conway," he replied, sitting up, rubbing his eyes, realizing he'd neglected to turn on his message machine when he'd left the apartment yesterday. No telling what calls he'd missed. "Who's this?"

"Viki Markham."

"Viki." He came quickly awake, heard traffic in the background and wondered where she was calling from. "Hi, what's up, honey?"

"Mr. Conway, I'm kinda lost," she said in a small, frightened voice. "Yesterday, when Mary Ellen and I were at the Seven Eleven, this man came up . . . well, he gave me something from Mommy and told me to go somewhere and I think I got on the wrong bus and I just used my last quarter to call you, Mr. Conway."

"Hold on, kiddo," he said gently, reaching for his pants,

carrying the phone over to the closet while he looked for a clean shirt. "Do you see any street signs around?"

"Yeah." She read it to him. "There's a Winn Dixie on the corner, that's where I'm calling from. Could you come and get me, Mr. Conway? Daddy left early this morning to play golf and he'd be awful mad if he—"

"Just wait out front and I'll be there in a jiffy," he assured her, the questions already stacking in his mind. *What* man? *What* did he give her? *Where* did he tell her to go?

"I'll stand right here. I won't move. I sure 'preciate this, Mr. Conway."

"Count to one thousand," he said, "and I'll be there before you finish." She was only a couple of miles from the apartment and at least fifteen miles from home.

"Okay," she promised.

A few minutes later, he pulled into the Winn Dixie parking lot and saw Viki sitting on the curb, holding her purse in her lap. She wore shorts and a sailor shirt and her hair was loose and shone in the sunlight. She looked so much like her mother that they might have passed for sisters. It was very warm already, and as he got out of the car he saw that her shirt stuck to her like adhesive and a line of perspiration crossed her upper lip.

"Hi," she said, clutching her purse in front of her, looking as if she might cry. "I only got to six hundred and forty-nine."

He laughed. "I live just a couple of miles from here." He opened the car door for her. "Hop in where it's cool."

She ran her hand over the top of the Porsche. "This is sure a neat car," she said. She patted her purse. "I saved your card, Mr. Conway. The one you gave me that day."

"Have you had breakfast?" She shook her head. "Fine, me neither. How about pancakes? You like pancakes, Viki?"

"I love them," she replied with a grin.

Once they were on the road again, Conway asked her about the man. She sat with her hands resting on her purse, which was in her lap, and her legs crossed demurely at the knees. The air from the vents rustled her hair and she brushed a strand from the corner of her mouth.

"I'd never seen the man before," she began. "But he drove into Seven Eleven just as Mary Ellen and I were getting on our bikes to go back to my house. He asked me if I was Viki Markham and I said yes, even though Mommy used to tell me never to talk to strangers. But he knew my name, so I figured it was okay. Anyway, he gave me this." She dug into her pocket. Conway looked over. *The second key. He'd been right about the second key.* "He told me to go to the Immaculate Conception Church and see Bishop Keating."

"What'd this man look like?"

"He had dark hair and it was wet, like he used Vitalis or something on it. He had a bad complexion, too, and didn't speak English too well. Oh. Yeah. He had a gold tooth."

Jose Panzo. It had to be. "Was that all he said?"

"He was kinda hard to understand. He told me not to tell anyone, that my mother had said I should never tell anyone about the key, except the bishop, who would know what to do. Then he said some other stuff. About Mommy." She turned her purse over in her lap, pulled at her shirt. "That she was wonderful and some other word in Spanish, I think, that sounded like sympathetic."

"*Simpática?*"

"Yeah, that's it. What's it mean?"

"Kind. Nice."

"Well, he kept saying that Mommy was . . . that word, and he looked like he was going to cry. Then he asked me if I understood what he'd said and when I told him yes, he drove away. I didn't call you before, Mr. Conway, because I wasn't sure what to do. I didn't think I should say anything to my dad. He's worried about everything right now . . . I mean, I hear him walking around the house sometimes at night because he can't sleep. I didn't want to worry him more. It's all this stuff about Mommy . . . that's what's keeping him up. So this morning after he left, I walked up to the main road and caught the bus, but I was supposed to get a transfer and . . ." She looked over at him, worrying her lower lip with her teeth. "I got it all mixed up. What do you think it means, Mr. Conway?"

"I think it means we should visit this guy."

"You know who he is?"

"I think so, yes. Your mother used to help him with his English. He's a janitor at the university."

"Did he love her?"

"Love her? I don't know. He apparently respected her, don't you think? To carry out her instructions?"

She lifted her eyes and glanced out the window. "I guess so," she replied. "Daddy says that Mommy was the kind of person men always love. She was real pretty, Mr. Conway. I mean, my mom was the main attraction, you know? When she was in a good mood, boy, I never saw anyone have so much fun. We took this trip once, to the Bahamas. On one of those cruise ships like the *Love Boat*. It took three days and I was just a kid then, but I can remember how she was . . ." She shrugged. "I don't know. She made the party, you know what I mean?"

Conway stopped in front of the pancake house. "Breakfast first," he said.

They ordered cheese blintzes. The waitress left a pot of coffee and Viki poured them each a cup. She stirred cream into her own, then passed him the cream and sugar and unfolded her napkin and smoothed it out on her lap. For an instant, Conway felt he was in the presence of a woman rather than a ten-year-old child.

"Do you know Bishop Keating, honey?" he asked.

"No, I'm not even Catholic. In the phone book, it said the church was down in the Spanish section of town. I thought I'd just take a bus down there and then see what I felt like doing. What do you think the key fits, Mr. Conway?"

"I think it goes to the box where we got that letter. The one from your mom. I have it in the car, too, I almost forgot."

"The letter and the money."

He began to feel uncomfortable, just as he had with Markham. He had no intention of shattering the girl's illusions about her mother, but neither did he want to lie to her. In the long run, a lie might be more damaging. But who was he to start the ball rolling? That was Markham's job, as her father.

The waitress brought their breakfast. Viki refilled their cups with coffee. After a few bites of her blintz, she dabbed at her mouth, said, "It's okay, Mr. Conway. I mean, I know I'm only ten and you think I'm just a kid, but I'm pretty grown up. Really. I've got it, too, you know. What my mom had."

He frowned. "What? What do you have, honey?"

She looked down at her plate. Her fork bit into the blintzes. "Mommy called it the Power. I don't have it like she did. I mean, it doesn't work with everyone. It doesn't work with Daddy Markham, 'cause he keeps things to himself so much, you know? Like my mom did. The only time it worked with her was when we did our experiments. But with you it works."

Conway felt a chill along his arms. He heard Fedora Hopkins asking, *"She got the Power?"* "How does it work, Viki? Describe it to me."

She sat pensively for a few moments, finishing her breakfast. "It's like I see pictures of what you're thinking. It works real well with my friend Mary Ellen."

"Does she know about it?"

"No, I think she just figures I'm weird." She wiped at her mouth, set her napkin on the table. "You're the first person I've told. My mom and I hardly ever talked about it. I guess for a long time I thought it was something everyone could do." She hesitated. Looked at him with her disturbing eyes, so much like her mother's in that photograph. "I know you don't like Mommy very much."

"I never met your mother, Viki."

"Yeah, I know. But since you've been working to find out who killed her, you've decided she wasn't very nice. It's not true, Mr. Conway. She was really a very good mom. I'm not just saying that because she was *my* mom, either. She never yelled at my friends, like Mary Ellen's mother does. She never hit me. And when I was a kid, she used to tell me stories every night. She wasn't just pretty, she was real smart and—" Her face suddenly fell in and she began to cry. "And I miss her," she whispered, sitting back in the booth, clutching her napkin and stretching it across her eyes until it ripped. The sight of her sitting there so helplessly, the tip of her nose growing red, her mouth quivering, cut into him and he put a hand on her arm.

"I know you miss her," he said gently.

She curled her fingers over his hand. "She really *is* dead. I mean . . . all that stuff about energy not dying . . . she's *still* dead, Mr. Conway."

"Her body's dead. But whatever it was that made your mother herself—her soul, if you want to call it that—isn't dead. I think that's what she meant by energy not dying, Viki. Do you understand what I mean?"

She nodded, blew her nose in her napkin and wadded it into a ball, then dropped it in her purse. "I think so." She finished her coffee. Conway lit a cigarette. Nothing he'd ever experienced in his life had set a precedent for how he should act around a telepathic ten-year-old girl who evidently read him like a comic. What pictures had she seen? What did his thoughts *look* like? And, just as Rita had explained, the transmission of information between *his* mind and Viki's had evidently been instantaneous; at the very moment she'd been telling him he didn't think her mother was very nice, he'd been thinking precisely that.

Conway wondered again about Ian's interest in the paranormal. Was it coincidental? The man *did* fit certain elements in the psychological profile: he was college-educated, in his early thirties, lived some distance from campus, seemed to be a tightly controlled individual, possessed above-average intelligence. But had he known Denise? Did he have unsatisfactory relationships with women? *Was he capable of murder?*

Ian had seemed quite certain, Conway recalled, that the Russians were planning to use telepathy in their spy operations. He might have read this somewhere, of course, except that he had uttered it with such conviction. But what did that prove? Besides, if Ian were their man, how could he have maintained such normalcy in the hospital? Would a man on the brink of psychosis be that lucid?

He thought back to Blanchard's descriptions of his wife, before her final psychotic break. Most of the time she had seemed fine.

"Listen," Conway said, "maybe it'd be better if I go see Mr. Panzo by myself. He might be hurt if he knew you had told someone."

"Don't tell Daddy, Mr. Conway. Promise."

"I promise."

"And you'll tell me what happens? About Bishop Keating?"

"I'll take you with me to see him, how's that?"

"It's a deal," she replied with a grin. Then she frowned a little, scrutinized him with those fey, compelling eyes. "Who's Rita, Mr. Conway?"

Okay, kid, I believe you. I believe Fedora Hopkins. "Rita," he began, laughing a little, a sick, nervous laugh, "is a friend of mine. Why?"

The girl sipped tentatively at her coffee, never taking her eyes from his, watching him over the rim of her cup as if his entire life were floating in the pools of his eyes. The back of his neck prickled. A moment before she spoke, he knew the gist of what she was going to say, as if their minds had suddenly connected like his and Rita's had that night, but without the nudge of Markham Magic. "She and her friend should be careful."

"Her friend?" *Say her name, kid, c'mon, I know you can do it. Laura. Got that? The name's Laura.* Conway sat forward, saying the name over and over in his mind, bombarding Viki with it, caught up in it now, knowing this was how Denise had felt when she and Viki played their "game." *Laura, Laura.* Then he realized what he was doing, realized it and was thoroughly embarrassed and sat back. *Laura. Shit. You're a grown man, Conway.* And he felt the name pop out of his head like a spit wad from a rubber band.

"Laura. Rita and Laura," Viki said, her cheeks flushing with excitement. "Right? Is that right, Mr. Conway?"

She got the power, John?

She got it all right, Fedora, she got it good.

2.

A bright, sunny Saturday morning, he thought, when women were home, catching up on chores like cleaning and ironing. As he stepped into the phone booth, he had a vivid image of his own mother on Saturdays, doing what his own women now did.

Suppose she was in bed with someone, a boyfriend, and he answered the phone? No, that was unlikely, he decided. It was an unspoken rule. A man didn't answer the phone in a woman's house. The same wasn't true of a woman, of course. Women seemed to believe they were free of laws, free of the rules in this game between themselves and men.

He dialed Nancy Ewill's number. It was perfectly quiet around him and the ringing was beautiful, not hollow, and that was a promising sign. Yes sir, he was a man who believed in portents. He knew she would be home.

But when she answered, her voice was so different from the crisp nurse of the other day that at first he couldn't speak. "Hello," she said cheerfully. When he said nothing, she chuckled. "Jack? Is that you? Are you fooling with me again?" Her voice was softer now, with a hint of sleep. She laughed, certain he was Jack, playing a game. Goddamned women and their games, he thought.

"Nance?" he said finally, his voice muffled. *Nance. Yes, so much nicer, more intimate, than Nancy.* His mouth grew dry, his insides tangled. "Nance?"

"Yes, this is Nancy. Jack, is that you? You have a cold?"

"Nance, it would feel so good up inside you, so deep up—"

The connection was broken. She didn't slam down the phone, she didn't yank the cord out of the wall. She just placed the receiver on the cradle, unafraid. This shocked and angered him, it frustrated him. *How dare she.*

Then he realized she wasn't afraid because it was light outside and the man, her boyfriend, was there. Sure, women were cocky when there was a man around to protect them. Even now, he imagined Nancy turning to this man, her loyal lover, touching his arm as she told him what had happened. *You'll never guess who* that *was: an obscene phone caller.* Maybe they were sitting on the edge of the bed when she said this, and she kissed him, kissed this man who was protecting her.

He picked up the phone again and did something he had never done before: he called her back. She answered on the first ring. He detected the caution in her voice.

"I'll lick yo—"

A terrible noise shrieked in his ear. It leaped into the soft mush of his brain, dug into his neck and shoulders, shot down his spine, and spread like fire as though it had caught on some essential nerve that reached every part of his body. He dropped the phone, wiggled his finger in his ear, snatched up the phone again. Now he could hear the noise going on and on and realized it was a whistle. In his mind's eye, he saw her, Nancy Ewill, R.N., blowing madly on her whistle, blowing until her cheeks were plump red balloons, her tight-ass dignity gone, and he burst out laughing and slammed down the receiver.

The noise rang in his head, it echoed. The humidity made it difficult to breathe. He pressed his palm to his forehead; the skin seemed hot, feverish. Like Nancy's, he thought, and smiled as he saw her still blowing on her whistle like a coach. And by now, her boyfriend was grabbing for the phone, shouting, *Nancy, Nancy, what's wrong? What the hell's going on?*

He walked slowly back to his car, got in, sat there for a few minutes until the ringing in his ears stopped. He squeezed his eyes shut, fighting back dizziness, a slight nausea, and the general malaise that had been plaguing him for days, weeks, maybe even months. He couldn't remember anymore. There seemed to be a gaping hole in his chest where his heart once was. A black hole, he thought, through which his life was slipping, where his memories would be pulverized. He thought of the drug stash he had and of how if he used it right now, this very minute, it would wash away the malaise and connect him with that essential part of himself.

Which essence, Bucky boy?

The drug would push him *there*, to the place, he thought, the special secret place where he and Denise had spoken without words, where their lives had braided so magically together. But the drug could kill. The cops said so, right?

Scare tactics. It was the heat, this terrible heat, that was all. He got back out of the car, walked over to the phone booth.

He reached into his pocket and glanced at the slip of paper where he'd written Nancy's number and address. He would just drive by, check out the neighborhood. With his felt-tip pen, he jotted her number on the wall of the phone booth and added: *Nancy Nurse, lonely, call me.*

22

1.

CONWAY FOUND PANZO sitting in the shade of an acacia tree, not far from the hibiscus where Denise had been found. His lunchbox was open in the grass beside him, a Thermos and wrappings inside. Panzo didn't seem surprised to see him and just nodded and kept on munching his apple.

"How're you, Señor Panzo?" Conway sat next to him in the grass, catching the whiff of coffee from the open Thermos.

"I okay. You find man yet, Señor Conway?"

"Still working on it." Conway broke off a blade of grass, nibbled on the end of it. "I have a feeling you can help me."

The Cuban was gazing off toward the control tower. He finished the apple, dropped the core in the lunchbox, raised the Thermos to his mouth, drank. He ran his hand across his mouth. "I help? How I help, señor?" He screwed the top on the Thermos, still not looking at Conway.

"For starters, you might tell me exactly what Denise Markham said to you when she gave you the key to give to her daughter."

Panzo brought his eyes slowly to Conway's face. "You think because I am Marielito, I do not know laws of this country. I know the law, señor. You can do nothing to me if I no answer your questions."

"I don't want to do anything to you, Señor Panzo. I only want some answers, that's all, so I can find who killed Mrs. Markham. You *would* like to see the murderer found, wouldn't you?"

"*Sí, claro.*" Panzo nodded. "But I gave the *señora* my promise. I no break it."

"Listen to me. Mrs. Markham was ill. She thought she was going to die. That's why she gave you the key and had you promise not to tell anyone. She didn't know she was going to be murdered. That changes things, cancels all promises. You understand?"

Panzo opened the Thermos again, drank, offered it to Conway, who shook his head. He slowly screwed the lid back on, returned the Thermos to the lunchbox. His movements were deliberate, Conway thought, and behind those dark, inscrutable eyes, he sensed a whirlwind of thoughts. "She only tell me key was for Viki. She say if something happen to her, I should give key to Viki in two or three weeks. I tell her to see Bishop Keating and I tell her which church. That is all she tells me, señor."

"You didn't ask her what the key was for?"

"No."

"You weren't curious?"

"No, not my business."

"That was all she said?"

"She gave me address of house, say it is verrry important, that her life is this key, that is all she say, señor. I promise." He crossed himself.

"Do you know Bishop Keating?"

"*Sí, sí, todos* . . . everyone know him. He is holy man. He has five churches in Meahme. He verry good to Marielitos. Help us get food, lawyers, doctors."

"How did Mrs. Markham know the bishop?"

"She not say."

"And you didn't ask."

"Not my business, señor."

"I wish you'd told me this when I first spoke to you. It would have . . ." He stopped. What was the point. He couldn't blame the man for wanting to keep his word to probably one of the few people on campus who had been kind to him. And Conway believed him. José Panzo knew only as much as Denise Markham had intended him to know, only what was necessary. The same old story, he thought. She had used him as she had used everyone else.

Panzo gazed off toward the control tower again. "She was good woman, Señor Conway. Many no think so, but from here"—he touched his heart, spoke softly, reverently—"*de mí corazón*, I tell you she a good woman."

After a time, Conway stood, thanked Panzo, and the man just raised his hand and continued to stare off into the distance, as if part of his life were frozen there.

It was ten-thirty when Conway drove up in front of the hospital. Rita stood at the door, holding a bag in one hand, her purse over her other shoulder. She had her thumb out and had hoisted her skirt. He rolled down the window, opened the passenger door.

"Need a ride, lady?" he asked.

She tossed the bag in back. "Nevada, please. And hurry."

"You sure do have magnificent legs, lady."

222

"Flattery," she said, touching his nose with the tip of her finger, "will not make me forget you're thirty minutes late. But driving this terrific little car might placate me. What d'ya say, mister?"

Conway chortled, threw up his arms, and went around to her side. Rita climbed into the driver's seat, revved the engine, looked at him. "Where to?"

"I'm not sure," he replied, and while they sat there on the small incline in front of the hospital, the engine running, Conway told her what had happened since eight that morning.

"No wonder I worry about you," she said, sitting back. Her hair was pulled away from her face with the tortoiseshell combs again, the way he liked it, and the one on his side was coming loose. He fixed it, and she smiled at him as if the gesture surprised her.

"So what do you think, Rita? Suppose this bishop has some hideous secret? I'm not fit to play God with a ten-year-old's life."

"You told her you'd pick her up. Seems to me she doesn't need any more lies."

"How come things always seem so clear to you?"

"Because so many other things aren't," she replied, then let go of the emergency brake and they were off, whipping downhill, out onto I-95. "Just tell me where to go."

Conway clutched the seat and kept his eyes on the road. This wasn't exactly the same as the campus runway.

The Church of the Immaculate Conception was like every other Catholic church Conway had ever seen: florid, absolutely quiet, as though it had been created for the dead, not the living. Windows were placed at strategic locations so that at certain times of the day, light shimmered through the stained glass as if to announce the arrival of the Lord Himself. People were lined at the confessionals, fingering rosary beads, their mouths moving in silent prayer. The place made him uneasy.

"A bishop wouldn't hang out here," Rita whispered as the three of them stood in the doorway. "Bishops don't do Saturday afternoon confessions. Priests do confessions. Bishops just extend their hands so sinners can kiss their rings and return cleansed to the world."

"Cynic," Conway whispered over Viki Markham's head.

"Catholic upbringing. It made me a heathen," she replied, gazing down the aisle toward the altar. "I bet he's in the rectory."

"Behind the rectory," Viki said suddenly, turning and running outdoors. Conway and Rita exchanged a glance, then followed Viki at a swift clip, through the courtyard, where birds twittered and fussed, then between two stone buildings to a huge field. There, some fifteen or twenty Hispanic youths crowded around an older man wearing jeans, a pale yellow guayaberra shirt, and a clerical collar. He was holding a soccer ball. He had the whitest, thickest head of hair Conway had ever seen.

"Okay," he called out, tossing the ball at one of the boys. "Play ball! Show 'em what you've got!"

The boys rushed out onto the field. The man stood there for a few moments, tall, slender, smiling to himself, then turned fully, as if sensing them there.

"Hi," he said as he approached. He removed his sunglasses. "May I help you with something?"

Conway suddenly understood. "Are you Bishop Keating?" he asked.

"I am."

"Is there someplace we can talk in private?"

"And who might you be?" Keating's voice was still pleasant, but a tiny frown had worked down between his eyes. He slipped his sunglasses into his pocket.

"Detective John Conway, Rita Lincoln, Viki Markham."

Keating's eyes moved slowly toward Viki, as if he were afraid to look but were compelled to do so. "We can talk in my office. Just the two of us, if you don't mind."

"No problem," Rita said, taking Viki's hand. "C'mon, honey, let's go to confession or something." She looked at Keating with something approaching contempt. *She knows,* Conway thought. But did Viki?

They didn't speak until they were in Keating's office. The man removed a pipe from a rack of pipes of varying sizes and shapes, filled it with tobacco from a small wooden container on his desk. "Have a seat, Mr. Conway. Would you like a drink?"

A drink? It was barely noon. Conway shook his head. "No, thanks."

The office was furnished in dark wood, leather, glass, and chrome. A picture of the pope hung directly behind his desk on the wall next to a crucifix. His chair sighed as he sat down and began to rock, slowly, puffing on his pipe. He unsnapped his clerical collar, tossed it carelessly on the desk.

"What may I do for you, Mr. Conway?"

"I think you already know the answer to that."

"Yes, I suppose I do."

Conway dropped the key on the desk. "Your daughter said you would know where this fits."

Keating stopped rocking. He stared at the key, set his pipe in the ashtray. "Box thirty-nine twenty-two, Key West Federal. Does that answer your question, Mr. Conway?"

His dark eyes latched onto Conway's. Denise's eyes, Viki's eyes, Conway thought, except that the bishop's eyes were absolutely cold. "I could have you subpoenaed, sir, which I suspect wouldn't do a whole lot for your career, so why don't you just tell me what's going on and we'll proceed from there."

Conway guessed the bishop was in his early sixties, although he looked at least fifteen years younger. His eyes were a shade darker than Viki's, and smaller, meaner, as if he were observing Conway from a distance and didn't like what he saw. He began rocking again, picked up his pipe, lit it. He seemed to be signaling time and the universe that it was okay to move forward again.

"And what is it you would have me say, Mr. Conway?" Keating asked, a note of amusement in his voice.

"You might start with the truth."

"Ah," He sighed. "Of course. The truth. You're still young enough to believe in truth." He got up, stuck his hands in his pockets, walked over to an old-fashioned gramophone sitting off by itself in a corner. He put on a record, cranked up the machine. A scratchy rendition of *The Blue Danube* waltz filled the room. "This is one of the loveliest pieces of music in the world," Keating said. "You ever been to Vienna, Mr. Conway?"

"No."

"Too bad. Every young man should know Vienna. Before I decided to enter the priesthood, I visited Europe, and Vienna was my favorite city, next to the Vatican, of course." He paused, his eyes assumed a dreamy, remote look. "This particular rendition was given to me by Sara Dobson's parents. They brought it with them from Hungary, when Sara was three or four. They were gypsies; Dobson is an anglicized name. I met them about six months before they were killed in an automobile accident."

"Sara Dobson. Denise's mother."

He nodded. "It's through her parents that Sara acquired what people in that godforsaken town of Cassadaga call the Power. You're obviously familiar with the term or you wouldn't be sitting here."

"I know the term, yes."

"Sara was an extraordinary woman, Mr. Conway. Gifted,

225

with a poet's soul, and lovely, much lovelier than Denise. I was about twenty-five when I met her. She was eighteen. I was stuck in a horrible parish in Winter Park, outside Orlando, and had been a priest long enough to be experiencing a profound crisis of faith. I'm sure even a man like you must know about a crisis of faith.'' His sarcasm was unmistakable; Conway bristled but didn't say anything, so the bishop continued. ''For a brief time, I fell in love with her. She got pregnant. But by then, I'd realized I loved the Church more.'' He spoke dispassionately, as if he were merely describing the events of someone else's life. ''She kept the child. I knew only that she had a daughter and they lived in Cassadaga from the time Denise was four until she was nearly seventeen, until Sara killed herself.''

He refilled his pipe, walked back across the room, and cranked up the gramophone again, which had run down. ''How did Denise find you?'' Conway asked.

''I don't know. But she did. About two and a half years ago, she came to mass one Sunday and waited for me afterward. I only had to look at her, of course, to know who she was. Just like with Viki. It's a face I dream of, you know. The high cheekbones, dark eyes, it's gypsy blood, Mr. Conway. It's primitive, older than civilization as we know it.''

''Tell me about the drug.''

Keating sat down again, fingered the collar on the desk. ''You want me to say I'm a fraud? Fine, I'll say it. And a coward? Okay, that, too. But I believe that within my capabilities as a bishop of this diocese, I have made a difference in a number of lives, Mr. Conway. And that's what matters.''

There it was again, Conway mused. The lament of the obsessed, mother telling her daughter, ''I may have hurt a number of people, but that couldn't be helped.'' In short, the end justified the means.

''My daughter contributed generously to this church. It was not my business to know where the money came from.''

''But you knew.''

When Keating didn't reply, Conway repeated himself. ''Yes, I knew,'' the bishop admitted finally, and then for the first time lost his composure. ''How could I not know when she gave me the number of the box and the name of the bank and asked me—no, *begged* me, Mr. Conway—to make sure her daughter got what was rightfully hers. I couldn't deny her such a thing. She was my blood, after all, and she *had* given generously to the parish.'' He stood, parted the blinds hanging at the window. ''That field out there, those bleachers, equipment, uniforms, emergency funds—those items were all contributed by my *daughter*, Mr. Conway.''

And you didn't even attend her funeral. ''You mean she bought you.''

Keating let the blinds fall back in place. He continued to stand there. A strip of sunlight fell across his nose, cutting it in half. ''A matter of semantics. It's your hang-up with truth, Mr. Conway. I know, I know, truth, justice, and the right way of doing things. But when you're my age, you realize there isn't any right or wrong way of doing things. You choose, that's all. You blunder through the best way you can. I intend to live well past a hundred, Mr. Conway. I intend to become a cardinal, to see Rome from within the inner circle. I've atoned for my turpitudes in more ways than you can ever know.''

Mea culpa, mea culpa: Conway felt like puking. ''What, besides your word that you'd comply with Denise's request, did she get in return for her contributions?''

Keating moved behind the leather chair, placed his hands on the edge. His ring shone in the ribbon of light. ''The pleasure of knowing her father. I also prayed for her soul,'' he added quickly.

''How touching.''

''Please. Spare me your judgmental arrogance. Her guilt was placated and so was mine. It's that simple. We had a business deal. Everything in life is a business. Even religion. Especially religion.''

Anger overcame discretion. ''Let me tell you the facts of life, *Bishop* Keating. That drug that bought your goddamned field and your equipment and uniforms and everything else, has also cost five people their lives and the tally could easily quadruple before I've figured out who murdered your daughter. Personally, I don't give a shit who did it, I think I agree with Fedora Hopkins—you *do* know the name, don't you, *Bishop* Keating?—that the guy ought to be applauded. Yes sir, a standing ovation for ridding the world of someone who infected everything and everyone she touched. And believe me, I *would* get out of this whole mess if the life of another woman weren't at stake.''

''That's quite enough,'' Keating snapped, coming around to the front of his chair, his cheeks pink with agitation.

Conway shoved the man into the chair. ''No, I don't think you've heard enough, *Bishop* Keating. Do you have any idea what that drug does? Huh? Let me tell you.''

''I suggest you remove your hands from my shoulder, Mr. Conway,'' Keating said, struggling to rise.

"Shut up. Let me tell you how the drug comes on you like heat from Hiroshima, *Bishop* Keating, and then how you suddenly find yourself in the Arctic. It takes root in the cerebellum like some kind of disease, making you think you're above the law of God and man and whoever else happens to be in the vicinity. And boy, you just want to fuck the living daylights outa someone, ever had that feeling, Keating? Maybe with Sara?"

Keating brought his arms up under Conway's, throwing them off his shoulders. He leaped to his feet, his face a radish red as he said in a tremulous voice, "Get out of here."

"You know the little white mice screwed themselves to death, Keating? Did you know the drug lets you climb inside other people's heads? That it not only taps the Power, but grabs it by the cuff of the neck and shakes hell out of it? With prolonged use, the drug that bought your precious field and uniforms and maybe even a mistress and a fancy penthouse on the Riviera and maybe even a ticket to the Vatican, damages the liver and the kidneys and triggers convulsions, hallucinations, and perhaps even psychosis. Have you ever seen anyone choke to death on their own tongue? Have you ever seen what a man looks like after he's fallen ten stories?"

Keating brought himself to his full height, some three or four inches above Conway. He was Thor, Zeus; he was impressive as hell. But he was also the embodiment of everything Conway abhorred. "You disgust me," he spat, and started out of the office.

"Mr. Conway."

"What."

"I could have you kicked off the force for what just occurred here."

Conway laughed. "I hardly think you're in a position to threaten me. Viki Markham's mere existence would be enough to ensure you never see Rome. Have a terrific day, *Bishop* Keating."

As Conway came out into the bright sunlight in the courtyard, his pugnacity vanished. He felt empty. He felt as if he were in a hot-air balloon in rapid descent through the clouds, the white heat, headed straight for electrical wires. He made his way over to the bleachers, sat back, lit a cigarette, waited. He didn't know what he was waiting for, but it seemed he should wait for something—an explanation, an epiphany.

But in the distance, the Hispanic youths played in their colorful uniforms, and inside, the parishioners fingered their rosary beads and prayed for salvation, and overhead, the sun burned holes in the sky. Nothing had changed.

Bishop Keating would probably see Rome from within the inner circle; Viki Markham would continue to be a telepathic freak; Truro would still want his facts, and Sanborn, his medical reports. Laura was still waiting, the sloop was still tied to the dock. He thought of the hopeless complexity of it all and wanted to run like hell.

Instead, he sat there smoking.

23

1.

"No," said Laura.

"No?" echoed Ian. "But babe, it's hospital policy."

She turned around, facing him. He stood behind a wheelchair and was waiting for her to sit down in it so he could whisk her out of the hospital and into no-man's-land again. "I'm not going."

Ian grinned. "Laura, everyone here leaves in a wheelchair. It's hospital policy."

"No, I mean I'm not leaving the hospital at all. It's safer here, Ian." The hospital had been her womb; she had grown into its heartbeat, been sustained by its placenta, and now she was supposed to descend through its birth canal and be expelled into the world. But the Man was out there, waiting.

He had succeeded in terrifying and unnerving her, and had it not been for the attic, he would also have succeeded in attacking, possibly killing her. Since he had failed once, she knew he would not fail again. And she could not second-guess him. Although the riddle of the Man was less oblique now, after all those hours in the attic, his behavior was too erratic for predictions. It would be like trying to foresee the movement of a hurricane. Which direction? Would it hit land or remain over water? Would the speed augment or was the storm going to stall? Would it double back?

Would he return to the scene of the crime?

For a few days, the Man had spun in orbit at the outer fringes of her life, distant as Neptune. By staying in the hospital, she could maintain that distance, a fact Ian evidently couldn't understand. "But you've been discharged," he said.

Laura shuffled back across the room in her thongs. Her feet and ankles were still swollen and it hurt to wear shoes, but the swelling in her face was gone and the doctor had told her she could return to work tomorrow. But she didn't feel safe on campus. Denise had been killed there. What guarantee did she have that the same thing would not happen to her? But what were her options? She couldn't just lock herself into Ian's condo when he left in the morning and then sit around in a state of paranoia.

"They'll just have to readmit me." She sat on the edge of the bed. Ian came up to her, kissed her on top of the head.

"Babe," he said quietly, patiently, "nothing's going to happen to you. I promise."

Did someone promise Denise the same thing?

"No," she replied stubbornly, reaching in her purse for a cigarette.

"You're being unreasonable," he said, stepping back, a trace of irritation in his voice. "You'll be staying at my place, you—"

"Let's go in here," said Tillis, plopping down into the wheelchair as he entered the room. He pushed a lever forward and buzzed across the room. "Isn't this something?" He laughed, his face pink, his cheek protruding with his customary wad of tobacco. "See, Laura? It's absolutely painless. If you don't want Ian to push you, then drive it yourself." He came straight toward her; she yanked her feet up off the floor.

"Tillis"—she laughed—"you're dangerous."

"It isn't the chair," said Ian, rolling his eyes toward the ceiling, "she just doesn't want to leave the hospital. Period."

The wheelchair sped away, turned abruptly, stopped. "I thought you were going to stay at Ian's," said Tillis, his small, dark eyes sliding close together as he frowned, then stood.

"I am. I was." She worried her lower lip. She was beginning to feel childish. She knew she would not be readmitted without justification, and what, exactly, was she going to tell her doctor? *I don't wanna go home?*

"Listen," said Tillis earnestly, "you'll be almost as safe at Ian's as you would be if we put you in protective custody. At night, there's a guard on duty and no one gets past him without a sticker on the car windshield. There are about a hundred condos spread through ten or twelve buildings. The place has a wall around it, a pink wall." He grinned. "Like Jericho."

"I know. I've seen it," she replied.

"And I'll even buy you dinner," Ian remarked.

If you cooperate, Laura, your allowance will be raised. "Okay, okay," she said, capitulating. "I'm outnumbered."

Tillis gave an exaggerated sigh of relief; Laura thought it sounded like air escaping from a balloon. "You may have just saved my marriage. If I'd spent one more night here, I think my wife might've filed for divorce and then I'd be out scouting around for lady number five."

"Five?" Laura laughed.

Tillis shrugged. "They can't stand me longer than two or three years." He swept his arm in front of him, motioning toward the wheelchair. "Your limo awaits you, ma'am."

She picked up her purse, felt the weight of the .38 in it as she sat down. "You driving?" Ian asked, coming around behind her. "Or should I?"

Laura dropped her head back, peered up at the underside of his jaw. She reached out, touched a finger to a dark spot. "You missed," she said.

He leaned forward and kissed her. She thought, suddenly, of the mysterious other woman and realized she hadn't crossed her mind since she'd been in here. Had he made his choice? Or was the other woman still waiting in the wings of his life, anticipating the moment when he would extricate himself from this relationship and rush to her with his confession? She righted her head. Perhaps, she thought, this secret hobby of his, this apparently sudden interest in psychic phenomena, was connected to the other woman. "You drive," she told Tillis. "Let's get the hell out of here."

"That's the spirit," Tillis replied, rubbing his hands together, setting her overnight bag in her lap. "You've got the spit and fire my third wife had, Laura. Yes sir, love to see it, even if it isn't easy to live with."

"Amen," Ian remarked, and pushed her out into the hall.

Thank you very much, Ian, she thought, and glanced back over her shoulder. Light fell through the window, onto the bed. The room had a look of peace and serenity about it, and the only evidence that anyone had been there was an unmade bed and a paper cup on the dresser. *Don't go,* it seemed to call after her. *Live in me, I'll protect you, don't go.* She hugged her purse against her and stared down the hall.

The place seemed as quiet as the hospital room had a while ago. Untouched, sitting off the road, the tips of the pines in back peeking over the roof of the house, the hedges along the side so thick, verdant, blooming. But even if Laura had been unaware of what had occurred inside, she would have sensed something was wrong. You developed an instinct about the place you lived in. It was as if the house were bleeding and she could hear its wails of pain in the susurrous rustle of the pines.

Ian stopped in the driveway. Laura walked down to the road, opened the mailbox, leafed absently through the mail. She was stalling, prolonging the inevitable. The mail was mostly professional journals and junk, except for a postcard from her parents, who were making their way around South America by cruise ship. She recognized her father's small, neat handwriting. *"Hi, honey, we're pulling out of Rio this afternoon and want to get this in the mail to you before. The trip's been magnificent. So far, no Montezuma's revenge. Only sore feet from all the walking. Wish you were here. More soon. Love, Dad."* On the front was a nighttime shot of the Copacabana. She suddenly longed for the sound of her mother's voice, her father's laughter, for all those small, intimate things that made up a family.

"Laura?" Ian called from the porch.

She lifted her eyes. He was waiting. She got out her keys. Her throat was parched and her skull was drumming. She forced her legs to move, heard dry leaves complaining underfoot. Her hand trembled as she inserted the key in the lock. When the door swung open, the smell of insecticide was pungent in the stale air.

"Conway and Ake cleaned it up some," Ian said, walking over to the wall and switching on the air conditioning. "Let's get some air circulating in here."

Laura dropped her purse and mail by the wall, moved slowly through the room, her sedulous resolve to take inventory of the damage draining from her. It was a nightmare, testimony of some profound malaise she could barely begin to comprehend. The couch and chairs were bleeding cotton. The drapes and carpet were ruined. She knelt in front of the books stacked along the floorboards, passed her hands over the spines, fighting back tears. Fitzgerald, Wolfe, Hemingway, sci-fi collections, several priceless first editions: all damaged. Two 1937 editions of *Scribner's* magazine had been torn apart. The bookcase was split down the middle. It was a violation worse than the Man touching her clothes because books had been the stuff of her profession, had peopled her world as a child, had at times been more real to her than anything outside herself.

She picked up several, wiped them clean with the tail of her shirt, carried them upstairs with her. She'd forgotten Ian's presence. She was unaware of anything except the crescive impotence of her rage, of the knowledge that she would never be able to walk through these rooms again without remembering. Terrify: unnerve. The Man had made sure there would be a juxtaposition of memories: closets and rainbows, ants and attics, roses and Denise, windshields and notes, mirrors and lipstick.

She stopped in the bedroom doorway. Conway had tried to prepare her for what she would see, but hearing about it from someone else was simply not the same as seeing it yourself. The heart had been ripped out of her king-size bed. The pillows lay limp as dolls against the headboard. Some of her clothes were draped over the chair, divested of identity, in shreds. She scooped her arms into the pile of negligees and sweaters and slips, then lay back on top of them and stared at the ceiling. *Why? Who?* Who could possibly hate her so much? Her gaze fell from the ceiling to the hall, to the closet. How many hours had she been up there? Eight? Nine? How many hours had *he* stolen from her since this had begun? "I intend to help you get that bastard before he gets me," she had told Conway. But how? Where to begin? The Man was faceless, nameless, ageless. The only thing she knew about him was his blood type.

After a while, she sat up. Her body was heavy with something like sleep, as though she'd been drugged. The light from the naked window was glaring and hurt her eyes. It seemed suddenly thick, tangible, as she tried to move through it to the closet. *Who? Who?* sang in her brain like the senseless cry of an owl in a forest of perils.

The things remaining in the closet were mostly older clothing that had gotten pushed to the back, things she'd intended to drop off at a local thrift store. The floor of the closet was littered with shoes, some on their sides, some sticking up at odd angles, as if their necks had been broken in the Man's rush to attack her clothes.

Laura found another overnight bag on the shelf, yanked some of the shirts from their hangers, began stuffing them into the bag. When the shirts were gone, she grabbed shoes, makeup, whatever was there. She would take everything with her. Everything. If he returned, he would find an empty house . . . and notes, yes, she would leave him notes. *Ha, ha, you sonuvabitch, beat you here.*

When the bag was full, she started toward the stairs, heard Ian on the phone, couldn't make out the words, hurried down, inexplicably anxious that she couldn't hear the words distinctly. The woman? Would he call the other woman from *here*? Would he dare? She rushed into the kitchen, clothes trailing out of the bag, things falling from her arms, heard him say, "Right. See you in an hour." She stopped, looked at him.

"I didn't hear the phone ring."

"It didn't ring, that's why. I was supposed to call Conway when you checked out of the hospital. He's coming by my place in a while. Just to see how you are." He paused. "Here, babe, let me help you with all that stuff."

As he came toward her, she pulled away. "No, I've got it." No one would touch her things. Then she looked up at Ian. His chocolate eyes fled beneath hooded lids. His mouth pulled back in an unforgiving line. He brushed a finger under his mustache, lowered his eyes to the floor. A moment or two passed. The quiet was as thick as the sunlight had been moments ago. If she balled up her fist and pounded at the air, she would hit it. And the quiet would neither break nor splinter, and she would not be able to pass through it, beyond it. The quiet would move as they moved. Then he spoke.

"You want to leave the air on?" He walked over to the wall. Laura buried her face in her bundle of clothes, into the odor of mothballs and perfume and childhood, and wanted to cry. She dug her face more deeply into the shirts and pants, hoping she would dig so far that she would eventually emerge on the other side of the nightmare.

Ian came across the room toward her, his footsteps sighing against the carpet, his breath quiet, shallow. He touched a hand to her hair. The clothes, bag, slipped from her and she finally let go of her rage and her fear and clung to him and wept.

They had just put the last of her things in Ian's car when Hank Lincoln drove up. He came across the lawn, looking dapper and distinguished in a suit and tie, and she guessed he'd driven over from work. "Hi, the hospital said you'd checked out, so I thought I'd try here." He said hello to Ian, who merely nodded, as if resenting the intrusion. "You're looking better than you were a couple days ago, Laura. I'm glad."

"Thanks, Hank."

His hands were deep in his pockets and now, in the unforgiving sunlight, she noticed he looked drawn, tired. It was the separation from Rita, she thought. It was wearing on him. He seemed a little nervous, too, as if he had something to say to her but felt inhibited by Ian's presence.

"Look, I just want you to know that even if Rita and I are, uh, separated, don't make yourself a stranger, Laura." He glanced down, the tip of his shoe kicked at some dried leaves. "If there's

234

anything I can do, just give a holler." His eyes darted toward the house. "I don't suppose you're going to be staying in the house for a while."

"I'm on my way to Ian's."

"Good. I think that's wise, real wise." A finger strayed to his lip, where perspiration had beaded. He brought his right hand out of his pocket; Diogenes nodded its head, said, "Right pretty you look, little lady. Now no fretting, you hear?" and Laura laughed.

"No fretting," she said, thinking of the state of the house inside, the evidence of the Man's rage.

"All bad things pass," Diogenes continued. "Yes ma'am, you can count on it."

"Okay, okay," Hank said, looking at Diogenes. "She doesn't need any more of your two-bit advice. Go back to sleep."

"Noooo, don't wanna go back inside," Diogenes wailed.

Hank rolled his eyes, whipped the puppet off his hand, folded it, and shoved it back in his pocket. "Damn thing always misbehaves," he said, and laughed. It was a forced, uneasy sound, and an awkward moment passed. "Anyway, just call if you need anything. Nice to see you again, Ian."

Then Hank turned and walked back toward his car. "Weirdo," Ian murmured.

"He's just trying to be nice," Laura snapped, and felt like adding, "Which is more than I can say for you."

"Maybe so, but I still think the man's strange, what with that deformed puppet and all. I can understand Rita's decision."

"He's a magician, Ian. That's what magicians do." But she knew what he meant. Hank *was* odd and it had always been something of a mystery to her that he and Rita had gotten married.

Hank honked and waved as he drove by. For a moment, standing there in the glare of the June heat, Laura felt an uneasy stirring inside. Ridiculous, she thought as Ian held the car door open for her. It was her paranoia; it had reached such tremendous proportions that if she wasn't careful, she'd be pointing the finger at everyone around her, Ian and Rita included.

She slid inside the car and stared off down the street where Hank's car had disappeared.

24

It was after eight on Monday morning and the temperature in the station felt like a hundred and five, Conway thought. The air conditioner had broken down last night and still hadn't been repaired. His office was stale and smoky, like a nightclub on Sunday morning. Even Pivot, accustomed to working in the gelid underworld of the dead, twitched and fussed as he sat across from Conway and kept removing his glasses and wiping them on his shirt, as if the heat were fogging them up.

"Couldn't believe that turd called me up at *home*," Pivot said. "He just wanted to tell me that since you'd been so remiss in sending him the reports he needed, he just knew he could count on me to get them in the mail by tomorrow."

Conway laughed. "You mean you don't *like* Evan Sanborn? I thought everyone liked him."

Pivot's small, dark eyes widened. "Too hot for jokes like that, Conway. Anyway, I stopped by to tell you I finally got the report back from the medical center. In layman's terms, they say that Denise Markham had use of about thirty percent of her liver, was already having kidney and respiratory problems, and if she hadn't died that night, Johnny, she would have died within a matter of months. That was their final determination. Case closed."

"I wish."

Pivot leaned forward, dropped his elbows on Conway's desk, brought his finger to his glasses, and pushed them back on his nose. "Say, I've been hearing rumors. True this drug taps psychic ability?"

"Where'd you ever hear a rumor like that?"

"Oh, word gets around, you know how it is."

Conway knew, all right. He could just see Dave Tillis having a few beers with the boys down in the traffic division, telling his stories, then those guys having a few beers with the boys in narcotics, and then . . . yeah, he knew all right.

"Yeah, it's true, I guess."

"That a fact," Pivot said with a grin, sitting back. "I'll be goddamned." He paused and dug a hand into the pocket of his lab jacket. "You know that for sure, Johnny? Or is that just what the Markham woman claimed?"

"Maybe I should recommend that Tillis be sent to AA," Conway grumbled, ignoring Pivot's question, wondering how much Tillis had told him.

"He doesn't mean any harm. Shit, he thinks you walk on water, Conway."

"Right."

"Really. I'm telling you. He says you were the first guy in the department who recognized he had brains."

Conway laughed.

Pivot smiled, something he didn't do very often. His face usually went from a frown to a grin with no steps in between. "He likes his beers and tall tales. That's why he became a cop. Want to hear my theories on why *you* became a cop, Johnny?"

"Now you're a chairside shrink, huh." Conway chuckled.

Pivot removed his glasses, flipped the sides together, and dropped them in his shirt pocket. "Sometimes my corpses need someone to talk to."

Conway moaned. "Terrific, Larry."

The door opened and a corporal walked in. "Say, Mr. Conway," he began, his face flushed with the exuberance of a neophyte, "you wanted all obscene phone call complaints fed through here, sir, and I just got this one that sounds like it's, uh, well, this woman said some perv slashed her tires, pinned a note to the deflated rubber, and this was after an obscene phone call on Saturday." He handed Conway the slip of paper with the woman's name and address on it.

"That's all she said?" Conway asked.

"No. She said to please hurry."

"Gotta run, Larry," Conway said, getting up as the corporal walked out.

"Me, too. See why I prefer corpses, Johnny? They don't talk back, they don't rape, kill, or mutilate or make obscene calls."

Conway gave him a funny look, chuckled, wondered if Pivot had ever been married, and if so, what the lady was like. "You're a weird bird, Larry. But I don't hold it against you."

"Gee, thanks." Pivot laughed. They walked outside and Pivot locked his fingers together, held them over his eyes like a visor. "You never answered my question, you know? Fact? Or just what the Markham woman claimed?"

"Fact, Larry. See ya." Let him discuss *that* with his corpses, Conway thought.

Nancy Ewill lived in an expensive neighborhood several miles from where many of the South Miami hospitals were located. The house backed up to a golf course, and a hedge ran from front to back around the sides, sequestering it from the neighbors. When she told him she was an R.N., he felt curiously elated. It meant if it was their man, he was feeling poorly enough to have visited a doctor. Even if he weren't using the drug now, it seemed likely he had in the past.

"See," she explained, sitting forward on the couch, still dressed in jogging clothes, "I found the note when I left the house this morning to run. Well, let me back up first. . . ." She twisted a strand of hair around a finger, then brought it over her shoulder. She sat back, her long legs crossed at the knees. "I got this call Saturday morning. The guy said the usual things—"

"What things?"

She told him. "Anyway, I hung up and got my whistle out of the drawer. I haven't used it since I left L.A. I didn't think he'd call back. At least not the same day. And not within a matter of minutes. Most pervs call once, you know, then that's it. But when the phone rang again and it was this same jerk, I was ready. Then this morning I found my tires flat and this note." She handed it to him.

Like the ones in Laura's house, it had been typed on a standard office IBM Selectric. "*Nance, it wasn't nice to blow a whistle in my ear. I don't forget things like that. I'll be watching you. Count on it.*"

"What time did you go out to run?"

"Around eight. I got home about ten last night and didn't use the car afterward." She spread her arms out, indicating the house. "I'm divorced, Mr. Conway. From a physician. Got this house in the settlement and although I love the place, it's too big for me, you know? Scary at night sometimes. Scary right now, actually."

The single woman's lament, he thought.

They went outside and Conway checked the tires. They had been punctured in the back and the diameter, no doubt, was an eighth of an inch. He got up, brushed his hands against his jeans.

"How come I get the feeling you know what this is about?" she asked him, folding her arms just under her breasts, squinting an eye closed against the glare of the sunlight on the hood of the car.

"I think you'd better find a place to stay for a few days. With a friend, relative, whatever, as long as it isn't here."

"That figures." She sighed. "I couldn't just get a run-of-the-mill perv, nope. Okay. Let's have it. What's the story on this guy?''

He explained about Denise Markham, Laura, the drug, and her face grew progressively paler as he spoke. "I see," she said finally. "A possible psychotic, right?" And he nodded. "So why me?" Her eyes rolled up toward the sky as though she were addressing the question to an unseen presence. "Huh? Why me?"

He asked her the routine questions: Did she know of anyone who might want to harm her, get even with her, and so on. "Could you give me a list of the patients you've seen in the last week or two?"

"Mr. Conway, I work in a large clinic. With twenty-five physicians. We sometimes get as many as two hundred patients through in a day."

"Specifically, for whom do you work?"

"Dr. Livesy."

"Then I need a list of patients he's seen in the last week."

"A lot of them are walk-ins, you know. There wouldn't be any record of them, except in the individual files."

"I'm looking for a man complaining of kidney problems, respiratory ailments, a general malaise, maybe. . . ."

She chuckled. "Mr. Conway, that's quite a variety of symptoms. But I'll see what I can do. It may take a few days."

Conway handed her his card. "Stay in touch and call me as soon as you have anything."

She looked at his card. "Murder's a business now?"

"People don't lose them as easily," he replied, thinking of Viki Markham. He wrote his home number down. "If I'm not in, leave a message, okay?"

"Will do."

On his way back to the department, Conway patched through a call to Tillis. "Yo, John, this must be important."

"Can you give me a rundown on Turnbalt's activities since ten last night?"

"Since ten?"

"Yeah. That's right, Tillis. Since ten."

Tillis hesitated. "Actually, no. I can't."

"Why not?"

"Because I fell asleep, Conway."

He hit the heel of his hand against the steering wheel, checked his anger before he spoke. "Christ, I don't have you out there for catnaps."

"Hey, man, I got three hours of sleep yesterday morning

when Laura was released from the hospital and then Jake called and asked if I would relieve him, because he'd been sitting out in front of Turnbalt's for nearly twenty-four hours. Get me some help.''

"There aren't any more men." *Asshole*.

"Look, I'm sorry, but—"

"What about the telephone bug?" Conway asked.

"Nothing unusual in either the penthouse or the store."

"Shit," Conway said, then added: "By the way, I'd appreciate it if you'd keep your mouth shut about this case."

"What's that supposed to mean?"

"It means shut up when you've been drinking, Tillis, that's what it means," and he slammed the mike down, ran a hand through his hair, muttered, "Shit," again. When the radio buzzed several moments later, he ignored it. He knew it was Tillis calling back in defense of what Pivot called the man's love of beer and tall tales. He'd heard it all before. Tillis never found new arguments for anything he did. It was always the same I-got-my-hand-stuck-in-the-cookie-jar routine.

As he sped down the interstate, he passed the hospital where Laura had been admitted several days before and thought of the odd conversation that had taken place about Bell's theorem. On impulse, he called Doris Lummond at Southern Bell and asked if she would provide him with copies of Ian Fletcher's phone bills for the last six months. He was not sure what he expected to find, if anything, but she told him to stop by later that afternoon.

"What the hell," he muttered softly to himself. It *felt* right.

As Conway came into the building, he saw Ake and Truro standing by the water cooler. He took one look at the captain's long, bulldog face, caught a whiff of his putrid cigar, and started to duck back out when Ake spotted him.

"Conway, hold on. You aren't going to believe this."

He joined them reluctantly, nodded at the captain, who averted his eyes and mumbled something. He was evidently still sore. "What's up?"

"C'mon, you've got to hear this." Ake opened the door to his office and the three of them entered. Truro sank into the chair nearest the ashtray, Ake leaned against his desk, flipped on the recorder, and Conway remained standing with his back against the wall, wishing Truro would disappear. "We had a visitor a while ago," Ake explained.

There was considerable static on the tape, the sound of people clearing their throats, scraping chairs across the floor, coughing.

Then Ake's voice, loud and clear: "State your name, date, and why you're here."

A brief silence followed. Truro expelled a cloud of smoke. It drifted across the room toward Conway. Harassment, he thought. The air conditioner still hadn't been repaired, and although the only window was open, it didn't do anything for the circulation in the room. The smoke seemed to hover between him and Truro.

"My name," said the voice, and Conway's arms dropped to his sides, "is Thomas Duncan. Today is June twenty-second, and this concerns the murder of . . . of Denise Markham."

Ake: "Okay. Go ahead with your statement, Duncan."

Duncan: "Detective Conway and Mr. Aikens here . . . they, uh, came to my place late Friday night and said that Peg and Howie Marshall died from an O.D. on, uh, the drug Denise manufactured. They said they knew I'd sold the drug on campus, that I'd sold it to the Marshalls, and I denied it. Mr. Aikens explained that I'd be, uh, doing a lot of time if I was charged with murder one . . . you know, like I wasn't going to be out of prison before I was a hundred and forty-five."

Ake: "We know that part, Duncan. Just get on with your statement."

Duncan: "Yeah. Right. Well. I just want to go on record as saying that I didn't kill Denise. I loved her. I wouldn't kill her. . . ." There were stifled sobs, coughs, the sound of Duncan blowing his nose. "She took me on as her assistant because I didn't know anything about chemistry and because I knew a lot of people on campus, you know, because I'm the basketball jock. About a . . . a week later, we became lovers. . . . Uh, we started experimenting with the drug . . . did it pretty often, as a matter of fact. I, uh, haven't been too well, you know. . . ." He paused; Conway and Ake glanced at each other.

Ake: "How often did you do the drug?"

Duncan: "Five, six times a week in the beginning . . . sometimes just snorting it . . . sometimes drinking it . . . and a couple times we shot up. . . . They say this drug . . . kills . . . you know?" There was a choking sound, sobs, then a heavy silence.

Ake: "Did you always meet in the lab?"

Duncan: "No. Sometimes at my place . . . sometimes at a motel. . . . Anyway, I started selling the stuff. Just friends at first, you know, people who were always lookin' around for a new high. . . ."

Ake: "How much did you sell it for?"

Duncan: "About a hundred dollars for a quarter of a gram. . . . We'd agreed to split it fifty/fifty. . . . But then later on, it went down to fifty-five/forty-five, then forty/sixty, and then . . . She said she had other people . . . investors . . . that she owed money to. . . . She said she had to think of her daughter's future, of her—"

Ake: "How much were you selling in a week?"

Duncan: "At first, maybe a gram or two a week, I don't know. Then it got to be more. I knew her so-called investors were pouring money into this because she was turning the stuff out by the barrels, so I upped the price to a hundred and fifty dollars a quarter of a gram . . . yeah . . . and started pocketing the difference myself. . . ."

Ake: "You mean you didn't tell Denise you had jacked up the price."

Duncan: "No."

Ake: "Who were these investors?"

A brief silence followed. Conway glanced at Truro, who was leaning forward in his chair, jowls sagging. He realized this was the first time the man had heard the tape.

Duncan: "Turnbalt was one of them and probably that Blanchard guy and then someone else, but I don't know who."

Ake: "How do you know there was a third investor?"

Duncan: "One night, when Denise left the lab, I followed her. She went to Marie Turnbalt's store in the Grove. It's got a basement. Not like the basements you find up north or anything, but big enough. I got in through a window, hid under the staircase. After a while, they came down. They were laughing . . . Marie Turnbalt and Denise. Then Denise says, 'I brought some if you want a snort,' and Marie says, 'Sure, but business first.' There was some rustling like, you know? And Marie says, 'Here's eight thousand, up front, and another twelve thousand next week. . . . We want to be your exclusive agents. . . .' Then she sort of laughed and they didn't talk for a while. I guess they were snorting. Finally Denise says she's obligated to her original backer, and then . . . ." A long silence.

Ake: "And then what, Duncan?"

Duncan: "Then there was some giggling . . . you know, little-girl-type giggling . . . and they made it. Together. The two of them. On the couch. It—" His voice broke.

Ake: "You said Frank Turnbalt was involved."

Duncan (sniffling, blowing his nose): "He came down after a while. Got the money. He said their backer was willing to double his investment and it was going to put them all on easy street.''

Ake: "Turnbalt had a backer."

Blanchard, thought Conway, glancing at Ake.

Duncan: "Yeah, I guess so."

Ake: "When was this, can you remember?"

Duncan: "November 1984. Right before Thanksgiving. I'd given her some roses for Thanksgiving. She loved roses, you know."

Ake: "Did Denise or Turnbalt ever know that you knew?"

Duncan: "No way, man. It's all in her notes, Mr. Aikens. In that notebook Mr. Conway found in her office."

Ake: "He never found the notebook, son."

Duncan: "Well, it's all in there. Notes she took when she was high . . . and every penny was recorded, too. . . . She was meticulous about money. That drug's . . . I don't know . . . it's bad . . . it does something . . . to your head. . . . Sometimes, I swear, I could hear what Denise was thinking, I know it sounds crazy, but I could, man, I swear it . . . and then . . . and then the pains in my side started and I . . . well, I'm always sick now. I stopped using the stuff a few months ago. . . . I was afraid that . . ."

Ake: "Did you continue selling it?"

Duncan: "Yeah, to some people. But I'd warn them, you know, like the Marshalls . . . I warned them about the pain, but they really enjoyed the stuff. . . . But by then, I wasn't Denise's assistant anymore. I'm telling you, Turnbalt killed her. . . . He was afraid of her, I think . . . because she was smarter than he was and he knew it and he knew she could also screw him royally if he ever tried to double-cross her. See, he wanted to buy the formula from her . . . said he could have it made in a lab in the islands . . . where it'd be safer, and Denise refused to sell it to him. . . ."

Ake: "You know that prolonged use of the drug can be fatal?"

Duncan (his voice cracking): "Yeah, I know. Look, I even called Mr. Conway a while back . . . made a date to meet him at the airport, and then . . . and then I got cold feet. . . . I didn't think he'd believe me. I knew he'd arrest me for dealing, you know, and I . . ." He began to cry. "I didn't want to spend what . . . what time I have left . . . in jail. . . ."

Ake: "Is that why you came forward now?"

Duncan (sniffling): "Lucia . . . well, she said it was the right thing to do . . . that maybe you'd grant me immunity or something . . . if I agreed to testify against Turnbalt. . . .''

Ake switched off the machine. Truro jumped up, his face bright red. "That's it," he said, slicing the air with his hand. "I've heard enough. We're going to issue a warrant for Turnbalt's arrest, get blood samples taken, then charge him with the murder of Denise Markham—"

"Don't be a fool," Conway said, stepping forward.

Truro shook his cigar at Conway. "Don't start with me again, boy. I've had it up to here—" He hit his forehead with the side of his hand. "Up to *here* with your shit. You fucked up bad on this one, Conway. Not to mention that you never got Evan Sanborn those reports, that you—"

"Hold on, Captain," said Ake. "Let's hear what John's got to say, all right?"

"I don't give a damn what he's got to say. We've got to sew this one up, and fast."

"Fine," Conway replied, clenching his fists, trying to hold on to his temper, even as he felt the last shreds of his patience going, "then let's do it right, so it sticks. I'd like to see this guy put away for the next fifteen or twenty years. But number one, we need more than just Duncan's statement and Blanchard's records to nail him, and number two, that *more* is either the notebook or possession of the drug."

"Has to be kept legal," Truro said, shaking his head, his jowls flushed from the heat, a ring of sweat under his arms, "can't have illegal search and seizures." He paused, puffed on the cigar. "Doesn't that daughter of hers know anything at all? Why the hell didn't that blasted woman just give the notebook and money to Markham in the first place? Huh? That's what I'd like to know."

Conway and Ake glanced at each other across the room. Ake rolled his eyes so only the whites showed. "Viki Markham doesn't know anything. She's just a ten-year-old girl" —*with the Power, Mike*—"who's trying to understand why her mother died, that's all. But Denise's father is another story."

"Her *father*?" exclaimed Ake. "Denise's father?"

Conway related the story of Bishop Keating. Ake sat down at the adding machine, thought a moment, began tallying figures.

"This is just a rough estimate," Ake said finally, "but I say we're talking maybe four to six million made off something manufactured in a university lab over a period of about two years."

"Impossible," Truro protested. "No one could manufacture

that much of a drug in a campus lab without someone knowing about it."

"Wrong," Conway replied. "Denise was primarily a researcher. That lab was her domain; she was queen bee. Second, Captain, the value of anything is determined by what people will pay for it, and people paid through the noses for Markham Magic, so quantity had nothing to do with it. It was the quality of the high which sold it."

"Quality, shit," mumbled Truro. "What the hell do you know about the quality of the stuff? You tried it?"

"Yeah, as a matter of fact, I did." He lit a cigarette and turned his back on Truro as he dropped the match into an ashtray. He was waiting for the explosion, the recriminations, the enumeration of ethical and legal violations. He was waiting for the shit to hit the fan.

Instead, Truro looked at him as if Conway had lost his mind and said, "I always knew you were nuts, Conway. I always knew it." He poked at his gut. "Always felt it right here, yes siree. But you say you know about the quality of the stuff? Okay, I believe you. Yup. I sure do." He ran his hands through his thinning hair. "Jesus. I need a vacation."

"Let us do it our way," Conway said. "And we'll keep you updated. Fair?"

"Sure. Fair. Okay."

"And keep Evan Sanborn and Tallahassee off our backs."

Truro stabbed out his cigar in the ashtray. "All right, all right. Just get me answers. What about Duncan?"

"I was getting to that," Ake said. "First of all, Karen Pauling finished the blood typing on the sperm. It's AB positive. That rules out any connection with the other two murders. And Duncan consented to a blood test while he was here. He's O, so he definitely didn't murder Denise."

So it goes, Conway thought.

"Well . . ." Truro sighed, getting heavily to his feet. "So much for the kid." In the doorway, he turned. "Updates, you two. I still want updates."

Conway clicked his heels together and saluted. When the door finally closed, he muttered, "I can't believe it. I finally got a point with him."

"You'll need it," Ake remarked, "when it comes to finding the guy who killed the other two women, Conway."

25

1.

LAURA STOOD IN front of her closet, biting at the side of a nail, perusing what was left of her wardrobe. The chair behind her was piled high with unsalvageables, and although insurance would probably reimburse her for the larger expenses, it wouldn't begin to replace her wardrobe.

Behind her, two men were setting up her new king-size bed, and she kept fighting the urge to tell them to just leave the mattress on the floor, so she could curl up and sleep while there were still people in the house. Her insomnia, and her dreams when she managed to sleep, had only worsened during her nights at Ian's. She'd spent most of every night on the couch downstairs, staring sleeplessly at the television, pushing away at the riddle of the Man, every sense on red alert for the slightest sound at the door.

"Ma'am," said one of the workmen.

She turned around. He was wiping his forehead with his T-shirt and his bare chest glistened with sweat. He was eyeing the old mattress, which rested against the wall as if awaiting execution. "Yes, what is it?"

"Mind if I ask what happened here?"

"Someone broke in," she replied.

"Well, it looks like he went to work on everything with a knife, that's what it looks like to me. I've never seen anything like this here bed, ma'am. And those curtains downstairs—" He shook his head. "Do the police know who did it?"

She shook her head. "No, not really," she replied curtly, not wanting to discuss it. She went into the closet and brought out an armful of clothes, put them on the chair.

"Probably some kid out on probation or parole, you know?" the man continued. "I'm telling you, the laws are made to protect the criminal, not the victims. Damn shame, ma'am. You want us to haul off the old mattress?"

"Yes, thanks. The sooner the better."

She watched the two men carry the mattress through the door, toward the stairs, then followed them down. More men were busy hanging drapes, ripping up the carpet. Once the tile was

246

laid and the burglar alarm installed, she would be able to move back in. It wouldn't be soon enough to suit her. The tension between her and Ian was so thick that they rarely conversed beyond monosyllables. And when they did, it was because Ian was discussing the mysterious Markham notebook, which he believed Frank Turnbalt had.

At first, she'd allowed herself to believe that Ian's interest in the notebook lay in his concern for her, in resolving this so they could get on with their lives. But she realized now this simply wasn't so. Yet what other explanation was there?

Questions. No matter where she looked, there were only more questions.

She went into the kitchen and put on a pot of coffee, shuffled through the pile of mail on the table that had been left there since Sunday, when she and Ian had stopped by to pick up clothes. On the cover of one of the professional journals was a photograph of three pyramids, shot through a telephoto lens, which rose two-thirds the way up the page. Just above the middle pyramid glowed the sun, plump as a grapefruit, a blurring ball of heat. In bold red letters across the top of the cover was written: MEXICO: SITE OF THIS YEAR'S UNIVERSITY TEACHERS' CONFERENCE. In smaller letters, just beneath that, was: Details Inside.

When this was over—*when? like a novel? a movie?*—she would go somewhere. Mexico. Tahiti. Didn't matter. Just away. And she would sleep. Lie in the sun. She would forget. She looked back at the picture. Something about it bothered her, but before she'd had a chance to think about it, one of the men called out, "Ma'am, you've got company."

She came out into the living room just as Marie Turnbalt rushed into the house in a cloud of perfume, glittering with gold and her salubrious optimism, those watery green eyes smiling.

"Laura, honey, how *are* you?" Then she looked quickly around, skewing up her face. "My God, I had no idea—"

"You should've seen it a few days ago," Laura replied, wondering what she was doing here. "You're just in time for coffee."

They went into the kitchen. Marie dropped her purse on the table, pulled out a chair, lit a cigarette with her small, delicate gold lighter, dropped her head back, and blew smoke into the air. Every movement was separate, but the overall impression was of a singular, fluid motion, like a dance.

"Rita said I'd probably find you here, that you were tired of being cooped up at Ian's. I went over to the campus to see Frank and ran into her. She told me she's separated?'' Her eyebrows shot up and Laura nodded. ''Too bad,'' Marie continued, then touched her hand to Laura's arm. ''And when are you going back to work?''

Laura set a cup of coffee in front of her. ''Probably toward the end of the week. I want the house livable before I go back.'' She pushed her mail to the other side of the table, glanced at the photo of the Mayan ruins again, wondering what it was about the picture that bothered her. She sat down. ''So what're you doing out of the store? I thought you never left.''

Marie smiled. ''Well, never say 'never' first of all.'' She laughed and reached into her bag. ''It's almost like a house-warming,'' she said, and set a small velvet box on the table. ''This came into the store the other day and reminded me of you.''

Laura opened the box. ''Good God, Marie,'' she said quietly, overwhelmed, suspicious, surprised. It was a small gold pendant, similar to the one she'd seen Marie wearing, and it hung on a thin gold chain. In the middle of the pendant were three bright emeralds, arranged like flowers on a raised gold stem. ''This is lovely, thank you.''

''Try it on,'' Marie said enthusiastically, undoing the clasp. She got up and secured it around Laura's neck. ''The minute I saw this, I knew it was made with you in mind.''

Laura looked down. The pendant hung low on her neck and caught the sunlight perfectly. Her suspicion and surprise gave way to a certain tenderness for this woman with whom she'd shared lean and simpler years and such complicated dreams. It supported her contention that if Frank *were* their man, Marie certainly didn't know about it.

Marie, still as restless as a ghost, sipped at her coffee, said, ''I hope you and Ian will be able to come to dinner after Frank and I get back from Juno next weekend.'' She glanced at Laura's arms and hands. ''It must've been terrible,'' she said softly.

''The welts are almost gone,'' Laura replied, and kicked out a foot. ''And here, too.''

''Well, it's over. It's always best not to think about ugly things once they're over. Let go. It's the only healthy way to live.''

Laura suddenly wanted to take Marie by the shoulders and shake her until her teeth rattled, shake her until she told the truth. *Did he do it, Marie? Did Frank do it? Are you covering up for him?* Something of what she was thinking must have shown on her face, because Marie frowned, fingered the gold chain at her neck, said, "You believe them, don't you, Laura." Her voice was flat, neither accusatory nor questioning, just a statement.

"Believe who about what?" she asked.

Marie looked down at the mug, stirred it with distraction. "I don't know what's wrong with me," she said quietly. "Lately, I don't know . . . I just haven't been feeling up to par. I get the feeling that . . ." She shrugged, touched a hand nervously to her hair. "Oh, don't pay any attention to me," and she laughed that polished laugh she'd picked up from Frank, put out her cigarette, stood. "I should be getting back to the store."

"Thank you for the gift," Laura said, walking Marie to the door.

"You know, sometimes I miss the old days." Marie raised her eyes. "Do you?" she finished softly.

"Sometimes, yes."

"I miss the Grove the way it was, I miss . . . You know, I never had a friend closer than you," she said, then leaned forward, hugged Laura quickly, and hurried out into the sunlight with a wave of her hand. Laura stood there until the Mercedes vanished around the corner, feeling both saddened and puzzled.

By six that evening, she was back at Ian's, fixing herself a bite to eat, hoping he'd be home before dark. There was a bag of clothes in the corner that she'd brought over from the house, stuff too torn to either wear or give away, but she'd been unable to drop it in a dumpster and be done with it. Silly as it was, the clothes were the last vestiges of her life before the Man had blown into it like a foul wind, and just seeing the bag in the corner—a sleeve, shirttail, a button sticking out—gave her a distorted sense of hope that there *would* be an end to this, that the dreams would end, the insomnia would stop, that the Man would either be caught or move on.

She sat down at the table with a bowl of soup and a sandwich, reached for the journal with the pyramids on front, studied it, glanced through the article, looked at the photograph again. Something about the picture had been nagging at her since she'd seen it. On the middle pyramid, the steps rising toward the top, toward the sun, were visible.

That's it. "Christ," she muttered, leaping up, running toward the phone. How could they have missed what was so simple, so obvious? She dialed Conway's number.

"I'll have to check if he's in, please hold." The receptionist buzzed Conway's office. She drummed her fingers on the table, her excitement barely containable.

When Conway answered, the words came out in a rush. "The magazine, John, there were pyramids on the front and—"

"Laura, slow down." Conway laughed. "What're you talking about?"

"You were on the right track all along, but it's not east or west of Hobbit's dune, it's *up*, John, *up* to the treehouse. Six steps *up* toward the sun!"

2.

The woman was asleep, her shoulders a pale gold in the afternoon light. He had just met her, in one of the bars near the college, and she was easy. Most women were easy once you understood what they wanted, he thought. But he had no affection for her, not like he did for Denise, not like he did for Laura. It was almost as though he were Laura's secret lover now, the man who sent roses, left her notes, the man who loved her from a distance.

The woman's eyes opened slowly and he wondered if she'd really been asleep. His mouth brushed her shoulder and she giggled, turned over, said, "Again?" She laced her fingers together behind her head. Her hair fanned out across the pillow. Her look was slightly coy, teasing, girlish. Her cheeks were flushed with excitement. She had a long, beautiful neck, like a swan's, and large, peasant hands with nails cut evenly across the top.

"Here, I've got something for you," he said, reaching into the nightstand. He brought out the fancy crystal container Denise had given him. "You'll like this stuff," he said, fixing the tiny tube at the top so she could snort it.

"Coke?" She held the container between her fingers, shook it, grinned. "My, my, you're just full of surprises, aren't you."

He touched a finger to her mouth, to that small place where her lips seemed to divide. Her tongue darted out like a lizard's again and she giggled. It annoyed him and he took back the container. He wouldn't do too much, he decided, just enough to experience that *space*, that *magic*.

"Leave enough for me," she said, watching him, her eyes ugly with eagerness.

When he finished, he passed her the container. Just one snort apiece, he thought. This was the last of the drug, and he wanted to preserve some for Laura, for when he and Laura would . . .

"Ah," the woman breathed, nodding, smiling, handing the container back to him. "Nice, real nice." She sat back against the pillows, humming softly to herself, tapping her fingers against the sheet where it covered her thigh. "Did you hear about that stuff that's out on the streets?" she asked, looking at him, touching the tip of her finger to his chest, then drawing it down, down. He gripped her wrist, held it tightly, held it until she grimaced and tried to pull it away. "Hey, that hurts. C'mon, stop it."

"Lies, all that stuff on TV is lies," he told her, loosening his fingers from her wrist, turning her hand over and kissing the imprint of his fingers against her skin.

"God, I feel so hot," she said, rubbing her free hand against her forehead.

Hot, then cold, hot, then cold, he thought; oh, yes, this was like the old times. He could feel the *space* approaching from a distance, could feel it fluttering in the air around him like wings. He squeezed his eyes shut as a wave of heat swept through him, a pulsating wave that centered in his groin. He looked over at the woman, saw that she was feeling it, too. Good, it was a promising sign; they would enter the space together, in synch, like he and Denise used to do, like he would do with Laura.

He gently pulled back the sheet covering the woman, her arms slid around his neck. Her eyes were sort of wild, glazed, and she murmured, "Oh, yes, now, right now, yes." His hand moved between her legs, which parted. She was ready for him, but he would have to teach her first, teach her to allow him to do what he did to Denise when they played the game. "I like you," she said, giggling, touching the tip of his nose with her mouth.

"You wouldn't betray me, would you," he said, his mouth moving from one breast to the other, her hand hard against the back of his head, urging him down.

"No, no, never betray," she whispered. "Hmm, that feels good."

His head filled with the faint scent of her perfume, of sex, of summer. She was saying something to him, but he couldn't grasp the words, they were echoing in his skull, and now pictures were flashing inside the darkness behind his eyes. Pictures of— He seized one, held it, suddenly pulled away and stared down at the woman. *Who is he? Who's the other guy?*

Her mouth opened and closed, but no words came out. Fear, confusion, and something else he couldn't identify painted her features a fiery red, then yanked the color away. *Whhaaatt iisss thiiss stufff?* Then she opened her mouth again, burst out laughing, clapped her hands over her mouth, said, "My God, I feel like . . ."

"It's the space. Relax. Enjoy it." He knew he was supposed

to be angry with her for something, but he couldn't remember what it was. Everything seemed to be moving too quickly for him now, like a movie speeded up. She was straddling him, nibbling at his neck, his ears. But when had she gotten on top of him? That wasn't how the game was played. No, it was wrong, his control was sliding away from him. He bucked suddenly and she rolled away, picked herself up, her hair a tangle around her face.

"What's *wrong* with you?" she demanded.

Confusing, everything had become so confusing. He didn't want her to run away, that would spoil everything. "I don't like it *that* way," he explained.

Her tongue flicked at her lower lip, her eyes were narrowed, scrutinizing him. She was *seeing* something in him, he thought, and quickly shielded his thoughts, slammed the doors in his mind. Her face softened, as if she'd suddenly understood something. She reached out, touched her open hand to the side of his face. *Who hurt you so badly, honey?*

There, her voice inside his head now, right? Wasn't that her voice? "I loved her," he said before he realized he was speaking aloud. "I loved her, lent her a lot of money, I . . . She was a thief."

"Well, I'd never do anything to hurt you," she assured him. She pushed her hair behind her ears, leaned over, took him in her mouth. *See? Only pleasure, no hurt.*

Good, she'd said the right thing. Now she would be rewarded. He was feeling in control again. This was how women were trained. He touched her shoulders, urging her up. Her soft cheek brushed like silk across his stomach, then he moved over on top of her, inside her. He loved the sound of her moaning, her whispers, as they moved slowly, fitting together nicely, nearing the space. Perhaps this woman would be different, someone whose youth he could mold, someone who would appreciate his teachings.

She pulled back from him a little, a frown forming a V between her eyes. *Not coke, this is not coke, is it.* She opened her mouth, but her words were garbled when she spoke, and he didn't want to listen, didn't want to talk now. He pushed up deep inside her; her head lolled forward, touching his chest. They were growing together, they would be locked like this forever. She was huge; a cavern. For an instant, the old terror returned: he would get lost inside her.

"So good," she murmured.

"Your reward," he said.

"What?" She laughed, pulling away again.

He caught her by the wrists, pinning her down against the bed, and pumped furiously inside her. Her eyes rolled back, her head whipped from side to side against the pillow, she made odd, deep sounds in her throat. He would like to tie her wrists now, tie her legs, but he couldn't remember where the scarves were. "We could . . . play a game. . . . Would you like that? Hmm?"

But she was thrusting against him, oblivious to everything but her own selfish pleasure, and he suddenly rolled away from her, leaving her high and dry. "What . . . ?" she sputtered, sitting up. "What's wrong?" She rubbed the heel of a hand against her eye, then gripped her arms against her body, shivering from the drug's cold.

"The game, the game, we're going to play the game," he said.

She gave a short, dry laugh. "*What* game? What're you talking about?"

He looked at her, at her ugly, red-rimmed eyes. "Lie down. You're not allowed to move."

She was sitting back on her heels, her hands flat against her thighs, hair dark against her white shoulders. "The game. Oh. Okay, we're going to play a game. Fine. Wonderful." She lay back. "Like this? Is this what you want?"

This was like the early days with Denise, he thought. The many lessons he gave her in fields, in the backseats of cars, in motels, and once in the shoals of a river. There was so much he and this woman would try together. And she said she wouldn't betray him. Didn't she say that? Promise it?

He got on top of her and she didn't move, not even her arms. She lay still as a corpse, watching him, waiting for the next part of the game. Now their heartbeats would grow together, they would allow the space to encompass them, permeate them, transform them. Yes, the space was a shrine, he thought, and they would pay homage. "You see? Do you see how good it can be when you behave?"

But she didn't hear him. Her head was thrown back, her eyes were closed, her hair wild, and for a distended, awful moment, he could not recall her name.

He drove into the white light, slowed as he neared the Seven Eleven where Viki Markham and her friend biked every day between three and four. He should have done this before, he thought, although even now a part of him still didn't believe in the existence of the notebook. Denise was an egregious liar. He, above all, knew this. He had seen her taking notes, but it might have been just part of her act, her invariable drama.

Just the same, he'd rehearsed what he would say to Viki: he was a close friend of her mother's, a fellow chemist. He would gain her trust, charm her. He had a way with women and children, sure, people had told him this throughout the years. He would feel her out, see if she knew anything.

He should have done this weeks ago and wondered if he was getting careless. He would have to watch himself. Even the business at the clinic was symptomatic of something. It alarmed him to have to backtrack. Yet it had been easier than he thought: heavy eye contact with the receptionist, a few flirtatious words, the calendar slipped out from under some papers while she was down the hall. His mother would have been proud of the way he had with women; he intuited how they were weak, vulnerable, malleable.

Take the receptionist, for instance, a replacement for Louise, who was on vacation; plump, shy, unattractive. He knew he had made her day. In fact, it would have been much tougher if Louise had been at the desk. She was older, hardened. She called all the patients "sonny-o" or "hon," like they were family. He would have found a way around her, certainly, but it wouldn't have been quite as simple.

And now the calendar was ashes, the evidence destroyed. Oh, yeah, he'd looked all right. He'd seen his name printed there in the little square and beneath it, "X-ray results, Livesy." Much too close, he thought.

He pulled into the parking space in front of the store and waited. It was warm in the car. Heat had stalled just inches above the pavement. His thoughts drifted back to the woman, the afternoon roll in the hay. He felt good, although he was still aware of the drug pulsing against his senses.

The woman he'd been with was simple, with fundamental needs. That had been the problem with Denise, he decided. Intelligence and education, drive and compulsion, ambition: those weren't the ingredients for happiness or obedience.

In the distance, he saw the two girls, a brunette and a redhead. They pedaled madly across the main road, materializing from the heat like mirages. They slid off their bikes, all summery, all youth, and walked them up to the window. Viki kicked the stand on her bike and followed it back until it balanced on the pavement. He wanted, just for a moment, to let the drug do its trick, to let him pop his mind out into the heat until it brushed against the child's. But suddenly she raised her head, fiddled with the hair at the back of her neck, opened a bobby pin with her teeth, and stuck it back in her hair, and he saw a miniature Denise. Dear God, he had no idea, he'd only seen her at a distance before. . . .

Was he imagining it? Was she looking at him oddly? Knowingly? With his disguise, he should have been safe, but . . .

His hand grappled for the key. He turned it, still watching her from behind his sunglasses. *Does she have it? Does she have it just like Denise told him she did?* Was it possible she *knew*? He threw the car into reverse, peeled out of the parking area. The tires shrieked. The engine wailed like a banshee. He didn't stop until he was miles from the girl, miles from anywhere.

His head dropped to the steering wheel. He was panting, as if he'd been running.

3.

The tea kettle sang.

The adding machine twanged like a banjo.

The typewriter tap-danced.

It was midnight and Conway's eyes ached from reading. He, Ake, and Rita sat at the dining room table, the contents of Denise's notebook spread out among them. Laura was across the room, the phone between her head and shoulder as she spoke to Ian and continued to type up Duncan's statement, notes from Blanchard's financial records, all pertinent data from the notebook that related to Turnbalt. Tomorrow they would present Truro with a detailed account of what had transpired and a warrant would be issued shortly afterward. It was just as Duncan had said: Denise had kept meticulous records.

Conway got up and went into the kitchen to fix another pot of coffee. He felt something close to admiration for Denise Markham's intellect—as calculated, involuted, and deliberate as it had been. To provide money for her research, she'd gotten involved with a kid sixteen years her junior and entered into a relationship with the Turnbalts that was more than just business. To ensure the survival of the research, she'd fostered a friendship with José Panzo, which resulted in the man's blind loyalty; had tracked down her father and essentially had bought him off; and in the event of an untimely demise, so her research wouldn't fall into the wrong hands, she had couched her life in riddles. The details had been orchestrated around a verse written more than two years before she'd died, before she could have had any inkling of

255

how things would turn out. She'd thought of nearly everything, except being murdered, and that had toppled her house of cards.

"A penny," Rita said, coming up behind him, slipping her arms around his waist.

He turned, kissed her quickly on the mouth. "Denise had almost everything figured out."

"Except for this Bucky character. You think it's Turnbalt?"

"I don't know."

"Hey," Laura called from the other room. "Ian wants to know if we need help."

"Tell him we know what his *real* motive is," Rita called back. "He just wants to be near you."

"You really think so?" Conway whispered.

She scrutinized him for a long moment. "*Ian?* Oh c'mon, Conway. You think . . . No, no way. Something would've happened by now. Now c'mon, we've got work to do."

Conway hoped she was right, but Fletcher bothered him.

They'd found the notebook several hours after arriving at Markham's. It was hidden between double panels under the south window in the treehouse. It was three-ringed, four inches thick, and most of the entries were typed, dated, cross-referenced. A detailed and scientific summary of her research was included, with numerous references to Bell's theorem—another connection to Fletcher that made Conway uneasy.

The notebook possessed the same quiet, almost obsessive neatness that had struck Conway the first day he'd entered Denise Markham's office. Besides the full accounting of drug sales to Turnbalt, there were copious notes on observations made while under the influence of the drug: references to her personal life, including mention of the mysterious Bucky; her thoughts on topics ranging from religion and politics to the relationship between fathers and their daughters. Except for the narrative about Bell's theorem, the scientific stuff was beyond him. He concentrated on the parts of the notebook that dealt with the woman's doubts and obsessions, her myopia and singularity.

Her descriptions of the drug "trips" bore some similarities to what he'd experienced that night with Rita but were tailored to Denise's particular way of perceiving the world. There were numerous references to heat, extreme cold, the obsession with sex, the arrogant omnipotence, and of course, the telepathy. The flaws in the drug were duly noted. There was a graphic description of an evening spent with the Turnbalts, presumably written when the effects of the drug had worn off. There was no mention of Duncan; he had evidently been too unimportant in Denise's scheme of things to even warrant a footnote.

In the front of the notebook was a second letter to Viki—the further instructions Denise had promised. It was succinct, straightforward, more Denise than the first letter, Conway thought. In his own mind, it was final proof that the woman had not been above using the very person for whom she'd proclaimed such love: her daughter. Love and sex had been her ultimate weapons.

> *Viki,*
>
> *Again, this excessive secrecy was necessary. By now, you've met and spoken with Bishop Keating. You're to entrust this notebook to him. Simply tell him you've brought the formula. He will know what to do with it. He has connections.*
>
> *I would prefer you not read this. There are many things in here you won't understand, so please, as a favor to me, to your memory of me, as tarnished and incomplete as it is, just take this to the bishop.*
>
> *I love you,*
Mom

The part about Keating hadn't really surprised him. Who else would she have given it to? An illiterate Cuban refugee? Turnbalt? Markham? No, Keating was the logical choice. As for whether or not he'd actually intended to give the notebook to anyone, well, Conway thought it was unlikely. Keating had gotten what he wanted. And yet Conway felt certain that even Keating had known only what Denise believed was necessary to accomplish her purpose. The sad and terrible irony was that the woman had not leveled with Viki about who the bishop really was. It was just another secret she'd intended to take to the grave with her. He suspected that Viki knew the truth, that she'd known it that day at the rectory, but in her unspoiled wisdom, perhaps she had sensed it was something better left unsaid, unconfirmed.

"What I don't understand," Rita said suddenly, pushing away from the table, "is why all these people aren't dead."

Ake glanced up from the adding machine. "Look at it this way," Ake said, "the medical center claimed Denise would have been dead in a couple of months. She'd been doing the drug four, five times a week for at least two years that we know of—drinking it, sometimes injecting it. Duncan had been doing it maybe six or seven months. I think if we knew the truth about the Blanchards, we'd find they were as excessive as Denise. But

257

I figure Marie and Frank and the majority of the people they sold it to use it occasionally, you know, as a weekend high." He paused as across the room Laura hung up the phone and cleared her throat.

"Don't forget, Turnbalt was selling a life-style, not just a high."

"I'd sure like to know who this Bucky is," Rita said, flipping through several pages. "He crops up a lot. Listen to this: 'I whisper, "Bucky, guess what. Hobbits and aardvarks need kisses." I test the extent of his anger with the words, the tenor of what this evening will be like, and they work on him like magic. He comes toward me smiling, like the old days, and for an instant, I can almost believe it will be good, that everything between us will be good again.' "

"Hobbits and kisses," Laura repeated, coming across the room. "That was the phrase from the first letter, wasn't it?"

"Yeah, except that in the letter, she said 'daddies' also needed kisses."

"Hobbits and aardvarks," Rita said, shaking her head. "I give Denise credit for imagination, anyway. What time tomorrow do you think you'll know Frank's blood type?"

Laura shrugged, looked down at her hands. "What's the difference? It won't be AB positive. I just know it."

Conway didn't reply. But he had a feeling she was probably right.

26

IT WAS EMBARRASSING, Conway thought, to watch a grown man, captain of the homicide division, acting as if he'd just climbed down out of the trees. He might as well have beaten his chest and howled and picked lice out of his hairy arms. Truro's face was bright red. His belly lolled over the waist of his pants as he came forward on the balls of his feet, then lifted himself up so that he was eye to eye with Clarence Zolar, the Turnbalts' attorney.

"Now you tell that pompous sleaze," said Truro, "that unless he consents to a blood test, we're going to charge him with three counts of murder one, in *addition* to the drug charges."

Zolar stood there nodding, listening politely, cool and slick in his suit, holding a black leather briefcase in one hand and an unlit pipe in the other. He was, Conway guessed, in his early forties, and his sleek good looks and composure exacerbated the lack of both in Truro. He was one of the best defense attorneys around, known for taking only "hot" cases, and this one was about as hot as anything that had come along in Miami in a long time. The man was originally from Texas, and when he spoke his voice was quiet, firm, with an undeniable Southern twang.

"Now Mike," he said, "Ah understand what you're sayin', believe me, Ah do. Ah'll see what Ah can do."

"What you *do*," Truro replied, rolling back on his heels now, "is tell him we've got a lab tech right down the hall who's just going to prick his little ole thumb, and if he's telling the truth, he'll do just fifty years for the drug charges, instead of a hundred and fifty years for murder."

"Ah wanted to ask you, is Marie in there, too?" He motioned toward the door with his head.

"No, we separated them."

"Ah see. Well, Ah'll be wantin' to talk to her, also. Ah'll be representin' the two of them."

"Whatever," Truro muttered.

Zolar opened the door. Conway heard him say, "Mornin', Frank, Ah trust you're doin' well?"

"Shipshape," Turnbalt replied, then the door closed and except for a "Bullshit" from Turnbalt a few minutes later, it was quiet. Conway moved on down the hall before Truro could say anything to him and ducked into the room where Marie Turnbalt waited. She sat at a table by herself, staring vapidly at her hands, which were folded in front of her. Light from the window brought out the rich brown of her hair, and when she glanced up it ossified her features.

"I don't have to speak to you," she said.

"I just wanted to know if I can get you coffee or something," he replied.

Her pale green eyes were ringed by circles like bruises. She sat back, her hands dropped into her lap, and she made a sound like a sigh. She seemed very young to Conway, and tired. "I'd like a cigarette," she said. "If I'm allowed to smoke."

"Sure." He handed her her pack, then lit her cigarette for her. She inhaled deeply, as if she'd quit only a few weeks before and now relished the first taste of addiction. She gazed at him none too kindly, fingered the gold chain at her neck.

"Are you waiting for me to confess?" she asked, cocking her

head, the hint of a dimple at her mouth. She reached back, removed a comb from her hair, and it tumbled to her shoulders.

"No, your attorney arrived. He's in with your husband."

She crossed her legs, swung her foot out, back, out again. The news seemed to buoy her confidence. "Clarence is the best, you know. He's expensive as hell, but he's the best." She paused, chuckled. "His first name is no coincidence; his mother planned it that way, I think. Clarence Darrow, Clarence Zolar, nice ring, huh."

"I've heard he's good," Conway replied.

"You can't prove anything, because we didn't do anything."

"Did Frank kill Denise?" Conway hadn't meant to ask it, hadn't come in here intending to ask it. Truro, in fact, would explode if he knew. But there it was and it loomed between them. She seemed to shrink before his eyes. Her gaze dropped and she leaned forward with her hands on the table again, passing her thumb over her wedding ring, as if recalling her vows.

"No," she replied quietly, "of course not."

She wasn't entirely certain, Conway thought. "I know that you and Denise were friends. Did she ever say anything to you about anyone she was seeing?"

Marie lifted her eyes again. A hint of a smile—mocking, hateful—tugged at her mouth. "Why should I tell you anything, Mr. Conway?" She stabbed out the cigarette.

"Because if it turns out your husband has AB positive blood, he's going to be charged with three counts of murder and it'll practically be an open and shut case unless someone comes up with another suspect."

The mockery fled. The pale green of her eyes darkened. "Once," she said after a while. "Only once. Someone named Bucky. I never knew his real name. He was just Bucky to her. Someone she'd been seeing off and on for maybe three years, you know, whenever she and Don split up. Oh, hell, maybe she saw him after she and Don would get back together, I don't know. She would screw anything, Mr. Conway, it was—" She stopped. "Yeah, even me." Her voice softened. "Denise and I were lovers, but I'm sure you already knew that. Women are more naturally inclined toward bisexuality than men, it's—"

"Is that Marie speaking? Or Frank?"

The glitter and sophistication dropped away. He knew he was seeing a Marie that had existed before Frank came into the picture. She covered her face with a hand and closed her eyes. "What," she whispered, "has happened to us?" She shook her head, as if the truth of the years had suddenly caved in on her. "What will I do without Frank, Mr. Conway? I don't know how to—"

He pulled out the other chair, sat facing her, and covered her hand with his own. "If you're convinced your husband didn't kill anyone," he said gently, "then please, tell me whatever you know about Denise and this man. Bucky."

She sighed deeply, and it held the tragedy of capitulation and muted relief. "Yes, all right."

"Was he single? Married? Does he live here in town?"

"I don't know. I swear. Denise never said. She was so secretive." Conway removed his hand, lit two cigarettes, and handed her one. She dropped her head back, gazed up at the ceiling, blew smoke. "I . . . I never knew anything about her family . . . except that she loved her daughter and didn't get along well with Markham . . . said he was too boring. . . . And as for Bucky, they apparently did extensive experiments with the drug. . . . She once said it gave them an unnatural closeness. I know that seems vague, but unless you've tried the drug, it's difficult to explain. You kind of grow together with a person if you do it together often." She hesitated. "Does that make sense, Mr. Conway?"

Perfect sense. "Yes. Anything else?"

"My own guess is that he lives in the area, because I don't think Denise would ever bother with a long-distance relationship. She simply wouldn't take the time out of her work. Whoever he was—is—he must've understood Denise's obsession." She stubbed out the cigarette, gestured at the pack on the desk. "May I?"

"Keep it," Conway told her, noticing that her thumbnail had been chewed down so far the blood had crusted around the cuticle. She hit the top of the pack with her index finger. He lit a match, held it to her cigarette, and she pushed away from the table and walked over to the window, an arm folded at her waist. She smoked silently for a few minutes. "Is there anything else you can tell me?" he persisted. "Did she ever give you any hint about what this Bucky does for a living? Anything about his background?"

"She said he was great in the sack," Marie said, her voice flat. She turned. "She also believed they had known each other before. In a previous life." She rolled her eyes toward the ceiling. "Whenever Denise started talking like that, I stopped listening. I mean, reincarnation, Christ, for that matter I could say Frank and I have known each other before.'' Then she added, ''I can't see how else I got into this mess.''

''You know it's true about the drug's effects,'' he said.

She turned toward the window again. ''Yes,'' she replied quietly. ''Although you'd never get Frank to believe it.''

''What did Blanchard say when he came to your place the night before he died?''

''The night he killed himself, you mean.'' She came back across the room, stubbed out the cigarette, stood with her hands gripping the back of the chair. ''I agreed to talk with you about Bucky, Mr. Conway. Not about Jerome or the rest of it. That's what Clarence is for.'' She smiled. ''To protect my innocence, right?'' The sarcasm was gone, but Conway thought her eyes seemed wary now, and fearful.

''Fair enough. Just tell me this, for my own information. How often were you using the drug?''

''More often than Frank. He and I used to indulge on weekends. With Denise . . . or the Blanchards. . . . Sometimes . . . I, uh, did it two or three times a week, depending on how I felt.'' She rubbed her hands along her arms. ''They say that coke is psychologically addicting, but nothing like Denise's little wonder is, Mr. Conway.'' She paused. ''Now it's *my* turn. Did you bug my store?''

''Off the record?'' he asked, and she nodded. ''Yes.''

She bit at her little finger. ''I thought so. Didn't find anything, though, did you, Mr. Conway.'' For a moment her voice held a trace of mockery.

''Nope.''

''Laura thought . . . for a while, anyway . . . that Frank . . . well, that Frank was responsible for everything that has happened to her, didn't she.''

''We all did.''

Marie nodded. ''I guess I can't really blame her. Funny, though. Frank always liked Laura.'' She sat again, sideways, a foot tucked under her. ''She was a good friend to me for a lot of the years that mattered. We went our separate ways after Frank and I were married, I guess. You know how it is.'' She rubbed her eyes with the back of her hand, shrugged. ''But we were talking about Denise. Denise and Bucky.''

''Can you remember anything else?''

''Yes. One thing. She once remarked that it was an ideal relationship because he 'wasn't around a lot,' whatever that meant. Her and Bucky's relationship didn't interfere with her marriage. Of course, I never understood why she and Markham stayed married for six years. Except that Viki loved him.''

"You mean that Bucky traveled a lot?"

"I don't know. She never explained what she meant by his not being around much." She stopped, ran a hand through her hair. "He used to give her things—gifts, clothes sometimes, expensive clothes. And there was a pair of gold earrings she wore constantly that he'd given her."

"Plain gold?"

"Yeah, eighteen karat."

And when she was found, he thought, the only piece of jewelry she was wearing was a wedding band.

Marie sat down, worried her hands in her lap. "God," she whispered, and shook her head. "I've heard prison . . . for women . . . is worse than it is for men. Is that true, Mr. Conway? I mean, do you think . . . do I have a chance?"

"I don't know. And I don't know anything about women's prisons." It was a lie, but what was the point of elaborating.

Her dimple surfaced momentarily. She laughed. The worry in her face dropped away and she looked like the woman he'd seen that first evening at the penthouse, as if nothing could possibly go wrong in her life. "Thanks just the same, but I've heard the stories, you know."

The door opened and Zolar stepped in, looked at Marie, smiled perfunctorily, frowned at Conway. "Sir, mah client cannot speak with you unless Ah'm present. If you'll pardon us now."

A Southern gent to the end, Conway thought. And he was probably charging them as if he were F. Lee Bailey himself.

Conway started toward the door. "Say, thanks for these," Marie said, holding up the pack of cigarettes. She looked back at Zolar. "Tell me, Clarence. Do you know what Frank's blood type is? Because I sure as hell don't."

Zolar stood mutely by the door until Conway left. He started toward the lab, but one of the secretaries said he had a call. He took it in his office and was surprised to hear Nancy Ewill. "Already? That was quick," he said.

"I'm afraid I don't have good news. The doctor's appointment calendar is missing. Our regular receptionist is in New Jersey for a funeral and the only thing we can figure is that a patient took it while the other girl was filling in. Either yesterday or the day before."

"Terrific," Conway muttered.

Another dead end, he thought, except that it provided confirmation that the man was the same, that he was in pain, that he was worried. "I appreciate your getting in touch. Would you happen to know if any of the doctor's patients goes by the nickname of Bucky?"

"Not offhand. And the doctor's on vacation. On a cruise, but I'll ask when he returns."

"And when will that be?"

"Two weeks," she replied.

"That figures."

She gave him her new phone and address. He'd no sooner hung up when Ake lumbered in to tell him Turnbalt was type O.

"So what's the next move?" Ake asked.

Conway laughed, shook his head, stuck his hands in his pockets as he got up and walked over to the window. *The next move, Mr. Bobby Fischer, is* . . . Police work, he decided, was part legwork and the rest was blind luck, the very thing that, if he'd known it two weeks ago, would have put him on the next plane to Colorado. "A date with the queen bee. Denise's notebook. I still think the answer's in there somewhere, Ake. I'm going to take two days off."

"You aren't going to see the bishop?"

"Not right away. I don't think the man ever intended to see that his daughter's formula got anywhere. Oh, I suppose he would've made sure Viki got her money, and eventually maybe he and Markham would've met, who knows how Denise intended things to work out. But basically, Keating got what he wanted out of the deal. He was her pawn and she was his. Wonderful relationship between father and daughter."

He picked his briefcase up off the floor, set it on the desk, opened a drawer, and brought out a stack of papers, which he put inside. "I'll call you," Ake said, "if anything comes up." He followed Conway to the door. "This sure ain't like you, white boy. What do you want me to tell Truro?"

"As little as possible."

"He'll ask."

"Shit, he always asks. Tell him I resigned. Took a sabbatical. In Bali. Or Colorado. I don't care. Tell him I'm tired of the case, Ake, and then tell him I've got the time coming and I'll be back when I've got some answers."

He pulled up in front of his building and saw Rita's Volvo in his usual spot. Grinning, he grabbed his briefcase off the seat and ran up three flights of stairs, taking them a pair at a time.

She opened the door before he'd reached the landing, stood with a hand on her hip.

"You make enough noise." She laughed.

"How come you're not in school?"

"Independent study. It's a term that means the teach is approaching burnout." He kissed her hello quickly on the mouth, hoping none of his neighbors were watching.

She snuggled up close to him, reached up on her toes, whispered, "The lady in twenty-four B is watching us. If we give her a show, she may have a coronary."

Conway laughed and they stepped indoors. "How long have you got?" he asked.

"All day," she replied. "And now, you've got to change into grubbies, Conway. I've got a surprise." He started toward her, but she pointed a finger at the bedroom. "Go. Grubbies, Conway. Hurry."

"Okay, sure," he said, backing toward the bedroom. "You aren't even going to give me a hint?" he called out.

"Nope."

"Disney World, we're going to Disney World."

"Nope."

"The Seaquarium?"

"Tacky, very tacky."

He went into the den, put the papers in his briefcase away, saw Rita standing in the front doorway, her hands behind her back, which was to him. She was rolling slowly back and forth, from her heels to her toes.

"Did I forget my birthday or something? Oh, wait a minute. You heard about the Turnbalts."

"Yup. I figured you'd be ready for some fun. A day of nothing but fun, Conway."

He came out of the study. "Anything else I need?"

Rita looked him up and down. "A cap. A straw hat. Something."

"Don't have either."

"Well, we'll just have to see what we can do."

As they were walking downstairs, he said, "I hate suspense, Rita. Is it far? How far do we have to drive?"

"Patience, Conway."

In the parking lot, he started to unlock the Porsche, but she shook her head. "Nope." She held out her hand, he took it, they continued across the street. He looked at her.

"You didn't," he said.

"I did," she said.

"How?"

They had reached the grass. The sloop wasn't three hundred yards away. It was secured by only one rope. "I asked, Conway. I just asked. We've got 'er for the day."

"For the day," he repeated, grinning.

She was his, all right. She stood against the blue of the morning sky like a promise, so smooth and sleek in her wooden skin, that single mast just waiting for its sails. They got on board, Conway dug his hands into the ropes that secured the boat, called over his shoulder, "Who owns her? Where are the owners? How come they never use her?"

"He's a little old man who says he keeps it around for when his son and his family visit. Says he's too old to use it himself now, being a widower and all." She paused. "Says he might be interested in selling it. For the right price."

Conway laughed. "What else did he tell you?" The rope dropped into the water.

"Says he's seen this fine little Porsche—"

"C'mon."

"Really."

"And?"

"Maybe he'd be willing to make some kind of deal. Says he's too old to sail by himself, but not too old to drive by himself. He says he sure likes that fine little Porsche."

As he moved toward the stern, he caught Rita around the waist. "I may not bring you back, you know." He reached down to start the motor so they could get out into the canal, and she leaned against the side next to him.

"Yeah, I know," she said, resting back on her hands now. "I was sort of counting on it. I've decided to divorce Hank, Conway."

They motored most of the way south, then put in at Pumpkin Key to wait for the wind to rise. Rita had brought along provisions and fixed them lunch on board. There were clean towels in the bathroom that smelled of Tide, clean sheets in the closet, fresh soap, a fridge stocked with beer and two pounds of plump, fresh shrimp, which she said was for dinner.

They went skinny-dipping in the inlet, where the water was that deep green of jade, of pine, where the trees drooped and formed an umbrella of privacy, and later they made love on the deck of the sloop, in the sun, the two of them thick with salt and desire, and it was much more than the drug had been. This had magic. The magic of the future.

Around four, they feasted on the shrimp. By then, Rita was

wearing a blouse because her shoulders were pink. The tip of his nose was bright red and she covered it with sunscreen, then rubbed the stuff on his shoulders and down along his arms and whispered, "I just like touching you, see." And when he turned around to kiss her, she gazed out from under a floppy straw hat that left jagged shadows on her arms and said, "You. I love you." His heart swelled. He felt certain that if he thrust out his arms and caught the currents just right, he would lift like a kite and soar.

She moved across from him again and began peeling shrimp. She spoke slowly, carefully, and when she smiled, she pushed her hat back on her head with her knuckles, because her fingers were wet from the shrimp. "I realized I've never had a relationship like this with a man. I mean, there were men before Hank. A lot of them. Some were friends, others I dated, others were there strictly for sex. But I've never—" She stopped, frowned. "You promise not to laugh at me?"

Conway almost choked. *Laugh at her?* "Why would I do that, Rita?" he managed to say.

She gave a small shrug, finished her shrimp. "I don't know. I guess I figure that men generally don't like to discuss stuff like this."

He had thought women didn't like to discuss stuff like this; his wife certainly hadn't. And Jen would simply have popped another pill and pushed everything underground in between explosions. "I promise not to laugh at you."

"Ever since that night we did the drug," she began, "everything has changed. It made a difference somehow. I feel as close to you, Conway, as I do to Laura. I've known her all my life; I've known you a matter of weeks."

A drop of cocktail sauce bloomed in the corner of her mouth like an exotic flower. Conway reached out, wiped it away with a finger, dipped his hand in the water. He moved over next to her. "I think it's only fair to tell you, Rita," and he put his mouth very close to her ear, nibbled at it, whispered something, and she laughed. "Does Hank know what you've decided?" he asked.

She shook her head. "I haven't told him, if that's what you mean. But I'm sure he suspects. I saw him earlier today." She paused, looked away, reached for another shrimp. "I went by to pick up some things." She stopped again. "The passbook, actually. I wanted to withdraw my half of the savings and invest it elsewhere." She stopped, rubbed her hands across her face, then dropped them in her lap as if in defeat. "Well, there isn't any savings."

"What happened to it?"

"Hank gambled it." She made an impatient gesture with her hand. "Can you believe it, Conway? Hank and I have been married about a year and a half and we've been separated four or five times because of money." She laughed and it was a bitter, sad sound. "He's a compulsive gambler. First, it was twenty-five thousand dollars he withdrew from the company's pension fund. Now this." She gazed out over the water. "I think I've stayed until now because . . . oh, hell, you're raised with this Cinderella dream, you know? And it's hard to shake it." She tugged at the brim of the hat, pulling it down lower over her eyes. "So, the first chance I get, I'm going to tell him I'm filing for a divorce. No-fault. Clean and simple." She paused. "Loss of money, wasn't that what Fedora Hopkins said?" Conway nodded.

It was twilight when they putted into the canal and tied up at the dock. George O'Keefe, the owner, was sitting on his back porch and lifted his cane, waving at them. He hobbled across the lawn toward them and Conway met him on the dock.

"So, son, how'd she handle? Nice, eh? Would you and the lady like a spot o' whiskey?"

"Love one," Rita and Conway replied simultaneously, then laughed.

O'Keefe grinned. "Stay right there and I'll bring some out."

Conway watched as the old man made his way back across the lawn, shoulders hunched, a bad limp to his right side. There in the twilight, O'Keefe was an archetypal figure, something that had sprung from myth or perhaps from the soup of his unconscious.

"Does he live there all by himself?" Rita nodded. "I wonder if he cooks."

"Cooks?" She laughed.

"Yeah, we could hire him on."

O'Keefe returned with a bottle of Irish whiskey and three shot glasses, which he lined up on the railing. "Lady tells me you might be interested in a trade," O'Keefe said.

"Lady tells me the same thing about you," Conway chortled, eyeing Rita, who was suddenly very busy unloading things from the boat.

"I say we drink to a trade," O'Keefe suggested, raising his shot glass with a twinkle in his clear Irish eyes.

When Rita left, Conway drove down to the all-night Pantry Pride, bought groceries, then stopped by a friend's garage for a preliminary appraisal on the Porsche. He didn't have the vaguest idea whether or not he was really going to go through with a trade, but he enjoyed entertaining the thought, particularly in light of Rita's announcement that she intended to file for divorce.

He was whistling as he let himself into the apartment nearly an hour and a half later. He set the bag of groceries on the table, hit the replay on the tape machine, filled the kettle, intending to make tea as soon as he showered. The only call he'd received had come in at four-thirty.

"Hello, Mr. Conway. This is Steve Jenkins, your ex-wife's attorney. It is imperative that we set up a meeting concerning the back alimony you owe Stella. I will await your call."

"Go suck an egg," Conway muttered, switching off the machine with an angry flick of his wrist. He walked down the hall into his den, immediately noticed that something seemed different about his desktop—rearranged—but before he could turn around, something came down over his head. There was a blinding moment of white pain, then the floor rushed up toward him in a blur and he blacked out.

When he came to, a cold liquid was dripping down the side of his face. It smelled like booze. It stung. It made the little men tromping through his head lift their hands and holler and stamp their feet. Pressure was building to a dull roar in his skull, preparing to explode. He opened his eyes. He was staring into the wizened, kind face of George O'Keefe.

"Stay put now, Johnny, and I'll be afinishin' with this in a minute."

"Ouch," Conway grumbled when the old man touched something to his head.

"First the whiskey and now the peroxide. I think you'll be among the livin' for a while, but that's a mighty nasty gash." He pressed a bandage over the wound, took Conway firmly by the shoulders, and hoisted him to a sitting position. The room spun like a Ferris wheel. Black dots danced behind his eyes. He gripped the edge of the couch.

"How'd I get up here?" Conway asked, patting the couch, dropping his legs over the side.

"My legs aren't worth a damn"—O'Keefe chuckled—"but my arms are. I came by to see if I could take the Porsche for a spin tomorrow morning, and I found the door open and groceries on the counter and you here, spilling blood all over the carpet." He paused and shook his head.

Conway leaned forward, with his arms resting against his legs. For just an instant, he was puzzled, then he knew what the intruder had been after. He stood, swayed unsteadily, held on to the edge of the desk until the dizziness had passed, then moved around to the front. He opened the right middle drawer. "Sucker"—he laughed—"that lousy stupid sucker." The notebook, of course, was gone.

"Somethin' missing?" O'Keefe asked.

"Yeah, but not the way this guy hoped."

"You know who's done it, son?"

"I'm slowly getting there," Conway replied as he knelt in the closet doorway and slid a tile away. The safe hadn't been touched. He dialed the combination, lifted the lid back, and removed a Xerox copy of the notebook. "Always pays to have duplicates of things, you know? My mother was a writer, O'Keefe. Kids' stories. She even kept copies of her rough drafts. I think I got it from her." He sat with his back against the couch and his legs stretched out in front of him.

"This be a case you're working on?" O'Keefe asked.

"This be a case all right," Conway replied, and began to tell him about it. O'Keefe pulled a pipe and a tobacco pouch from his pocket, and in a few minutes the air was swollen with the rich, sweet scent of it. O'Keefe poured the two whiskeys, and by the time Conway had finished telling him the story, his pipe was dead and the whiskeys were gone.

"Quite a story," said O'Keefe. " 'Course, you go spendin' any time on the sea, Johnny, and you know about what your Fedora Hopkins calls the Power. M'thinks it goes back to when we lived in caves, when we were hunters and needed the Power to survive. Technology has made us a lazy bunch. Me, that's why I always took to sailin'." O'Keefe paused to refill his pipe and light it. "Now how about another spot o' whiskey, Johnny."

They sat and chatted for over an hour. The whiskey dulled the ache in his head and gave Conway a chance to turn things over in his mind, but at a distance from the problem. It was like trying to make out something in the dark and findi it, that you had better luck if you looked slightly to the right or left of the matter.

When O'Keefe left, Conway made his cup of tea and sat at his desk, paging through the notebook, immersing himself in Denise's world. He concluded there were only three possible motives for the theft of the notebook: the murderer was afraid he'd been mentioned; someone wanted the formula to the drug; the third investor (Bucky?) didn't relish the thought of joining the Turnbalts in jail. He decided the murderer and the thief might or might not be the same individual. It seemed imperative that he keep this in mind, in light of his previous certainty that Turnbalt was their man.

He listed the people who'd known about the notebook's discovery or had suspected it because of news of the Turnbalts' arrest, jotted notes to each name, studied the list, then went to bed and slept on it.

At six, he got up, looked through his notes, fixed himself a bite to eat as he thought about it, hoping he was wrong. Then he placed a call to Fedora Hopkins in Cassadaga, New York.

"Hullo?" said a sleepy female voice.

"Mrs. Hopkins? This is Mr. Conway. I'm sorry to bother you so early in the morning."

"Mr. Conway. Oh. My. Give me a minute. Who—what time might it be?"

"Six-thirty. Listen. The reason I'm calling is about the man Denise was with that day when you saw her. Could his name possibly have been Ian Fletcher?"

She hesitated. He could hear her breathing softly. "Why yes, Johnny, Ah think that was his name. Real polite young man, young man, like Ah said."

"Can you tell me anything about him? I mean, what you talked about?"

"Jus' about things, you know. Ah think Denny had brought him jus' so she could show him off like, to get my 'proval, Ah s'pose. He seemed mighty fond of Denise, Ah do 'member that clearly."

"Thanks again, Mrs. Hopkins. I'm sorry to have awakened you."

"Don't worry about it, Johnny. Hope Ah've been some help. You keep in touch now, hear?"

"Yes, yes, I will. Thanks again."

27

1.

FOR THE THIRD time, Conway went through the copies of Fletcher's phone bills, which Doris Lummond had given him several days before. And again, he found nothing irregular. In six months, the man had made only a handful of long-distance calls, and these were to members of his family in Indianapolis.

A call to the Chamber of Commerce confirmed that Word

Systems, Inc., the firm for which Fletcher worked, had been in business for several years. Long enough, Conway thought, for the man to establish himself as a computer salesman for the university.

His second call was to Ake's contact at the credit bureau. He requested a credit check on Fletcher and his company and was told it would take a few hours.

On his way back to his apartment, Conway reviewed what he knew about Fletcher, and it wasn't much. Most of it was second-hand, through Rita. It was anyone's guess how much of it was fictive. He and Laura had met in Key West about six months ago, at an educational conference of some sort. He was born and raised in the Keys, his family was now in Indiana, he'd lived in Florida the last ten years, had an undergraduate degree in business, a master's degree in education, had sold real estate, used cars, and had entered the computer and word processor business through a family friend.

Or so he said.

Closer to home, Ian had supposedly been on the road when Denise was murdered; had never been around when Laura was terrorized; and had mentioned that day at the funeral that he'd met Denise—something that had surprised Laura sufficiently for her to comment on it. Then, of course, there was Bell's theorem— the notes of Ian's that Laura had found and his obvious familiarity with it that day in the hospital. And he couldn't ignore the fact that since Laura had moved in with him a week ago, the terror campaign against her had ceased and had turned to Nancy Ewill instead. Coincidence?

Was Ian Fletcher on the verge of psychosis?

When he returned to the apartment, Conway called Ake and asked him to put a tail on Fletcher. "I'm wondering if we shouldn't have done it before."

"Before, we didn't have much to go on."

"Thing is, if Fletcher's our man, then he's had a whole week to get at Laura and hasn't."

"That'd be too easy," Conway replied. "And it's why I don't think she's in any immediate danger."

"Let's hope you're right, white boy."

Conway gave Ake a list of things he needed. "Can you get over here within the next hour with that stuff?"

"Okay. See you in about forty-five minutes," Ake said, and rang off.

Conway called O'Keefe, and fifteen minutes later the old man strolled in with his cane hooked over his arm. "Well, Johnny, how do I look?"

He wore a beret, pulled down low over his forehead, a madras shirt with jeans and sandals. "Like a made-to-order eccentric." Conway laughed.

O'Keefe twisted the ends of his mustache, grinned. "I brought along a dark shirt and other shoes, just as you instructed. Say, is this legal? I mean, with your department?"

Truro's face loomed like a soft, pink sun in Conway's mind. *You what?* he imagined the man screaming. *That's against regulations, Conway.* Screw regulations, he decided. "Don't worry about it, George. I need your services."

O'Keefe rubbed his hands together and gave an impish laugh. "This will be the most fun I've had, lad, since . . . well, since I don't know when."

"The need may not arise, but have you ever handled a Smith and Wesson?"

"Done my share of rum-running on the high seas, Johnny boy, before the dope and refugees came along. So yeah, I've handled one."

Conway explained what he had in mind. "Any questions?"

"Nope."

Promptly at nine-thirty, a woman from the credit bureau called. "Mr. Conway, I checked on that information you requested. And I was wondering, is that company American-based?"

"As far as I know, yes."

"Well, in checking through his records, I found out that every month money is wired to Mr. Fletcher's account from a bank in Zurich."

"*Zurich?*"

"Yes, sir. There's never been a check deposited to his personal account, just wire transfers from Zurich." For a moment, Conway was a little surprised that a single phone call could yield so much information. But Big Brother was here all right, he was stored in computers, Conway thought. He simply worked less blatantly than ole Orwell had imagined.

"I assume his credit checks out then, right?"

"Yes, sir. These monthly deposits are sizable, usually between four and five thousand."

"Right. Four or five thousand. Well. Thank you. Thank you very much."

Shortly before ten, Conway let O'Keefe off just around the corner from Word Systems, Inc. Inside the old man's pocket was a transmitter coil shaped like a spring in a ballpoint pen. Originally invented by a CIA think tank, it had a range of half a mile and had proven a particularly effective tool in recording drug transactions. The world of microelectronics, Conway mused, had certainly made his own job easier. Orwell had envisioned *that*, too.

He drove around the block and pulled in behind the Word Systems building, where Ake was waiting for him. He parked four cars away. Several minutes later, the receiver picked up O'Keefe's Irish voice, quiet, charming, infinitely affable. "Mornin' ma'am," he said. "I'd like to see Mr. Fletcher, if he's abein' here."

"And your name, sir?" asked the receptionist.

"O'Hara, George O'Hara."

"I'll ring him, just a moment." Pause. "Mr. Fletcher, there's a gentleman here to see you. . . . I don't know, sir, I'll ask. Mr. O'Hara, is this concerning the purchase of a word processor?"

"Sure is," O'Keefe replied. "That *is* what you people sell, isn't it? I haven't come to the wrong place?"

She laughed. "No, this is the right place. . . . Yes, Mr. Fletcher. I'll take you back, Mr. O'Hara."

Footsteps. The sound of O'Keefe's cane tapping along the floor. Then the usual introductions and amenities and Ian saying, in his best PR voice, "Have a seat, Mr. O'Hara. What may I do for you?"

O'Keefe played his part well. He explained that he was a writer and interested in purchasing a word processor to use in his work. "I need someplace to store facts, you see. The old noggin isn't what it used to be."

"What kind of writing do you do?"

"Nonfiction. About the sea," he replied, and Conway almost laughed. Only an Irishman could get away with a line like that. "This bum leg here . . . well, it wasn't always like that. I've done some sailin' in my time."

"We don't usually do business with individuals, because we're such a small firm, but let me show you what models we have."

Papers rustled, as though Fletcher were showing O'Keefe a selection of brochures. The old man hemmed. He hawed. He finally said, "Let me put your number on my calendar, Mr. Fletcher. I always lose these little cards. I'll call you in a day or two when I've made up m'mind." A moment passed. Something crashed to the floor. "Oh, my," O'Keefe breathed softly. "I'm sorry. I get clumsier and clumsier in my old age. . . ."

Conway smiled. He could imagine O'Keefe leaving his pen on

the desk while Fletcher picked up whatever he'd knocked to the floor. He thought how Tillis or one of the other men would have bungled the job royally.

"I'll be waiting to hear from you," Fletcher said finally. Conway heard footsteps, a door opening and closing. For a moment, there was silence, then Fletcher muttered, "Stupid old coot even left his pen."

Conway saw O'Keefe emerge from between two buildings. He pulled his cap down on his head and was grinning to himself. "How'd I do?" he asked eagerly as he got in.

"Perfect."

"Now what?"

"We wait."

O'Keefe nudged the cap back on his head. "Johnny, just an observation. The man didn't appear the least bit psychotic to me. I mean, I'm no expert, but that's my observation."

"Yeah," Conway replied, wishing he could forget the fact, "I know what you mean."

For the first few hours, nothing much happened. Ake joined them in the car for a while, and he and O'Keefe played a game of chess. Then a tapping like Morse code broke out over the receiver (Fletcher flicking the pen against the edge of the desk?), and all three men sat forward as they recognized the sound of dialing.

"Dr. Perkins, please," said Fletcher's voice. "Babe? Hi, it's just me. How's it going your first day back? . . . Really? . . ." Conway glanced at Ake, who rolled his eyes. "Great. . . . Say, it looks like it's going to be another long night. . . . Between ten and eleven, probably," Fletcher said in an appropriately weary voice. "Babe, I'm sorry, but all these new salesmen are so green. . . . Are you sure you'll be all right alone, babe? Good . . . go shopping, get out a little. Is Rita going with you? . . . Laura, you can always go down the hall and stay with Mrs. Reynolds if I'm not home when you get back. . . . She is *not* a hundred and five years old. . . ." Impatience, thought Conway. *You bastard.* "It'd be better to stay with her than by yourself. . . . Babe"—his voice was a whisper now—"I'm sorry. I didn't mean to snap at you. It's just that things have been so . . . uneasy between us . . . What? Oh, right. Babe, I'll see you tonight. Good luck in class."

More tapping. Then, for nearly another hour, the sound of typing filled the squad car. Ake and O'Keefe played another game of chess. And when the sound began again, Conway could imagine Fletcher sitting at his desk, tapping the pen with distraction, arranging his deceptions, his dark eyes narrowed and pensive and waiting.

"Ian?"

O'Keefe glanced up at the sound of the woman's voice. "The receptionist," O'Keefe said.

"What's the story?" the woman asked.

"I haven't called yet. At four."

"It's ten of," she replied.

Fletcher laughed. "You must be anxious to move on."

"A civilized country is what I want. Maybe I'll be lucky enough to make the Oktoberfest this year." Her voice dropped. "C'mon, Ian. Try now."

"Okay, okay." A chair scraped across the floor. There were footsteps, the sound of a door squeaking open, then Fletcher's voice: "Sam, this is Eddie. Do you copy?"

"What is it?" Ake asked. "A ham radio?"

"Probably," O'Keefe replied.

"Sam, this is Eddie, do you copy?" Fletcher's voice repeated. Then a distinctly foreign voice replied, "I copy, Eddie."

"I've got some loose ends to tie up," Fletcher continued, "then on to Zurich. The weather here is three double oh in the afternoon shade, like the air over France. Unbearably warm."

"When are your classes finished?" Sam asked.

"Tuesday. Wait until you see me in my trench coat and clerical collar, carrying my notebook, like any diligent student. I'll be glad to get out of Miami."

"I copy," Sam replied. "Say, did J. M. Bell come through?"

"Sure looks like it," Fletcher replied, and signed off.

"Great," said the receptionist. "I can't wait."

Fletcher and the receptionist chattered about how crowded Europe was in the summer. Conway turned to Ake. "The air over France? What do you make of that?"

Ake was scribbling on a scrap of paper. "How about a three P.M. Air France flight from Miami to Zurich?"

Conway grinned. "Sounds good to me." But what was in Zurich besides the bank that issued Fletcher's checks? And why was he going to be dressed in a trench coat and clerical collar?

"When do you think we'll be leaving here?" the receptionist asked.

"I figure four to six weeks, then we'll just disband Word Systems," Fletcher replied.

"Who's the courier going to be?" the receptionist went on.

"Bishop Keating. I'm going to drop the notebook by the

rectory later. It'll be safer there." Fletcher sighed. "This would've been so much easier if Denise had just complied in the beginning."

Conway looked at Ake. "I owe that bastard a knock on the head."

"Who's J. M. Bell?" O'Keefe asked.

Conway and Ake exchanged a glance and laughed. "My man," Ake said, his teeth lining up in his grin like a white picket fence, "J. M. just happens to be the guy who created Bell's theorem. Seems Mr. Fletcher thinks he's got it all planned."

2.

Laura stood at the long window in her office, gazing down at the walk where only several weeks ago Denise Markham's body had been found. It was beginning to drizzle, and the incipient gloom matched her mood. The hibiscus seemed anemic and undernourished in the pale gray light where umbrellas were popping open, where students were hurrying to class, where life was proceeding just as it always had. Up here in her tower, raindrops hit the glass like hail.

It was ironic that her own nightmare had begun with the death of a woman she had barely known, that her death had, in fact, transmuted so many lives. Now the nightmare had nearly outgrown itself. More people were dead, the Turnbalts were in custody, another woman had been stalked, and when Laura tried to imagine herself at some point in the future, it was like being in the attic again, pounding against the barriers of the present just to see her way to the end of it all.

Waiting was the worst part of it. A week had passed since the Man had made any move. Her life was in a holding pattern, circling within the eye of the storm; it was his way of mocking her, showing her he was still in control. This was the *unnerve* part of his strategy, she thought, his way of telling her she was her own worst enemy. The horror was that he might wait another month or perhaps several months, wait until she was beginning to believe he'd vanished from her life as suddenly as he'd entered it. Then he would swoop in like a vulture for the kill, and the element of surprise would be in his favor.

Every so often, a scene from *Psycho* would careen through her mind: she would be standing in a shower, perhaps humming softly to herself, and suddenly the Man's shadow would fill her vision and his knife would plunge through the curtain and sink into her ribs and she would struggle to retain consciousness long enough to see his face.

She shivered and turned away from the window. Fatalities, victims, tolls. She didn't want to dwell on the other fatality, but it was in the very air that she breathed. The death of her relationship with Ian was evident wherever she turned. It lay in his eyes, in their separate beds, in the voice of his lies. Maybe there was someone else in his life and maybe there wasn't. She wasn't even sure that it mattered anymore. The point was she had never bought his story about the credit card receipts, new salesmen, about all the traveling. Oh, maybe she'd bought it for a while because she'd needed to believe in him, because her myopia had prevented her from seeing the truth. She, after all, had been like the woman who discovers she has breast cancer after months of avoiding self-examination for fear of what she'd find. Since that first lie that he was married, her trust, she knew, had been only superficial. If she had scratched a little deeper, she would have touched the fistula, named it, been done with it. But now . . . well, now, here she was.

The months had passed. Now she needed the rituals, the final parting, a brief grieving for what might have been, for whatever it was she'd seen in him that very first morning in the Keys. Now the untangling would not be so easy.

"Laura? You ready?"

She turned around. "Rita, hi."

"Let's go shopping, kiddo. Neiman Marcus is having a sale. Everything is thirty percent off."

"Just let me get my purse."

"You all right?"

"I'm indulging in a little self-pity."

Rita gave her a quick hug. "Well, I think you're entitled."

Since Laura had driven that morning, they took her car and drove down through the Grove, past Marie's store. Business was evidently booming. The usual number of cars was parked out front, the curious were still stopping to admire the expensive items in the window, and the same would probably be true a year or two from now.

"You think they'll sell the store?" Rita asked.

"I doubt it. Frank will probably work out a deal with Zolar or someone else to keep it going while he's doing time. I bet the business triples. He's got the Midas touch, Rita."

It wasn't Frank she was worried about; it was Marie. Laura felt a stab of remorse that the friendship had thinned so pitifully over the years. Perhaps if Marie had had a close friend, Frank's hold on her would not have been quite as strong, and so much could have been averted. She touched the gold pendant at her throat, wondered if Marie had known that day what was coming. Maybe she had even welcomed it as the only way she could jump off the mad carousel her life with Frank had become.

Or was she just making excuses? Laura still couldn't reconcile the very vivid picture Conway had drawn from Duncan's testimony of Marie with Denise and from Markham's statements about orgies. It was a side of the woman Laura had not known existed until all this had happened. But she felt it was also something Frank had encouraged, nurtured, part of that web of dependency and need he had spun.

"I hope you're not blaming yourself for what happened to Marie," Rita said.

"No, not really. I just feel it could have been avoided. What happens to a woman like that in prison?"

"She may not go to prison," Rita said. "Zolar's shrewd and I'm sure his defense will be convincing. Personally, I think it's a mistake for him to represent both of them. Marie would have a better chance standing trial alone, with another attorney altogether. But if she does have to do time, then"—Rita shrugged —"I'm sure she'll survive. Assuming, of course, that she survives the effects of the drug."

"The odds don't seem very encouraging for that, do they."

"Who knows. Seems to me Marie's biggest problem is going to be trying to make it without Frank. And without money. In prison, you receive an allowance." Rita rested her elbow in the window and drummed her fingers against the roof of the car. "You just never know when it comes to the law, Laura."

Victims, Laura thought, more victims. "This is a depressing conversation."

Rita didn't speak for a few minutes, but when she did, her voice held a tone Laura recognized. "When we finish shopping, I've got to go by the house and see Hank."

"You're going to divorce him, aren't you."

"Am I that transparent?"

Laura laughed. "Just to me."

3.

They had followed Fletcher to a travel agency. It was raining hard now, and O'Keefe, driving the Porsche, kept the windshield wipers on so they could see. The receiver wasn't picking up anything, but Conway guessed Fletcher was picking up an Air France ticket for the flight to Zurich.

When he came out of the building, he stopped, looked

279

obliquely into the rain as if it were a complete surprise, then darted out to where his car was parked. They waited until two or three vehicles had pulled into the road behind him, then O'Keefe put the car in gear and they followed.

"Where do you think he's headed, Johnny?" O'Keefe asked.

"The bishop's."

As Fletcher turned left onto Loyola Boulevard, which led straight to the church, Conway told O'Keefe to turn at the next left and pulled into the rectory parking lot. He repeated the directions to Ake over the walkie-talkie.

"Hey, Conway," said Ake. "I've been thinking. What else can we get him for besides robbery, B and E, and assault with a deadly weapon?"

"Maybe murder."

It was shortly after six, but darker than it should have been because of the rain. Conway cracked the window and remembered the night he and Rita had tried Markham Magic. It seemed like so long ago, maybe months or years, he didn't know. His sense of time had been distorted almost from the moment Truro had called him and he'd taken his first step into the closed and shadowed world of Denise Markham.

O'Keefe swerved to avoid a puddle as he pulled into the rectory parking lot and winced when mud splashed on the hood. The old man handled the car with the same deftness and care that Rita did, Conway thought.

"This rain's not cooperatin'," he grumbled.

The lot was filled with enough cars so they wouldn't be conspicuous, Conway thought, pulling the hood of the raincoat over his head. He realized he was wearing the same leaky sneakers he'd had on the day he'd met José Panzo. It had been raining then, too. How pitifully little he'd understood that day. He had expected just another homicide. Instead, he'd climbed inside the box with Pandora and nothing in his life had been the same since.

He got out of the car. His sneakers squeaked. Ake was already moving swiftly across the lot, through the crowd of people hurrying in for evening mass. Conway quickly followed.

28

1.

THEY STOOD JUST inside the rectory doorway, out of the rain. Dry leaves blew through the courtyard, scratching across the cement, flapping against the edges of the benches. From somewhere upstairs, organ music sprang from an open window, and the long, heavy chords merged with the sound of the rain. Young, enthusiastic voices echoed in the hallways behind them as a bell began to peal, and the stairs thundered with the rush of neophytes from the upper floors of the rectory. They waited, he and Ake, with their backs to the hallway, until the area had cleared, then turned right and moved toward Keating's office. Halfway there, Conway stopped, removed his sneakers, and hid them under the stairs. They made too much noise. Ake, he noticed, was already barefoot, his pants rolled up to his knees like a farmer.

The melancholy, scratchy notes of *The Blue Danube* waltz slid along the shaft of light from the partially opened door. They positioned themselves on either side of the door, and from where Conway stood he could see the bishop, standing at least a head taller than Ian, fixing two drinks. He wasn't wearing his clerical collar. Apparently the collar wasn't something to be worn when he was conducting "the business of religion" outside the pulpit.

"Toast to success," Keating said, handing Fletcher a drink.

Conway saw Fletcher's hand reaching for the glass, then his other hand setting the notebook on the surface of the desk. "To Zurich," Fletcher replied.

Ake looked over at Conway and mouthed, "Bullshit," as the two men inside clicked glasses. "It would have been much easier if Denise had just accepted our proposition in the beginning," Fletcher said.

"*Your* proposition," Keating corrected him. "The only reason I consented to help you was because her work would have fallen into worse hands sooner or later. Better you than the Russians."

Fletcher laughed as he moved into Conway's line of vision. "I'm the lesser of two evils, right?"

"Something like that."

"You're being paid well for what you're doing. I just happen to be the highest bidder."

"The *only* bidder," Keating said.

"Only because the others didn't know about you."

"Did you read any of the notebook?"

"Five or six hours' worth. I'm not a scientist and I'm certainly no chemist, but her personal entries are elucidating. The money aside, Bishop, you won't regret your decision. My people believe Denise's work is brilliant, although flawed, and a mammoth step toward achieving our goals."

"The day Conway was here, he said the drug had all sorts of serious side effects. That concerns me." He said this, Conway thought, as if it caused him about as much concern as a hangnail.

"Those are immaterial. We have chemists who can perfect the drug. Swiss chemists, the best." Fletcher lifted his glass to his mouth, Keating studied his pipe rack, chose one, filled and lit it. "Did you know," Fletcher continued, "that the Russians are so far ahead of us in psi research that it makes us look like we're still in the Stone Age, Bishop? There's every indication that any psi research with military potential is well financed by the secret police, the Soviet army, and other paramilitary groups." Ake shook his head, mouthed, "He's bonkers." "I'm telling you, Bishop, you name it, the Russians are studying it. Telepathy, clairvoyance, dowsing, eyeless sight. The Third World War isn't going to be fought with missiles. It's going to be fought with thought control. We have every reason to believe Denise's research will bring about a balance of power between the Soviets and the West. You should be proud of your part in all this."

A ghost of a smile crossed Keating's face. "You missed your calling, Ian. You should have been a preacher."

"Don't insult me." Fletcher laughed.

"I mean it. You would be terrific decked out in white, screeching in a tent somewhere. Look, I don't know what this drug does. I have only your word and what Conway told me. And of course"—he tapped the notebook—"this. But whether the next war is fought with thought control or acupuncture, Fletcher, it's not my concern. The money you're paying me will buy things for this diocese, for orphans, it will . . ." Conway thought he was going to puke.

"Spare me the sanctimonious bullshit. Let's have another drink."

"How will I know my contact?"

"He'll know you. Wear a trench coat and your clerical collar and carry the notebook in full sight. You'll be approached in the

Zurich airport.'' Ian had moved out of Conway's sight again, but he saw the bishop take the ticket. "Round trip, but the return flight is open. You may want to stay on a few days. You'll be paid the remaining half of what we agreed on when you get there.''

The gramophone was wearing down. Keating cranked it up again, finished mixing the two drinks, and passed one to Ian. "Tell me something, did you love Denise? Or was it just the formula you wanted?"

"It doesn't really matter now," Fletcher said.

"Motives always matter."

Fletcher walked into Conway's view again. He saw the pen sticking up out of his pocket, hoped O'Keefe was getting an earful. "At first, it was just the formula. That's why I came over here. The people I represent, a group of independent multinational businessmen, had known for some time about her research. As far back as five years ago, she published some of the preliminary results under an assumed name. That was a long time before she started marketing the drug.'' Fletcher paused, sipped at his drink, and seemed to be weighing his words carefully, like an actor. "And before I'd met her.''

"And after?'' The bishop stirred his drink, then drank it in several gulps and fixed himself another.

Ian ran a finger under his mustache, then dabbed at it with a handkerchief. "After," he said quietly, "it was different. I fell in love with her. In fact, I wanted to marry her, but she wouldn't divorce Markham. Most men who knew Denise fell in love with her, Bishop, did you know that? She was . . .'' He paused. "She was mythical, in a sense.''

"Mythical,'' Keating repeated.

Fletcher continued as though Keating hadn't spoken. "She wouldn't divorce Markham because she was concerned about Viki. She said the girl had lost her father because of her mistakes and that she needed time. The truth is that she resented my work and it eventually came between us. Also, I don't think she loved me. Maybe the only man she ever really loved was Bucky. You'll read all about Bucky in the notebook, Bishop. Yes sir, Bucky.''

Keating's body seemed to sway to the music, and for a few minutes Conway had the impression the man wasn't really in the room. Then he moved toward the gramophone, cranked it again. "Why can't you deliver the notebook yourself?''

"It would look too suspicious.''

"To whom? The police?''

"I *do* have a life of my own, you know," Fletcher replied a bit defensively. "I can't just take off without arousing some suspicion."

Keating faced him, puffed on his pipe, sipped at his drink. Softly, he asked, "Did you kill her, Fletcher?"

Conway glanced at Ake as Fletcher replied, "We're a peaceful organization, I told you that. We don't kill unless it's absolutely necessary, Keating. And it hadn't gotten to that point yet. I still believe that in the end, she would have accepted our offer."

"That doesn't answer my question." Keating's voice was edged with impatience. His composure was developing fissures. "I asked if *you* killed her, not your goddamned organization."

Fletcher freshened his drink. Keating downed half of his. "I think you'll find your answers in the notebook, couched in another one of your daughter's riddles."

The bishop swayed slightly. When he spoke again, his words were slurred. "Hobbits and aardvarks," he said softly, "do you know about them? She used to tell such wonderful stories. She'd sit out on the field sometimes, with my boys, all my boys, and she would tell them stories, Fletcher. These kids barely spoke English, couldn't understand a word of what she was saying, but she communicated something. It was as if . . . as if God were with her. . . . Denny could've been great at whatever she did, Fletcher. My daughter . . . she . . ." His voice broke and he pressed the palms of his hands flat against the desk, his head hanging, chin against his chest, and began to cry. Conway realized the bishop's libations had started long before Fletcher had arrived. He wasn't just buzzed; he was bombed. His cries turned to sobs.

Fletcher simply stared at him. "You didn't even attend her funeral," he said contemptuously.

Keating sat back in his leather chair, his hands covering his face. "How . . . how could I risk such—" He sobbed. "I—I loved her, Fletcher, in spite of what you or anyone else might think. She . . . she was my blood . . . she was . . ."

"And you wouldn't even have known her if she hadn't tracked you down." Fletcher turned his back on the bishop. "You'll find some rather interesting entries on her thoughts about the relationship between father and daughter, Bishop. Don't read it unless you have a strong stomach."

Conway saw Keating drop his hands. "I should never . . . never have consented to help you," he whispered. "Never. You are . . . you are . . ."

"Now, now, Bishop. We both know you don't really have a choice in the matter. Not if you want to see Rome. We both know it wouldn't do to have a cardinal who not only broke the vows of celibacy, but also fathered a daughter." Fletcher sat on the edge of Keating's desk, touched the ice in his glass with a finger, and ran it slowly around the crystal rim until it made an eerie, high-pitched sound. He was evidently enjoying himself now. "It would be so simple, too. Just a few words to certain members of the papal community, documentation . . . No, I don't think it would do much for your career. You're a weak man, Bishop. But you aren't a stupid one."

Keating pushed back from his desk, raised himself to his full height. His thick white hair was disheveled. His shirt was wrinkled. He looked, Conway thought, slightly mad. "What gives you the right to—to—"

"To tell the truth?" asked Fletcher, remaining where he was.

"Truth," spat Keating. "What the hell do you know about truth?"

Conway nodded to Ake. He'd heard enough. He pushed the door open with his foot, walked in with his gun drawn, Ake directly behind him. "Evening, gentlemen," he said.

2.

"If I were you," Rita was saying, "I'd take the rest of my sick and annual leave for what remains of the quarter and with that and the month we'll have before the fall term begins, I'd put my life back in order. Go somewhere, Laura. It'd make the break with Ian easier and would put an end to all of this for you."

They were sitting outside Waldenbooks in the mall, finishing ice-cream cones. "I could join my parents," Laura said, "or go to Mexico. It wouldn't matter where, as long as it was miles from Miami."

"Maybe I could go with you."

"You've got Conway here."

She smiled, said, "Conway, yes. Although I'm sure he wouldn't mind."

Laura looked over at her, wondering at all the years they had traveled together. "Well, Rita, when we're old and gray and all that, we'll . . ."

"I know, I know." She laughed. "I'll look at you and say, 'Hey, remember when . . .' Right?"

But would it happen? Would she live long enough to get old and gray? Of course she would. Everything would turn out fine in the end, like a fairy tale where everyone lived happily ever after. "What made you decide to go through with the divorce?" Laura asked, deciding it was time she thought about someone besides herself for a change.

Rita shrugged. Her tongue darted out to catch a rivulet of ice cream inching down the side of her cone. "A lot of things, I guess. The missing money, his . . . I don't know, his distance from me. He isn't the man I married, Laura. I didn't tell you, but he stopped by my sister's the other night and he started acting . . . sort of crazy. You know, how could I do it to him and if I hadn't asked so many questions about the money, things would've worked out for us. . . ." She raised her eyes to Laura's. "You get the picture."

"He stopped by the house to see me the day I got out of the hospital. Ian and I were on our way over to his place. I felt sort of sorry for him."

"Sorry for him," Rita repeated, her voice soft, dreamy, as if she were remembering something. "Yeah, he's good at that. And he probably whipped out that gross puppet, huh."

Laura nodded.

"Maybe that's what I should enter in my divorce petition. Irreconcilable differences due to intervention by Diogenes. Shit. He hides behind that grotesque thing. In the beginning, when he was honing his ventriloquist skills, I kinda liked Diogenes. But now the whole thing's gotten . . . I don't know, weird."

Weird: like Ian said, Laura thought.

Rita glanced at her watch. "I should really get going. I know Hank's going to be home this evening and I'd like to get this part over with."

"It's probably for the best, Rita." But she wished it didn't sound so trite.

3.

Fletcher spun around the moment the door creaked open and his hand flew to his shoulder holster, hidden under his jacket.

"Don't!" Conway shouted, and Fletcher's eyes darted from Conway to the towering figure of Ake behind him. His arm dropped to his side. Keating's bloodshot eyes sank into his ashen face. The glass he held slipped away from him, hit the arm of the chair, and shattered, the drink spraying his already wrinkled shirt. He gaped, slumped back heavily into his chair, hands folded on the desk, as if in prayer.

"Dear God," he mumbled. "Oh, Christ, what—"

Ake took Fletcher's gun, and Conway picked up the notebook. "I'll take this back now, thank you very much," he said, then reached over and removed the pen from Fletcher's pocket. "And this, too. Can't have either of these things finding their way to Zurich, now can we, Ian."

"I haven't broken any laws," Fletcher protested. "I want to see my attorney. I demand to see an attorney. I get one call, Conway, and I'd like to make it right now."

"You," said Ake, stepping forward, pushing his large index finger into Fletcher's shoulder, "are going to be lucky if we let you take a leak." Fletcher stumbled back into the chair behind him. "For starters, there's assault with a deadly weapon, breaking and entering, theft of state property. Then, of course, if your blood type checks out, there could be a murder one charge, intent to commit murder. . . ." Ake handcuffed him.

"Murder?" Ian exclaimed, as though he'd never considered the possibility. He started to his feet and Ake pushed him down into the chair again. "I didn't kill anyone," he insisted, his voice louder now. "I didn't kill anyone and I can prove it!"

"You *did*," Keating yelled, "you did! You said you killed my daughter, my Denny," and he lunged toward Fletcher. Ake caught the bishop around the neck, twisted his arms behind him, cuffed him, and sat him down once more. "You—you can't treat me like that, you—you nigger!"

Ake touched the tip of his gun to Keating's neck and very quietly said, "Your Eminence. It would give me the greatest pleasure to blow your head into kingdom come, so why don't you just shut up?"

Keating's mouth dropped open. He whined. In a soft, obsequious voice, he said, "I haven't done anything, I haven't—"

"I want to see my attorney," Fletcher said. Conway ignored him and recited the Miranda Act.

"Any questions?" he asked, reaching for the phone.

"I didn't kill Denise," Fletcher insisted. "How—how could you think I'd do those things to Laura, Conway? *How?*"

"Let's see," said Conway, "if I've got this right. You wanted to marry Denise, you're disbanding your little company in four to six weeks, you represent some lunatic organization that believes the secret of psychic power will be the ultimate weapon, and you've been using Laura. Are those the facts, Ian? You might have gotten away with it, too, except that you were too anxious to get the notebook."

"Anxious?" He laughed. "You call waiting five years being

anxious?'' He rubbed the side of his face against his shoulder. ''As for Laura, I love her.''

''Right.''

''Conway, you're way off base about everything. Don't you *see*? If someone else gets their hands on that formula, there's no telling what—God. You don't understand the importance of what my people do, you don't—''

''This notebook and its duplicate are going to be burned.''

''You've got the wrong guy in custody. I didn't kill Denise and I didn't kill anyone else. I wouldn't hurt Laura. Conway, Jesus, my blood type is AB positive.''

''Prove it,'' Conway snapped.

''Fine,'' Fletcher said, ''prick my thumb. C'mon, take me to a lab and have them prick my thumb and you'll see.''

''One question. Did you or your organization offer financial assistance for Denise's research?''

''We wanted to buy the formula from her, Conway. And no, I'm not the man she calls Bucky. I don't know who the hell Bucky is. I'll tell you what I think, though. I think this dude Bucky might have been someone Denise made up.''

''He was the third investor,'' Conway replied, and wondered why the remark bothered him. There seemed to be something he was not remembering, but before he could think about it, Ake picked up the phone.

''We'll get you over to a lab, Mr. Fletcher, and find out just where you're coming from.''

4.

She'd left Rita off at the campus, where her car was, and was on her way back to Ian's with her baggage full of purpose and a suddenly limitless future. She would tell Ian tonight, speak to her department head tomorrow, and would leave Sunday, after the burglar alarm system had been installed in the house and the tile laid. She would wire her parents, realized she wasn't sure where they were now. Santiago? Buenos Aires? It didn't matter. For the first time in weeks, she could see her way clear to the end.

Laura stopped at a light, lifted the packages on the seat beside her, looking for her purse and cigarettes. Then she realized that in the shuffle of separating purchases, she and Rita had inadvertently switched bags. The keys to Ian's place were in hers, on another key ring; she didn't have a spare. She made a right turn when the light flashed green. She would swing by campus on the off chance Rita had gone inside, and if she hadn't, then she'd head over to Hank's.

5.

The rectory parking lot swelled with the phantom blue of the squad car lights. Radios squawked. People were rushing about, Truro was barking orders, his heavy jowls flopping from side to side as he moved. Curious priests emerged from the dorms, parishioners wandered out of the church, and people from neighboring streets were lining up along the sidewalks. A regular zoo, Conway thought.

Keating and Fletcher, still handcuffed, looking miserable, leaned against opposite squad cars. The bishop's head drooped like a wilted flower's, chin touching his chest. He'd either dozed off, Conway thought, or was conducting business with the Almighty, perhaps arranging corbans for more equipment and uniforms for his boys, in return for freedom.

"Conway," Fletcher shouted, "could you step over here before they haul my ass away?"

"Now he wants to confess," muttered O'Keefe, lighting his pipe. "Say, Johnny, when you have a free minute, I want to show you something."

"Hey," Fletcher yelled again. "Please."

"Hold on, George, I'll be back in a minute." He walked over to where Fletcher stood. "What is it?"

"It's Laura," Fletcher said. "She and Rita went shopping, and she's going to be in the apartment alone. She—"

"What do you want me to tell her, Ian? That she can visit you in jail?"

Fletcher looked down at the ground, shuffled his feet, said, "I didn't do anything to her. Nor did I kill Denise. I am not Bucky. Hell, I never even tried the damn drug, Conway."

"Who was the third investor?"

"How the hell should I know?" Fletcher said loudly, his cheeks reddening.

Conway stared at the man's bulging chocolate eyes, at the tendons standing at attention in his neck, at the way he kept rubbing his cheek against his shoulder, struggling with the cuffs that held his hands behind his back. And he knew Fletcher was telling him the truth.

Something shifted inside him, something as huge as Australia, and he took one last look at Ian, then hurried over to where O'Keefe was sitting.

"What'd the bugger have to say?" O'Keefe asked. He was sitting sideways behind the wheel, his feet flat against the ground, the notebook open on his lap. He was scribbling on a sheet of paper.

"He's telling the truth," Conway said, reaching for the car phone.

"Hmm," O'Keefe muttered, "I thought he was confessing. Say, do you—"

Conway held up a hand as he dialed Rita's number at her sister's. He let it ring and ring, then hung up quickly and called Ian's number. It, too, rang emptily. "Oh, boy," he whispered, "I sure hope to hell I'm wrong." He rested his forehead against the steering wheel.

"Listen, Johnny, to what I've been trying to tell you. I've been going through this notebook and—"

"George," Conway interrupted. "There was a gambling debt and this—"

"If you just look at this real carefully," O'Keefe said, interrupting him, flapping a sheet of paper. "I've been sitting here going through the notebook, you know? I wrote down the list of phrases which appear more than once in the notebook." He tapped the fourth one down. Conway, obsessed with his own conclusion, felt a surge of impatience, but O'Keefe didn't seem to notice. "If you look real careful now, Johnny, you'll see this is the only phrase which forms an acronym." Conway heard O'Keefe as if from a great distance, through the obsecration of his own silent screech of denial. It was the nameless thing that had pursued him, taken root in him, and now it had been identified. Somewhere on that remote mountaintop, lying in shadow, the incubus in the box was laughing. "See?" O'Keefe said. "Hobbits and aardvarks need kisses. An acronym, like I said. H-A-A-N-K. You know anyone by that name, Johnny?"

6.

Hank said Rita had run up to the store for wine and cigarettes and would be right back, so why didn't she have a drink and wait? Considering what Rita had come here to do, it seemed a little strange to Laura that she'd make a cigarette run, but she needed her purse so she stayed.

She thought Hank seemed a bit edgy and wondered if Rita had already mentioned the divorce. She hoped he wouldn't ask her opinion, but he was so sullen at the bar that she suspected he probably wouldn't say anything at all. She tried to make polite conversation. Hank nodded and murmured, but his eyes kept darting to the door, as if his senses were straining to hear Rita's car returning. He was acting . . . *weird*. Yeah, that word again, she thought.

He excused himself after a few minutes to make a phone call and Laura sat there staring at the TV in the corner. After three commercials, she wondered what was taking Rita so long and whom Hank was talking to.

She got up and poured the drink down the bar sink, left the glass on the counter, and wandered over to the sliding glass door which looked out into the backyard. The moon and the few brave stars she'd seen earlier had retreated behind a bank of clouds and shimmered uncertainly in the immense blackness. She remembered the first time she'd stepped into his house, before Hank and Rita were married, she'd been fascinated by the electronic wizardry, the gadgets, the glass that was impervious to almost everything. Moon glass, Hank had called it, because it was the same stuff that had accompanied the astronauts into outer space. Hank's fortress, she thought.

It was too dark in the yard to see anything except the bulky shapes of the trees, but during the day it was one of the loveliest sights she'd seen—a gallimaufry of color and tropical foliage: flaming vine and passion flowers, mango and orange and acacia trees, ivy, roses, jasmine. Hank was accomplished at almost everything he did.

Her thumb pressed the lock down. She felt like walking around outside, but when she tried to open the door, it wouldn't budge. The damned computer, she mused. As soon as it got dark, the house invariably became a living, breathing testimony of the man's paranoia. True, she felt safe here, safer here than she had at Ian's or in her own home. It was reassuring that no one could get in, but it alarmed her that she couldn't get out. It brought back the claustrophobia of the attic.

Laura walked into the bathroom adjoining the guest room downstairs, found a clean towel under the sink, soaked it with water, and wrung it out. She held it against her face. Her head was throbbing. She walked into the bedroom with the towel pressed to her head, wishing Rita would hurry up and get back. She sat on the edge of the bed, staring at the rug. Her eyes burned from lack of sleep. The headache had climbed into her temples. She smoothed down her blouse as she stood, and when she lifted her eyes she was looking into the closet.

The towel fell to the rug.

She blinked, stepped cautiously forward, and opened the door all the way. A small, choked sound smacked the air and she stumbled back. The dreams and the days and the questions slammed down from the closet and into her sleepless nights. Her hands bunched into tiny fists under her chin. Her arms tightened in on her body, her elbows pressed to her sides, and no words came out because the Man finally had a name, a face. There were rainbows in the closet.

29

1.

COMPUTER: ON. ALL systems go. They were sealed in, as if into a spacecraft. Doors and windows were locked, phones were on busy, the fence was electrified, the video cameras were humming. This was his kingdom after all, and here his word was law. He took a final look around the room. The green words printed on the screen were reassuring somehow, like signposts that marked the *rightness* of what had happened.

He held the crystal container up to the light, flicked it with his fingers, loosening the powder. Just a little more, he thought, and the rest he would save for Laura. They would move into the magical space together, as it was intended that they should. Already, the first few snorts he'd had a while ago were coursing through his blood. He could see the grand design of their braided lives, all the minute pieces fitting together like a lovely mosaic.

But first, he would test Laura. If she learned quickly, like his other women, then he would be good to her, very good. But if she dawdled, complained, lied, then he would have to punish her like he did the others. Reward and punish: Pavlov always knew the answer.

When he returned to the living room, she was gone. He noticed the empty glass on the bar, smiled. Wherever she was, she couldn't be far. Perhaps she was in the bathroom, freshening up. He wondered if she was still feeling the effects of the ant bites. He would have to apologize to her for that. But if she hadn't hidden from him that night, if she'd cooperated, it wouldn't have happened.

He fixed himself another drink, walked across the room,

turned the radio on low, and dimmed the lights. He drew the curtains across the windows, the sliding glass door, and shut off the TV. The important thing was that she'd finally come to him. There would be time for talk, explanations, and fun, yes, most of all that, he thought, shivering as the first wave of the drug's arctic air swept through him.

He caught sight of himself in the line of small mirrors over the couch. He was a handsome man but didn't look his age. He brushed a hand through his hair, admired the fit of his clothes. He smoothed down his shirt, felt the letter in his pocket, and it triggered the cloacal impotence of his fury. *How dare she*. How dare Rita betray him. He'd treated her well, hadn't he? He'd taken her into his home, given her his name, and then she'd betrayed him, like Denise.

How much had Denise taken from him in all? Forty or fifty thousand? Or was it more? He couldn't remember. But she'd deserved to die. She'd been punished. And now Rita would be punished.

And Laura . . . well, poor Laura, he thought. He didn't know why he was so angry with her, but he must've had a good reason. He wasn't a man to act without reason.

Now the drug was taking root in his brain, blooming like bougainvillea. His eyes fluttered closed; part of his mind stepped free, roaming the rooms for Laura. He could feel her nearby, could sense that pulse, that essence which was uniquely her. But he could not hone in on it, not like Denise used to do. He opened his eyes and padded to the bedroom doorway. "Laura? You all right in there?" She was so pale earlier, he thought, so pale and thin. This worried him, nagged at him.

He called her name again, stepped into the room. It was empty and the bathroom door stood open. "Laura? Where are you?" His voice was trembling now, the fury thickening inside him as a flood of heat coursed through his veins. He threw back the foot of the spread, got down on his knees, looked under the bed. He rushed into the bathroom, checked the shower, the linen closet, clenching and unclenching his hands, the fury sloughing along his tongue, then suddenly escaping. "*Laura!*" he shouted, and hurried toward the bedroom closet.

Rainbows, she saw the rainbows. She was hiding from him, just as Denise had. He recalled how Denise had avoided his calls, broken dates, how she'd finally withheld the money that was rightfully his—the loan plus profits. She had hidden from him with other men—that stupid jock, Duncan, then Turnbalt, and others he didn't know about.

Laura wasn't permitted to hide unless they were playing a game, and only *he* would decide what the game would be. *The tenacity of women*, he thought, it was something they were born with, the singular strength in the evolutionary flaw that had produced them.

He kicked the closet door shut. She was ruining things now, they were supposed to move into the space together, experiencing the magic. But the only thing he felt was his fury. He left his drink on the dresser, shouted, "Laura! You can't get out! And the phones won't work!" She couldn't escape, but the house was large, there were so many places to hide. He dug into his pocket, slipped the puppet over his hand. "What do you think, Di?"

"You're sweating," the puppet replied flatly.

"About Laura. What do you think about Laura?"

"She's looking for Rita."

"Of course." Insightful Diogenes, he thought. "She'll have to be punished."

"Yes, punishedpunishedpunished. Lemme watch, please. I wanna watch."

"No."

"You let me watch with Rita," it whined. "You let me watch with Rita when—"

"No." Hank yanked the puppet off his hand, stuffed it back into his pocket.

"*Please*," it screeched from inside.

Gimme, gimme, everything was gimme with Diogenes. It would have to be punished, too. Its screams grated on his nerves, sucked at his patience. God, how he hated the whining.

"Laura," he called again, then hurried down the long hallway to the other end of the house where Rita was. He opened a door, smiled with relief. She was still there, alone, splayed out like a frog, ankles and wrists bound to the bed. Now she was conscious, too, and lifted her head.

Why, Hank, why? her voice whispered in his head.

She was Denise as she gazed at him, yes, he could see Denise's eyes shining from Rita's face. Her right cheek was swollen where he had hit her, and blood had dried on the bone like a rose petal. She wore only her bra and panties and was grunting, moving her head from side to side.

"Should I remove your gag, Denny? Will you be good if I remove the gag?"

Her eyes followed him as he approached the bed. He untied the gag, whipped it away from her mouth. "Nothing to say in your own defense, Denny? C'mon, spin your magic, c'mon."

"I'm Rita, Hank. What have I done to you? What—"

"Denny, Denny," he cooed softly, placing the smooth, cool side of the knife against her belly. A muscle twitched there and he smiled. He brought the knife up under her bra, sliced it in half. Such a handy knife, he thought, so sharp, so convenient to have around, so wonderfully handy. He reached into his pocket and brought out the gold earrings. "See these, Denny? Remember when I gave you these? Now you've been careless and gone and lost them and here they are. I have them."

"*I'm Rita*," she screamed, "*Rita!*" Her face was red, so ugly and swollen. He stepped back, squinted at her, clenched his hand around the earrings. She *did* look like Rita, but those eyes— Denise's eyes . . . It was a trick, just another one of Denny's clever tricks.

He dropped the earrings into his shirt pocket, remembered the letter. Rita, of course, it was Rita he had to punish for this. He removed the letter carefully, unfolded it. "Does the cop like your body, Ree?" He pushed her bra aside with the edge of the knife, so her breasts were exposed. Lightly, very lightly, he circled a nipple with the tip of the blade. She squeezed her eyes shut, made a sound deep in her throat, a *Denise* sound, he thought, and smiled, a sound of terror. Good, terror transformed, and Ree definitely needed some transformation in her life.

"Let me read you something, Ree." Her head was to the side, away from him. He grabbed hold of her chin, yanked her face toward him.

"Please," she whispered.

"You must look at me when I speak to you, Ree. I must have your full attention." He began to read: " 'Your lovely wifey is making it with Detective John Conway. Just in case you're wondering how I know, I found them together. And in case you don't understand the precise meaning of *making it*, let me clarify: screwing, nooky, copulating. They were doing it in *my* bed, Mr. Lincoln, and chances are they have also done it in *your* bed.' " He raised his eyes. She was crying. Her lashes stuck together, mascara had smudged under her eyes. Her mouth quivered like the throat of a singing bird. "*Were* you doing it in my bed, Ree?"

"If you're going to . . . to kill me . . . just do it . . . just get it over with."

He shook a finger at her. "You were bad, Ree. Very bad, just like Denny. Did you know Laura is here, too? Did you know it's just the three of us? Isn't that nice? Like a little private party."

"Laura?" It was a choked sound, and now he saw it, the

genuine terror, crouched in the back of her eyes, stealing the color from her face.

"You two switched purses by mistake. She came to return yours. Isn't she a good friend, Ree? I think she's such a good friend, in fact, that she might just come to your rescue. See, she was bad, too. She saw the rainbows, so now she's hiding." He chuckled as he brought Diogenes out of his pocket and fitted it over the top of the bedpost, where it could see everything.

"Hank. Please. You're sick. The drug has . . . We'll get you help, I promise. The best help that—"

"I arranged the rainbows tonight, Ree, just for you. When I received this filthy . . ." He crumpled the letter, tossed it across the room. "When I got that filth, I arranged the rainbows."

She whimpered. "We'll get you help, please, Hank. . . ."

"Shut up. You always thought you were so smart, didn't you. Just like Denise. And Laura. The three of you." He felt himself growing hot, flushed. An image flared in his mind: Laura crouched somewhere in the house. Yes, he could see her, her head pressed up against a shelf, her arms pulled in at her sides like broken wings. If he concentrated a little more, he knew he could pinpoint her location, but then Rita screamed and his head snapped up.

"*Laura, it's a trick, Laura. . . .*"

He slapped his hand over Rita's mouth, grabbed the handkerchief, forced it between her lips, retied it. "That wasn't very nice, Ree. It was bad, very bad. What do you think, Di?" he asked, glancing at Diogenes.

"Badbadbad. Punishpunishpunish. Shabbyshabby."

Rita's eyes widened with terror, watching as he unbuckled his belt, stepped out of his slacks. She began to thrash her head from side to side, struggling against the ropes that bound her. Her impotent screams rumbled like thunder deep in her chest. He cut through the ropes that held her legs. She kicked in her newfound freedom, frisky as a colt, all fire, all spit, lovely, absolutely lovely. He sat on her legs to hold them down, closed the knife, set it on the floor, eased her underwear down and off.

"Denny and I used to play this game," he told her. "She loved it. It's a nice game, you'll see, Ree. You haven't been very nice to me, you know. All those times we separated . . . how you turned away from me . . . and then this last separation, when I needed you most, when I . . . I had to find others, Ree. There were others, besides Denise." He touched the tangle of dark blond hair between her legs. She turned her head to the side, as though it were too horrible to watch, as though it were happening to someone else.

"I was tired of you, Ree. Maybe I'll marry one of the other ladies. . . ." His hand moved across her stomach, a beautiful tummy, a beautiful woman, his Ree, his little whore, little liar. He touched his mouth to her breasts, then yanked her face toward him and looked deeply into the fields of deception, into those eyes like Denise's, all the way into her execrable, shriveled soul.

"Bad, so bad," he whispered. "How does Conway do it, Ree, hmm?"

She stared past him, at Diogenes sitting on the bedpost, watching with its one ugly eye.

2.

A scream and then nothing, Laura thought. *Was he torturing Rita?*

The sound of her heart filled the room, house, perhaps even the world. She was squashed up inside the bathroom cabinet, beneath the sink, inside with cleansers and guest towels. She gripped the cool, slick pipes, fighting back the white panic that was spreading over her mind like butter. *Think, dammit, think.* How long had it been since the scream? Five minutes? Ten? She pushed the door open a crack. A strip of light fell as far as her toes. It was quiet, much too quiet.

Where did Rita leave her purse? The gun was in there. And without the gun, she didn't have a chance. Okay, think, where did Rita usually leave her purse when she came into the house? Kitchen? Bedroom? She was a creature of habit, Laura knew, so if she could just remember where she usually left it, then it would be there now.

She crawled out of the cabinet, her muscles screaming. She felt the cold tile against her bare feet, came as far as the guest room, peered out into the dim, empty silence of the living room. *Where was she? Where did he have Rita?* Laura grabbed hold of the doorjamb, steadying herself, shaking away the memory of rainbows, of the attic.

First, a weapon, then the computer; yes, it would help to have some sort of plan.

But how much time did she have?

She ran soundlessly through the living room, into the kitchen. It was dark. She heard something. Her hand froze on a drawer. Was that the sound of bed springs? *Was he raping her?*

Whimpering, fighting back panic, she pulled the drawer open slowly, feeling the throb of a pulse at her neck. The dry, hot shoots climbed all the way into her brain. Nausea whipped through her as her hand closed around a knife. She brought it out of the drawer. She remembered, suddenly, stupidly, a cool Sunday in February when she and Ian had come here for a barbecue. Maybe this was the knife Hank had used to carve the chicken. Or was it roast? Was it even a Sunday?

''Oh, Jesus,'' she whispered, patting her hands along the counter, looking for the purse. She padded through the dark until she reached the breakfast table. Nothing, it was empty.

The rachitic sounds from the bed ceased. Her heart leaped into her mouth, drummed along the parched runway of her tongue. Someone was saying something. *Hank? No, no, Diogenes.* The sound started up again. If he was raping her, if she was still alive, then there was hope, she thought.

She gripped the knife. Could she possibly overpower him? Or should she try the computer instead?

The computer, stupid, the computer.

Her body trembled as her foot touched the first stair, then the second. She winced when the wood squeaked, strained to hold on to the sound of the bed springs, to the puppet's voice. The noises were like the ticking of a clock, marking time, gutting her insides. Her muscles ached; her temples pounded with the overture of a major headache.

On the landing, she stopped. Her heart filled the silence like the hiss of escaping gas. The bedroom was directly over the room where Rita was. There were no back stairs. Once he left Rita, she would have only minutes.

She moved along the wall, slowly at first, seizing on the image of the computer as it filled the screen of her mind. She tested the floor before each step, always listening for Diogenes' voice, every sense straining, pushing for overload. Boldness mixed with desperation. Her steps were long. *Mother, may I? . . . One giant step. . . .*

Laura fixed her eyes on the glow from the bedroom lamp, coming closer, then closer, until she flew the last few feet, sucking in her breath as she gripped the knob, moved the door a little. She winced at the sound of it scraping against the carpet. Had he heard? She stopped, started, stopped again like a reluctant engine.

When the door was closed, she quickly locked it, stood with her back against the door, breathing hard, curling and uncurling her toes against the carpet. Her eyes darted about, taking in the

298

neatly made bed, the nightstand, the closet door cracked open, a pair of slippers peeking out from under the foot of the bed. Such order, she thought dimly, as if by surrounding himself with it, Hank hoped to contain his madness.

There was the computer, perched on the dresser in such sweet repose, its screen as blank as the sky at high noon.

30

1.

THE COMPUTER WAS smaller than she'd imagined, a suitcase-sized portable model with milky smooth sides and a monitor that could be easily folded over the keyboard. Like Denise and the house, it was as impervious as moon glass.

Laura slid a hand along the sides, back, searching for a switch. She was unfamiliar with this Japanese model but finally found the power switch, attached like an appendage, an after-thought. The monitor glowed green and a cursor blinked off and on in the upper-left-hand corner. Laura tapped the space bar and the cursor moved across the top of the screen. She returned it to its original position, typed in HANK, hit the execution button.

PLEASE LOG ON.

She stared at the screen, tapped LOG, hit the space bar, spelled HANK again. As she pressed the execution key, the green letters flashed ENTER PASSWORD. She smashed a hand down against the keys, muttering, "C'mon, c'mon," then clawed at the machine, tried desperately to dig the tip of the knife in between the keys. *C'mon, dammit, c'mon.*

The green words shone proudly, testimony of Hank's added insurance that the world outside couldn't penetrate and that those within could not get out. He had probably made certain that even a loss of power would not release the house, that nothing would release it except the proper command.

The air stank of inertia; panic bristled in the room. It would end abruptly, yes, she could see this happening, the weeks screeching to a halt as he crashed through the bedroom door with that knife, that thin, careful knife, and slid it between her ribs before she even knew what had happened. This was how it must have happened with Denise.

Laura scurried over to the door, listened, strained to catch the smallest sound, something that would tell her he was still downstairs. She licked her lower lip, tried to swallow. But her mouth was as dry as the Mojave; she was burning up inside.

She looked around for something heavy enough so that one swift blow, delivered to the skull of the thing, would kill it. *No guarantees.* The bright green words glowed: ENTER PASSWORD. The words *saw* her, she thought, they possessed consciousness, knew what she was thinking.

How long had it been?

The balcony, perhaps she could escape through there. But when her hand pushed down against the handle, nothing happened. The computer held it, too. And the glass would be impossible to break. She turned back to the computer, staring at it, willing it to cough up the password.

2.

Something was different in the air, Conway thought. The dark was strained, as it sometimes was in a dream the moment before it became a nightmare. The only clear sound was the hum of the electric fence. It sent shivers along his spine.

No cars in the drive, no moon in the sky, no breeze. But there were lights on both upstairs and down. He listened tensely as they drove by the house, headlights off, and felt himself being sucked up into the box, into no-man's-land. He started to think of Rita, of how his own myopia had prevented him from piecing the clues together that had been there all along. But a door slammed shut in his mind. Not now, he thought. Now wasn't the time to dwell on what might be going on inside. He needed a plan.

"Circle around back," he said quietly to Ake, keeping his gaze on the upstairs window where light glared like a full moon. Nothing would happen while he watched the window, he told himself. He wasn't too late. He had to believe that.

They drove around the block and into the alley behind the house. Ake coasted to a stop just inches from the humming fence. The upstairs light was visible from here. The master bedroom, he decided. Was that where the computer was? A streetlamp flickered uncertainly at the end of the alley, too dim to make them vulnerable, but bright enough so he could see the trees in the yard had been trimmed, making it damned near impossible to drop over into the yard from the alley.

"I don't think you should go in there alone," Ake said.

When Conway replied, it seemed the words came from somewhere outside himself, outside that door which had shut in his head. Fear pounded against it. "You've got to help me get over the fence. We can't wait around for squad cars, and we can't just sit here." He secured the gun in his holster, tightened the laces on his sneakers. He swallowed. His Adam's apple bulged against the skin of his throat, parched and huge.

They got out of the car and Conway scrambled up over the hood, onto the roof. Ake followed. They crouched there for a moment, and through the forest of thick branches, he saw the upstairs light. Crickets cried out in the melancholy dark. If only he'd seen the inside of the house, had thought to ask Rita more about the computer; if only . . .

"No basement," Ake remarked.

"But there's an upstairs balcony and sliding glass doors upstairs and down. Can't just sit here. Ready?"

"All set, white boy." Conway scooted around behind him, grabbed hold of Ake's head, put one foot firmly on a shoulder, then the other foot. Ake's immense hands clasped him at the ankles. He wobbled as the giant beneath him raised up, moved his hands from ankles to calves, and finally stopped at Conway's knees.

"Oh, Christ," Conway whispered, suddenly dizzy from the height. The air touched the sweat on his face, gobbled it up. He eyed the electric fence, where a post protruded like a spear. He was more worried about the post than the electricity. Since he wouldn't be grounded, there would be no shock. But that would be little consolation if he were impaled on the spearhead.

Conway catapulted through the warm air, the dark curve of the sky sliding past him, lights from the house frozen in the vacuous antiquity of space. Had he cleared the fence? He looked. The ground was rising to greet him—hedges, leaves, branches enlarged and distorted and unclear. A patch of grass yawned open like arms. *Sky diving: take the brunt of the landing in your knees*.

When he hit, his knees gave like rubber and he rolled into the hedge, caught himself on his hands. He glanced over his shoulders, astonished that he'd made it. The car wasn't visible, and neither was Ake. He was alone in the damp earth of Pandora's box, and the lights in the upstairs window held him like a tractor beam.

3.

Hank tugged at his slacks, pulling them up. He watched Rita. She neither moved nor opened her eyes. Her chest seemed still. Blood spotted the sheets. Did he stab her? Or was the blood already there?

He squeezed his eyes shut, trying to conjure the recent past. She came here from shopping with Laura. He was in the living room. The letter was in his pocket. She said she wanted a divorce—no-fault divorce, Hank, she told him, so there wouldn't be any hassle over money or property. "What's yours is yours, Hank. I just want what I came into the marriage with."

"Meaning your half of the savings?"

"That'd be nice, but not very plausible . . ."

"I didn't gamble it, Rita."

He couldn't recall what had happened after that, until Laura's arrival. He moved closer to the bed, peering down at Rita. If he watched her closely, the answer would come to him, the bits of his life that had slipped away would reappear in her face, he would—

"Punishpunishpunish," Diogenes whispered, chanting the words. "She's betrayedbetrayedbetrayed. She is shabbyshabby-shabby."

He ordered Di to shut up. He couldn't remember while the puppet was mumbling. Its singular eye stared at him impudently.

"Nonono," it said. "Hahaha."

He yanked it off the bedpost, threw it to the floor, brought the heel of his shoe down over its face, its ugly little face. He ground it into the floor like a cigarette butt. "I told you to be quiet," he wheezed, grinding the heel harder now, wondering why his head hurt, why his lungs were filling up with holes. "You've been bad, very bad, like Ree, like Denny and Laura."

"*Nonono!*" it cried. "Hurtshurtshurts."

It was the shriek of his own wretched soul as it split open, spilled through his blood, and dug into his cells like a cancer, poisoning everything. The pain circled his waist in a flash of white heat, sprang up into his lungs and throat. He rocked back on his heels, slapping at the pain, wanting to pull it out of himself. He came forward, found the knife once more, brought his arm back and then down, again and again, stabbing Diogenes, killing the noise. "You . . . you filth, you would tell lies, you would tell my secrets, you would betray everything."

Its patch slipped away. The empty eye socket gazed up at him. Like Denny, that eye, gazing at him from under the hibiscus. He knew that look; he had always known it. The pyramid of his women loomed like a hopscotch of faces and crashed in on him. He leaped toward Diogenes, then rushed back over to the bed, pulled back Rita's eyelids, gazed into the blue. He smelled sex, the past, blood, and death. From the end of the knife, Diogenes whispered, "Laura didn't do anything and that's the truth. Laura didn't do anything and that's the truth." Then it screeched, "*Laura, all ye, all ye, in come free!*"

He grabbed the knife, yanked it out of the floor, impaled it and the puppet in the doorjamb, then jerked open the closet door, fished around on the top shelf until he found his .44. A good, solid weapon, he thought, capable of blowing a hole in the side of a boat, one of his father's favorites.

"Yesyesyes," Diogenes urged, its voice a blinding pain in his skull. "Yesyesyes, punishpunishpunish," and the words stuck in a groove, repeating themselves over and over again as he loaded the gun. "*Laura!*" the puppet shouted.

Hank jammed a cartridge into the gun, turned, aimed, fired.

The puppet was blown off the wall. Part of the doorjamb fell away. *You made me do it, Di, you made me do it.*

4.

The explosion shook the dark, rattled the floor where she stood, and knocked loose the word she needed. Laura's hand danced across the keyboard. DIOGENES. She struck the execution button.

READY.

DIR. The directory appeared: accounts, bills, Denise, house. She stared at Denise's name, hesitated, then moved the cursor to the text and stopped it in front of house.

Her hands shook as she tapped COMP CALL. A sense of unreality gripped her when the screen lit up and a list of words flashed bright green. The heart of the monster, she thought, was here, controlling every facet of Hank's fortress: LOCKS, LIGHTS, FENCE, VIDEOS, SPRINKLERS, GARAGE, DOORS, WINDOWS, and on and on. She played the keyboard for a long moment, certain she heard the fortress shutting down with a whimper, a sigh.

Laura ran across the room, threw open the sliding glass doors, hesitated as she stared into the abyss below. None of the trees was close enough to the balcony. There were no ledges in sight, no stray branches she could have leaped toward. She opened her mouth to scream, realized there was no one close enough to hear. The white panic oozed around her, freezing her, then she shoved it back, away, and ran through the bedroom into the bathroom. She locked the door behind her, praying she had chosen correctly, knowing she was dead if she hadn't.

5.

The explosion of the .44 had paralyzed him. Unspeakable visions pummeled Conway's brain: shoulders without heads, heads without bodies, yawning abysses where bodies had once stood. He would find nothing but dust and blood inside the house.

Then several things happened in quick succession: the lights in the house blinked off, the noise of the fence collapsed around him, and the sprinklers jerked on in spasms, rolled in death throes, gulping at the air. They rallied. They whirled in the dark like ballerinas, and the spray hit him in the back, neck, flaying the hedge, flowers, pounding furiously, erratically, against the house and trees. Little by little, the geysers lessened, then sank back into the grounds and finally vanished altogether, like a vein of oil going suddenly dry.

He gripped the handle of the sliding glass door and was surprised when it gave so easily, so soundlessly. He stepped inside the inky black deeper than a nightmare.

6.

Four and a half bathrooms in the house, Laura thought, two of them upstairs. Her chances were reduced to fractions. But this had to be the right one. Her hands slapped the walls. She bit down hard, tasted the blood on her lip, heard the sharp, startled noises around her as the memory of the attic swelled, ready to clamp down and sink into her like stone.

She pulled on the first knob she touched and dared to hope. Distantly, as if coming from a television in another room, she heard Hank kicking at the bedroom door, loud and hungry as a giant. It flew open, banged against the wall. *Fee fie, fo, fum . . .*

Her hands grappled in the dark. Cool air nipped at her fingertips. She scrambled up on the edge, sat, stretched her legs out on the aluminum slide, lay back with her arms straight over her head, and shoved off into the dark, down the laundry chute, swift as Alice through her hole.

She bumped. Her shirt caught on something and tore. Her throat was tight. The tiny space was pushing in on her, would crush her. The muscles in her neck strained, hurt, she couldn't breathe, she would—

Then she popped out of the chute and into a pile of dirty laundry in the utility room, next to the garage. She sucked at the air, sobbed as the basket tumbled over. She scrambled to her feet and grabbed onto the edge of something cool and smooth. The washing machine, she thought, and pulled herself to her feet. Dizzy, she was so dizzy, she was floating again in the wet dark of nowhere, no time. She flung her arms across the machine to fix herself in space, and then she felt it.

The purse.

It was there on the machine where Rita always left it when she came into the house. Laura clutched it. Small cries, like gasps or hiccups, raced down her tongue as she dug inside the purse and then popped against the air as her hand found the .38.

She raced down the hall to the room where Rita was, knowing now that Hank was right behind her.

7.

He spat, gagged at the odor of the dirty socks and underwear, weeks of laundry. He was hot, very hot, and his vision was fuzzy. But he was only seconds behind her, yes, he could feel the heat of her body, of her terror.

"Hank, can you hear me?"

The sound of his name, of a male voice in the house—it stopped him cold. *The wife fucker, here, in his kingdom.* He slipped through the utility room door, flattened against the wall in the kitchen. He listened as the idiot detective shouted something from the stairs. *Fool, you bloody fool. Down here.* He wanted to laugh at the simplicity of it. *Come to visit the cuckold? Good, you've made it just that much easier.*

This would be his best performance ever. Quickly, in an urgent voice like Rita's, he called, "John, please, help!" and the voice was far enough away to give him time to complete what he had to do. What women always made him do: punishpunishpunish.

When the women were finally dead, then he would settle the score with Conway.

8.

Her heartbeat filled the room, her breath came in short, quick spurts, silent sobs as she dragged Rita over to the closet. *Was she alive? Was she alive?* The words pounded against her skull with a terrible rhythm. But there was no time to check for a pulse, no time to do anything but push Rita inside the closet door, out of the line of fire. She knew what Hank would do. Here, now, in this house, they were connected, and when she heard his voice imitating Rita's, she realized she had only a few seconds. And she couldn't warn Conway, because Hank would kill him before he ever reached the hall.

Laura scurried across the room, yanked the sheets up over the pillows, then ran back to the wall, her eyes on the door. Now he was coming, just as he had always come for her, in the dark, hissing soundlessly, the heat of his breath in the very air she breathed. But now they were equal, both armed, both in the dark. This time she was prepared.

A terrible calm fastened over her. She conjured an image of the silhouette, remembering the call, the mirror, the drawers, the attic, the rainbows, remembering the hours of her life she had lost to this man. And she waited, her eyes on the door.

9.

Conway turned back. *John? When had Rita ever called him John?*

His legs wouldn't move quickly enough. His mind was three miles in front of his body. The box was letting loose its one final peril, and the dark was worse than any he had ever known. The house and the hall were larger and longer than any future, and when the explosions and shots ripped through the air, he heard the wail of the thing, now named, stirring up death, stirring up rainbows, tearing into his life, just as he knew it would.

EPILOGUE

September 15
10:00 A.M.
Key West

CONWAY, STRETCHED OUT on the roof of the cabin in his swimming trunks, opened his eyes into the hot, blue sky. The sloop rocked gently beneath him. The noises of the marina were muted, and for a moment he lay there picking them apart in his mind: the screech of birds overhead, the shouts of children on the other side of the pier, a truck rolling to a stop nearby. Then he heard, "Ahoy, Conway!"

He raised his head, shaded his eyes, reached for a towel, and wiped his face as he sat up. He saw Ake and Rita hurrying along the walk, Ake's movements like the gallop of a stallion while Rita struggled to keep pace with him.

"Hey," he called back, waving his towel in the air like a flag. He stepped down onto the deck, slid into his thongs, and grinned as Ake and Rita neared. "Black boy, you stealin' my woman?"

"I thought I'd surprise you and this is how you act?" Ake laughed as he stepped on board and grasped Conway's hand, nearly crushing it. "You get any more sun, white boy, and youse gonna be my color."

"This must have been planned," Conway said, glancing at Rita.

"Nope. I swear it. I was on my way into town for some groceries and there he was in the marina office, trying to track us down. How about beers, guys?"

While Rita went below, the two men settled into low canvas chairs. "Truro let you come to Key West on duty time?" Conway asked.

"They need you to testify at Turnbalt's trial and later, at Fletcher's. They were both arraigned about three weeks ago." Ake paused. "I don't guess you've been reading the papers."

"Nor have I seen a TV since I left Miami."

"You sound so smug." Ake laughed and Conway grinned. "Truro figured that was important enough to allow me a visit on company time."

"Is Turnbalt copping a plea?"

"Nope, I don't know what angle Zolar's using, but it must be good. As for Fletcher . . . well, his organization has hired some fancy attorney out of Tallahassee. No telling what'll come of all this."

"What about Marie Turnbalt?" Conway asked.

"She's still in intensive care, hooked up to machines, and in a coma. They're trying a new medication, but no one can say for sure whether she'll make it."

Conway nodded. "It's Frank who will come out smelling like a rose."

In the six weeks since he and Rita had sailed out of Biscayne Bay, he'd thought a lot about the characters in Denise Markham's drama and knew that none of them had escaped completely unscathed. Laura had fled to Ecuador; Viki Markham had been shoved out of childhood; Marie Turnbalt was hooked up to machines; Rita awakened nights, stricken with terror that she was back in that room with Hank; and yes, he had his own dark places.

"Fletcher admitted to writing that letter you found in Denise's office, Conway," said Ake. "That first love letter. I asked Turnbalt about the other letter, but he just laughed and said you'd have to figure it out."

"Arrogant to the bloody end," Conway replied.

"We played around with Hank's computer. I swear, the man recorded everything—favorite murder mysteries, legal cases, his sex life, everything. He lent Denise somewhere in the vicinity of fifty thousand, over a period of two years, and she never reimbursed him a penny. Between that, her other lovers, and his past use of the drug, he just went off the deep end." Ake paused. "I should have figured he was bonkers from the beginning because of that puppet."

"What's the story with Duncan?"

"He and the redhead are getting married. He has periods of remission, which the docs say are due to his youth and incredible fortitude. He might make it, after all. He's still on medication."

"Did he cop a plea?"

"Yeah. He got five years of probation."

Rita came topside with the beer and sat on the warm deck near Conway. "What happened to Bishop Keating?" she asked.

"Ah. His Eminence pleaded no contest to receiving stolen property. He got a year suspended sentence and—get this—was demoted to a priest and sent to an Eskimo village in the Arctic Circle."

Conway laughed. "So much for Rome."

They sat quietly for a few minutes in the hot light, watching a flock of gulls making their way east toward the Atlantic, where the fishing was better. Conway spread suncreen on his nose, slipped on his T-shirt. He touched a finger to his leg, and when

he removed his hand a white dot appea_____
cancer before we ever get out of Florida,"

"O'Keefe said he was coming down for a_____
leave for Panama in October. I thought I mi_____
off and join him." He grinned. "Maybe I'll b_____
can all go to the South Pacific."

"Gawd, spare me."

Ake reached into his pocket, brought out a long _____velope.
He tapped it against the edge of his palm. "I guess I'd better deliver
this." He passed it to Conway. "It's a warrant for your arrest."

"*What?*" Rita laughed.

"Poor joke, Ake."

"Read it."

Conway read it. "I can't believe Stella would do this."

"She must've read about your marriage," Ake remarked,
"and wanted her due." He tipped his beer to his mouth, set it on
the deck.

"I'm not paying her a dime."

"Truro said if I couldn't find you, I could rip it up."

"Truro said *that*?"

"On one condition."

Conway gazed up into the sky. "That I come back to work,
right? That I come back now."

"Three choices. First, there was a murder two nights ago in
Hialeah and the woman who—"

"Forget it."

"Number two, that your leave of absence is over as of now."

"Nope."

"Number three, that you pay her by the end of the week, so
you show up clean in court when you testify against Turnbalt and
Fletcher. He says he—and I quote—'don't want no kinda bullshit like this staining the department's good name.' "

"Equitable choices," Conway muttered.

"That's dog face, equitable all the way."

"Okay. I'll pay her. Then I'm taking her back to court."

Ake laughed. "I sort of figured you'd say that." He reached
for the warrant, ripped it in two. Rita picked up the pieces,
ripped them until they were the size of confetti, and let them
loose in the hot breeze. All three watched as the bits floated out
over the water, then ascended up over the web of trees on the
opposite shore, up toward the sun, finally scattering against the
cerulean blue of the September sky.

On that remote mountaintop in Conway's mind, he heard
Pandora's box whispering closed at last.

About the Author

TRISH JANESHUTZ was born and raised in Caracas, Venezuela. She now lives in South Florida with her husband, Rob MacGregor, also a writer, and their two cats. IN SHADOW is her first novel.